D0101463

Pandora's Helix

Also by Ken McClure

Pestilence
Requiem
Crisis
Chameleon
Trauma
Fenton's Winter

Pandora's Helix

KEN McCLURE

SIMON & SCHUSTER

LONDON · SYDNEY · NEW YORK · TOKYO · SINGAPORE · TORONTO

06968796

First published in Great Britain by Simon & Schuster Ltd, 1996
A Viacom Company

Copyright © Ken Begg, 1996

This book is copyright under the Berne Convention
No reproduction without permission
All rights reserved

The right of Ken McClure to be identified as author of this work has
been asserted in accordance with sections 77 and 78 of the Copyright,
Designs and Patents Act 1988

Simon & Schuster Ltd
West Garden Place
Kendal Street
London W2 2AQ

Simon & Schuster of Australia Pty Ltd
Sydney

A CIP catalogue record for this book is available
from the British Library

ISBN 0-684-81635-0

Typeset in New Caledonia 11/14pt by
Palimpsest Book Production Limited, Polmont, Stirlingshire
Printed and bound in Great Britain by
Butler & Tanner, Frome & London

This book is a work of fiction. Names, characters, places and incidents
are either products of the author's imagination or are used fictitiously.
Any resemblance to actual events or locales or persons, living or dead, is
entirely coincidental.

Ken McClure would like to thank the many friends and colleagues in science and medicine who helped him with the groundwork for this book. Particular thanks must go to Doctors Susan and Gordon Dewar and to Heather Davidson. Last but not least, he would like to express his continuing affection for Dolly Daydream who remains . . . a class act.

If a little knowledge is dangerous, where is the man who has so much as to be out of danger?

Thomas Henry Huxley (1825–1895)

Pandora/*paendo:ra*/ *Gk. Myth.* Said to be the first mortal woman, created by Zeus and sent to earth with a box of evils, which she let out to infect the earth (see Pandora's box)

Helix/*'hi: liks*/ *n.* Anything of spiral form, esp. advancing round an axis, like a corkscrew; shape (as double helix) of the DNA molecule, which carries genetic information necessary for organization and functioning of living cells, and control of the inheritance of characteristics.

One

Michael Neef, consultant in pae-
diatric oncology at St George's Hospital, checked his watch as he
descended the spiral staircase to the Pathology Department. He was
running late but felt he had to respond to Frank MacSween's request
that he 'pop down' to the PM suite for a moment. He and MacSween
had known each other long enough to respect each other's opinion.
If Frank said there was something worth taking a look at, it usually
meant there was.

Neef, a tall, well-built man in his middle thirties with swept-back,
dark hair and a handsome face, marred only by the legacy of a
broken nose after a motorcycle accident in his teens, pushed
through the swing doors of the path lab and nodded to the duty
technician before entering the changing rooms. He helped himself
to a green cotton gown and tied it loosely behind him. He didn't
bother with the footwear option, leaving the row of wellington boots
under the wooden bench undisturbed; he wouldn't be staying long
if he could help it.

He didn't like pathology; he never had. He appreciated that it had
to be done but that was as far as it went. The sights and smells of the
place made him feel claustrophobic – and not just the post-mortem
suite. The dark wooden shelving in the labs with their jars and bottles
of hellish contents put his teeth on edge and everywhere there was
the sickly sweet smell of tissue fixatives. While the upper world of

medicine smelt of antiseptic and ether, the underworld of pathology smelt strongly of alcohol and formaldehyde. He did, however, pause to slip on a plastic apron over the gown – always a wise precaution if you were going to be standing close to the table.

Neef entered the PM suite. It was a long, low-ceilinged room, white-tiled and lit by fluorescent lighting that gave everyone prison pallor and highlighted every pore on a human face. He saw MacSween at work at the furthest of four pedestal tables. He was crouching over a cadaver with his spectacles perilously close to the end of his nose but retained by his mask. His bushy, eyebrows hooded his eyes. Water gurgled down the drain channels of the steel table, preventing him from hearing Neef come in. It wasn't until he reached up to reposition the overhead lamp that he saw Neef approach.

'Ah, Michael, thank you for coming,' he said in his pleasing Scottish lilt, straightening up and putting his gloved hands to the small of his back as if to emphasise his stiffness.

'What have you got, Frank?' asked Neef.

'Put a mask on and I'll show you.'

MacSween looked down at his subject and for a moment the only sound in the room was that of the extractor fan in the ceiling above the table. There was a fault in it – the even sound of the motor was marred by an intermittent metallic click that defied syncopation. The fan stooped briefly, then started again.

MacSween said, 'This is Melanie Simpson, aged thirteen.'

Neef looked at the child's body. 'I'm sorry, I don't seem to —'

'No, she's not one of yours. She was brought over from University College Hospital. They're short-staffed in pathology at the moment; Eddie Miller's not well.'

MacSween looked up briefly and caught Neef's eye. They both knew that Eddie Miller, one of the pathologists at University College Hospital, had a serious drink problem. But he was close to retirement and his colleagues were covering for him. The general view was that a career of over thirty years in pathology deserved a dignified end. A black-tie dinner, a crystal-decanter presentation, speeches of appreciation, a bouquet for his wife, the whole bit. In the meantime his workload was being channelled towards routine post-mortems. Pathology on the living – the screening of biopsies and urgent tissue samples from the theatres – was carried out exclusively by his more sober and competent colleagues.

Eddie seemed to have accepted the situation. He had no choice. Any attempt to concern himself with a live patient and he would hit the pavement, thirty years or not.

'So what's the problem?'

'I've never seen anything quite like this,' said MacSween. 'Melanie had severe pneumonia. Both lungs.'

'Pneumococcal? Klebsiella?' asked Neef.

'Surprisingly, neither. It wasn't bacterial at all, so they assumed it was viral.'

'Unusual for viral pneumonia to be this virulent.'

'It is,' agreed MacSween, 'but that isn't why I called you. Look closely at her lungs. She should have been one of your patients.'

Neef looked at the lungs, which had been removed and were lying in two adjacent steel dishes. They were covered in small tumours.

'Good God,' whispered Neef. Have the lab examined them?'

'I've just had Charlie Morse do some quick sections; they're malignant all right. If the pneumonia hadn't killed her, the lung cancer would have done.'

Neef picked up a probe from the tray at the side of the table and examined the lungs more closely. 'Strange,' he murmured. 'No obvious candidate for a primary focus. What about her other organs?'

MacSween shook his head and said, 'Only the lungs are affected. That's why I called you down. I've never come across this in a child. As you say, it clearly wasn't just a case of a single tumour and then metastasis. There are multiple primary foci but all in the lungs.'

'So what do you think?' asked Neef, still mesmerised by the sight of the diseased lungs.

'I was hoping you were going to come up with a suggestion,' said MacSween. 'You're the cancer expert.'

'Neef shook his head. 'It clearly wasn't spontaneous. Apart from

3

anything else, kids this age simply don't get lung cancer. And the degree of tissue invasion suggests that some powerful carcinogen must have been involved – or maybe even a radiation source.'

'Like an atom bomb in the high street, you mean,' said MacSween wryly.

'I take your point,' said Neef. 'Radiation sources capable of causing this amount of damage are few and far between, so my best guess would be intimate contact with some sort of powerful carcinogenic chemical.'

'And they're *not* so few and far between.'

'Unfortunately not. It seems like every day we hear about a new one.'

'Thirteen years old, and look at her. She was just a bairn.'

Both men looked at the ivory white face of the dead girl, eyes closed, blonde hair held tightly behind her by the head block on the table. Her cheeks were unblemished and translucent giving her an ethereal appearance. She wouldn't have looked out of place on a stained glass window.

'She didn't even have a taste of life, damn it,' muttered MacSween.

Neef glanced sideways at him and saw that his eyes were moist.

'You're not supposed to think like that,' he said – as a friend as well as a colleague. 'You're a pathologist, remember? You're supposed to stand at the table eating your sandwiches and being cynical, like they do on television.'

'Sod television,' said MacSween.

Neef gave a shrug as if possibly embracing the philosophy, and MacSween gave a slight grin. 'So what do we do?' he said.

'We'll have to call the public health people in,' replied Neef.

'You don't want to wait until the lab have had a chance to identify the carcinogen?'

'It's too serious,' said Neef. 'They're going to have to trace the source so they might as well start looking while the lab do their tests. This is going to make some epidemiologist's day.'

'We'll have to tell University College. She's one of their patients, remember? We don't want to stand on anyone's toes.'

Neef nodded. 'It'll be interesting to hear what public health say,' he said thoughtfully. 'It's hard to think what carcinogens a thirteen-year-old schoolgirl could possibly come up against to cause this much damage.'

'She'd have to have had a Saturday job stripping blue asbestos out of factories single-handed,' said MacSween.

'Our present government would probably call that, work experience,' said Neef.

'Sod them too,' said MacSween.

'I've an awful feeling that before too long I might be adding the gentlemen of the press to your list,' said Neef, looking at his watch.'

'Problems?'

'The Torrance case. A reporter's coming to see me.'

'Oh yes, 'Little Tracy'. I read about that. You're on a hiding to nothing, laddie.'

'Tell me about it,' said Neef with a wry grim. 'I'd better go.'

Neef's secretary, Ann Miles, came into his room as soon as he returned. She was looking anxious. 'Ms Eve Sayers is here from the *Evening Citizen*,' she said. 'I don't think she's too pleased about being kept waiting. She kept reminding me that her appointment was for three o'clock.'

The clock on the wall of Neef's office said eight minutes past. He shrugged and said, 'Let's keep it quiet or someone'll come up with a charter about it . . .'

Ann Miles smiled conspiratorially and said, 'Shall I show her in?' Neef nodded.

A confident young woman in her late twenties, slim, good figure and wearing smart but casual clothes, came into the office. She looked about her as if the occupant of the office was of less interest than the decor. As Neef's room was a plain, standard-issue, NHS consulting room with little in the way of furnishings save for a desk and two filing cabinets, this gambit was doomed to failure. Neef assumed this was her way of showing her displeasure at being kept waiting. He waited

5

until he had her attention before smiling and saying, 'I'm Michael Neef. What can I do for you, Ms Sayers?' He indicated a chair in front of his desk.

The reporter sat down and swung her shoulder bag round to rest it on her knees while she extracted a small tape recorder; she placed it on the desk in front of her.

'Whatever happened to shorthand?' smiled Neef.

'Does it bother you?'

Neef shook his head. Sayers hit the record button and came straight to the point.

What do you say to accusations that you and your colleagues are not doing all you can to help little Tracy Torrance, Doctor Neef?' The voice was cool, confident, even intimidating.

Neef eyed the good-looking woman in front of him for fully five seconds before saying, 'Tracy Torrance has an incurable condition. My colleagues and I have done all we can for her. To suggest otherwise, as her mother did recently through the columns of your paper, is really quite irresponsible.'

'Isn't it true that money was a consideration in your decision not to offer Tracy further treatment?' Sayers asked.

'No,' replied Neef bluntly.

'My information is that there is a further treatment for Tracy's condition but you decided against it because it cost too much. What's your response to that, Doctor?'

Neef swallowed his anger and steeled himself to keep calm. He watched as Eve Sayers fiddled with the recording-level control on her tape machine. 'I would say that was a gross distortion of the facts.'

'Are you denying the existence of the treatment I'm referring to?' demanded the reporter, looking down at her level-indicator again.

'I know exactly which treatment you're referring to. It's not appropriate in Tracy Torrance's case.'

'Not appropriate?' repeated Eve Sayers challengingly.

'Not appropriate, as in "won't have any effect".'

'How can you be sure, Doctor?'

Neef shrugged and opened his palms in a gesture of concession.

6

'No one can be absolutely sure of anything in a case like this. None of us have a crystal ball to look into. I had to make a decision based on professional expertise and experience and that told me – after much consideration – that the treatment you refer to would not benefit this particular patient.'

'But if you admit you can't be absolutely sure, surely it's worth giving it a try. What have you got to lose?' asked Sayers. 'What has *Tracy* got to lose?'

'The treatment is very expensive. It would be a waste of resources. Other patients would suffer because of it.'

'So money *does* come into it?' said the reporter, making another adjustment to her recorder.

Neef was finding the constant fiddling with the machine annoying. It was as if the woman wasn't talking to him at all. She was trotting out questions like a speak-your-weight machine while her mind was on something else. This time he did not reply until she looked up and he felt he had her attention.

'Doesn't it?' she repeated.

'In that sense, of course it does,' Neef replied. 'My unit, like every other, has finite resources. We have to work within our means.'

The reporter's face took on a look of triumph. She said, 'So little Tracy will not get the treatment that could save her life because you have to work within your means. Isn't that what you're saying, Doctor?'

'No,' replied Neef coldly. 'Tracy Torrance will not get the treatment you refer to because I don't think it would do her any good.'

'Ah yes,' replied Sayers. 'Inappropriate.'

'Precisely,' said Neef, fixing her with a cold stare.

'Well, I think it only fair to tell you, Doctor, that my paper has decided to finance private treatment for Tracy. We'll be running the story in tomorrow's edition.'

Neef shook his head slightly and shrugged. 'You people have no idea of the damage you do, have you?'

'What damage? It seems quite straightforward to me, Doctor. Tracy can't get the treatment she needs on the NHS so my paper will give it to her privately.'

'Come with me,' said Neef, suddenly getting up out of his chair. He came round the other side of his desk and took the reporter's hand, almost dragging her out of the door. His abruptness seemed to have an effect. Sayers's self-confidence evaporated.

'Where are you taking me?' she gasped.

'You'll see.'

Neef led her up one flight of stairs and and opened the door of a ward marked ONCOLOGY ONE. There were some surgical gowns hanging on pegs behind the door. He handed one to her and told her to put it on.

The reporter did as she was told and followed Neef through the ward.

'There are sixteen kids here at the moment,' said Neef. 'All of them have tumours of one sort or another. How many others would you and your paper like to treat while you're at it?'

'Now, wait a minute,' stammered Eve Sayers. Tracy is a—'

'Special case?' interrupted Neef. 'No she isn't. There are lots of children here in the same position. So come on, how many?'

Sayers held up her hands as if warding off Neef's attack. 'We're a newspaper. It's not our job to provide treatment that should be provided as a matter of course. We can only afford to highlight the occasional case in the public interest. We couldn't possibly afford to—'

'You mean money comes into it?' Neef cut her off, feigning outrage. 'You mean your resources are finite, Ms Sayers? You have to work within your means? Good Lord, what an admission and when children's lives are at stake.'

'All right, you've made your point,' said Sayers quietly.

'I haven't finished,' said Neef. 'Take a good look.'

Sayers looked at the children in the ward through the glass walls of the cubicles. They looked so vulnerable, like refugees from some distant war. Many had no hair, a side effect of drugs and radiotherapy. The posters of Disney characters on the walls and the toys lying around served only to accentuate their isolation from normal childhood.

'Come and meet Neil,' said Neef. He led the way to a small side room where a little boy of about four was playing with a toy fire engine. He had his back to them when they entered. 'Hi Tiger!' said Neef softly and the boy turned round. Eve Sayers took in breath sharply when she saw the huge, disfiguring tumour on the left side of his face. It extended from above the cheek bone to the jawline and pulled his mouth out of alignment. 'Hello,' she smiled, regaining her composure. 'What have you got there?'

The boy tried to say 'fire engine' but the words were malformed by the pressure on his mouth of the tumour. Eve pretended he had said it anyway and repeated the words. She got down on her knees to admire the toy and wheeled it back to him. There was a pause while the boy appraised the stranger, then he giggled and pushed the toy towards Eve again. The game continued until a nurse came in and interrupted proceedings.

'Time for your sweeties, Neil,' she announced. 'Are you going to be a good boy and eat them all up?'

Neil gave a slow silent nod and got to his feet. The nurse fed him his medication and praised him with a cuddle when it was over.

Neef indicated to Eve that it was time to go. 'See you later, Tiger,' he said to Neil, and ushered Eve out of the room.

''Bye, Neil,' said Eve, looking backwards.

Neil made a gurgling sound.

'Why did you do that?' demanded Eve through gritted teeth as soon as they got outside the ward and were standing on the landing.

'Upset you, did it?'

'I was thinking of the boy,' she retorted. 'I wasn't prepared for it. He must have seen the reaction on my face.'

Neef paused for a moment before saying, 'Well, that's *something* in your favour. It was *his* feelings you were concerned about, not your own.'

'You haven't answered my question,' insisted Eve. Some of her former hostility seemed to have returned.

9

'You came to see me about a patient called Tracy Torrance,' said Neef.

'Yes.'

'But you didn't call her that, did you? You constantly referred to her as, "little Tracy".'

'Well, that's what the readers of the paper have come to know her as.'

'Thanks to you.'

'What are you getting at?'

'I mean you and your paper have been hitting the cuddly-bunny button from the word go and you knew exactly what you were doing.'

'I accept that there's been a certain emotional aspect to –'

'What about kids like Neil? Or should I say, "Little Neil" or maybe, "Baby Neil"? Do you think he'd fit the bill?'

Eve Sayers looked uncomfortable as she searched for an answer.

'Maybe not,' Neef continued. 'Neil doesn't have a mother to call the papers on his behalf and he doesn't look very pretty, does he? He's been in care since he was two years old, ever since his mother's boyfriend threw him at a wall when he dared to cry through a football match on the telly. And now he's got a tumour that's going to kill him before he's five. Not much of a life, Ms Sayers. Not much of a crowd-pleaser?'

Eve shook her head. 'Surely there's something that can be done for him.' she said. 'If it's a question of money perhaps it might be possible to—'

'And the others?' interrupted Neef, with a wave of his arm in the general direction of the children behind him.

Eve shrugged her shoulders but didn't say anything.

Neef waited a moment then said, 'Well, we've established that your paper has limited resources – just like my unit – and we both have to make decisions. I make mine on medical grounds while you and your paper prefer cuddly star quality. Tracy Torrance did not get a further course of treatment because I and my colleagues thought it medically inappropriate. The press, in the form of your paper, have decided she *will* get it because she looks adorable and will appeal to their readers. They, like you, can conveniently ignore all the other children. I and my staff cannot. We have to do our best for all our patients in this unit, Ms Sayers, and now, if you'll excuse me, I've got a lot to do.'

Eve Sayers turned on her heel and left without saying anything further. Her heels clicked on the stairs as she descended to the main corridor and gradually faded off into the distance. Neef stood for a moment on the landing, pretending to look out of the window at the courtyard below. He felt no sense of satisfaction over what had happened, just a kind of numb sadness. He returned to his office, sat down at his desk and rested his arms in front of him. Ann Miles came in and put a cup of coffee in front of him. 'I thought you might need this,' she said.

'Thanks,' said Neef.

'Can I take it Ms Sayers has gone?'

Neef said, 'Yes.'

Ann Miles sensed Neef's demeanour and said, 'Things didn't go well?'

'I lost my temper,' said Neef.

'Oh dear.'

'Oh dear, indeed,' sighed Neef. 'Now we'll have to wait and see how much damage she's going to do to us.'

'You think she will?'

Neef shrugged uncertainly. 'She came to do a cuddly-bunny story about Tracy Torrance. You know the form, penny-pinching doctor condemns baby to death. Local paper rides to the rescue accompanied by the cheers of its readers.'

'I hate it when they do that,' said Ann. 'Surely they can't really believe that anyone would allow a child to die to save money.'

'I don't know what they really believe,' confessed Neef. 'Maybe they do it without thinking. I don't know.'

Ann looked at the clock on the wall and said, 'You're not going to thank me for reminding you, but you have a meeting with management at four.'

'Jesus,' sighed Neef. It was three minutes to.

'Ah, Michael,' said Tim Heaton, the hospital chief executive, as Neef entered and saw that he was the last to arrive.

The monthly hospital management meeting had become an unpleasant fact of life as far as Neef was concerned. Administrators seemed to have blossomed like weeds after rain over the past few years. This was partly due to changes in political philosophy, but mainly down to the fact that the hospital had taken NHS trust status under government guidelines. They were now responsible for their own finances. Individual consultants had to fight their corner in order to achieve the funding they needed for their own units but tended to form alliances against the 'suits' – non-medical managers brought in from outside to run 'the business' of purveying medicine to the sick. The situation often reminded Neef of the constantly warring factions of Renaissance Italy.

As always, Heaton was dressed immaculately, dark suit, dazzlingly white shirt and trendily patterned silk tie. This always made Neef aware of his own sartorial shortcomings. The mere sight of the man made his suit feel uncomfortably old and his trousers more than a little baggy. Another thing that Neef noticed was that, at whatever time of day one met Heaton, he always looked as if he had just shaved. His perennially tanned skin never betrayed a hint of stubble. He had come to the trust from the business world, having been chief executive of a large engineering firm with extensive overseas contracts. Although loath to admit it at first, Neef had come to concede that the man had 'people skills'. He was a good administrator.

'I think we're all here now,' said Heaton.

Neef took his seat at the table with ten others, including Heaton. He smiled briefly in the general direction of everyone and gave a special nod to Frank MacSween. The papers for the meeting had been placed in front of him. Neef noticed that this appeared as a minor triumph of desktop publishing. Laser-printed text and a brand-new logo for the hospital – healing hands lightly holding a dove, done in pastel blue – had taken over from the xeroxed, typewritten, much-Tipp-Exed scripts of the past.

Heaton turned to his left and said, 'I'm going to call upon our finance director to make his report, just in broad general terms if you would, Phillip?'

Neef gave silent thanks for the 'broad general terms' rider. Phillip Danziger had an accountant's love of figures that he found hard to share. In the red or in the black was really all he wanted to know.

The tall, gangly accountant got to his feet and donned a pair of horn-rimmed glasses before nodding to Tim Heaton and saying, 'Of course.' He shuffled some papers before beginning 'Basically, ladies and gentlemen, we've got problems,' he said.

There were groans around the table.

'We're holding our own for the moment but the future doesn't look good.'

'But what about the extra business we took from the old General when it closed?' asked Carol Martin, the director of nursing services.

'Our financial position has been artificially sweetened by the closure of our nearest rival, said Danziger, enunciating, formal, every gangling inch the accountant. 'But patient projections seem to suggest that we may lose much of the extra business when the new surgical centre at University College Hospital comes on line in November. As usual, their marketing has been excellent and it looks like being a big success. GPs will be falling over themselves to get what they see as the newest for their patients.'

'Doesn't mean the surgery will be any better,' said Mark Louradis, one of the consultant surgeons, his Mediterranean features betraying irritation.

'Of course not,' said Heaton, 'but image is important. We have to face it: University College has been very successful in promoting itself as a hospital at the very cutting edge of medical science.'

'True,' conceded Neef. 'There's scarcely a week goes by without some newspaper doing a feature on them. Last week, their lithotripsy programme, this week, their new surgical facilities. Pharmaceutical companies must be queuing up to pour money into the place to get a bit of reflected glory.'

'They don't even do transplants,' said Louradis.

'The trouble is, said Heaton, 'that the public aren't intrigued by transplant surgery any more, Mark. The newspapers have used up all the angles and the chattering classes are getting a bit bored with it. We need new treatments to give our image a bit of a boost and capture their imagination.'

Frank MacSween gave a slight snort.

Louradis said with a tight-lipped smile, 'It's getting to the stage when we'll be spending more on advertising and marketing than we do on nurses.'

'A slight exaggeration, I feel,' said Tim Heaton. 'But I say again, image is important. We are a big hospital and we're good but we can't afford to rest on our laurels. We have to move with the times, think of new ways of projecting ourselves, new ways of generating income.'

As usual, this kind of talk left Michael Neef feeling bemused. He had been a reluctant convert to NHS trust philosophy. In the beginning he had wanted to shout, 'We're a hospital, not a bloody supermarket' – but time had mellowed him and he had come to accept that things had changed in medicine and this was the way they were going to be in future. Ironically, he had given up a lucrative appointment in the States and come home to England because he wanted to return to 'real medicine' instead of finance-orientated treatment. A revolution had occurred during his three-year absence; a service had become a business.

It had been like that from the beginning in the States of course, where he had been chief of paediatric oncology at Gregor Memorial Hospital in New York. His initial sense of freedom at having apparently unlimited resources and the best of equipment to practise medicine as he saw fit had been gradually eroded by the knowledge that it was not available to all those who needed it. His patients were those whose families could afford to pay.

His initial belief that personal health insurance, which most people had, was just an alternative to the national system at home had to be modified in the light of what happened when such personal cover ran out, as it almost invariably did where terminal illness was concerned. Family grief was too often compounded by financial ruin as parents struggled to do their best for dying children.

Danziger continued with his report, outlining which requests for ex-budget equipment had been approved and which had been declined for the moment – put on hold, as Heaton liked to say. Each unit in the hospital was allocated an annual budget but it was accepted that medical advances or simple circumstances might dictate that requests for special funding outside this budget would be made. Neef had not lodged any request for equipment in the past few months but he had made out a case for special funding for a new chemotherapeutic drug. There were several new ones coming on to the market and he was keen to try this one after reading the clinical trial results in the journals.

As if reading his thoughts, Danziger looked at Neef and said, 'Michael, I'm afraid we've had to decline your request for that the new American drug to be made available to your patients *en masse*. The sub-committee thought the benefits would be marginal and that the extra costs could not be justified.'

Neef turned his pen end over end on the table for a moment while he considered his response. This was shaping up to be one awful day.

'I see,' he said. 'Perhaps I can remind the sub-committee that I've been particularly restrained in my requests for new chemotherapeutic agents. I don't routinely request every new preparation that becomes available, because I do my homework on them first. If I think the benefits will be marginal I don't ask for them. However – Neef paused for effect – 'if I *do* ask for a drug to be made available its because I do believe that the benefits to my patients would be tangible. Antivulon has shown itself to be thirty-per-cent less toxic to normal tissue cells when it's used against tumours, and it's much less distressing in terms of side effects. This is a very important factor where children are concerned.'

15

'We understand your disappointment, Michael, believe me,' said Heaton, 'But with so many competing causes . . .'

'I will re-lodge my request this month,' said Neef.

'As you wish,' said Heaton anxious to defuse the situation. He looked across the table and said, 'Perhaps our commercial contracts manager will have something to cheer us up. Andrew?'

Andrew D'Arcy, a small, puckish man wearing a blue pin-striped suit and a pink bow-tie smiled and said, 'I have two pieces of good news.'

'Thank God for that,' said Frank MacSween in a stage whisper.

D'Arcy either didn't hear, or *pretended* not to hear, and continued, 'Verner Mann – you know, the pharmaceutical people – have asked us to carry out the clinical trial work on their new third-generation cephalosporin. They reckon it'll be particularly effective in clearing up urinary tract infections. They're offering a pretty generous package, too, and it could lead to further collaboration.'

'Excellent,' said Heaton. 'I take it our consultant urologist knows all about this.'

'Peter's giving a seminar in Manchester today,' replied D'Arcy, 'but the deal has his full approval.'

'Good. What about your second piece of news?'

'D'Arcy looked at Michael Neef before saying apologetically, 'Unfortunately I haven't had time to discuss this with Michael beforehand. I understand he was tied up with the press when I rang him but I've had a call from a biotechnology company called, Menogen Research.' The name did not appear to mean anything to anyone at the table. 'They're a small local company. They were funded by venture capital about ten years ago. They've been developing gene therapy strategies for tumour treatment and they feel they're now at the stage of moving to human clinical trials and want to begin discussions along these lines.'

Heaton beamed and said, 'Gene therapy! Genetic engineering! Now that would capture the public imagination. The Sunday papers are always full of it. This sounds exactly like the sort of thing we need to raise our profile. What do you think, Michael?'

'I think we need to know an awful lot more about Menogen Research before they get anywhere near our patients, but I'd certainly like to talk to them.'

'Excellent,' said Heaton.

'I do have to stress that there's not going to be much in the way of financial gain for the trust in this, said Danziger, 'but, as Tim says, it's a high-profile project. We could get lots of media attention.'

'It's also a high-risk area,' said Frank. 'University College Hospital got involved in it last year with a cystic fibrosis trial that didn't do terribly well as I remember.'

'But it got them a lot of attention,' said Heaton.

'And that's the main thing,' said MacSween, under his breath. He gave Neef a furtive smile.

Neef stayed behind for a few minutes with Andrew D'Arcy and Tim Heaton to discuss suitable times for a meeting with the people from Menogen Research.

'How come we've never heard of them?' Heaton asked D'Arcy.

'Because,' said D'Arcy, 'they're one of many biotech companies set up in the early eighties when venture capital flowed in like champagne at a wedding. Genetic engineering was the thing to sink your money into and everyone wanted to get in on the act. Unfortunately for most of them, things didn't move as fast as the hype suggested. Many companies went to the wall when funding was withdrawn.'

'What went wrong?' asked Neef.

D'Arcy shrugged his shoulders and said, 'I suppose a number of things were to blame. Investors were looking for quick profits and when that didn't happen they started getting restless. They felt they'd been conned but that wasn't really true. The scientists had just been overoptimistic; they kept hitting problems they hadn't envisaged and everyone had underestimated the amount of red tape involved in moving research from the science lab into the real-life environment of a hospital. This hurdle's much higher for the biotech people than the drug companies because of the moral implications involved in gene swapping. Everyone wants to have their say. Ethics committees abound.'

'But Menogen obviously survived,' said Heaton.

'They did,' said D'Arcy. 'They were bright enough not to get into competition with the big boys. A big problem at the beginning was that a whole lot of companies tried to do the same thing. They all wanted to clone interferon and human insulin and there could only be one winner's name on the patent when it was filed. Menogen opted out at the very start and concentrated on less ambitious projects. They did very nicely out of cloning blood factors and coming up with new diagnostic kits. That not only kept them in business, but enabled them to employ some hot-shot molecular biologists to develop the business. It seems this investment has paid off. They've come up with several new gene delivery vectors and they are running strongly in the gene therapy race.'

Heaton leaned forward conspiratorially and said, 'I know that gene therapy is the latest thing and all that but . . . what exactly is it?'

'Neef smiled and said, 'It's a technique where a functioning gene is inserted into a patient's cells in order to correct a deficiency in their own genes. Alternatively it can be used to introduce a new function altogether to the patient's cells.'

'But surely that means you'll be altering the genetic make-up of the patient?' said Heaton.

'To a very limited extent,' said Neef. 'No one's trying to alter germ cells like sperm or ova. There's no question of introducing heritable changes, just localized ones to help individual patients – and believe me, that's proving difficult enough. The whole business is still in its infancy.'

'But it's going to be big in the future,' said D'Arcy.

'There seems little doubt about that,' agreed Neef.

'So Menogen Research would like to try out this technology on our patients,' said Heaton.

'That's the general idea,' replied D'Arcy. 'They were honest enough to admit that they'd approached University College Hospital first but had been turned down on the grounds that Uni

College have their own gene therapy initiative run by their medical school.'

'Did you ask them about the paperwork?' asked Neef. 'It's all in order as far as licences and safety certificates are concerned. Of course, it will have to be passed by our own ethics and safety committee, once we find out the details of what the company have in mind.'

'Exciting,' said Heaton. 'Don't you think so, Michael?'

'Absolutely,' agreed Neef, feeling that this was the response that Heaton required.

'The cutting edge, that's where we want to be.'

D'Arcy looked at his watch and said he had to go. Neef took the opportunity of being alone with Heaton to warn him about the imminent bad publicity he felt Eve Sayers was about to bestow on them.

Heaton shrugged philosophically. 'It's been coming. Ever since the interview with Mrs Torrance last week, I had the feeling that the paper was going to get involved. It looked too good an opportunity for them to miss. I imagine it was a toss-up between sponsoring a trip to Disneyland or lashing out on private medicine. Unfortunately for us it's going to be the latter. Still, we'll survive.'

Neef didn't mention anything about losing his temper with the journalist but he reminded himself that Heaton wouldn't have done that. He was far too smooth.

'Incidentally, Michael,' said Heaton as they left the boardroom and he ushered Neef out first. 'I am aware that you've remained within budget for the last year and a half. I'll make a point of bringing this point up at the next meeting of the pharmacy sub-committee.'

'I'd be grateful,' said Neef. 'I feel sure the American drug is worth trying.'

'That's good enough for me,' said Heaton. 'We've got to do our best for our patients, even the poor little blighters in your unit. Let's hope this thing with Menogen works out. It could be good for everyone.'

Heaton gave a last smile and walked off with his usual confident gait. Neef watched him go and permitted himself a wry smile. That was how it was done, he thought. Heaton would get him the new American drug if he played ball with Menogen.

Two

Neef looked at his watch and saw that it was five thirty. He walked slowly back to the unit and looked in on Sister Kate Morse in the duty room of Oncology One.

'Hello stranger,' she said when Neef put his head round the door.

'It is getting a bit like that, isn't it?' said Neef, pulling out a metal-framed chair and plumping himself down wearily in front of her desk. 'How are our patients? Maybe I'll get round to seeing them soon!'

Kate Morse smiled indulgently. She was a pleasant-looking woman of an age with Neef, married with two children of her own. Her husband, Charlie – also in his mid-thirties – was chief technician in the pathology lab.

'The Martin boy has had a bad day and Lisa Short has started going downhill as we feared. Lawrence called her parents this afternoon. They're coming in. Lawrence said he'll see them and sit with them; he's on duty this evening.'

Neef nodded. Lawrence Fielding was his senior registrar and largely responsible for the day-to-day running of the unit.

'Everyone else is holding their own. Freda and Charles have shown definite signs of improvement.'

'Good. I looked in earlier with a visitor but I didn't have time to talk.'

'I heard,' said Kate meaningfully. 'A journalist.'

Neef saw the knowing look on her face. He said, 'It's brace-yourself time again, I'm afraid.'

'I'll have a word with the younger nurses,' said Kate. 'They always take it worst when they suddenly find out they're part of a uncaring organization that always puts money first and doesn't give a hoot about the patients.' There was more than a hint of venom in her voice.

'I'd be obliged, Kate,' said Neef, getting to his feet. 'Maybe I should have a word with our junior doctors. How are they getting on, by the way?' There had been a staff rotation two weeks before when two new housemen had been appointed to the unit for six months. Neef had not seen much of them.

'They'll do,' said Kate. 'They're taking it all to heart but that's no bad thing at this stage. It's the ones who take it in their stride that I worry about.'

'Me too,' agreed Neef. 'I'll have a walk round before I go.'

Kate Morse got to her feet to accompany him but Neef raised his hand. 'No,' he said. 'Just a little walk round on my own.'

Neef went first to the side room to where Lisa Short had been moved. One of the nurses was with her, making her more comfortable, although she seemed too sleepy to notice. The nurse stood up when she saw Neef enter but he held up his hand to indicate that she should continue. 'I just popped in to say hello,' he said. 'How is she?'

'Dr Fielding increased her painkillers earlier but he wanted to keep her conscious if at all possible. I understand her parents are on their way. She seems fine at the moment, just pleasantly drowsy. No pain.

'Never-never land,' said Neef, his face tinged with sadness.

Lisa's eyes flickered open and he smiled and took her hand. 'Hello there,' he said gently. 'Mummy and Daddy will be here soon.'

The child's mouth made an attempt at a smile but she was very weak and her eyes closed again. Neef lifted her medication chart from the hook at the foot of her bed and noted what Lawrence Fielding had written her up for and at what time it had been given. He checked his watch and said, 'Let's hope her parents make it within the hour.'

The nurse nodded, allowed herself a brief moment for reflection, then set about busying herself rearranging toys along the back of Lisa's locker. She had worked in oncology for eight months. She had learned how to cope.

Neef continued round the unit checking charts and scheduled treatments for the following day. John Martin was supposed to start a course of radiotherapy in the morning but, as Kate Morse had reported, it had been a bad day for him. One of the housemen, Tony Samuels, was with him.

'How's he doing?' asked Neef.

The houseman hadn't heard Neef approach and was startled. He got to his feet, nervously feeling at his tie.

'Sorry, I didn't mean to startle you,' said Neef. 'How is he?'

'Comfortable for the moment,' replied Samuels, regaining his composure. 'I think it's just been a bad reaction to chemotherapy. We may have to consider changing it. What do you think, sir?'

'Not just yet,' replied Neef. 'We'll keep him on standard primary regimen for another couple of days. See how he gets on. If he still reacts badly, we'll think about changing then.'

'What about his radiotherapy tomorrow?'

'Cancel it,' said Neef. 'Poor kid's got enough on his plate right now. We'll think again about that in a couple of days as well.'

'Very good, sir.'

Neef saw that Tracy Torrance had been moved to a side room and guessed why. He looked round the door and had his suspicions confirmed. The floor was almost covered in cuddly toys that had been sent in by readers of the *Evening Citizen* after the first story. He knew Tracy's parents wouldn't be here this evening: they were appearing on a local television programme. He himself had been asked to appear but had declined, preferring that a 'hospital spokesman' be used instead. 'Hello Tracy,' he said.

The little girl smiled up at him and he felt pleased that she knew nothing about the political and show-business wranglings going on over her illness.

'Who have you got there?' he asked.

'Mr Raggins,' replied the child, holding up the rag doll she had come in with. She hadn't come to terms with the host of brand-new cuddly strangers surrounding her. This was a feature of terminal conditions in children. They lost their interest and excitement in new things, preferring to cling to the old and familiar.

Neef saved looking in on Neil Benson till last. He tried not to have favourites among the children, or at least not to show it, but he did have a soft spot for Neil.

'Hello, Tiger,' he said when the boy saw him. Neil held his arm up in the air and Neef knew this was the signal to present him with his own open palm. Neil brought his hand down on Neef's in his own version of a high-five. Neef smiled. There was something about Neil, an inner strength, a resilience that went way beyond his years – or prospects, come to that.

There seemed little doubt that Neil's tumour, a malignant melanoma, was going to end in his death, but for the past three weeks it had stopped growing. Daily measurement of the affected area had shown a plateau on the graph. Unfortunately, the tumour had not shown any sign of regression but they had been afforded a breathing space and there were so many non-medical factors at work in cancer therapy that it was unwise to predict anything with an air of complete certainty.

Neef finished his round and popped his head round the door of the duty room to say good night to Kate Morse.

'You're off, then?' she said.

'Some days feel like they've had thirty-six hours in them. This has been one,' said Neef.

'Chin up,' said Kate, smiling. 'Most people know that you can't believe all you read in the papers.'

'I hope that's true, for all our sakes,' said Neef.

'Don't take it to heart, Mike,' said Kate softly. 'It's what's really true that matters, not how these people twist or misrepresent things.'

Neef nodded and said, 'Thanks, Kate. Maybe you and Lawrence and I could have a meeting tomorrow? There's a biotech company interested in carrying out a gene-therapy trial on our patients. I'd like to know your feelings before I talk to them.'

'Sounds interesting,' said Kate. 'Anything resembling progress is always welcome.'

Neef drove home slowly. The evening rush hour was long past, the sky had cleared, the wind had dropped and evening sunshine was filtering through the leaf canopy on the long narrow lane leading down to where his cottage nestled at the foot of a steep single-track road. It was no more than eight miles from the hospital. Getting this cottage was the luckiest thing that had ever happened to him, Neef reckoned.

He had just come back from the States to take up the job at St George's and was desperately looking for somewhere to stay. He had spent another fruitless evening looking at overpriced flats in the area when he had taken a wrong turning on the way back to the hotel where he was staying and found himself at the foot of the hill. He had been looking for a place to turn the car round when he had come across the cottage lying derelict among tall grass and wild rose bushes that were threatening to engulf it.

Intrigued, he had looked around and discovered that a railway had once run along the base of the hill. The track had long since been removed but he found evidence of ballast and it was possible to follow the route of the line through the undergrowth. The location of the cottage said that it had probably had something to do with that railway, had perhaps been the home of a signalman or level-crossing operator. After checking with British Rail and discovering that they had forgotten about the existence of the line and the cottage, Neef had badgered them until they had come up with the deeds to the property and, after a lot more prompting, they had finally agreed to sell it to him. He had spent the last three years making it habitable and comfortable.

Neef parked his Land Rover Discovery on the piece of land he had cleared beside the cottage for that purpose. He needed a four-wheel-drive vehicle to get up the hill in winter. This neck of the woods was definitely not a priority on the local council's gritting schedule.

As he opened the door, the 'lady' of the house came to meet him. Dolly was soft and sleek and very elegant. She moved silently and with a graceful sinewy gait that always evoked his admiration. She also had a beautiful, thick, furry tail. Dolly was a cat – but not just any cat, as Neef was always keen to point out. Dolly was a Maine Coon.

Dolly brushed up against Neef's legs and then again as he stooped to stroke her. 'I take it this means your bowl is empty,' he said. He was more used to being ignored. 'Let's get you something.'

Dolly followed Neef to the kitchen where he opened a tin of cat food for her and carried it out to the back porch where her bowl was kept. Dolly scampered round his feet and waited impatiently until Neef had emptied out the contents; she almost pushed him out the way in her anxiety to start eating. Neef stood up and looked down at her. 'I take it I'm no longer required,' he said. Dolly did not interrupt her meal.

Neef poured himself a large whisky and settled down in an armchair that looked out through french windows to the back garden. The evening sunshine was now deep yellow, almost orange, and he wished it could have been the end to a better day. He toyed with the idea of not watching the TV programme featuring the Torrance couple but throught better of it. It would be as well to know the worst. He turned on the TV.

The Torrance report was the third item in the local news bulletin and started with a summary of the facts, then the camera moved towards Mr and Mrs Torrance sitting, facing a reporter.

'But you don't accept that your daughter's condition is beyond help, do you, Mrs Torrance?' the reporter asked.

Mrs Torrance, a slight woman with dyed red hair and gimlet-hard eyes, held a handkerchief to her face while her husband, much taller and broader and with a vacant expression, put his arm round her. 'No,' I don't,' she almost whispered.

'You say you believe there's a treatment that would help Tracy but that she is not getting it. Is that correct?'

The woman nodded silently, keeping the handkerchief to her mouth.

'Why not, Mrs Torrance?' asked the reporter gently.

'Money. They won't treat my little girl because it's too expensive.'

'They're going to let her die,' Mr Torrance butted in.

'I know this must be very distressing for you,' continued the interviewer, 'but the hospital of course, deny this. They maintain that the decision not to treat Tracy was made entirely on medical grounds. Money was not a consideration. What do you say to that?'

'They bloody would, wouldn't they?' retorted Mr Torrance. 'Ever since they became – what do they call it? – a trust, a bloody trust, it's money, not people, they're interested in.'

The scene changed then to an outside shot of St George's Hospital, with a familiar voice out of vision for a few seconds before the picture cut to the hospital press officer, John Marshall, looking as smooth as the TV professionals themselves, with a caption telling viewers who he was.

'Obviously, our deepest sympathy goes out the Torrances,' he said smoothly to an unseen interviewer – presumably the one who had been with the Torrances. 'But unfortunately health professionals have to make decisions that won't always be popular with everyone. While we fully understand the Torrances' situation, I have to say that the decision was made for medical reasons and medical reasons alone.'

Neef silently gave thanks.

The filmed report ended, and the studio anchorman came into shot.

'John Marshall, press officer for St George's, ending that special report by Naomi Harrison. Well, in the last half-hour – since that report was compiled – we've learned that the local newspaper, the *Evening Citizen*, has offered to step in and pay for private treatment for little Tracy. And we've been joined live in the studio, at short notice, by Mr and Mrs Torrance, who you saw on that film a short time ago.'

The camera moved back to reveal a red-eyed Mrs Torrance sitting next to the presenter, her husband alongside her. Then the picture cut to a close-up of her, clearly contrived to capture the tears as they flowed down her face. Her shoulders shook silently.

'What's your reaction to what must surely be very heartening news, Mrs Torrance?' asked the presenter.

'There are no words . . .' she began, as the camera moved back once more to bring her husband into the shot with her.

'No words,' he agreed, with a shake of his head.

After a few more unspectacular and rather obvious and, to Neef's mind, indulgent questions and the predictable answers, the shot cut to the presenter, who, with a look of practised concern, allowed just a second of silence before moving on to the next item.

Neef had watched the whole thing without a flicker of emotion. He turned off the TV using the remote and gave a sigh of resignation before downing the remainder of his drink. 'Momma told me there'd be days like this,' he groaned as he got up and went through to the kitchen. There was a decision to be made. Should he make himself something to eat or should he have another drink? He poured the whisky and paused to put some music on the CD-player before settling down again to gaze out at the garden. The music was the Albinoni *Adagio*. In a few minutes the sadness would come as thoughts of Elaine returned.

Neef's wife, Elaine, had died nearly four years before of cancer of the liver. They had been married for seven years. There were no children. His rehabilitation had been slow but time had done its bit and taken the edge off the pain he had once thought unbearable. Still, when he listened to the Albinoni, Elaine's favourite, waves of sadness would wash over him and rekindle the pain of her loss. He put his head back on the chair and looked up at the ceiling. 'I still miss you,' he whispered.

The music finished and left a sudden vacuum in the room. Neef brought his head up from the chair back and felt as if he had just landed after a long flight. He was back on the ground; there were adjustments to be made. His drink was finished and he had things to do. He had a life to get on with. He would make himself something to eat and then he would catch up on reading the medical journals, particularly those dealing with gene therapy.

Just after nine thirty, the telephone rang. It startled Neef, who had been deeply into an article on the gene-therapy treatment of cystic fibrosis. It was this treatment that University College Hospital had come to grief over when they had tried it last year. The results had not been good, with none of the patients on the trial showing lasting improvement and several of them showing strong inflammatory reactions to the treatment. It had all been a big disappointment, not only for the patients and their relatives but also for the hospital, which had attracted a lot of publicity at the time for its pioneering work, and for David Farro-Jones, a friend of Neef's and the leading molecular biologist from their medical school, who had set up the trial.

'Neef.'

'Dr Neef?' asked a woman's voice. 'Dr Michael Neef?'

'Yes, who is this?'

'It's Eve Sayers. I found you through the phone book.'

Neef felt his heart sink. Hadn't this woman done enough damage? What more could she possibly want? He tried to work out what new scheme she might have come up with to pay him back for what he had said to her. 'Why?' he asked bluntly.

'I know I'm not exactly flavour of the month as far as you're concerned . . .'

Neef remained silent as if to affirm this.

'But it's been preying on my mind . . .'

'What has?'

29

'Everything really. You, the unit, the little boy, Neil. What you said. Everything.'

Neef was still very much on his guard. 'Would you please come to the point, Ms Sayers,' he said. 'I'm a bit busy at the moment.'

'Dr Neef, I'm finding it very hard to say what I want to say on the telephone. Could I possibly come over and speak to you personally?'

'I think not, Ms Sayers. I really don't understand what it is that you want from me.'

'It's simple really, but oh so difficult. I just wanted to say that I was sorry.'

Neef could hardly believe his ears. 'Sorry?'

'It's true,' said Eve. 'For the first time in my professional life I've been feeling ashamed of something I've done and I wanted to apologize. I just didn't understand.'

Neef couldn't rid himself of suspicion, which made a response difficult.

'I'm sorry, I can't stop the second story going into the *Citizen* tomorrow – the one about the paper's offer to sponsor treatment. Things have gone too far already. My editor saw his chance to announce the private-treatment angle early and get publicity for the paper on television this evening. The Torrances were being interviewed.'

'I saw them.'

'But I've done my best to tone it down for the paper's version tomorrow.'

'Well, thanks for that,' said Neef.

'I really am sorry.'

'Perhaps I took one hell of a leap onto the moral high ground if truth be told,' said Neef.

'You were entitled to. There's one thing I must ask you?'

'What?'

'What will happen to Neil? You will note I said, "Neil", not "little Neil" or "baby Neil".' Eve added disarmingly.

'Neil has a malignant melanoma. There's nothing we can do for him except deal with the pain and keep him as comfortable as possible.'

Eve paused as if she had found the finality of Neef's reply difficult to cope with. 'There's nothing you can do?' she asked.

'I'm afraid not.

'It must be absolute hell for his mother,' said Eve when she had recovered her composure.

'Neil's mother abandoned him,' said Neef. 'He cramped her style.'

'How do you do it?' Eve asked in a quiet whisper. 'How can you go on working with kids who are dying, day in day out, when there's nothing you can do for them.'

'There's actually quite a lot we can do for them,' said Neef.

'But it's cancer you're dealing with,' said Eve. 'You've got chemotherapy and radiotherapy and not much else. Some even say the treatment's as bad as the disease.'

'There's also surgery and exchange transfusion and various other techniques.'

'But you must lose a lot,' said Eve.

Neef conceded the point. 'Yes, we do.'

'I'm sorry,' said Eve, 'I just don't understand how you and the nurses can bear it.'

'Sometimes we can't,' said Neef, 'We owe it to each other not to show it.'

'We don't cry out loud.'

'Pardon?'

'It's a song . . . Elkie Brooks.'

Neef said, 'Look, we're not saints. We're just well-trained people doing the best we can with the resources we have. I don't like people glamorizing the staff any more than I do the patients.'

'But it's not something everyone could do,' said Eve.

'When staff tell me that they can't bear it, that they want to transfer, I point out to them that the kids they leave behind are still going to die. Wouldn't it be better if they stuck around and did their best for them? Medicine isn't just about dealing with

31

curable conditions: it's also about doing our best for the patients who can't be cured. If the best we can do for them means keeping them pain-free and comfortable up until the end, so be it. We owe them that. But things are getting better all the time.'

Eve took a moment to digest what Neef had said then she asked, 'Are things really getting better all the time?'

'Maybe not as fast as we'd like but yes, and gene therapy is about to come into its own in the next few years. In fact, there's talk of us doing a clinical trial in the very near future.'

'But cancer isn't a genetic problem,' said Eve.

'No, but it doesn't have to be for gene therapy,' said Neef. 'The strategy will be to introduce genetic change in the tumour cells, which will make them vulnerable to other killing agents.'

'I see,' said Eve. 'And you say you're going to be trying this out?'

'It's possible but nothing's been decided yet. There's still some negotiating to be done.'

'But supposing you do get the go-ahead . . .' said Eve. 'Is it possible that Neil might be given this new treatment?'

'Whoa,' said Neef. 'We're a long way from deciding things like that.'

'I'm sorry,' said Eve. 'That was unfair and I've been taking up too much of your time.'

'Not at all. It was nice of you to call and say what you did.'

'Dr Neef?'

Neef noticed the nervousness that had suddenly appeared in Eve's voice. 'Yes.'

'Do you think I could come and visit Neil?'

Neef was taken aback. 'I really don't think that's a good idea,' he said. 'Forming an attachment to a child in Neil's position is asking for a whole lot of heartbreak.'

'I'm aware of that,' said Eve. 'I've just had a short lecture in how to handle it. It's just that I think he liked me and if I can play with him and make him smile a little then I'll have done my best too?'

'I'm really not sure . . .'

'I wouldn't have asked if he'd had a mother or anyone else interested in him.'

'I'll think about it. Give me a call in a couple of days,' said Neef.

'I will,' said Eve.

Three

'You look tired,' said Kate Morse, when Neef came into the duty room.

It was hardly surprising. He hadn't slept well. The day's events had thrown up a montage of images that had haunted the margins between sleep and wakefulness, making sure that complete rest did not come. Mrs Torrance's gimlet eyes accused him. 'Going to let her die,' said her husband over and over again. 'Just a bairn,' said Frank MacSween as his face materialized from Melanie Simpson's empty chest cavity.

It had not been until the first reassuring grey light of morning sneaked in through the V in the curtains that Neef had fallen soundly asleep. Little more than an hour later, Dolly had woken him with her paw on his cheek, having decided it was breakfast time.

'I didn't sleep well,' Neef told Kate as he picked up the night report.

'Lisa died at three this morning,' Kate announced. 'Her parents and Lawrence were with her.' Neef nodded. 'And a solicitor employed by the *Evening Citizen* called to say that arrangements had been made to transfer Tracy Torrance to the Randolf Clinic this afternoon.'

Neef nodded again.

'Did you see the TV report last night?' asked Kate.

'I did,' said Neef. 'I also had a call from Ms Sayers.'

'Who?'

'Eve Sayers, the *Citizen* reporter who's doing the story.'

'Hasn't she done enough damage?' exclaimed Kate. 'These people are beyond the pale!'

'Actually, she phoned to apologize.'

'She what?' exclaimed Kate.

'She wanted to apologize for what she was doing to us.'

'Do you think she was genuine?' asked Kate.

'I was suspicious at first but I think maybe she was. I couldn't figure out an alternative angle.'

'A reporter apologizing? Whatever brought that on?'

'I think Neil may have had something to do with it,' said Neef. 'She met him during the course of a somewhat forced guided tour I subjected her to yesterday. The pair of them hit it off. She wants to come and visit him.'

'And what did you say?' asked Kate in tones that left Neef in no doubt about what she thought of the idea.

'I said that I didn't think it was a good idea.'

'It isn't.'

'She was persistent. I said I'd think about it.'

Kate Morse's look said what she thought.

'I know, I know,' said Neef. 'But Neil doesn't have anyone and he obviously took a shine to her yesterday.'

'You're the boss,' said Kate. 'But have you thought how having a journalist like her around the place is going to affect the staff? Everyone's going to be on their guard in case they make some little mistake and find themselves on the front page of the *Citizen*.'

'I must confess, I hadn't considered that. I was assuming that she'd be coming here in a strictly non-professional capacity.'

'At the very least, I think we'd have to be assured of that,' said Kate. 'And another thing.'

'What?'

'If she visits Neil and they do hit it off, she has to keep coming back. She doesn't visit a couple of times and then disappear when the novelty's worn off.'

'Absolutely.'

'Even when the going gets tough,' added Kate with a meaning-ful look.

'That goes without saying.'

'I still think you should make sure she understands all the implications.'

'It may not come to that,' said Neef. 'I won't decide anything until I've seen the story in the *Citizen* this evening. She said she was going to do her best to back-pedal on it.'

'I think you have to consider . . .'

'What?'

'Ms Sayers may have decided to get herself a story about a child oncology unit. She may be using Neil to get on the inside, so to speak.'

Neef nodded and said, 'To my shame, I thought of that too. I even considered that the whole apology scenario was part of some con.'

'The safe course—'

'Is to say, no. I know, Kate. It's just that I'm not sure. She may be entirely genuine and to dismiss her intentions unfairly—'

'Would be unforgivable and not you at all,' said Kate, smiling. 'Up to you.'

'Let's forget it for the moment. I'm sure there are more pressing things to consider?'

Kate Morse nodded, adjusted her spectacles and opened her day folder. 'Lawrence suggested we have the meeting you wanted at four this afternoon when he comes back on duty?'

'Fine.'

'We have an admission at eleven this morning, a twelve-year-old boy with a brain tumour, referred to us by Dr Sleigh at the infirmary'.

'Yes, I remember. He phoned me. There's some indecision about whether surgery is possible or not.'

'That's the one,' said Kate. 'Thomas Downy. And of course, Tracy Torrance. Will you be here for the handover?'

'Yes,' said Neef, without hesitation. 'I think I'd better be.'

'They're coming at two. We can expect a media circus outside, I suppose.'

'I don't doubt it. Do we have Thomas Downy's notes?'

'I put them on your desk.'

Neef walked round the unit before going to his office. He preferred this informal approach to ward rounds, rather than the traditional scenario of consultant followed by entourage of juniors, still favoured by many of his colleagues. Or maybe that was being unfair to them. The special nature of his own unit permitted a different approach. In a high-turnover general ward it was probably necessary for consultants to be continually briefed on whom they were seeing and what was wrong with them. The population in his own unit was more stable. He knew all his patients well and liked wandering round on his own.

By ten thirty, Neef had made a thorough examination of Thomas Downy's case notes, his X-rays and CT scans. He understood the problem. Here was a borderline case for surgery with a cerebellar tumour in such an awkward position that attempts to remove it might well cause irreparable damage or even death on the table. He would have to pass the buck entirely to the neurosurgeon. In the meantime, he would assess the boy's physical condition when he was admitted and get some MRI scans done just in case the surgeon decided to take the chance. He called Ann Miles on the desk intercom and asked her to contact Norman Beavis, the neurosurgeon contracted to the trust.

There weren't enough neurosurgical cases in St George's to warrant the full-time services of a neurosurgeon so the trust had contracted for the *part*-time services of Beavis. Ann called back to say that Beavis's secretary had been informed. Mr Beavis was operating this morning but would return his call this afternoon.

The Downy boy was admitted at eleven and made welcome and comfortable by the nurses before the two housemen examined him and ran preliminary tests. Neef was in attendance but took a back seat. He was pleased with the way the new housemen were shaping up. They both chatted to the boy, disguising the clinical nature of their task with talk of football. On finding out that Thomas Downy was an Arsenal supporter, good-natured rubbishing of his allegiance broke out with Samuels favouring Manchester United and John Duncan, who came from Glasgow, rooting for Celtic. Neef noticed the boy smile for the first time as Samuels and Duncan argued with each other in true pantomime fashion.

Neef ate lunch in the hospital restaurant. He was feeling slightly nervous about the afternoon encounter with the Torrances and this had dulled his appetite. He opted for a cellophane-wrapped salad from the self-service counter and a cup of tea. He was joined at the table by Frank MacSween.

'I called University College about the Simpson lassie,' said MacSween.

'You told them about the tumours?'

MacSween smiled wryly and said, 'I think at first they thought I was complaining about the patient not being sent here in the first place. They were at great pains to assure me that no one had realized she had cancer. She was admitted as an ID case with pneumonia.'

The University College Hospital Trust and the St George's Trust had a set of agreements about what kind of patients they could deal with. Infectious diseases went to University College, child cancer cases came to St George's.

'Probably your Scots accent,' said Neef. 'They'll be expecting a bill.'

'I shall treat that with the contempt it deserves,' said MacSween. 'Anyway I explained that the public health people would have to be informed as the cause of the cancer would have to be identified quickly. They said they'd be quite happy about that so I did – this morning.'

'Good.'

'Public health are sending someone over this afternoon to take a look at the pathological material and then they'll get on to it. University College also sent Melanie Simpson's notes over this morning just in case the PH people want them.'

'Anything interesting?'

MacSween shook his head. 'Not a thing. Bairn hardly had a day's illness in her life and then, zap, she's dead.'

Neef played with his fork thoughtfully. 'You said the bugs lab failed to find any evidence of bacterial pneumonia, so they were assuming it was a virus?'

'That's right.'

'Are you happy with that?'

'I think so; it's always a bit iffy when a diagnosois has to be made through a process of elimination but the bilateral consolidation was classic so I wouldn't argue against it. Why do you ask?'

Neef shook his head as if dismissing some vague notion he had no wish to expand on and said, 'Just a thought.'

'Well, we'll see what the virology lab has to say and then we'll get a clearer picture,' said MacSween.

Neef and MacSween looked at each other and broke into grins. 'No, we won't,' they both intoned together.

'They'll find half a dozen everyday viruses of the cold and flu variety and invite us to pick one as the cause,' said Neef.

MacSween nodded. Viruses were always much more difficult to pinpoint than bacteria.

Neef looked at his watch and rose from the table. 'They're coming for Tracy Torrance this afternoon,' he explained. 'She's going to the Randolf Clinic.'

MacSween nodded. 'The show must go on,' he said.

'Keep me informed about the Simpson case will you?'

'I will. Betty wants you to lunch on Sunday. Bring a friend, if you have any left when the newspapers are finished with you.'

'And with that happy thought . . .' said Neef, getting up. He smiled his goodbye.

At five minutes to two, Neef straightened his tie and put on his jacket. He went over to his office window and saw activity round the front gate. A television camera crew were in place and technicians were milling around with their hands in their pockets. He saw a woman holding a microphone look at her watch and then primp at her hair with her free hand.

A few minutes later a black Ford Granada swept into view and turned in through the gates. It stopped outside the front door and Mr and Mrs Torrance got out, accompanied by a tall, fat man with thinning hair which he kept plastered across his scalp with the palm of one hand. In the other, he carried a briefcase. He shepherded the Torrances inside and turned to face reporters alone. He was standing on the second step leading up to the front entrance. The reporters below him looked like seals waiting to be fed, Neef thought.

As the brief interview ended and the fat man disappeared inside, Neef checked with Ann Miles that Tracy was ready.

'All ready,' she affirmed. 'Shall I show them straight in when they arrive?'

'Please.'

A few moments later, the door opened and the Torrances were ushered in, accompanied by the fat man, who introduced himself as Lewis Milligan.

'I represent the *Evening Citizen*,' announced Milligan. 'In this instance, I'm also acting on behalf of Mr and Mrs Torrance.'

'Tracy is all ready for you,' said Neef. 'We're all sorry to see her go. We hope everything goes well for her at the Randolf Clinic.'

'Thank you Doctor,' said Milligan. 'I'm sure it will.'

The Torrances seemed content to leave everything to Milligan. They stood in the background with a barely suppressed look of smugness on their faces.

There was a knock on the door. Kate Morse came in holding Tracy in her arms. Another nurse stood behind her with a plastic bag containing Tracy's belongings.

Mrs Torrance made a great show of taking Tracy into her arms and smothering her with affection. Tracy seemed unimpressed, preferring instead to chew a corner of Mr Raggins. As she was hoisted over to her mother's other shoulder, Tracy dropped the doll and stretched out her arm in silent anguish. Milligan picked it up and eyed it distastefully.

'You're going to have lots of new dollies at the Randolf,' he said in what he imagined were child-friendly tones. Tracy did not respond. When it began to look as if he wasn't going to return the doll, Kate Morse stepped in and took it from him. She gave it back to Tracy and said to Milligan in tones that threatened to freeze him, 'Mr Raggins goes.'

As the party started to troop out of Neef's office, Mrs Torrance handed Tracy over to her husband, who seemed equally determined to mount a display of affection for the onlookers. Mrs Torrance was the last to leave the room in front of Neef. She paused for a moment to let the others get ahead then turned round to face him. He saw the gimlet eyes that had haunted his dreams the previous night.

'You must really hope she dies,' she hissed.

'You can't believe that, Mrs Torrance,' said Neef, trying to appear calm when he felt as if he'd been kneed in the groin.

'Stands to reason. If she dies, you were right. If she lives, you were wrong.'

'No one's infallible, Mrs Torrance. I certainly don't pretend to be. I would be absolutely delighted to be proved wrong over your daughter. Please believe me.'

Mrs Torrance gave a sneering look of disbelief then left to catch up with the rest.

Neef closed the door of his office and went over to the small washbasin in the corner. He splashed water up into his face for a few moments, then rested his hands on the edge of the basin. He saw that they were shaking slightly.

He heard the door open quietly behind him but didn't turn round. He knew it was Ann Miles.

'Are you all right?' she asked.

'With water dripping from his face, he looked at Ann in the mirror and said, 'That bloody woman really believes I want her daughter to die.'

'She's distraught,' said Ann. 'She doesn't know what she's saying. You have to make allowances. You know that.'

Neef nodded, still with his back to her. He patted his face dry and said, 'Sometimes I think my capacity for "making allowances" has been stretched to its limit.'

Ann said, 'My husband's an accountant. He thinks his job is stressful. He doesn't know the half of it.' With that, she backed out of the door.

Neef's phone rang. It was Norman Beavis. He would come in to see the Downy boy on the following morning if that was convenient. 'I've pencilled him into the theatre schedule for Thursday,' said Beavis.

'Good,' said Neef. 'I think he's borderline but see what you think.'

Kate Morse and Lawrence Fielding arrived promptly at four. Lawrence, a sallow-skinned, serious-looking man, good at his job but lacking in humour, stood aside to let Kate enter first, then closed the door behind him with meticulous care before sitting down beside her. He always reminded Neef of a deferential butler but he was a clever man and a good doctor.

'I just wanted to have a word with you both about a proposed trial that would involve our patients.' said Neef.

'Kate said something about gene therapy,' said Lawrence.

'That's right. A company called Menogen Research have developed a genetically based strategy for tumour treatment. They've satisfied the relevant control bodies and safety committees and obtained permission for human trials to commence. They still have to present their strategy to our own safety and ethics committee but, assuming they cross that hurdle, what do you think?'

'I'm not at all sure what it would involve,' said Kate.

'Nor me,' agreed Lawrence.

'Then we're all agreed on that.' Neef smiled. 'It's a brand-new area for all of us. I'll know more when I meet the people from Menogen. I think the best we can do in the meantime is agree in principle if we can.'

'I'm all in favour of trying new things, providing they have a reasonable chance of success and aren't just being used to provide data for some boffin's pet project,' said Kate.

'There's the parents to consider too,' said Lawrence. 'It's so easy to give people false hope as soon as you start talking about "new treatments". The words immediately translate into "miracle cure".'

'And our parents are particularly vulnerable,' added Kate. 'They're on a hair trigger to clutch at any straw.'

'Good points,' said Neef. 'So we can agree that, unless there is a real chance of our patients' condition being significantly improved, I should say no?'

Both Kate and Fielding nodded.

'Is the treatment itself distressing?' asked Kate.

'I believe not, but that's something I'll verify. The kids have enough on their plate with chemotherapy and radiotherapy. There'd have to be a terribly good reason to ask them to cope with anything more.'

Fielding said, 'I've been doing some general reading about gene therapy since Kate told me about our possible involvement.'

'Me too,' said Neef.

'There seems to be an element of danger involved in it. People keep stressing that it's an unknown quantity.'

'That's true,' agreed Neef. 'But the major concern seems to centre on the possibility of actually causing cancer in patients undergoing therapy.'

'And ours already have it,' said Kate.

'A strange comfort to take, I admit,' said Neef. 'But I do think that the fact that the kids who might be involved in any such trial would probably be the ones with the worst prognoses must play a part in our thinking.'

'Nothing left to lose,' said Fielding.

'Yes,' said Neef.

'As long as that's not the only consideration,' said Kate. 'They're not laboratory animals to be as used by these Menogen people.'

'Absolutely not,' said Neef.

Fielding nodded.

'Can I take it, then, that we're all in favour of the trial, providing that there's a real chance of tumour regression and that the new

43

treatment doesn't put our children under unreasonable stress or have any horrendous side effects?'

'Yes,' said Fielding.

'Good. I'll let you know when I have more details.'

As soon as Kate and Fielding had left, Ann came in to report that Andrew D'Arcy had called to say that the people from Menogen Research would be coming the following day. 'He wanted to know if you could be free at ten a.m.? I told them you could,' said Ann. 'I've marked it in your diary.'

'Thanks, Ann. By the way, Mr Beavis has pencilled Thomas Downy in for surgery on Thursday. I'd better see his parents beforehand. Could you have them come in tomorrow afternoon?'

'Will do.'

Ann had scarcely left the room when she was back in again. She closed the door behind her before saying, 'There's a Doctor Lennon from the public health service outside. He's come on the off-chance of having a word with you?'

'Send him in,' said Neef. 'I think I know what it's about.'

A short, bald man in his late fifties, wearing a dark suit and carrying a briefcase with combination locks on it, came into the room and held out his hand. 'I'm Lennon,' he said. 'I'm an epidemiologist. I've just been having a word with your Dr MacSween.'

'About Melanie Simpson?'

Lennon nodded. 'A disturbing case. I understand from Dr MacSween that you were present at the post-mortem. You saw the girl's lungs for yourself?' Lennon had a West Country accent that belied his appearance. He spoke like a farmer but looked like a bank manager.

'That's right. Frank called me down when he came across the tumours,' said Neef.

'As you're a cancer specialist, Doctor, I thought I would ask if you have had any thoughts on what might have caused Melanie's condition?'

Neef shook his head slowly. 'I'm afraid not,' he said. 'As you know, it's practically unheard of for a child to develop bronchial carcinoma. Apart from that, the tumours were present in such numbers that it couldn't have been spontaneous. There must have been some highly carcinogenic agent involved.'

Lennon nodded his agreement. 'No doubt about it,' he said. 'The puzzle is that the cancer was confined to the lungs,' he added thoughtfully. 'If a powerful carcinogen was involved one might have expected tumours throughout the body.'

'A good point,' conceded Neef. 'And if it had been a radiation source we might reasonably have expected to see some signs of epidermal damage. But as far as I could see the girl's skin was unblemished.'

'A puzzle,' agreed Lennon. 'That leaves us looking for some powerful carcinogen that Melanie must have inhaled,' he said.

'Like a gas, or fumes of some sort,' said Neef. 'Or maybe dust particles.' He remembered MacSween's comments about asbestos.

'The lab didn't find any evidence of fibrous material in her lungs,' said Lennon. 'So I think we can rule out particulate matter. That just leaves chemical fumes.'

'So where will you begin to look?' asked Neef.

Lennon smiled and said, 'Good question. Where would a perfectly ordinary little girl, living with her mum and dad in a semi on Langholm Crescent come across a highly toxic gas?'

'These days you hear so much about poisonous chemicals being dumped here, there and everywhere that I suppose we shouldn't be too surprised when this sort of thing happens,' said Neef.

'Sad but true,' agreed Lennon, getting up. 'Well, it's my job to find and identify the damned source before anyone else is harmed.'

'Are you working alone?' asked Neef.

'There'll be three of us. My colleagues are interviewing Melanie's parents at this very minute. With the information they collect, we'll try to build up a picture of her movements over the past few weeks and from that we may get some clue as to where she might have contaminated herself.

'I sincerely wish you luck,' said Neef.

45

'Thanks,' said Lennon. 'I'll keep in touch.'

Kate Morse appeared, holding the first edition of the *Evening Citizen*.

'How bad is it?' Neef asked her.

'Well they ran the story but it's not nearly as awful as it might have been. She's toned it down quite a lot.'

'Good,' said Neef.

'They've also included an interview with the director of the Randolf. He more or less says that it's a chance in a million that Tracy's going to benefit from the treatment, but of course the paper has to point out that even a chance in a million must be taken if a child's life is at stake. What price life?' she added in a deliberately pompous, self-righteous tone of voice.

'We can probably tell them that, right down to the last penny,' said Neef wryly.

'Anyway, I don't think the nurses will lynch Ms Sayers if you decide to let her visit Neil,' said Kate. 'It could have been a whole lot worse.' She put the paper down on Neef's desk.

'I haven't decided finally,' said Neef, 'but thanks for the assurance. I'm meeting with the people from Menogen Research tomorrow morning so I should have some more gen about the trial.'

'Good,' said Kate. 'I was just saying to Charlie last night, it would be a wonderful boost to morale if something good came out of this.'

'Wouldn't it just?' Neef smiled.

He read the article for himself when Kate had left and agreed with her interpretation: it could have been worse. He drove home feeling much more relaxed than he had the previous night.

Dolly was nowhere to be seen when he got inside the cottage but this in itself was not unusual. She had a number of favourite hiding places. He looked in each in turn. Third time lucky. She was in the linen cupboard, snuggled up on the highest shelf, peering down at him.

'Hi, Dols? How was your day?' he asked. He heard Dolly's paws hit the floor gently behind him as he walked away. She had dropped from six feet with hardly a sound. He filled her bowl then had a drink while his microwave dinner cooked. He turned on the television, reassured by the thought that this evening no one he knew was going to be on the news. 'A better day all round, Dols,' he said as he drained his glass and got up to open his briefcase. He had a lot of paperwork to catch up on.

Neef arrived early for the meeting with Menogen next morning. He had been late for the last three management meetings and didn't want to develop a reputation for it. Andrew D'Arcy arrived shortly afterwards and then Tim Heaton, immaculate as ever, being lobbied on the move by Carol Martin over nursing budgets.

'Have a word with Phillip,' said Heaton, adeptly detaching himself from the nursing director and wishing the others good morning. The hospital press officer arrived with two strangers in tow. They were introduced as Steven Thomas, managing director of Menogen Research, and Dr Max Pereira, research director.

Thomas looked like a businessman: he was conventionally dressed in suit and tie and sounded English; but Pereira wore jeans, a striped T-shirt, leather jacket and a beret. Phillip Danziger arrived last and apologized for being late.

Tim Heaton took easy charge of the meeting, welcoming the men from Menogen and saying how pleased he was that St George's had been approached. He hoped that everyone would benefit from the association. Neef wore a neutral expression. He was thinking that Heaton would have made an excellent diplomat, an ambassador even. He could hear him saying, 'The ties that bind our two great countries ... Valdovia has always had a special place in our hearts ...'

'This is Dr Michael Neef, consultant in paediatric oncology,' said Heaton, breaking Neef's train of thought. 'It is his unit, of course, that you would be working with.'

Neef smiled at Pereira and got a nod in reply. Thomas was more effusive.

With the introductions over, Heaton said, 'I suggest the following schedule. First, Mr Thomas outlines in broad general terms what he has in mind and what he would like from us. This should be in non-technical terms as at least half of us here are neither medical nor scientific. Then Doctors Neef and Pereira consult over medical matters while Mr Thomas and Mr Danziger discuss figures. We can then reconvene over lunch. If we've made progress we can go ahead with a meeting with the ethics and safety committee. They've been warned about this possibility and would be ready to convene this afternoon if called upon.'

Heaton looked at Thomas and Pereira and explained, 'We are subject to scrutiny by a local ethics committee that oversees both St George's and University College hospitals. It comprises lay people as well as selected medical staff from both hospitals. You'll be expected to provide evidence of approval by the relevant safety bodies.'

'All here,' said Thomas, touching his briefcase.

'Good,' said Heaton.

'Can I ask which medical staff University College have on the committee for this application?' asked Neef.

Heaton looked at the paper in front of him and said, 'The dean of the medical school, Dr Alan Brooks, and the head of their molecular biology section, Dr Farro-Jones.'

'David Farro-Jones?' asked Pereira.

'Yes. Do you know him?' asked Heaton.

'We were post-docs together at Johns Hopkins in Baltimore,' he said in what sounded to Neef like a New York American accent.

'Then you'll obviously speak the same language this afternoon,' said Heaton.

Ostensibly, Heaton had been referring to technical language but Neef wondered if Heaton hadn't said what he had as an in-joke for those present who knew David Farro-Jones. Although he and Pereira spoke English, there was a world of difference between Farro-Jones's Oxbridge accent and Pereira's New York patois. He also wondered about the expression on Pereira's face when he heard Farro-Jones's name mentioned. Maybe it had been surprise – or maybe there had been more to it.

'Is that all right then?' asked Heaton, looking round the table at everyone in turn. 'Good. Over to you, Mr Thomas.'

Steven Thomas gave everyone a potted history of Menogen Research along the lines that Andrew D'Arcy had already reported to Heaton and Neef two days before.

'It has been our good fortune over the last three years to have had the services of Max Pereira here and several of his colleagues whom he brought with him from the world of academia. These brilliant researchers have designed a range of vectors and strategies which we believe will be successful in delivering functional genetic material to where it's most needed in the body. Testing in lab animals has given encouraging results and now the time has come to use the technology for real.

'We have obtained all the relevant safety certificates and ethical approval at national level. What we need now is the collaboration and cooperation of a first-rate hospital like St George's and its staff – in particular, Dr Neef and the paediatric oncology unit. I think it is not outside the bounds of possibility that here, together, we might make significant strides forward in medical science.'

'Thank you, Mr Thomas,' said Tim Heaton getting to his feet as Thomas sat down to polite applause. 'I think we all echo these sentiments.'

Neef smiled at Pereira and said, 'If you'd care to come with me, Doctor. I'll show you round the unit and you can meet the patients.'

Four

'Maybe we should talk first and then I'll show you around the unit,' suggested Neef.

'Whatever you say,' replied Pereira.

Pereira was nearly a foot shorter than Neef, despite the fact he was wearing cowboy boots with Cuban heels. Neef had to modify his stride to allow him to keep up as they crossed the courtyard from the administrative block to the unit. Pereira was also weighed down by a large battered briefcase which had the remains of many airline stickers plastered over one face of it.

Neef introduced him to Ann Miles and asked if coffee was possible.

'Of course,' she said. 'How do you like yours, Dr Pereira?'

'White, lots of sugar,' Pereira replied without turning to face her. He had taken off his leather jacket but had kept his beret on.

Ann Miles exchanged an amused look with Neef before closing the door behind her.

'Are you medically qualified, Dr Pereira?' asked Neef.

Pereira shook his head. 'My first degree was in medical microbiology, then a PhD at UCLA followed by post-doctoral fellowships at Harvard and Johns Hopkins, then I joined Menogen.'

'You're a molecular biologist?'

'I am, but people tend to come to molecular biology from a

range of scientific backgrounds. I was primarily a virologist, David Farro-Jones has a medical degree, I think.'

'He has,' agreed Neef. 'But he keeps telling me that molecular biology is the science of the future.'

'He's not wrong,' replied Pereira.

'But without a medical degree there's no question of you being let loose on the patients on your own.'

Pereira laughed out loud. 'That's understood,' he said. 'I couldn't stick a plaster on a cut finger. On the other hand, I've forgotten more about viruses than most medics will ever know.'

It was Neef's turn to smile. 'I'll gladly concede that,' he said. 'So we work as a team.'

'Absolutely.'

'Then I have to know exactly what you have in mind. I must insist on understanding the theory behind everything you propose to do before I agree to it.'

'How much do you know about gene therapy?'

'I know that it involves introducing new genes into patients' cells and that getting them in there can present problems. Beyond that, not a lot.'

Pereira nodded. 'Constructing the working gene in the lab is the easy part. As you say, it's getting it into the patient's own cells that gives us the problems. We obviously can't inject copies of the new gene into cells one at a time; we'd have to do it a hundred million times to even make a start on a tumour. So we have nature do it for us. We use viruses as transport vectors.'

'Live viruses?' asked Neef.

'Live but disabled,' said Pereira. 'We disable the virus genetically so that it can't replicate itself inside the patient, then we introduce the new gene to the virus in the lab and let the virus carry it into the patient's cells for us.'

'A sort of localized infection?'

'You got it.'

'It sounds straightforward,' said Neef. 'So what are the pitfalls?'

'Lots,' admitted Pereira. 'Viruses are still viruses, disabled or not.

51

If we use too many virus particles the patient may react badly against the introduction of foreign protein, particularly if we have to repeat the treatment.'

'Anaphylactic shock?'

'That's a possibility. On the other hand, if we use too few the whole strategy might not work. There are a couple of other things you should be aware of if you're not already.'

'Tell me.'

'Although the viruses we use are disabled by removing their replicating machinery, some researchers have suggested that they might reactivate themselves inside the body by finding their missing bits.'

'I don't think I follow. How?'

'Many of the viruses we use as gene-carrying vectors are pretty common. Most of us have been infected with them before through having colds and flu. The worry says that many of us will still have the odd live virus particle lurking around inside us. If the disabled vector virus should come up against one of these old particles it's just possible that it could reactivate itself through DNA recombination.'

'You mean it could get back its missing bits and set off a full-scale infection?'

'Yeah. But being aware of the problem is halfway to solving it, as Grandma used to say. We at Menogen use retrovirus technology, which doesn't have that problem but it could have others.'

'Anything I should know?'

'Yes,' said Pereira. 'The advantage of using retroviruses is that they integrate into the host cell's chromosome; the disadvantage is that some people think they could trigger off cancer.'

'I had read about that possibility,' admitted Neef.

'But this wouldn't be a problem with *your* patients,' said Pereira. 'They've already got the big C.'

Neef looked at Pereira, who had opened his briefcase and was rummaging inside.

Neef looked at Pereira long and hard. He couldn't make up his mind about the man. He was certainly different.

'What exactly are the chances of gene therapy actually helping my patients?'

'As opposed to what?'

'As opposed to just providing you with more data about your virus vectors.'

'Hopefully it will do both,' said Pereira.

'I have to know the chances,' insisted Neef.

Pereira seemed to sense that this might be the big-money question. He stopped sifting through his papers and said, 'All right, I admit, it would be nice to include some neomycin tag experiments just to see how the vectors are distributed in the body.'

'No,' said Neef firmly.

'Why not?'

'Adult cancer patients are able to make up their own mind about helping medical science when there's nothing in it for them. Kids can't.'

'But their parents—'

'Will snatch at anything without fully understanding the implications, so it's me who has the final say-so round here and I say no data experiments.'

Pereira sighed and let his head drop for a moment. 'So what's the deal?' he asked.

'The deal is that, if we inject any gene-therapy vector into my patients, it has to carry a viable gene with a real chance of improving their condition. Do you have such vectors?'

'Yes, I believe we do,' said Pereira. 'And I believe that they'll work. Given the right patients and the right conditions, I think we can pull off the big one here. I think we might be able eventually to zap cancer.'

'You honestly believe that?'

'I honestly do.'

Neef nodded non-committally. 'Good. Now tell me about the side effects of this kind of therapy.'

'There really shouldn't be any – certainly nothing like the side effects of standard chemotherapy.'

'Good. Can we get down to specifics? What gene do you intend introducing and why?'

Pereira separated a couple of diagrams from his pile of papers and pushed them in front of Neef. 'For suitable tumours we would use a disabled murine leukaemia virus with altered envelope proteins and carrying TDK – you know, a thymidine kinase gene. This would be injected directly into the tumour. The virus only infects dividing cells so, in the case of a brain tumour only the tumour cells will take up the TDK gene. We then treat the patient with Gancyclovir. This drug will only kill cells containing a working TDK gene.'

'It sounds simple in theory. Are you sure that only the tumour cells will be killed?'

'That's what the theory says.'

Neef wondered if Pereira's answer had been evasive but didn't press the point for the time being. 'What about different types of tumour?' he asked.

'Menogen's success has been in developing a range of pseudotype viruses based on the virus I mentioned. They all have altered envelope proteins, which gives them different affinities. It's just a question of selecting the right vector for the right tumour.'

'Okay,' said Neef, after a moment's thought. 'That's enough science. Let's go and meet everyone.'

After noting the unit nurses' somewhat puzzled and muted response to meeting Pereira, Neef wondered what the patients were going to make of him. In the event, they treated Pereira with much the same caution as the nurses had displayed. They seemed to sense that his smile was less than sincere and didn't respond to his clumsy attempts at making jokes.

'I hope he'll grow on me,' confided Kate Morse as she stood beside Neef, watching Pereira through the window of her office.

'That's my hope too,' agreed Neef with a slight smile. 'God knows what the ethics committee are going to make of him.'

'Mr Beavis was here earlier to see Thomas Downy,' said Kate. 'He's going to speak to you personally but—'

'Not operable?'

''Fraid not.'

'Damn. I hoped Beavis might give it a try.'

'Thomas's parents are coming in at four. Will you be around or do you want Lawrence to tell them?'

'I'll do it,' said Neef with a sigh of resignation. 'I should be back by then.'

Neef called Tim Heaton from his office while Pereira was still with the children. 'So far, I think I'm in favour of the trial,' he told Heaton. 'Pereira's a bit hard to take but he seems to know what he's talking about.'

'Good,' said Heaton. 'I understand from Phillip and Andrew that they are quite happy with the financial arrangements. I'll try to convene the ethics committee for two thirty. Can we all have an early lunch – say twelve thirty?'

'Fine.'

Pereira returned to Neef's office after giving up on making meaningful contact with the patients. 'Okay,' he announced spreading his hands out from his sides, 'Michael Jackson, I ain't. I'm a scientist.'

'Not everyone gets on with kids,' said Neef with a smile.

'I don't dislike them,' replied Pereira. 'But I don't go all misty-eyed over them. Is that a problem?'

'I suppose not, but I like to understand people's motivations when I'm going to be working with them.'

'That must be difficult when most people in this game don't tell the truth in the first place,' said Pereira.

'A cynical view.'

'A realistic one. In my experience, doctors become doctors because they figure it'll provide them with a good living, social standing, nice car, membership of the golf club and so on. Any thoughts about fixing sick folks come way down the list. But they've got a good PR thing going for them, I'll give them that. Most people believe they care.'

Neef was taken aback by Pereira. He was also puzzled. The words sounded as if they had been born of bitterness, but Pereira didn't sound bitter. He said it all quite dispassionately.

'So what motivates a medical scientist?' he asked.

Pereira smiled and said, 'People like to believe it's an unswerving desire to cure man's ills and alleviate pain and suffering but it ain't. No sir. Scientists are people like everyone else. They're fired by notions of career advancement and increased academic status, all mixed up with the prospects of fame and fortune.'

'That sounds pretty awful.'

'It only *sounds* awful,' said Pereira. 'In practice the system works very well from the patients' point of view.'

'How so?'

'Researchers work their butts off, not because they want to help sick folks but because they want to be first past the post; there are no prizes for coming second. They know there's a whole bunch of guys out there doing exactly the same sort of experiments. That means that the work has to get done as fast as possible. It's also done as thoroughly as possible because every researcher knows that his competitors are just waiting to go through his published work with a fine-tooth comb to pick fault with it. And, if they find any mistakes or unjustified assertions, they'll crucify you. So no short cuts. The patient gets a good deal.'

'You paint an honest if somewhat depressing picture,' said Neef with a wry smile.

'I just face facts,' said Pereira. 'Human nature is what it is. I accept it. Lots of folks don't. They have to endow their actions with all sorts of noble-sounding bullshit.'

'Between you and me, Max,' said Neef, 'I wouldn't come out with that to the ethics committee this afternoon. They just might take it personally.'

'Thanks for the warning.'

Halfway through lunch Neef's bleeper went off. He excused himself and went to call the unit.

'We've just had a referral from East Side General,' said Lawrence Fielding. 'I think you should come over.'

Neef hurried back to the unit and found Fielding in the light-wall room. This was a long narrow room next to the duty room. One entire wall was translucent plastic with a fluorescent light source behind it. Scans and X-rays could be pinned up on it for examination.

'What have you got?' asked Neef as he entered and found Fielding examining a series of three X-rays with the aid of a hand-held lens.

'Jane Lees, aged fourteen,' replied Fielding. 'I've not seen anything quite like this before, especially not in a child. She has multiple tumours on both lungs.'

Neef felt a sudden sense of foreboding come over him. Fielding had more or less said what Frank MacSween had said the other day about Melanie Simpson.

'I have,' he said, as he took the lens from Fielding and took a closer look at the X-rays. 'I saw exactly the same thing in Pathology on Monday. Frank MacSween was doing a PM on a patient from University College, a thirteen-year-old girl. She'd been admitted as a bilateral pneumonia, but the lab couldn't find any bugs. She died and they called it viral.'

'They didn't realize she had cancer as well?'

'Nobody did until Frank opened her up. We've had to call in the public health team because of the extent of the malignancy. This looks like number two.'

'In more ways than one,' said Fielding.

'How so?'

'Jane was admitted to East Side General, as a bilateral pneumonia! They didn't find any evidence of bacterial involvement so *they* called it viral, too. Unlike your girl, Jane recovered from the acute pneumonia but her clearance X-rays showed up the tumours, so she was transferred here. The early X-rays were clouded by excess mucous and inflammation caused by the pneumonia. I suppose that must have been the case with the first girl too.'

'I suppose it was,' said Neef thoughtfully. 'I want you to call the public health people. Ask for Dr Lennon and explain what's happened. The sooner he traces the cause of this thing the better.'

'Will do,' said Fielding.

'How is the girl?'

'We've made her comfortable for the moment but once these tumours get a real grip there's not going to be much we can do for her.'

'We'll do our best,' said Neef, putting his hand on Fielding's shoulder. 'Like we always do.'

Lunch was over by the time Neef got back to the administrative block. He had opted to see Jane Lees himself before leaving the unit and this had taken a good thirty minutes. Although the girl was very ill, she was conscious and Neef had hoped she might have been able to shed some light on the nature and source of the carcinogen that she and Melanie Simpson must have been exposed to.

But she hadn't. Jane Lees lived in another part of the city and she had not known Melanie Simpson. Neef was thinking about this as he ran up the steps of the administrative block in time for the ethics committee meeting.

'Problems?' asked Tim Heaton who was just about to leave along with Phillip, Danziger. They would not be required to attend the ethics committee meeting.

'I've never known a day without them,' replied Neef. He didn't want to get into conversation with Heaton about the two girls before he himself had had time to consider the implications.

'Life's rich pattern,' said Heaton, who smiled and swept out, checking his watch as he did so and almost leaving Phillip Danziger in his wake.

The ethics and safety committee on this occasion comprised two churchmen, the Roman Catholic chaplain for University College Hospital and the Church of England chaplain for St George's; Alan Brooks, the dean of University College medical school; Major Ronald Jackson, a local magistrate; Dr David Farro-Jones, reader in molecular biology in medicine at University College medical school; and Miss Emma Taylor, area organizer of the Women's Royal Voluntary Service. Major Jackson was in the chair. Steven Thomas,

Max Pereira and Neef were present throughout. Andrew D'Arcy was available to be called upon. All members of the committee had copies of the formal written application in front of them.

Jackson opened the proceedings by requesting evidence of Menogen's successful application to licensing authorities at national level.

Thomas handed over a series of documents, one at a time, announcing each in turn. 'Our formal application, which I think you already have, approval certificate from the Medicines Control Agency, and certification from the National Gene Therapy Advisory Committee.'

'Thank you, Mr Thomas. A necessary formality, you understand.'

'Of course.'

'As I understand it, no transfer of human genetic material is involved in the proposed therapy. Is that right?'

Max Pereira replied, 'Quite right, sir.'

'I think that makes our task considerably easier,' said Jackson. 'So what gene do you intend transferring to our patients?'

'It's the thymidine kinase gene, taken from herpes simplex virus, sir. The TDK gene for short.'

'Isn't that dangerous?' asked the WRVS woman, Emma Taylor.

Neef thought for an awful moment that Pereira was about to be rude to her, but he controlled himself.

'No, ma'am, it's only a single gene from the herpes virus, not the virus itself. It's presence will render the tumour cells sensitive to a drug called Gancyclovir, so that when we give the patient the drug it will kill the tumour.'

'I see,' said Taylor vaguely.

Major Jackson turned to the two churchmen. 'Is there anything you gentlemen would like to ask?'

Both men shook their heads. 'Nothing here to concern us,' said the Roman Catholic priest. 'I hope it works.'

'Then perhaps I should hand over to Dr Farro-Jones as our expert in this case. I'm told you two chaps know each other?'

'Indeed we do, Major,' said Farro-Jones; then to Max Pereira, 'How are you Max? It's been a while.'

'Fine, David. Good to see you.'

Neef could not help but be aware of the striking physical differences between the two men. Farro-Jones was tall, blond and athletic-looking. He had the easy charm and accent that often come from a public-school and Oxbridge education, while Pereira looked like a small, swarthy sailor and spoke like a New York cab-driver.

'Max, I'm a bit worried about the gene transfer vector you intend using to take the TDK gene in; it's a leukaemia retrovirus, isn't it?'

Ears pricked up around the table at the mention of the word leukaemia.

'It's the standard Moloney vector,' said Max. 'It's been around for a while. It's never given any problems in the lab and we've disabled it even further.'

'Yes, I see that,' said Farro-Jones hesitantly. He looked down at the papers in front of him. 'But you've also altered its envelope proteins?'

'We've made it much more effective and, because we have a range of them, much more specific. That's what we've all been working toward, efficient transfer vectors that can be targeted at specific tumours?'

'Yes indeed,' agreed Farro-Jones. And it all sounds very effective on paper but I really do worry about safety . . .'

Neef hadn't expected David Farro-Jones to be so lukewarm towards the proposal. If anything, he had expected his support, Farro-Jones and Pereira being fellow molecular biologists – and Farro-Jones having already been involved in the introduction of gene therapy at University College Hospital. He thought he would point this out.

'Is the Menogen vector significantly different from the one you and your colleagues used in your cystic fibrosis trial, David?' he asked.

'It is, Michael,' replied Farro-Jones. 'We used a liposome delivery system on our patients because we felt it was safer than using a live virus.'

'And it didn't work, right?' said Pereira.

'No it didn't,' conceded Farro-Jones with a smile. 'And I take your point. We're having to move towards virus vectors too, but there are safer ones around.'

There was an uneasy pause before Steven Thomas took the initiative and said, 'I think there has to come a point, ladies and gentlemen, when you've carried out all the trials and safety checks possible without actually moving to a human subject. I think we are at that point with the Menogen vectors.'

'I just worry about the safety aspects,' Farro-Jones confessed. He turned to his colleagues with a slight grimace. 'The patients' welfare must be our first consideration. After all, as Florence Nightingale once said, "The first duty of a hospital is that it cause its patients no harm".'

There was polite laughter.

'There are no named patients on the application,' said Jackson. 'You're asking for open permission?'

'Dr Pereira and I will agree this between us,' said Neef.

'I take it the request for open permission is because the subjects will be terminally ill,' said Jackson.

'Yes sir,' said Neef,' 'but I have made a stipulation that no child will be used for the sole purpose of gathering scientific data. Every child given gene therapy will be given it with the sole intent of improving his or her condition.'

Jackson nodded, turned to his colleagues and said, 'I think I'm inclined to agree with Mr Thomas in this instance. I think the time has come.'

Permission to proceed was approved. The committee members rose and David Farro-Jones came over to speak to Pereira and Neef.

'I'm sorry, Max, if I appeared a bit sticky there. I just worry about the dangers of these new vectors.'

'You've got to call it like you see it David,' replied Pereira.

'No hard feelings, I hope?'

'None. I appreciate your concern but we're sure that they're safe and we've got the go-ahead anyway.'

'Then let me be the first to wish you the best of luck,' said Farro-Jones. 'And if you need any help with equipment or lab space just give me a call. Michael will tell you how to get in touch.'

'Of course,' said Neef.

'Thanks a lot, David, I appreciate it,' said Pereira.

'We must have dinner soon, talk about old times, eh?'

'I'd like that.'

'Nice chap,' said Neef as Farro-Jones hurried off.

'Yeah,' replied Pereira. 'So when do we start in earnest?'

'How about Monday?'

'That sounds okay. I'll start moving in stuff at the weekend. I may look in on your unit then if that's all right with you?'

'Of course. I'll tell the others to expect you.'

'Maybe I could take a copy of some patient notes before I go, ideally the ones you think might benefit from the therapy.'

'We can do that now if you like. I've just got time before I meet some parents.'

'Bad news?'

'I'm afraid so. Their boy has a brain tumour. It's inoperable.'

'A bitch,' said Pereira. 'Inaccessible?'

'It's in the cerebellum. I thought it was borderline but our neurosurgeon gave it the thumbs-down.'

'Afraid of litigation, huh?'

'I don't think that came into it,' said Neef, mildly annoyed at Pereira's interpretation.

'Whoops. Sorry,' said Pereira, sensing that he had offended Neef. 'Maybe things are different in England.'

Neef didn't reply but it was food for thought. Maybe surgeons weren't as afraid as their American counterparts of an action being raised against them in the courts but things had been heading that way – and not just for surgeons. His own insurance premium for that sort of eventuality had risen dramatically over the past few years.

'If you thought the kid's tumour was borderline, it must have been reasonably accessible?' suggested Pereira, making it sound like a question.

'Yes but my hand wasn't going to be wielding the knife. Why do you ask?'

'Do you think it could be reached with a needle?'

'I hadn't thought about that,' said Neef. 'You think we could include the boy in the trial?'

'Sounds like he might be a possible candidate to me,' said Pereira.

Neef suddenly felt better. He was always uneasy before an interview with parents when it was bad news he had to impart, despite the fact that he'd had to do it hundreds of times before. It produced an unpleasant, hollow feeling in his stomach. This was compounded today by the fact that he'd had no lunch. Pereira had introduced an unexpectedly welcome ray of hope into the proceedings but he reminded himself, if he felt this much better, how would Thomas Downy's parents react when he threw them such a lifeline? He would have to be very careful. Raising false hopes would be unforgivable.

Neef and Pereira were going through the patient notes when Lawrence Fielding put his head round the door.

'I managed to catch Lennon at the Public Health Department,' he said. 'He was pretty shocked to hear the news about the second case.'

'I'll bet,' replied Neef. 'Did he say if he'd made any progress with the Melanie Simpson case?'

'None at all,' replied Fielding. 'But he feels that having a second case might help if he can just find out what the two girls had in common. He was going to speak with Jane Lees's parents this afternoon and maybe Jane herself later if that's all right with you?'

'As long as she's well enough to see him,' said Neef. 'I talked to her myself at lunchtime but I couldn't find out anything. She'd never heard of Melanie Simpson.'

'Jesus,' exclaimed Pereira who had been reading through the notes and had come to Jane Lees's X-rays. 'Is this the kid you guys are talking about?'

'Yes, we've had two like that in the past week. The girls have obviously been exposed to some powerful carcinogen. Our public health people are trying to trace it. I don't suppose Jane Lees is a possible for gene therapy?' Neef asked Pereira.

Pereira shook his head. 'No siree,' he said. 'Not too much lab work has been done on lung cancer and the fact that we're looking at multiple tumours would tend to rule it out anyway. Apart from that it looks like time is not on this kid's side. What a mess.'

Pereira left at five minutes to four and Neef went to his office to prepare himself for the meeting with Thomas Downy's parents. He put on a clean white coat, straightened his tie and made sure a box of tissues was close to hand on his desk. At precisely four o'clock Ann Miles showed in the Downys. They were a pleasant-looking couple and huddled together for comfort as they entered. It was something Neef had seen a lot of. As they sat down they drew their chairs closer together so that they could hold hands while they listened to what Neef had to say.

'I'm afraid I have some bad news for you,' said Neef. He could almost feel the hopes and prayers of the couple evaporate into nothingness. 'Our neurosurgeon, Mr Beavis, examined Thomas this morning and reluctantly concluded that his tumour was inoperable.'

'Oh my God,' whispered Mrs Downy. Her husband put his arm round her and manfully kept eye contact with Neef. 'I see,' he said. 'So there's nothing can be done for him then?'

'Other than keep him comfortable, I'm afraid not.'

Mrs Downy started to sob and tears started to roll down Mr Downy's own face, although outwardly he strove to remain impassive. Neef felt a lump come to his own throat.

'How long, Doctor?'

'Hard to say. Weeks rather than months,' replied Neef. 'I'm desperately sorry.'

'Thank you, Doctor,' said Mr Downy.

Neef pushed the box of tissues across the desk.

'That is the reality of the situation, I'm afraid,' said Neef. 'And I'm sorry I've had to be so brutally frank but it's important that you understand this before I say what I'm about to.'

'What's that, Doctor?'

'This unit is about to participate in trials of a new and largely untested cancer treatment known as gene therapy. It's experimental and may even be dangerous but, with your permission, I would like to include Thomas in these trials. I must stress that I can't offer you any realistic hope of a cure for Thomas. We have no way of knowing what to expect. But, if you agree, we can at least give it a try.'

The tears stopped and hope replaced pain in the Downys' eyes.

'Of course, Doctor,' said Mr Downey. He seemed to be speaking for his wife, too.

'I must just stress again,' said Neef, 'it's all right to hope for the best but I think it would be wise to prepare yourself for the worst.'

Five

Ann Miles had been holding a call from Eve Sayers. Neef put a hand to his forehead and made a face when she told him; he had forgotten that the journalist was due to call back today. He nodded to Ann and picked up the receiver.

'Well, do I get to come and visit him?' asked Eve. She sounded anxious.

'To be quite honest, Eve,' confessed Neef, 'I haven't had time to think about it. We're about to start out on a trial of the new therapy I mentioned. We just got final permission this afternoon.'

'Sounds exciting. Anyway, about Neil . . .' asked Eve, returning to her original question.

'There would be certain conditions.'

'Like what?'

'I'd need your assurance that you were coming here as a private individual, not a journalist.'

'You have it.'

'And if you start visiting Neil, you don't stop.'

'I don't understand. What do you mean?'

'It's not unusual for people to want to visit sick children, especially the terminally ill, but usually they want to do it on their own terms: they want to come when it suits them and not when it doesn't.'

'I'm not one of them,' said Eve.

'I didn't imagine you were but if Neil forms an attachment to you, as well he might considering how well you two got on the first time, you would have to respect it, even when his condition starts to worsen. You *will* have to be around for him, however distressing you personally might find it.'

This time there was a long pause.

Neef said, 'I'm glad you're taking time to consider.'

'I suppose I hadn't thought that one right through,' said Eve.

'Think about it on your own for a bit,' said Neef. 'Call me back tomorrow. Better still . . . come to lunch with me on Sunday?'

'Lunch?'

Neef had voiced the invitation on the spur of the moment and was suddenly filled with doubts. He felt slightly embarrassed and more than a little vulnerable. But it was too late to change his mind. He explained, 'One of my colleagues, Frank MacSween, and his wife have asked me to lunch on Sunday. They said I should bring a friend if I had any left after you and your paper had finished with me. They'll be most impressed if I turn up with the assassinating journalist in question.'

'I see,' said Eve. 'Tangled web and all that. All right, I'll come.'

Neef wrote down her address and said he would pick her up at twelve thirty.

'What does your colleague do?' asked Eve as an afterthought.

'He's a pathologist,' replied Neef.

When Neef put down the phone he wondered for a moment what he had done. He couldn't remember the last time he had turned up at a function other than on his own. Certainly not since Elaine's death. Four years was a long time. Depending on who else was at the MacSweens' on Sunday, tongues might start wagging. Did it matter? He supposed not. Apart from anything else, he had asked Eve along only as a sort of riposte to Frank's joke about having no friends, it least, this was how he reassured himself.

On Friday morning Neef held his weekly meeting with his unit's medical and senior nursing staff. He was able to give them the good news that his application for the latest American anti-cancer drug, Antivulon, had been approved after further consideration by the pharmacy sub-committee. Tim Heaton had kept his word; the unspoken *quid pro quo* had been honoured. The news had come by way of an internal memo from Heaton's office; it had arrived just before the meeting.

'The question now, of course, is who do we treat?' said Neef. 'Our problem's compounded by the fact that Menogen will be starting *their* trial on Monday and I'd like your views on candidates for gene therapy as well.'

'I suggest that John Martin be changed to Antivulon as soon as possible,' said Tony Samuels, the young houseman.

'He hasn't settled on standard chemotherapy then?' asked Neef.

'No sir. He's had a pretty unpleasant week all round. Things just aren't getting any better for him.'

And we've still not been able to start him on radiotherapy,' added Lawrence Fielding.

'Then he sounds like our first Antivulon patient,' agreed Neef. 'I called the Pharmacy Department as soon as I got the go-ahead. There's no local agency handling the drug so they'll have to order it directly from the States. They're faxing the request.'

'What about Thomas Downy, sir?' asked John Duncan, the other houseman, 'now that Mr Beavis has decided against surgical intervention.'

'I'm marking Thomas down for gene therapy,' said Neef. 'Dr Pereira thinks he's a good candidate, always providing we can reach the tumour with a needle. I think we can. I've already had a word with his parents, so we have their permission, but I've still to arrange a surgical team.'

'I see, sir.'

'Some of our kids are doing really well on the regimen they're on at the moment,' said Fielding. 'I suggest we leave them out of the reckoning and concentrate on the ones that aren't doing so well.'

'That's imperative in the case of gene-therapy candidates,' said Neef. 'Our open licence dictates we confine therapy to those with very poor prognoses. So let's eliminate our success stories from the list of potential candidates.'

Fielding read out a list of names he thought should be excluded from consideration, asking for occasional confirmation from Kate Morse.

After a further half-hour's discussion and with eight children assigned to either gene therapy or Antivulon treatment, the group reached a stage where there were just two patients left for consideration: Jane Lees and Neil Benson.

'I hate saying this about any child,' said Neef, 'but I fear Jane may be a lost cause. The tumours are just so widespread in her lungs.'

'She's been fading fast since she was admitted,' said Kate. 'I think maybe her pneumonia left her debilitated but she has very little in the way of fighting spirit – and that's working against her.'

'She would be totally unsuitable for gene therapy according to Max Pereira but I think I would be in favour of giving her Antivulon,' said Neef.

'Nothing to lose,' said John Duncan.

'Maybe everything to gain,' added Tony Samuels.

'Then we're agreed?'

There were nods all round.

'That just leaves Neil,' said Neef. 'The bravest of hearts in the smallest of bodies. Is he still in remission?'

'No increase in tumour size,' replied Fielding. 'He's still on the plateau.'

'Then we let well alone for the moment,' said Neef with an air of finality.

'And when it starts to grow again?' Fielding asked.

'We'll cross that bridge when we come to it.'

Frank MacSween had gone off to a pathologists' meeting up in University College Hospital leaving his chief medical laboratory scientific officer, Charlie Morse, in charge of the path lab. Knowing that the PM suite would not be in use for the next few hours, Morse decided that this would be a good time to get the faulty extractor fan above table four fixed. He called hospital maintenance and asked for the electrical foreman, Doug Cooper.

'Any chance of one of your lads fixing a faulty fan in the PM room?' Morse asked.

'Not occupied is it?'

'No, nor liable to be for some time. There's some kind of meeting on up at Uni College.'

'In that case and seeing it's you asking, Charlie, I'll come myself,' said Cooper.

Cooper, a jovial-looking man with red hair and freckles, was there within five minutes. He wore a royal-blue boiler suit, open to the waist, exposing a Fair Isle pattern sweater with a hole in it; he carried a silver-coloured metal toolbox. He chatted with the young female technician at reception while he waited for Morse to appear. He was telling her that his daughter was about to start out soon on a nursing career, when Morse finally came through the swing doors. 'Maybe she'll be a unit sister one day, like this man's wife,' he said, and smiled towards Charlie Morse.

'Good of you to come so quickly, Doug,' said Morse. 'Come through, and I'll show you the problem.'

Morse unlocked the PM suite and clicked on the lights. They stuttered slowly into life and settled down to a constant background hum.

'This place gives me the creeps,' said Cooper as he entered. The uncertainty showed in his step.

'It's all in the mind,' said Morse.

'I suppose you're right, but you can't help but think what happens on these tables, can you?' Cooper paused by the first one to run his fingers lightly along one of the drainage channels. His eyes strayed to a bank of heavy-clasped doors along the far wall. 'Is that where you keep them?' he asked, his voice falling to a whisper.

'That's the body vault,' said Morse. 'But nobody's going to jump out at you, I promise.'

They had reached table four and Morse pointed up at the fan. 'That's the offender,' he said. 'It sounds like it's fouling something

70

and I think there's a bad electrical connection. It keeps starting and stopping. It annoys the boss; this is his favourite table.'

Cooper gave a look that suggested he couldn't imagine anyone having such a favourite object. 'Do you have stepladders down here?' he asked.

'No, but I'll get you one. You could always stand on the table if you like?'

Cooper looked down at the metal table with distaste all over his face. 'I'd rather not if it's all the same to you.'

'Okay,' Morse chuckled. 'Won't be long.'

Cooper looked uncertain at being left alone but managed to smile manfully. He started whistling loudly as soon as Morse was out of sight. He favoured a Beatles selection.

Charlie Morse returned with a small pair of aluminium stepladders and positioned them beside the table. 'There you go.'

Cooper took a screwdriver from his box and climbed the steps to begin undoing the grill over the fan housing. When he had removed the last of four retaining screws, the grill still refused to budge. He tried using the screwdriver as a jemmy but found it difficult to insert it far enough to get any purchase.

'Problems?' asked Morse.

'Can't budge it,' replied Cooper.

'Maybe if I supported the grill you could use a hammer on the end of your screwdriver?' suggested Morse.

'Worth a try,' replied Cooper, now grunting with the effort of working with his hands over his head.

Morse found a small hammer in Cooper's box and got up on to the PM table to pass it to him. He stretched up to support the grill; he didn't want it falling down on to the table should it break free. Cooper started tapping with the hammer and managed to insert the end of the screwdriver far enough for him to start using it as a lever. He no longer required the hammer and passed it to Morse who accepted it and stooped down to lay it on the table. As he straightened up to restore support to the grill, he was just too late. The grill, complete with its dirty cowling, broke free and fell away,

71

showering both of them with all manner of dirt and dust. As they had been looking upwards at the time, they got it full in the face and started coughing and spluttering. There was so much dirt in his eyes that Morse had to kneel down blindly to find the edge of the table to help him find his way to the floor.

'Sorry about that, Charlie,' said Cooper when he had finally stooped coughing and descended the ladders to join him. 'Bloody thing hasn't been off in years.'

When Cooper had stopped apologizing, he burst out laughing and said, 'We look like something out of *The Black and White Minstrel Show*. Remember that?'

Cooper gave an impromptu rendition of 'Swanee'.

'Very funny. Let's get cleaned up and then you can get on with it.'

Morse led the way to the changing room adjoining the PM suite and elbowed on the taps. He allowed Cooper to wash first. While Cooper was drying his hands and face he looked at his surroundings. The rows of plastic aprons and wellington boots put his imagination into overdrive again. His attention was caught by a blackboard on the wall. There were two names on it in pale-blue chalk.

'Are these the next customers?' he asked Morse.

'Yes,' replied Morse.

'I don't understand how anyone can do this for a living,' said Cooper, shaking his head. 'What a way to spend your life, cutting up dead people.'

'They probably don't see it that way,' said Morse.

'It's what they do, isn't it?'

'It's what goes on in your head that's important,' said Morse. 'Have you ever heard the story about the three stone masons?'

Cooper shook his head.

'When they were asked what they were doing, one replied, "I'm earning a living." The second replied, "I'm building a wall." But the third answered, "I'm building a cathedral." They were all doing the same job; they just saw it differently. The pathologists here investigate the causes of death and the effects of disease and injury to the body so that medical science can learn from it and hopefully improve things for the rest of us.'

'If you say so, Charlie,' said Cooper with a sigh. 'Let's get back to that fan. The sooner I'm out of here the better.'

Neef woke early on Sunday morning before even Dolly had given him his regular alarm call of a paw in the face. He lay thinking about whether it had been a good idea to have invited Eve Sayers along to the MacSweens' before deciding finally that, as he'd already done it, there was no point in wondering. He got up and filled the kettle to make coffee before going off in search of Dolly. She tended to sleep in different places around the house. He found her curled up on the settee. There had been a time when Neef had tried to discourage Dolly from sleeping on the furniture but in the end they had come to an arrangement: Dolly slept where she liked. Over the past couple of years Neef had accumulated a wide range of implements for removing cat hair from his clothes.

Dolly opened one eye when Neef stroked her but, seeing it was only him, closed it again. Neef smiled and went off to fill her bowl before making his own coffee and returning to sit in his favourite chair, looking out at the garden. Maybe he'd cut the grass before he went out to lunch. He liked having a garden but didn't enjoy gardening. He did what was necessary to keep it tidy but that was as far as it went. Luckily there were no neighbours for him to offend when the grass sometimes got more than a little too high. By the same token he could make as much noise as he liked. He could begin cutting grass with a petrol-engined mower at eight on a Sunday morning if the notion took him. And it did.

When the mowing was done, Neef changed to using a petrol-powered strimmer to attack the long grass where the mower couldn't reach before finally changing to manual shears to keep the encroaching shrubbery at bay. He was sweating freely by the time he came back indoors and showered leisurely before making himself two slices of toast, two boiled eggs and some more coffee. After this he set about tidying up the house. He usually did this on Sunday morning.

Neef dressed casually in navy slacks and a denim shirt with a cream-coloured Arran sweater on top. He picked up Eve at twelve thirty as arranged and discovered that she lived in a well-appointed, third-floor apartment of a modern block on Durham Road. The walls were plain white with occasional splashes of colour provided by a series of modern prints, which Neef found difficult to decipher as anything other than splashes of colour. He was no great fan of modern art. There were two black leather sofas facing each other on opposite sides of an Adam style fireplace, which hosted a living-flame gas fire, and each had a small table alongside, both with identical ceramic lamps standing on them. The main carpet was cream and there were three strategically placed rugs of North African origin. Neef guessed at Tunisia because of the blue element in them. French windows led out to a small balcony, where four slow-growing conifers braved the elements from terracotta pots.

'Would you like a drink before we go and spring the joke?' asked Eve. She had said it with a smile but Neef imagined he detected a slight edge in her voice.

'I'm sorry,' he said, 'I shouldn't have put it the way I did. It was clumsy of me. I didn't mean to imply that I was only asking you to lunch because I . . .' Neef paused then said, 'I'm being even clumsier . . .'

Eve nodded with an amused look on her face. 'I'd quit if I were you.'

Neef nodded. 'Sorry.'

'Are you sure you still want me to come?'

Neef nodded. 'I'm certain.' He was thinking how attractive she looked.

'About that drink?'

'I'll wait.'

The MacSweens occupied the lower half of a red sandstone mansion in Collingbourne Crescent. They had lived there all their married life – some twenty-three years – and photographs of their family's progress over that time occupied most flat surfaces in the comfortable

74

drawing room that Neef and Eve were shown into. Neef liked the room; he knew it well. He had spent many happy evenings there since coming to St George's. He had great affection for Frank and Betty; they had been particularly kind to him when he had first arrived at St George's and hadn't known a soul.

'You're a dark horse,' said Frank MacSween to Neef, when he was introduced to Eve.

'Hello, my dear,' said Betty, smiling at Eve and taking her hand. 'So glad you could come.'

Neef thought it typical of Betty. She always spotted who needed looking after and made it her business to put people at their ease. She was kindness itself.

'Eve is a journalist,' said Neef. 'In fact, she's *the* journalist.'

Frank MacSween looked surprised. 'You can't mean, the Torrance story?' he asked.

'I'm afraid so,' said Eve.

'Then you and I have a lot in common,' said Frank, recovering his composure.

'How so?' asked Eve. 'I thought you were a pathologist.'

'We both perform autopsies, only I tend to confine my activities to the dead.'

'And that will be enough of that, Frank MacSween,' scolded Betty. 'This young lady is our guest and she's very welcome, as any friend of Michael's always is.'

'Thank you,' said Eve.

Despite the fact that Eve and Betty seemed totally different in terms of personality, they appeared to get on like a house on fire. It pleased Neef.

There were four other lunch guests, Kate and Charlie Morse, and the MacSweens' daughter, Clare, who was there with her husband Keith. They had their baby son, Nigel, with them. The baby slept through lunch in a moses basket placed on the bench seat in front of the bay window. Kate Morse gave Neef a knowing look when she realized who his lunch date was, but that was as far as it went. She was polite if not overly friendly towards Eve.

After lunch, Kate and Charlie fell to conversation with Clare and Keith about the state of their garden. They had discovered during the course of lunch that Keith ran a landscape gardening business up in Yorkshire. They were now discussing ornamental pools and whether plastic liners or preformed fibreglass was best. Eve disappeared into the kitchen with Betty, leaving Frank and Neef with each other for company.

'Fancy a walk round the garden?' asked Frank.

'If you like.'

The MacSweens had a large garden with well-tended lawns and shrubbery. Betty looked after it. Gardening was one of her passions. Frank acted as a labourer when necessary but took no part in the planning, apart from one feature he was particularly proud of. He showed Neef a tunnel he had created in a dense beech hedge leading to a small circular clearing deep inside the hedge run. 'Do you know what that is?' he asked Neef.

Neef shook his head. 'No idea,' he said.

'That's going to be my grandson's gang hut.'

Neef smiled. 'Ideal,' he agreed.

'I'm looking forward to the day he discovers it,' said Frank. 'I won't ever tell him I deliberately made it. I've also plans for a tree house for him. It'll go in the chestnut up there.' He pointed to the friendly-looking tree at the top of the garden with lots of spreading horizontal branches. 'I've started collecting the boards and I've managed to lay my hands on a rope ladder.'

'It sounds like you've got it all worked out,' said Neef.

'I have. Having children gives you the chance to turn back the clock and relive part of your life all over again. See things through their eyes, things you'd forgotten. Having grandchildren means the same all over again, only it will be more relaxed. I'm looking forward to it.'

Neef nodded. He was thinking of Elaine.

'That's a good-looking young lady you've got there,' said MacSween as they continued their walk. 'How come you're walking out with the enemy?'

'I wouldn't put it quite like that,' said Neef. He told MacSween of the series of events.

'So that's why the story in the paper wasn't as bad as I expected,' said MacSween. 'Ms Sayers was pulling her punches.'

'I think if it hadn't been for her editor's insistence, she might have pulled the story altogether,' said Neef.

'So you're going to let her visit the boy in your unit?'

'I think so. Neil liked her, I could tell. He's got nobody else.' MacSween gave a non-commital grunt. 'You don't think it's a good idea, do you?' said Neef.

'It's not my decision,' said MacSween. 'But have you considered the possibility that Ms Sayers may have sacrificed the impact of one tear-jerker story in order to get several? The inside story of a children's cancer ward. There's a lot of journalistic mileage in that one. Second-hand emotion by the barrel. Enough tears to fill a river.'

'Kate has expressed similar doubts,' admitted Neef, 'but Eve's promised me that she will not be working when she's in the unit. Neil's having a remission right now; his tumour's stopped growing. I think if he develops a relationship with Eve, it might help him. We can't quantify the importance of mental state in terms of prophylaxis but we both know it matters. Cancer doesn't like happy people. It prefers depressives; it kills them faster.'

'I hear you're starting a gene therapy trial next week?'

'Tomorrow,' said Neef. 'I'm optimistic about it. We're working with a company called Menogen Research. Their scientific director, a chap called Max Pereira, has convinced me it could work.'

'We were all led to believe that about Farro-Jones and cystic fibrosis when Uni College tried it out last year,' said MacSween. 'But the results were very poor. A pity – I think Farro-Jones might have got a personal chair out of the university if things had gone better, but the powers that be were a bit miffed when it didn't work after all that publicity beforehand.'

'That's show business,' said Neef. His own comment suddenly made him think of Max Pereira. It was the sort of thing he would have said. 'Menogen's strategy is very different,' he said. 'They're not trying to replace a defective gene, like Farro-Jones. They're introducing a foreign gene which will make tumour cells susceptible to treatment with Gancyclovir.'

'If I were you I would have our press officer ... what's his name?'

'John Marshall.'

'Aye, Marshall. I'd have him keep the lid on things until you have a success story to tell. Otherwise, if it fails, you'll have the press back on your doorstep with tales of Dr Michael Mengele, the beast of St George's, using wee sick children as experimental animals.'

'I know the dangers,' said Neef.

'Did you have any trouble getting the trial past the ethics committee?'

'Surprisingly little, but I suppose the fact that there's no human genetic material being exchanged stopped the Frankenstein brigade from getting too upset. The Church didn't seem to think it was too far away from God's will and the chairman was positively friendly. The WRVS woman thought for a moment we were going to give everyone herpes but Pereira managed to put her right. Only David Farro-Jones was a bit cautious, but his concern was for patient safety. I suppose he's a bit hypersensitive after his own trial.

'It's all new,' said MacSween. 'No one knows what to expect and that's frightening enough in itself. You're only a hero when things work. Remember the Jenner factor and consider.'

Neef looked puzzled. 'Jenner, of vaccination fame?' he asked.

'Precisely,' said MacSween. 'Think about what he did. He believed that injecting a little boy with cowpox virus obtained from a milkmaid would protect him from smallpox. It did and he became a legendary figure in medicine, a national hero.

'Yes,' agreed Neef, still puzzled, 'I'm familiar with the cowpox—'

'But consider what he actually *did*. To prove his point he had to inject the child with smallpox. What if his idea hadn't worked? How would society have viewed that?'

'A diabolical crime,' replied Neef.

'And some of us think it still was,' said MacSween. 'But vaccination has succeeded in wiping out smallpox from the face of the earth. A wee moral dilemma wouldn't you say?'

'Medicine is full of them,' said Neef.

'Well, just remember Mike, if you should be put to the test in the next few weeks, you'll have a journalist sitting right there in your unit,' said MacSween. 'But then, some people keep piranha fish as pets.'

The sound of young Nigel crying put an end to the conversation and the two men made their way back to the house. When they got inside they found Charlie Morse walking up and down with the child on his shoulder. Nigel had stopped crying and was nestling into Charlie's neck. Charlie was whispering sweet nothings to him.

'He was always good with our two,' said Kate Morse. 'It was always Charlie who got up at night.'

'Did you hear that?' Clare jokingly asked her husband. Keith pretended not to hear.

Neef smiled at Eve, realizing that talk of babies was isolating the pair of them. She held his gaze for a little longer than necessary and he felt uncomfortable for a moment. As he looked away he wondered why. He concluded that it was some kind of vulnerability. His growing attraction to Eve Sayers was making him feel uneasy. But the feeling was oddly pleasant.

Nigel had fallen asleep on Charlie Morse's shoulder. Morse returned him gently to the moses basket. He was still whispering to the child as he brought up the covers. Suddenly, as he straightened up, he sneezed violently and then again. The second one woke the child, undoing all his good work.

'Bless you, Charlie,' murmured Betty. 'It sounds like you've got a cold coming on.' She lifted the child herself and patted him gently on the back as she soothed him back to sleep. 'Granny's here.'

'It's time we were starting back, anyway,' announced Clare as she got up to take the child from her mother. 'It's been such a nice weekend.'

This was the general signal for everyone to start preparing to leave.

Frank and Betty were thanked for their hospitality with genuine enthusiasm. Laughter and goodbyes gave way to the sound of car doors being slammed.

'Was that okay?' Neef asked Eve as they joined the main road.

'I had a great time,' said Eve. 'They're a nice couple, especially Betty.'

'I noticed how well you two were getting on,' said Neef. 'I think Betty was single-handedly responsible for me not starving to death when I first arrived at St George's.'

'Where had you come from?' asked Eve.

'The States.'

'I thought you chaps did that thing the other way around,' said Eve. 'Aren't you supposed to go to America in protest against the poor conditions in the National Health Service?'

'That's usually the way,' agreed Neef. 'But personally, I didn't like America.'

'Why not? You probably earned three times what you get here.'

'I did,' agreed Neef. 'And the facilities were the best in the world.'

'So why?'

Neef thought for a moment before saying, 'As soon as I started my job in the States I was sent on a course run by the hospital. It was called Reimbursement Maximization.'

'Doesn't sound too medical,' said Eve.

'It wasn't. It was a course designed to teach the hospital's doctors how to extract the maximum payment possible from their patients' health insurance. We were instructed to provide treatment after treatment until all their insurance money was used up and then to continue as long as their families would pay.'

'That sounds awful,' said Eve.

'I'm a children's tumour specialist. Many of my patients weren't going to get better at all. But the treatment went on until their families in many cases went bankrupt. Do you know that money owed on medical bills is the leading cause of bankruptcy in the United States?'

'I didn't,' admitted Eve.

'Well, it is, and it all got a bit too much for me. Medicine is the second largest industry in the States. It's big business and somewhere along the line people have lost sight of the fact that money shouldn't automatically be the first consideration.'

Eve nodded but didn't say anything.

'And so I came home,' said Neef, 'to discover we've started out along the same road.'

'The government says not,' said Eve.

Neef snorted his disbelief and brought the Discovery to a halt outside Eve's apartment block. He turned to smile at her. 'I'm sorry, I've been shooting my mouth off. I'm really glad you came today. I enjoyed it.'

'Me too,' said Eve. 'And I'm glad you told me these things. I like hearing insiders' views.'

Neef found himself wishing that Eve would ask him in but she didn't. He hadn't really had a chance to talk to her properly during the afternoon because of the way things had worked out. As she opened the door to get out she turned and said, 'Am I to be allowed to visit Neil?'

'You've thought about the conditions we spoke of?'

'Yes. I have and I agree.'

'Then come tomorrow. Make it in the afternoon.'

'Is there anything special he likes?'

'He's obsessed with fire engines.'

'Fire engines?' exclaimed Eve.

'It's the only toy we've ever managed to interest him in.'

Eve smiled briefly and said, 'I'll see what I can do.'

Six

After feeding Dolly, Neef settled down to read the Sunday papers he'd bought on the way back from lunch. He was interrupted by the phone. It was David Farro-Jones.

'Hello Mike. I thought I'd just call and wish you luck with the trial tomorrow.'

'That's very nice of you, I appreciate it,' replied Neef.

'I also wanted to repeat my offer of help and facilities should you need them.'

'I'm most grateful, David. I'm sure Max will be as well.'

'About Max, Mike . . .' Farro-Jones began hesitantly.

'Yes? What about him?'

'God, this is difficult . . .'

'What is?'

'You and I have known each other quite a while, Mike. I'd like to say something to you in confidence.'

'Go ahead,' said Neef.

'I know Max Pereira.'

'Yes, I know you do.'

'I mean, I know him well; we worked together for two years in the States. He's ambitious, ruthless and determined to get to the top. Nothing is going to stand in his way. This trial is important to Max and to Menogen, much more so than they've let on. They all stand to become millionaires if they get a good result.'

'And good luck to them too,' said Neef. 'If they've come up with a gene therapy that destroys tumours, they deserve all the success that comes to them.'

'Agreed, but I just thought you should be aware of the pressures they're working under. If their new vectors succeed, the sky's the limit; they'll have all the fame and fortune they ever dreamed of. But if they fail they could lose everything, and the chances are that Menogen would be in real trouble. They've gambled so much in developing retroviral vectors that if they don't work out it's doubtful whether they could get back in the race with an altered strategy. Someone else would almost certainly beat them to it.'

'So where does this leave me?' asked Neef.

'I just thought you should be aware of this,' said Farro-Jones. 'Strong financial considerations are not entirely compatible with the care and concern for patients that you and I take for granted. I think you should be on your guard at all times. Question everything Max tells you. Don't allow him to take any short cuts – and if you're unsure of anything give me a call; maybe I can advise you. There's one simple rule in all this at present: the more efficient the vector, the greater the potential danger to the patient.'

'Thanks, David, I appreciate the warning; but I think Max and I have an understanding,' said Neef. 'He admitted at one point he would have liked to do some tracer experiments on the children to check out the spread of his vectors but I said no. All the patients are to be treated therapeutically. Apart from that it's either me or my medical staff who'll be administering the viruses. Max won't be allowed near the patients.'

'But you will be dependent on Max giving you what he *says* he's giving you to inject into them,' said Farro-Jones.

'But the various safety committees have examined both the viruses and the strategy and passed them.'

'They examined what Menogen proposed on paper and examined the vectors Menogen gave them to examine,' said Farro-Jones.

'Surely you're not suggesting that—'

'No I suppose not,' conceded Farro-Jones. 'Maybe I worry too much and probably I'm doing it unnecessarily; but, if you do have any qualms at any time, I'd be happy to carry out a molecular analysis for you to verify anything you're not sure of.'

'Thanks, David. I can't say you've exactly put my mind at rest but I appreciate your concern.'

'Good luck, Mike.'

'Thanks.'

Neef put down the phone; his good mood had completely evaporated. He took little comfort in remembering the look on Max Pereira's face the first time he heard that David Farro-Jones would be on the ethics committee. He had interpreted it at the time as being something short of pleasure. This also made sense of David's behaviour when questioning Max Pereira. He didn't trust the man an inch.

'That, Dolly,' said Neef, getting up from his chair, 'is just about all I need.'

Neef was in early next morning. He examined the report from the night staff nurse and spoke to Tony Samuels, who had been on call. There were no new problems. Max Pereira arrived at eight thirty. He had changed his T-shirt but still wore jeans, a leather jacket and cowboy boots. He plonked his briefcase down on Neef's desk and put his beret on top. He asked, 'Any coffee?'

'I'll have a look,' replied Neef. 'I could do with some myself.'

Neef put his head round the door of the duty room and found the night staff nurse still there. 'No Kate?' he asked.

'Not yet. It's most unlike her.'

Neef frowned then asked, 'I don't suppose there's any coffee?'

The staff nurse smiled and said, 'It's against all my feminist principles but I'll make some while I wait for Sister.'

It was very unusual for Kate Morse to be late, thought Neef. He hoped she hadn't been involved in a car accident. It had to be said that she wasn't the best driver in the world. The last time she had given him a lift had been the equivalent of a white-knuckle ride on Blackpool Pleasure Beach. It was totally out of character but a fact nevertheless. Her husband Charlie had given up on trying to slow her down. 'Born to be wild,' he had said, tongue in cheek.

'So where are the viruses?' Neef asked Pereira when he returned to his office.

'They're in the unit fridge. I came in yesterday,' replied Pereira. 'There's also a back-up supply down in your Pharmacy Department.

'Anything else I need to know?'

'The high-tech stuff has all been done back in the lab,' replied Pereira. 'All you have to do now is administer the vectors, wait seven days, then start the patients on Gancyclovir.'

'I made a provisional list of five patients I though suitable candidates under the terms of our open licence,' said Neef.'

'Your houseman, Samuels, showed it to me yesterday.'

'Any problems from your point of view?'

'I don't think so.' Pereira opened his briefcase and took out a series of tracings made on what looked like acetate sheeting but seemed infinitely more pliable. 'I made up these,' he said, passing them over to Neef. 'They are exact tracings of the tumours from all angles available on the scans. From these, I've done volume calculations and estimated the amount of vector suspension we need to inject.'

'Good. For my part, I've calculated the best angle of approach using the keyhole gear,' said Neef. 'I've done that for four of them.'

'That just leaves the brain tumour kid, let me see . . . Downy.'

'Thomas Downy,' said Neef. He disliked anyone referring to the children by their last names.

'Yeah, Thomas Downy,' drawled Pereira. 'Has a surgical team been briefed for that one?'

'Norman Beavis will be ready in theatre at two thirty,' replied Neef.

'Good. Accuracy is going to be really important. We've got to hit the centre of the tumour.'

'I thought you said your vector would only infect dividing cells,' said Neef.

Pereira screwed up his face and said, 'It's possible we may get a bystander effect.'

'A bystander effect, Dr Pereira?' repeated Neef coldly, his features hardening.

'It's just conceivable that normal cells situated right next to the tumour could be damaged.'

'So Thomas Downy is at some risk of brain damage after all?'

Pereira hunched up his shoulders and spread his palms as if wrestling with a difficult concept. He said, 'Not really, if the procedure is carried out correctly and the virus goes to the heart of the tumour. Let's face it, Mike, when it comes right down to it, this kid's tumour itself isn't exactly doing his brain a whole lot of good as it is, is it?'

'Whereas you might kill his tumour but turn him into an brain-damaged idiot?'

Neef was struggling to keep his temper but the stress he was feeling wasn't helping. He kept thinking about what David Farro-Jones had said. 'You told me at the outset there was no risk of healthy brain cells being damaged.'

'And there isn't, in theory,' soothed Pereira. 'Normal brain cells don't divide so they can't become infected by a retrovirus. Our gene delivery system is based on a retrovirus, so normal brain cells can't become infected.'

'But?'

'In practice, it can happen . . . occasionally. It's just a phenomenon, that's all.'

Neef stared at Pereira as if he were looking through the back of his head. 'How many more phenomena haven't you told me about?' he asked.

Pereira held up his hands and tilted his head to one side. 'None, Mike, absolutely none.'

Neef was trying to decide whether Pereira was capable of using a strategy which would destroy a tumour but leave the patient brain-damaged in order to claim a technical 'cure'. He thought of the old surgical joke: the operation was successful; the patient died.'

'Have all the Menogen virus vectors been passed by the Medicines Control Agency?' Neef asked.

'Not all of them, no.'

'But the ones you're using in this trial have?'

'Of course. That was a condition of the National Gene Therapy Advisory Committee.'

'You said that the viruses are in the unit fridge?'

'Yeah.'

'I'm going to ask David Farro-Jones to come over here and take samples from all the vials. I'd like to be assured that the viruses are what you say they are and that they are present in the concentration you say they are in.'

Pereira's face darkened. His eyes flashed with anger but he kept control. 'And if I refuse?' he asked quietly.

'I'll stop the trial before it starts.'

'Then, in the circumstances, I have no option,' said Pereira. 'Go ahead. Do what you have to.'

Neef made the call to Farro-Jones, saying that he'd like to take him up on his offer of help. Farro-Jones said he'd be there within ten minutes.

Kate Morse knocked and came in smoothing her uniform front and then her hair. She stopped when she saw Pereira sitting there and sensed the tension in the room. 'I'm sorry,' she said, 'I didn't realise you were with—'

'It's okay, Kate, we've finished for the moment.'

'I just wanted to apologize for being late. Charlie's come down with flu or something and you know what men are like. I had to make sure a complete life-support system was within arm's length.

'No problem,' said Neef.

David Farro-Jones arrived from the medical school. He looked uncomfortable and embarrassed. 'Morning, Max; Morning Mike. So, what exactly is it you chaps want me to do?' he asked.

'I would like you to take pre-treatment samples of the viral vectors that Dr Pereira has prepared for my patients and analyse them . . . as a formality,' said Neef. 'Can you do this?'

'Of course,' replied Farro-Jones. 'I did say I'd be happy to help you chaps with any lab work you feel necessary.' He smiled at Pereira, who did not smile back.

'Look, Max, I hope you and I won't fall out over this?' said Farro-Jones. 'It's really just a sensible control measure when you think about it. Don't you think?'

Pereira gave a small smile and nodded. 'If you like,' he said.

'There's no reason at all for you two to fall out,' said Neef. 'This request is entirely down to me.'

'So where are these viruses?' asked Farro-Jones.

Pereira went to fetch them from the fridge. He returned with a wire rack containing five glass vials. He put the rack down with slow deliberation on Neef's desk.

'I can't open them here,' said Farro-Jones. 'They could become contaminated with bugs from the atmosphere. I'll have to take them back to the medical school. We have a laminar air-flow cabinet there. We can open them safely with full aseptic precautions.' He turned to Pereira and asked, 'Is this okay with you, Max?'

'I'd be kind of pissed off if you'd tried to open them here,' said Pereira. 'On you go.'

'I just thought, maybe, you'd like to be present when I open the vials?' suggested Farro-Jones.

'That won't be necessary, David,' smiled Pereira. 'I trust you.'

Neef knew the comment had been made for his benefit but he remained unrepentant. When Farro-Jones had left he said, 'We'll continue with the trial when David confirms the contents of the vials.'

'As you like,' said Pereira wearily, getting up to go. 'Maybe you can give me a call when it happens.'

'Of course,' said Neef. 'And Max . . .'

'Yeah?'

'You and I don't know each other so we don't have a foundation

88

for a relationship based on trust. Let's not bother to pretend. We do have to work with each other, however, so there should be some ground rules.'

'Like what?'

'If there's a choice to be made between what I see as my patients' interests and the possibility of offending you, I'm liable to offend you quite a lot. Is that understood?'

'I haven't heard a line like that since *Dr Kildare*,' said Pereira – and with that he left. He brushed past Kate Morse on the way out.

'Was it something I said?' she muttered. Neef didn't comment. He waited for Kate to speak. 'I think you should take a look at Jane Lees,' she said. 'Her breathing's very laboured and she's having a lot of pain.'

'I'll be right there,' said Neef. He got up to put his white coat on.

'You haven't said what you'll need for the trial patients,' said Kate.

'There's going to be a delay on the trial,' said Neef. 'A technical hitch.'

'Oh,' said Kate, remembering the manner of Pereira's departure. 'I see.'

Neef examined Jane Lees and made a change to her medication to ease the pain. He saw that Lawrence Fielding had written her up for an antibiotic. He was sounding her chest when Fielding joined him. 'You examined her this morning?' Neef asked.

'First thing,' replied Fielding. 'I thought the pneumonia might be coming back.'

'I agree,' said Neef. 'That's what it sounds like, but I'm not convinced it's pneumonia.'

'That's what she was admitted to East Side General with in the first place,' said Fielding.

'Viral pneumonia,' said Neef. 'So the antibiotic wouldn't do her any good.'

'I'm aware of that,' said Fielding, uncharacteristically curtly.

'I prescribed the antibiotic as cover against secondary bacterial infection.'

Neef looked up at Fielding and said, 'Sorry, Lawrence, I'm a bit on edge today. About this pneumonia . . .'

'What about it?'

'Supposing it isn't pneumonia at all. Supposing it were some kind of inflammatory response to the cancer agent she was exposed to and it only *looks* like pneumonia.'

'It's possible, I suppose,' agreed Fielding. 'That would explain why there was no response to the initial antibiotic therapy.'

'Precisely. Let's try her on a steroid, see if we can suppress the response. We've nothing to lose.'

Eve Sayers appeared at two thirty. She was carrying a parcel that Neef would have bet a month's salary contained a fire engine.

'You got one then?' he asked.

'I got one,' said Eve, smiling. 'It wasn't easy. The shop assistant told me they're not as popular as they used to be but I got one.'

Neef suddenly realized that she was nervous and it pleased him. He took this as a sign of concern for Neil. 'Why don't you just go right in then?' he suggested.

'If that's all right.'

Neef nodded. 'You remember where he is?'

'I remember.'

Neef followed Eve to the side ward and watched as she entered and said hello to Neil. Neil, who had been looking through a large picture book of animals that the nurses had given him, looked up and stared at Eve. Neef thought for a moment that he didn't recognize her but suddenly his eyes sparkled and he made a sound of pleasure. He put down the book and looked around for his fire engine. He picked it up from the floor and held it out to her. Eve nodded, obviously relieved and pleased that Neil had remembered. The pair of them settled down to play and Neef left them to it.

An hour later Kate Morse put her head round Neef's door to say that Jane Lees's parents were demanding to see him. He asked her to show them in.

'I want to know what the hell's going on!' said the small, pugnacious man wearing blazer and flannels, who entered first. His wife, much more timid in demeanour, trailed in behind him looking apologetic rather than angry. She fiddled with the catch of her handbag, which was draped over one arm.

Neef indicated they should both sit down.

Lees sat down but did not take his eyes off Neef. 'First the other hospital tells us our Jane has pneumonia, then they decide that she's got cancer and now we've had the public health at the door asking us all sorts of personal questions. What's going on?'

Neef's first thought was to wonder why the hell Lennon had not explained all this properly to the man in front of him. But maybe he had, he considered. 'As Dr Lennon probably explained to you, Mr Lees—'

'I didn't see any bloody Dr Lennon. The wife tells me some joker from public health's been round. There's nothing wrong with our house, dammit. Who sent him? The wife's right upset over it.'

Neef looked at the mousey woman, who had clearly failed to understand what Lennon had told her. She was looking down at the floor. A visit from anyone saying 'public health' obviously, in Mrs Lees's book, implied some criticism of her house and her capabilities as a mother.

'I think there's been a misunderstanding,' said Neef.

'I'll bloody say there's been a misunderstanding,' said Lees, launching himself on another offensive which Neef tried to halt by holding up his hands.

'Please, Mr Lees,' Neef appealed. 'Give me a chance.'

Lees paused and took a breath. He rubbed the back of his neck and hunched his shoulders a few times.

'Dr Lennon's visit had nothing to do with any supposed shortcomings on your part,' said Neef. He said it firmly and conclusively and it appeared to have the desired effect. He sensed Lees begin to relax.

'We're agreed about that then,' said Lees.

'Jane does have cancer, I'm afraid, and Dr Lennon and his colleagues are trying to find out how she got it?'

'What do you mean, how she got it?'

'We think Jane was exposed to some highly carcinogenic substance and that's how she got the disease in the first place. The public health people are trying to establish what it was before anyone else is affected.'

'Lees's eyes opened like organ stops. He looked mutely at his wife and then back at Neef. 'Let me get this straight,' he said. 'Are you telling me that Jane getting cancer was somebody's fault? It wasn't just one of those things?'

Neef suddenly wondered what he was getting himself into but it was too late to withdraw. 'We think that Jane came into contact with some gas or chemical that gave her the disease.'

'Gas or chemical?' repeated Lees slowly. 'Bloody hell.'

Mrs Lees spoke for the first time. She said to Neef, 'You can do a lot with cancer these days, can't you, Doctor? I mean it's not like it used to be, is it?'

''Course they can,' interrupted her husband, 'They've got all sorts of drugs these days.'

Neef looked at them both and felt his heart sink. That bloody awful moment was here again. 'I'm afraid Jane has lung cancer,' he said. 'She has extensive lesions on both lungs. The outlook is very poor.'

'Are you telling us our Janey is going to die?' asked Lees as if he couldn't believe he was uttering the words.

'I'm afraid so.'

Lees shook his head mutely, his mouth opening and shutting without any sound escaping as he struggled to find words. His wife buried her face in a handkerchief that she took from her handbag. Anger surfaced in Lees like an erupting volcano. 'If what you say is true, why the hell are the police not out looking for this chemical or gas or whatever it is? They're covering it up aren't they? That's what they're bloody well doing!' Lees had risen from his chair and was leaning on Neef's desk, accusing him.

'There's no question of anyone covering anything up, Mr Lees,' said Neef calmly.

'Then why aren't they all out looking for it? One poxy drain inspector? A lot of bloody good that is!'

'Dr Lennon is an epidemiologist, Mr Lees, not a poxy drain inspector. He's an expert in tracing the sources of disease. Policemen aren't. Dr Lennon came to ask your wife personal questions about Jane because he's trying to establish some common factor between Jane and the first girl.'

'First girl!' exploded Lees. 'You mean there's been another?'

'Jane is the second victim,' admitted Neef, feeling as if he'd just stepped deeper into the mire.

Lees took his wife's arm and led her towards the door. He opened it and turned round to say, 'Do you know what I'm going to do now, Doctor?'

'Tell me,' said Neef.

'I'm going straight to the bloody papers, that's what I'm going to do. They'll get some bloody action. It's a bloody disgrace, kids getting cancer from some bloody gas and nobody's doing a blind thing about it!'

The Leeses left, brushing past Eve Sayers, who was waiting at the door.

'Can I come in?' she asked, tapping lightly on the door.

Neef realized that she must have heard what Lees had said. 'Of course,' he said.

'I won't ask,' said Eve.

'Good.' Neef smiled. 'How did you get on with Neil?'

'Like a house on fire.'

'Appropriate for someone with two fire engines at his finger tips. Did he like the new one?'

'He certainly did. Can I come back tomorrow?'

'Of course.'

Eve hesitated as she got to the door. 'You said something about starting a new gene therapy trial this week.'

'We've had to delay it,' said Neef.

'Will Neil be one of the patients?'

'No. Neil's in remission at the moment. His tumour's stopped growing so we're leaving well alone. Apart from that there's some doubt about whether Neil would be suitable for this kind of therapy.'

'I see,' said Eve. 'Just thought I'd ask.'

Neef saw the disappointment on her face. He said, 'You're probably the best medicine for Neil right now.'

'Me?'

'The state of mind of a patient can often be an important factor in the prognosis of cancer cases,' said Neef. 'Happy, positive people do better.'

'It must be quite hard to be happy and positive when you know you've got cancer,' said Eve.

Neef nodded and said, 'Neil's too young to know what he's got. That's an advantage.'

'I'll do my best.'

At four o'clock on Wednesday afternoon David Farro-Jones appeared in Neef's office. He was carrying an ice box containing the Menogen viruses.

'Well?' asked Neef.

'They are exactly what Max said they were,' said Farro-Jones.

'I see,' said Neef, feeling a bit foolish.

'If it's any comfort, I think you did the right thing in asking for a check. You were only acting in the best interests of your patients.'

'Thanks,' said Neef. 'That doesn't make it any the less embarrassing, I'm afraid.'

'The right road is sometimes the hardest to travel,' said Farro-Jones. I don't think you should become any less vigilant because everything was okay this time. It's no bad thing for Max to think we're keeping an eye on him.' He got up to go, adding, 'If there's anything else just give me a call.'

'Thanks, David,' said Neef.

Neef put the virus vials in the unit fridge and looked up Max

Pereira's phone number on the desk pad. There was no reply. He called an alternative mobile number.

'Pereira.'

'Max, it's Michael Neef. Your viruses have been cleared by the medical school people.'

'No kidding,' said Pereira.

Neef winced but kept his resolution. He wanted to apologize to the man but he still felt that he'd done what needed doing in the circumstances and Farro-Jones had been right: it was no bad thing for Max to believe he was being watched. 'We could start tomorrow if I can get theatre facilities,' he said.

'Fine by me,' said Pereira.

'It's probably too short notice to get Mr Beavis for Thomas Downy but I'll see what I can do.'

'Whatever,' said Pereira dryly.

Neef put down the phone and went in search of Kate Morse. He found her with Thomas Downy and told her about the start of the trial. 'Do you think we can be ready?'

'Of course we can,' replied Kate. 'What about theatres?'

'I'm on my way to see about that. I thought I'd check with you first.' Neef thought that Kate was looking pale and drawn. He took her gently to one side and asked, 'Is everything all right?'

Kate put her hand to her cheek nervously and said, 'I'm sorry. It's Charlie. He's still off work. We got the doctor in yesterday. He said it was flu but I'm worried it might be more serious.'

'I see,' said Neef. 'What makes you think that?'

'Charlie's never ill. He gets the occasional cold and makes a meal of it but he's never really ill if you know what I mean.'

'Maybe that's the problem then,' said Neef. 'This time maybe he really has come down with a dose of the flu. There's a world of difference between what people call flu and the real thing. You can really be quite ill with it.'

'You're probably right,' said Kate.

'Why not give it until the morning? And if you're still not happy call your GP again. Tell him you're a nursing sister if he doesn't know that already. You know what you're talking about.'

Neef managed to book enough theatre time for the following day to start three patients off on gene therapy. He decided that the first two would be Rebecca Daley, who had liver cancer, and Martin Liddle, a pancreatic-tumour patient. They would require only the small theatre. The big theatre was available in the afternoon. He booked it, hoping that Norman Beavis would be free to carry out the operation on Thomas Downy. Beavis's secretary confirmed that this was so. Beavis was operating at University College Hospital in the morning but would be free in the afternoon. The remaining two patients were booked into the small theatre, both on Friday morning.

Feeling that he was on a winning streak, Neef telephoned the Pharmacy Department. 'Has my Antivulon arrived yet?' he asked.

'Half an hour ago, Dr Neef. It's on its way up to you now.'

Neef sought out Lawrence Fielding and told him the good news. Fielding said he'd get the relevant patients started on the drug as soon as it appeared.

Neef was walking back to his office, feeling better than he'd done for a few days, when he bumped into Eve Sayers. She had been visiting Neil and had just come out of his room.'

'Everything okay?' asked Neef.

'Just fine,' replied Eve. 'I was hoping I might bump into you. I have a problem.'

Neef led Eve back to his office and closed the door behind them. 'What's up?'

'A man named Lees called my paper yesterday and the editor's asked me to check up on his story. I think he was the man who was in your office yesterday when I arrived.'

Neef nodded. 'His daughter has cancer; he was very upset.'

'I told my editor that I had an agreement with you and couldn't break it. He said he understood but that it was an important story of great public interest if true. If I didn't feel I could take it on he'd ask another reporter to cover it. I'm sorry.'

'I see,' said Neef. 'Well, Mr Lees approached your paper directly so if it has to be anyone it might as well be you. What do you need to know?'

Eve related what Lees had told her editor. 'Is this substantially correct?' she asked.

'It is true that Jane Lees has cancer and we think she must have been exposed to some carcinogenic gas or chemical. She's the second within the space of a week.'

'Good Lord,' said Eve.

'Mr Lees feels that not enough is being done to trace the cause but I suspect it is. The public health people are investigating and they are the experts. Mr Lees would prefer lots of uniforms combing the streets.'

'Wouldn't that help?' asked Eve. 'I mean if it's a chemical spillage or something dumped illegally?'

'I don't think so,' replied Neef. 'It would be like looking for a needle in a haystack. This sort of thing calls for clever detective work. With any luck the PH people will have pinpointed the source by the end of the week.'

Eve nodded and said, 'In that case I'll do my best to stall for a couple of days to give them a chance.'

'Thanks,' said Neef.

Eve got up to leave and Neef escorted her to the door. As he turned the handle Eve suddenly said, 'Have dinner with me this evening?'

Neef was taken aback. 'Eeer . . . all right,' he said.

'Good. Come around eight.'

Neef sat in his chair for a few moments doodling on the phone pad while he thought about the invitation; it had come as a complete surprise, so his first reaction was to look for an ulterior motive. When he failed to see one he concluded that he should stop being paranoid and just look forward to spending a pleasant evening with Eve. He picked up the phone and called

Lennon at the Public Health Department. Luckily, he was in his office.

'Any joy with the investigation?' he asked.

'Nothing yet,' replied Lennon. 'I thought we'd be sure to crack it when we got two cases, but it hasn't turned out that way. We haven't found any factor that links them at all. Still, I suppose we should be grateful that we only have two cases. The cancer source can't be too accessible or we'd have more.'

'There is one problem on the horizon, however,' said Neef.

'What?'

'Jane Lees's father's gone to the papers. He's demanding action over what he sees as some kind of cover-up. The story's been stalled for a couple of days but probably not more.'

'Damnation,' sighed Lennon. 'Thanks for the warning. How is the girl, by the way?'

'Not good,' replied Neef. 'Not good. And if she dies it won't just be her parents demanding answers.'

Seven

Neef stopped at a Thresher's off-licence on the way over to Eve's apartment and picked up a bottle of Australian Chardonnay from the cold cabinet; the assistant told him that wines from Australia and New Zealand were very fashionable; he himself had little interest in wine. Suddenly worrying that white might not be appropriate, he also bought a bottle of Côtes du Rhone. He arrived at Eve's just before eight.

Eve was wearing a cream silk blouse over black cord trousers, which emphasised her good figure. She was wearing her hair loose again and swept it back from her face as she opened the door and invited Neef in. She accepted the wine with a 'Thank you' and said, 'I'm just about organized. Why don't you help yourself to a drink while I do things in the kitchen.'

Neef was left alone in the room he had first been in on the previous Sunday. This time the curtains were closed, muted jazz was playing on the stereo and the air was lightly perfumed with the smell of incense emanating from a small brass burner on the mantelshelf. Neef guessed that the burner had the same origin as the blue rugs, Tunisia. If the conversation dried up he could always ask about it. There was a silver tray with a selection of spirits on it and some bottles of mixers. A red plastic ice bucket had its lid displaced to the side by matching tongs. Neef helped himself to gin and tonic and called through to Eve, 'Can I get you something?'

'Gin would be nice,' she replied.

Eve returned from the kitchen, picked up her drink and said, 'We've got about ten minutes. Do you mind if I ask you something?'

'Go ahead.'

'You said earlier that there'd been two cases of cancer caused by this chemical or whatever it turns out to be?'

'Yes.'

'Were the two victims from the same part of the city?'

'Not as far as we know,' replied Neef. 'But it's reasonable to assume that their paths must have crossed at some time. This is what public health will be trying to establish. Ironically, their job's been made easier by the appearance of a second victim.'

'How so?'

'From interviews with the families, the investigators will build up a picture of each girl's movements over a period of time and then compare them. They should be able to spot any common factors like a park that both girls visited or woods or even a building. Then they can home in on it and mount a comprehensive search with the aid of the police if necessary.'

'I see. Sounds straightforward when you say it like that,' said Eve.

'It should be,' said Neef. He did not add that, as yet, public health had failed to come up with anything. 'Did you have trouble sitting on the story for the time being?'

'No. I convinced my editor that Mr Lees is under great emotional strain and that we really would have to be sure of our facts before we go to print with the story.'

'Good,' said Neef. 'I'm grateful. This kind of story can kick up a lot of public alarm.'

'What's wrong with public alarm?' Eve asked. 'It's the only thing that can galvanize some public bodies into action.'

'I suppose you're right,' conceded Neef. 'But it would be nice if PH were to clear this business up before it appears in print.'

°   °   °

Dinner was good and Neef complimented Eve on her cooking. He said with a contented sigh, 'That's the best meal I've eaten in ages.'

'If you come to my place more than three times you start getting the same things all over again,' said Eve.

'I'm sure you're being too modest.'

'Liqueur? Drambuie, Amaretto?'

'No, I need a clear head tomorrow. We're starting the gene therapy trial.'

'It must be very exciting to be in at the start of something new like this,' said Eve.

'It's also worrying,' said Neef. 'Anything new always means unforeseen problems, "teething troubles", as people like to call them, and gene therapy's been having its fair share of these.'

'I didn't realize it had been used before.'

'Several trials have been carried out internationally with varying results. University College Hospital tried it on cystic-fibrosis patients last year without any great success.'

'Is that the disease where kids have to have physiotherapy all the time to get all the mucous out of their lungs?' asked Eve.

Neef nodded. 'The condition's caused by a genetic defect in a gene that scientists have now identified. The challenge now is to put a normal working copy of the gene into the patient's own lung cells so that they'll start making the missing substance.'

'And cure themselves?'

'More or less. Cystic fibrosis affects more than the lungs, but the lung condition is certainly the worst aspect of the disease, and that should clear up once they get the treatment working.'

'So how do they get a working copy of the gene?' asked Eve, clearly warming to the subject.

'That's the easy bit, once you've identified it,' said Neef. 'The difficult bit is getting it into the patients' lung cells. For that, you have to use some kind of intermediate vector to carry it in, usually a virus.'

'A virus? You deliberately infect the patients with a virus?' asked Eve, with a horrified look.

'It's not as bad as it sounds,' said Neef. 'They disable the virus first so it can't cause infection.'

'But you say it didn't work at University College?'

'They didn't actually use a virus vector,' said Neef. 'They opted for a liposome system. That's safer than using a live virus but not nearly so effective in delivering the new gene to the patients' cells.'

'So it failed?'

'Unfortunately, but the word is they're going to try again soon with a new vector.'

'A virus this time?' asked Eve.

'Almost certainly.'

'So it'll be more risky?'

'As David Farro-Jones put it, the more efficient the vector, the bigger the risk.'

'Who's David Farro-Jones?'

'He's the molecular biologist in charge of gene therapy at University College.'

'But not at St George's?'

'No,' said Neef. 'St George's is run by a different hospital trust, although in practice we still talk to each other! Our entry into gene therapy's coming through a commercial company called Menogen Research and their chief scientist, a chap called Max Pereira.'

'Who's going to be the first patient?' asked Eve.

'Rebecca Daley. She's eleven. Hepatoma patient – cancer of the liver. We're treating her tomorrow morning.'

'Here's to Rebecca,' said Eve, raising her glass.

Neef nodded.

Eve topped up Neef's coffee cup and changed the subject. 'Do your patients ever get out at all?'

'What do you mean, out?'

'Day trips, home visits, that sort of thing.'

'Yes, that's quite common.'

'But not Neil?'

'Neil comes from a children's home. It would be awkward for the routine of the place.'

'Would you let me take him out?'

'I suppose—'

'Maybe to the zoo or something like that.'

'If he's feeling well enough, I can't see any harm in it. In fact, it might do him the world of good.'

'Good,' said Eve. 'I was just thinking how perky he seemed today. It would be nice if we could go out somewhere away from the hospital.'

'People will stare, remember. His face isn't a pretty sight, though *you've* probably got used to it.'

'You're right, I have,' said Eve, as if she'd just realized it. 'I don't notice the tumour now at all.'

'Maybe a crowded place like the zoo isn't such a good idea,' said Neef.

'Well, a run in the car perhaps, or a picnic in the country.'

'Sounds good.'

It was raining heavily when Neef left Eve's place just after eleven thirty. The big tyres on the Discovery made such a noise on the now flooding roads that Neef turned off the Vivaldi tape he'd inserted and listened to the hiss of spray instead. The sound of an English summer, he mused as he turned off the main road and dropped a gear to negotiate the steep hill down to the cottage. He could see the lights, partially blurred by the river running down the windscreen, but nonetheless welcoming. He had fitted random time switches in three of the cottage's rooms so that it would always appear inhabited to the eye of an opportunist burglar.

Neef poured himself a nightcap of whisky and sat down on the couch with a sigh. Dolly positioned herself at his feet. Eve was still very much in his mind; if he closed his eyes and put back his head he could see her smile. She put her head a little to one side when she laughed; it was a mannerism he liked a lot. He felt a pang of guilt at the thought, something to do with Elaine's ghost. But there was no denying the fact that he had enjoyed the evening very much. His only regret was that it seemed to have flown by. But there would be other evenings. He felt sure of that.

Neef woke with a start as the telephone rang. He clicked on the bedside light and looked at his watch. It was two thirty a.m.

'Mike? It's Kate Morse. I'm really sorry to disturb you.'

'What's the problem?' asked Neef, rubbing his eyes. He was trying to remember if Kate was on duty tonight. He felt sure she wasn't.

'It's Charlie,' said Kate. 'I'm worried sick.'

'Charlie?' repeated Neef.

'He's a lot worse. I called in the GP again as you suggested but he said there was nothing to worry about. It was just a bad dose of flu. He'd be right as rain in a couple of days. He should stay in bed and take aspirin – you know the routine. But he won't be, I know it, Mike. He's really sick and I don't know what to do for the best.'

Neef could hear that Kate was very worried and it meant some-thing. She was a very experienced nurse and used to modulating her voice through all sorts of crises, but she was having a hard time doing it this time. 'I'll come over, Kate. Give me fifteen minutes.'

'Thanks Mike. I'm so grateful.'

Neef pulled on jeans, a T-shirt and a warm sweater while Dolly opened one eye to watch the proceedings. 'Keep my place warm, Dols,' he said as he put on a waterproof jacket and pulled his medical case out from beneath the bed. Dolly closed her eyes again. She didn't move.

The journey to the small bungalow where Kate and Charlie Morse lived took twelve minutes. During the day it would have taken half an hour but at three in the morning the streets were virtually free of traffic. A couple of taxis and a police panda car were the only other signs of life as he negotiated roads that the heavy rain was rapidly turning into rivers.

'Thanks for coming, Mike,' whispered Kate as she answered the door. 'He's through here.'

Charlie Morse didn't turn to look at Neef as he entered the room.

He continued to stare up at the ceiling while taking rapid shallow breaths. He had the bedcovers down at waist level. His skin was pale and a thin film of sweat coated it. There was an unpleasant, sweet smell in the room – nothing specific, just the universal smell of illness, thought Neef.

'I won't ask you how you're doing, Charlie,' he said. 'I can see that for myself.'

Neef took out his stethoscope and warmed it briefly on the palm of his hand before applying it to Charlie's chest. When he'd finished, Kate stepped in to help support her husband in a sitting position while Neef sounded Charlie from the back.

'Okay,' said Neef.

Kate let Charlie sink back down on the bed. She tried to bring up the covers but Charlie stopped her with a vague push of his hand.

Neef moved back from the bed and Kate joined him, looking apprehensive.

'We're going to have to get him to hospital,' said Neef. 'He has severe pneumonia, both lungs.'

'The phone's out here,' said Kate. She led Neef out into the hall where he dialled 999.

'That bad?' said Kate.

'The quicker the better,' said Neef. 'And if you'll take some advice, Kate . . .'

'Yes?'

'Change your GP. He's an idiot.'

Kate nodded. Her mind was racing ahead to the next problem. 'Mike, could I possibly ask you to stay here for a few minutes in case the kids wake up. I'm going next door to see if I can a get a neighbour to look after them. I'd like to go to the hospital with Charlie.'

'Of course,' said Neef.

Kate threw a coat round her shoulders and disappeared out through the front door. Neef returned to Charlie's room and told him the ambulance was on its way. Charlie acknowledged with a slight nod of his head. He was breathing more rapidly than ever. A long way off in the distance, Neef thought he could hear the wail of a siren.

As the ambulance drew up outside the house, Kate came running up the path. 'Mrs Redpath's going to come over,' she said to Neef. 'Could you hang on till she comes?'

'Of course.'

Neef watched the two green-clad technicians load the stretcher bearing Charlie Morse into the back of the ambulance. Kate stood beside the open doors, her coat draped over her shoulders against the rain. She glanced up at Neef and he saw the worry on her face. The sodium streetlights were being unkind. She had aged ten years.

'Mrs Redpath won't be long,' said Kate.

'Don't worry about it.'

Kate climbed into the back, the doors were closed and the ambulance moved off into the night, its blue light flashing mutely through the rain.

'Where are they taking him?' asked a well-modulated woman's voice behind Neef.

Neef turned to find a small, stout woman standing there. Her fair-skinned face was fringed by a halo of pure white hair. She had a coat on over her dressing gown but was still wearing carpet slippers. Neef could see the wet ring around the outside edge of them. 'Mrs Redpath?' he enquired.

'Yes, and you must be Dr Neef. Kate told me you'd wait.'

'University College Hospital,' said Neef, remembering that she had asked him a question.

'He'll be well looked after there,' said the woman.

Neef left Mrs Redpath in charge of the house and the Morse children, who had slept throughout the proceedings, and drove home. He had abandoned any hope of getting much sleep.

Neef actually slept for three hours before the alarm went off, but it felt as though his head had hardly touched the pillow. He got up and took a long, hot shower before making himself plenty of strong coffee and two slices of toast. It was seven forty-five when he set off for the hospital and a scheduled early-morning briefing with staff. This was held in a small seminar room beside the theatres. Neef was last to arrive; he pulled a paper cup off the stack and poured himself some coffee from the Cona flask.

'Good morning everyone,' he said in a voice loud enough to quieten the hubbub. He managed a polite smile or Max Pereira, who he'd known would be there right and only. 'I just thought I should say something about the gene therapy trial we're starting this morning and how it affects you. There'll be five patients in all and we'll be using more or less standard surgical procedures throughout so we won't be asking anything new of you at all; that's why I could leave this briefing so late.

'Our first patient this morning is Rebecca Daley. Rebecca has a hepatoma and it will be our task today to inject the tumour with a virus suspension provided by Dr Pereira here. The virus carries a gene which hopefully will make Rebecca's liver tumour sensitive to Gancyclovir, which we will start giving her in seven days' time. I'll be doing the injection myself under ultrasound guidance. It should be quite straightforward.

'The second of today's three operations will be on Martin Liddle and this will be performed by one of Mr Louradis's surgical team. I'm afraid I haven't been briefed on who exactly. Martin has a pancreatic tumour and we'll be introducing Dr Pereira's virus through ERCP. In case anyone's forgotten, that is endoscopic retrograde cholangio pancreotography. In this instance, of course, we won't be using the technique to extract a tissue sample: we'll be injecting the virus.'

Neef turned to Pereira, who this morning was wearing a T-shirt advertising a Scuba-diving school on Crete. 'Basically they'll be inserting an endoscopy tube equipped with light and video camera down the patient's throat, through the stomach and duodenum, until we reach the pancreas. We'll be able to follow its progress all the way on a video monitor.'

'Sounds a breeze,' said Pereira.

If anyone else had said this there would almost certainly have been laughter, but people were unsure of Pereira. There were only a few uncertain smiles.

'There's no reason why it shouldn't be,' said Neef. 'Any questions?'

'I'd like to ask Dr Pereira what exactly his virus does,' said one of the theatre nurses. There was a murmur of assent.

Pereira stopped picking his teeth with his thumbnail and looked lazily about him before scratching his head. 'Basically, the virus does nothing,' he said. 'We're just using it to transport a new gene into the patient's tumour cells. The gene is called the thymidine kinase gene, the TDK gene for short. Once it's inside the cells it will start producing thymidine kinase and it just so happens that any cell producing thymidine kinase will be killed by the drug, Gancyclovir. In a week's time we'll give the patient Gancyclovir and kill the tumour. Simple huh?'

'Sounds a breeze,' said the nurse. There was general laughter.

'Our third patient today will be Thomas Downy and his case will be handled by Mr Beavis and the neurosurgical team in the main theatre. Thomas has an inoperable tumour of the cerebellum. Injecting the virus into the tumour will almost certainly not be a breeze. Video and ultrasound are, of course, out of the question. The progress of the needle will be monitored by CT scan at staggered intervals. The cerebellum, as many of you will know, is a bit of a minefield. Any damage to the normal cells around there and the patient's equilibrium and balancing function may be totally destroyed. Are there any questions?'

'What's to stop Dr Pereira's virus getting into the patient's bloodstream and putting this kinase thing into all his cells?' asked one of the radiology department's team. 'Surely there's a danger of making all his cells vulnerable to Gancyclovir.'

'Good point,' said Pereira. 'Firstly, the virus is actually disabled. It can't replicate itself so there's no question of spiralling viral infection. Secondly we've engineered the kinase gene to suit the tissue it's being injected into. That's why there are several variations of the virus being used today. For instance, the version we'll be using for the hepatoma kid has an alpha fetoprotein promoter sequence in front of the kinase gene. It can only be turned on by liver cells.'

'Isn't science wonderful?' said one of the nurses.

'That, I think, is what we're about to find out,' said Neef. 'Any more questions?'

There were none.

Rebbecca Daley's body looked very small and fragile as Neef prepared to begin the procedure that would end with eight millilitres of Pereira's virus suspension being injected into the heart of her tumour. Pereira had asked to be present at all the injections. Neef explained what he was doing for his benefit.

'We'll just rub a bit more jelly on her abdomen to make sure that we have a really good contact for the ultrasound probe,' he said. He smeared the conductive gel over the exposed area of Rebecca's stomach and then applied the head of the probe, moving it to and fro several times until he was satisfied with what he saw on the monitor screen in front of him. 'There we are,' he said. 'Can you make out the liver?'

'It all looks a complete blur to me,' replied Pereira. 'Sorry.'

'I suppose we're used to it,' said Neef. He stretched out one arm towards the screen and pointed. 'That's the liver there,' he said. 'And that' – he manoeuvred the probe a little to get a better picture – 'is Rebecca's tumour.'

Pereira leaned closer to the screen to get a better view. 'Now I see,' he said. 'I guess you use this gear a lot these days.'

'We certainly do,' replied Neef. 'In many ways it's revolutionized medicine. It's just so good to be able to see inside your patients without the need for invasive techniques.'

Neef made a mental calculation of the angles involved in introducing the needle that was to carry the virus. He said to Pereira, 'I'm positioning the probe so that the needle will cross its path and show up on the screen. That way we can follow its progress.'

There was a moment's silence while Neef pushed the needle

through the wall of Rebecca's abdomen and started to feed it slowly inside.

'I can see it!' exclaimed Pereira as a solid white line appeared on the screen.

Neef continued to propel the needle on its journey towards the tumour, watching the screen all the time instead of the patient. 'Almost there,' he said as the tip of the needle reached the outer edge of the tumour. 'And now we're about to go into it.'

Based on the volume of the tumour calculated from Rebecca's CT and MRI scans, Neef knew that he had to advance the needle one centimetre further to be at the heart of the tumour. He did this by watching the lumen of the needle, which had graduations etched along it. 'We're there,' he announced.

'And now you pull the trigger,' said Pereira.

Neef injected the virus and the operation was over. He withdrew the needle slowly and let out a sigh as he pulled it out. 'Our first patient,' he said. 'Good luck, Rebecca.'

There was a one-and-a-half-hour gap before the next operation was due to begin. Pereira decided to take himself off for a walk and get some fresh air. Neef wondered if he was feeling queezy. If Pereira was having problems with a simple needle op he was going to be in real trouble by the time the afternoon came. Neef asked in the duty room if there had been any word from Kate Morse. Staff Nurse Collins shook her head and said, 'Sister's not on duty till two.'

'Her husband was taken ill last night,' explained Neef. 'I thought she might have phoned to say how he was.'

"Fraid not,' replied the nurse. 'But Mr Louradis was trying to get in touch. Did the switchboard tell you?'

Neef shook his head and the nurse rolled her eyes skywards. 'Maybe you should call him.'

Neef returned to his office and called Mark Louradis. He was hoping that there wasn't going to be any problem with the surgical team due to operate on Martin Liddle.

'Mark? It's Michael Neef. No problem I hope.'

'None at all, Michael. I just thought I'd tell you that I plan to carry out the ERCP on Martin Liddle myself this morning.'

Neef was slightly taken aback. 'I'm sure we're very honoured. Isn't it a bit routine for a surgeon of your standing?'

'I just thought I'd like to be part of a little piece of history in the making at St George's. Our first gene-therapy trial and all that. You don't mind do you?'

'No, of course not,' replied Neef, still a bit puzzled. 'I hope you won't object if Dr Pereira and I observe.'

'Not at all.'

Neef put the phone down. Mark Louradis had actually sounded as if he was in a good mood. Not often that happened, he mused. Neef checked his watch and saw that he had plenty of time. He called the emergency-admission ward at University College Hospital.

'Staff Nurse Mellor. Can I help you?'

'Good Morning, Staff. It's Dr Neef at St George's. You had an emergency admission last night. I was wondering how he was this morning?'

'We had two last night, Doctor. Which one are you interested in?'

'Charles Morse. He's our chief path technician.'

'Mr Morse had a rather uncomfortable night, I'm afraid. He's not well at all.'

'Has there been any word from the lab yet?'

'Perhaps you'd better speak to Dr Clelland, sir.'

'Rules is rules,' muttered Neef under his breath as he waited. He did not have to wait long.

'Dr Neef?'

'Good morning, Doctor. I was responsible for having Charles Morse admitted to you last night. I was wondering if you'd had any lab results yet.'

'Not yet, Doctor. There were a few atypical features, but he's been provisionally diagnosed as a Klebsiella pneumonia because of the severity. He's been put on ampicillin.'

'I suppose it's too soon to say how he's responding,' Neef probed.

'We've certainly had no encouraging response as yet,' agreed Clelland. 'He's still very ill but, as you say, it's early days.'

'Thank you, Doctor.'

Neef put down the phone and reflected on the unpleasant sense of foreboding that had come over him. Maybe he was just hypersensitive to the word pneumonia these days, but Clelland's additional qualification of 'atypical' had only heightened his unease. He thought for a moment about the GP who'd called Charlie's condition flu, and then he called Kate Morse's home number.

'Kate? I hear Charlie's not so good.'

'Hello, Mike. Good of you to call. He's really ill. In fact, I think if you hadn't come out and called the ambulance when you did, he mightn't have made it through the night. He had to have oxygen in the ambulance. He's still on it this morning.'

'The ID unit at University College think it's a Klebsiella pneumonia. That would certainly explain why it's so severe. The ampicillin should get it under control, though. He should start getting better soon.'

'God, I hope so, Mike. It gave me a real scare.'

'I'll bet.'

'I'm on at two. I'll see you then.'

'Look, Kate, if you don't feel up to it today, we'll manage.'

'I'll be there,' said Kate. 'Sitting around worrying doesn't help anyone, least of all Charlie.'

'As you wish,' said Neef. 'I probably won't see you until after Thomas Downy's op. We're going to theatre at two thirty.'

'That had completely slipped my mind,' said Kate. 'I hope it goes well for Thomas. He's such a nice kid.'

Pereira returned from his walk and Neef asked him if he still wanted to attend the next operation.

'You bet,' replied Pereira.

Neef wasn't convinced, but he shrugged his shoulders and suggested they start making their way down to theatre. Mark Louradis was already in scrub when they got there. Neef introduced him to

Pereira. 'Mr Louradis is our chief surgeon here at St George's. He's going to inject your virus into Martin Liddle.'

'It's nice to have the best,' said Pereira, lathering his hairy arms.

Louradis looked sideways at Pereira as if searching for signs of sarcasm but didn't find any there. Pereira had obviously meant the comment to be taken at face value. How like Louradis to have doubted it, thought Neef. Despite a faultless reputation as a surgeon, Louradis suffered greatly from some unfathomable Mediterranean inferiority complex. Neef sometimes wished he had a fiver for every time he had seen Louradis's features darken with suspicion over something everyone else present would regard as innocent.

'What a colour!' whispered Pereira to Neef as he saw Martin Liddle's yellow skin hue.

'That's due to the tumour,' replied Neef. 'Pancreatic tumours are notorious for being advanced by the time they're diagnosed. The bile duct gets screwed up as the tumour spreads.'

'This isn't ultrasound, right?' asked Pereira, nodding at the monitor positioned to the side of the table.

'No, this time it's a real video picture. There's a small camera positioned just to the side of the end of the endoscope.

Louradis inserted the endoscopy tube and everyone watched its progress through Martin Liddle's alimentary canal.

'Now we come to the tricky bit,' whispered Neef to Pereira. 'He's reached the duodenum.'

Louradis coaxed the control levers at the head of the tube until he had negotiated an awkward turn and was satisfied with the picture on the monitor. 'Almost there, Dr Pereira,' he said. 'About here do you think?'

Neef sensed Pereira's discomfort at the question. He had obviously not been expecting to be asked for his opinion.

'What d'you think, Mike?' Pereira asked.

Neef smiled behind his mask. 'Maybe another half inch,' he said.

'Here?'

'Fine.'

Louradis injected the virus and started the process of extracting the tube.

'I need a cigarette,' said Pereira with feeling as he and Neef left the theatre together. 'That's it till two thirty, right?'

'That's right,' said Neef. 'Two down, one to go.'

After changing out of gown and gloves, Pereira disappeared outside for his cigarette and Neef walked back to the unit alone. As he crossed the courtyard past groups of chatting nurses a vehicle parked on the far side caught his attention. It had a press sticker in the windscreen. Two men with notebooks at the ready were standing nearby; they were talking to a man with a camera bag slung over his shoulder. What was that all about? he wondered with an uneasy feeling.

When he got back to his office he called the hospital press officer, John Marshall. 'You *are* remembering our agreement about no publicity for the gene-therapy trial aren't you?' he said.

From the first faltering syllable of Marshall's reply, Neef knew there was something wrong. He closed his eyes in anticipation of hearing something unpleasant.

'It didn't come from this office, Michael, I promise. But the press got it from somewhere. Mr Louradis is giving an interview about the Martin Liddle case at this very moment.'

'Oh shit,' said Neef. He put down the phone. So this was why Louradis had been keen to carry out such a routine procedure himself. He wanted some media attention. He must have set the whole thing up for himself. The man bitterly resented all the press coverage the surgical teams at University College had been getting. He must have seen this as his chance to grab some of the limelight for himself.

Neef's first thought was to have it out with Louradis and give free rein to the tide of adjectives that were springing to mind, but he began to see that what was done was done. It seemed likely they were now going to have to conduct the trial under press scrutiny as University College had done the year before. Nothing was going to change that. He decided not to say anything to Louradis.

In the event, Louradis phoned him some twenty minutes later.

'Michael, I'm calling to assure you that I had nothing to do with the press being here this morning. I was as surprised as everyone else.'

'Of course, Mark.'

'There were a couple of reporters waiting for me when we'd finished with Martin Liddle this morning. I don't know how they possibly got wind of it but I felt I had to say something. You know how it is.'

'Quite.'

'I know you didn't want the press to know about the trial until you knew how it was shaping up, but I'm sorry, there it is. There was nothing I could do without being rude. I played it down as much as I could. No hard feelings I hope?'

'Of course not.'

'Good. I look forward to hearing how our young friend progresses.'

'I'll see that you're kept informed.'

Neef heard the line go dead and tried out some of his adjectives anyway.

Who else would have called the press?

Eight

Neef saw that Pereira was looking apprehensive as they entered the main operating theatre where Norman Beavis would carry out neurosurgery on Thomas Downy.

'Are you sure you want to be present?' he asked. 'It's not for the faint-hearted.'

'I'm fine,' replied Pereira, running his tongue over lips that had gone dry.

The theatre was twice the size of the minor surgical facility that had been used in the morning and was packed with much more technical equipment and people. Beavis – a tall serious-looking man who favoured rimless glasses and a severe side parting in his hair that made him look like a Gestapo officer to Neef's way of thinking – was very much in charge. There was no first-name familiarity in his theatre. The 'Yes, Mr Beavises' and 'No, Mr Beavises' came thick and fast as he fired questions at the assembled team.

Thomas was positioned face down on the table, his small body draped in surgical sheeting and the back of his skull painted near the base with a yellow antiseptic solution in preparation for the first incision. Two technicians were making last-minute adjustments to the CT scan equipment.

'Is everyone ready?' asked Beavis.

There was general assent.

'Is anyone not ready?'

Silence.

'Do we have the virus to hand?'

'The theatre sister replied, 'All ready, sir.' She indicated a glass vial that sat in an ice bucket by the side of her instrument tray.

'Let's get started then.'

Beavis cut into the back of Thomas Downy's head and Neef leaned over to explain to Pereira what was going on. 'He's cutting back a flap of skin to expose the skull.'

Pereira nodded mutely.

Beavis discarded the scalpel in favour of an electric drilling tool, which he tested in the air before applying it to the base of Thomas's skull to start drilling out a plug of bone. The air was heavy with the smell of burning by the time he'd finished. He dropped the plug into a waiting bowl. Neef heard Pereira swallow.

'Will he put that back?' Pereira croaked.

'No,' replied Neef. 'He'll close the skin flap over the opening and in time the hole will fibrose and virtually close itself.'

Beavis inserted a long needle gently through the opening in Thomas Downy's skull and stopped. 'First scan!' he ordered.

The CT scan team moved into action and a few seconds later the image the scan had produced was displayed on a screen. Beavis moved the needle in deeper and repeated his request. The record of the needle's progress came up on the screen.

'What's happening?' asked Pereira.

'We can't use ultrasound for brain surgery and we can't get a camera inside the patient's head so we have to take a series of CT scans as the operation progresses.

'You get the picture *after* the event?' asked Pereira.

'It has to be that way,' said Neef.

'Jesus,' said Pereira softly.

The needle continued its monitored progress towards Thomas Downy's tumour until Beavis said, 'We're there. Can I have the virus please?'

The theatre sister reached out a gloved hand to pick up the glass vial from the ice bucket. Unfortunately its outside was wet from being in the ice and it slipped from her grasp. It bounced off the edge of the instrument tray and fell to the floor where it shattered. It sent tiny shards of glass everywhere and created a jagged wet splash where the virus had spilled out. Her gloved hands flew to her face in anguish and her eyes above her mask went as wide as saucers. Beavis couldn't turn his head to see what had happened. His hand was holding the needle steady inside the patient's skull. 'What's going on?' he demanded.

'We've lost the virus,' said Neef. 'It's fallen on the floor.' He stepped forward to put a hand lightly on the shoulder of the hapless sister as everyone else seemed paralysed by shock.

'Is there any danger?' exclaimed Beavis.

Neef looked at Pereira, who shook his head.

'No danger,' said Neef. 'The virus has been disabled but we'd better have some disinfectant on it anyway.'

One of the theatre technicians poured antiseptic solution on to the puddle on the floor and then swabbed it up with cotton-wool pads. The glass was collected into a small metal bowl.

'So now we don't have any virus to inject. Is that right?' asked Beavis. His voice was controlled but the implications to everyone were obvious. The operation had been a waste of time. Beavis still concentrated on keeping the needle steady inside his patient's head while he waited for an answer.

'There is some more,' interjected Pereira. 'There's a back-up supply in Pharmacy.'

'Will someone please get it,' said Beavis. 'Quickly!' There was no mistaking the anxiety in his voice. There was no question of his extracting the needle and then going back in again. The risk of serious brain damage was too great. He was faced with holding the needle *in situ* until the new virus arrived.

As the minutes passed, Beavis said, 'I think my hand's starting to shake. Could someone please prepare to take over here?' He said it matter-of-factly but everyone knew the seriousness of what he was saying. There would be danger as the needle changed hands but this would be preferable to the brain damage caused by an involuntary hand tremor. Beavis's assistant for the operation moved round into place at his elbow. 'Ready when you are, sir.'

'The virus has arrived,' announced one of the nurses at the back of the theatre.

'I think I'll be all right,' said Beavis. In the interim, he had piled up a number of surgical swabs under his scalpel hand in order to give himself some support. His assistant moved back round to the other side of the table.

The tray of glass vials was passed through the theatre doors and a nurse brought them to the table.

'Which one?' asked the theatre sister.

Pereira moved in to the table and selected one of the vials. 'This one,' he said. 'Five millilitres.'

The virus suspension was measured out into the barrel of a syringe and handed to Beavis who attached it to the needle already inserted in Thomas Downy's tumour. He slowly applied pressure to the plunger until the contents disappeared, then permitted himself a slight sigh of relief as he withdrew the needle slowly out of the back of his patient's skull and dropped it into one of the steel discard dishes.

He took a few moments' rest during which he flexed his fingers to free them of the stiffness that had developed during the long wait. He nodded to his assistant, who took over and carefully sutured the flap of skin back into place over the opening in Thomas's skull.

'All done,' he said.

'Heavy stuff,' Pereira whispered to Neef, rolling his eyes above his mask.

'We could have done without the drama,' agreed Neef.

The sister who had dropped the virus was still flushed with discomfort and embarrassment. She moved towards Beavis as he stripped off his gloves and said, 'Mr Beavis, I'm so terribly sorry about—'

Beavis stopped her in mid-sentence and said, 'Don't worry about it, Sister. It could have happened to anyone. No harm done.'

Neef decided to try to kill off the Gestapo officer image he had of Beavis.

The relief in the sister's eyes was obvious to all. One of her colleagues put an arm round her shoulders and, as Thomas Downy was wheeled out to the recovery area, it seemed as if the whole theatre suddenly relaxed as tension evaporated.

Neef walked back to the unit with Max Pereira. Pereira had been subdued all day but now he seemed to have perked up again. 'There was more to it than I thought,' he confessed. 'I thought you could just stick a needle in and that was that.'

'So we medics have our uses then?' Neef smiled.

'I guess I really need you guys to get the vectors in,' replied Pereira, without a trace of humour. 'Two more tomorrow?'

'Two more,' agreed Neef. 'And then we're all up and running.'

Neef went straight to the duty room to see Kate Morse. 'How's Charlie?' he asked.

'He's not good,' replied Kate. 'The lab haven't come up with a confirmation of the klebsiella diagnosis and he doesn't seem to be responding to the ampicillin treatment.

'Damnation,' said Neef. 'What are they playing at?' He diverted his eyes so that Kate would not see any signs of the alarm bells ringing inside his head. An atypical pneumonia that wasn't responding to treatment? It seemed too much like revisiting a bad dream. He looked sideways at Kate and saw that she was under great strain. It was etched in worry lines round her eyes.

'How was Thomas's op?' Kate asked in a brave attempt to change the subject.

'He's fine,' replied Neef. 'The operation wasn't exactly smooth but he came through it okay. Now we'll have to hope for the best for all of them.'

'Tracy Torrance died in the Randolf Clinic this afternoon,' said Kate. 'You were in theatre at the time.'

Neef nodded sadly. 'I hope to God her mother doesn't still believe I wished it on her.'

Neef was happy to see that the leaked story about the gene-therapy patients at St George's wasn't too sensational, in spite of the headline: NEW HOPE FOR CANCER KIDS. Although he still thought Mark Louradis had sought the publicity himself, he had apparently played out the role of reluctant academic being interviewed by an intrusive press. He had trotted out the usual platitudes about things 'being at a very early stage' and it being 'too soon to say' if the patients were going to benefit. He himself was only 'part of a team' and a lot of dedicated people were involved. It would be some time before the therapy would be generally available.

All mind-numbing stuff that the press and public had heard so often before, thought Neef. The press, however, did now know what was going on and he could expect their continued interest.

On the evening of the following day, the *Citizen* ran Eve's story about the two cancer girls, based on Mr Lees's complaint to the paper and her own subsequent investigation of the facts. She had waited two days, as she promised she would, to see if Lennon's people would come up with anything but they hadn't and had admitted as much in an interview. The story made the front page: CITY FEAR AS CANCER KILLER BAFFLES BOFFINS.

Neef suspected that the public health people were not going to be so enthusiastic about being the baffled boffins in question, although Lennon seemed to have been quoted fairly enough. Lennon had obviously said much the same to Eve as he had to Neef in their last conversation and it was unfortunately true that the investigation was going nowhere at present.

Neef thought that the facts had been reported accurately. He wondered what would happen now. He suspected that there were going to be a lot of worried parents out there. There was, of course, a chance that there would be no more cases and that the incident would fade away to be written off as just one of those things.

But, if there should be another case, the seeds of panic had possibly been sown by this article.

On the following Monday, Lawrence Fielding reported to Neef that Jane Lees had responded well to steroid treatment and her 'pneumonia' was under control. 'What made you suspect an immune response?' he asked.

'I wasn't entirely happy about the original viral-pneumonia diagnosis for Melanie Simpson,' replied Neef. 'I asked Frank MacSween about it at the time. I thought maybe the underlying cancer had given the appearance of viral pneumonia when it was really some kind of immune response, an inflammatory reaction to the tumours. Frank thought the post-mortem appearance was typically viral and I accepted what he said. But then Jane Lees presented with exactly the same symptoms as Melanie Simpson and, well, my suspicions were aroused again. I thought steroids were worth a try.'

'And you were right,' said Fielding. 'Steroids suppressed the lung symptoms.'

'Not that it's going to do her much good, I'm afraid,' said Neef. 'Her cancer's too well advanced.'

'No, but at least she's a lot more comfortable on Antivulon and steroids in the meantime,' said Fielding. 'And, to quote a source not a million miles from here, "If that's the best you can do . . . so be it."'

Neef smiled at having his own philosophy quoted back at him.

When Wednesday came and went without any follow-up to the interview Louradis had given, Neef felt well pleased. The public health people were still under daily scrutiny but most of the coverage of that particular day went to Tracy Torrance's funeral. The *Citizen* gave it mass coverage with, BRAVE LITTLE TRACY LOSES LAST BATTLE, using colour photographs of the wreaths with their poignant messages to wind up second-hand emotion. 'Recouping their investment,' as Tim Heaton put it when he called to ask Neef how the gene-therapy trial was progressing.

'So far so good. The patients start on Gancyclovir tomorrow,' replied Neef. 'Then it's just a question of waiting and seeing.'

'Fingers crossed,' said Heaton. 'This could really put us in the big league.'

Neef gave a non-committal grunt.

'Did you get supplies of your American drug?' asked Heaton.

'Antivulon. We've started using it,' said Neef. 'It's a bit too soon to say but one of our patients, John Martin, is coping with it much better than his previous chemotherapy. Thanks for your help in getting it. I appreciate it.'

'Not at all,' said Heaton. 'That's what team work is all about.'

Neef suddenly felt defensive. Heaton was after something.

'I understand from John Marshall that you don't want any press involvement with the gene-therapy patients until the trial is virtually over?' said Heaton.

'That's right. I didn't want any false hopes being built up for the children's parents. They're very vulnerable people.'

'Oh absolutely,' said Heaton – unconvincingly, Neef thought. 'It's just that as something did however manage to find its way into the press last week, however regrettable, I was wondering if it might not be a good idea to keep the papers sweet with some more formal announcement of what's going on. Perhaps a press release composed by John and yourself? Maybe a photograph or two? Put the record straight so to speak?'

'I'd rather not have any press involvement at all at the moment if it can be avoided.'

'That's the thing,' said Heaton hesitantly. 'I'm not sure it can. As the press know about the trial through Mark Louradis's interview, we really have to answer their questions, otherwise they might start assuming the worst. And we don't want that, do we?'

'All right,' Neef conceded. 'I'll keep Marshall informed and he can feed them information, but I don't want the press anywhere near the unit.'

'Good,' sighed Heaton. 'I'm sure John can keep them at bay while presenting things in a positive light. Anyway, glad you got your American drug all right.'

Neef put the phone down and cursed under his breath. The man was a master at making him feel guilty.

❖   ❖   ❖

Jane Lees died early on the following Friday evening. Her pain was under control and her end was peaceful. Her mother and father were with her, as was the hospital chaplain, Geoffrey Keys. The Leeses were not churchgoers but had agreed to Keys being present and luckily took comfort from what he had to say.

Neef spoke to both parents afterwards in his office. It was a very different occasion from the last time he had seen them. Mr Lees's anger had entirely disappeared and had been replaced by grief over his daughter and bemusement at why it had to be her.

'Why?' he asked with tear filled eyes. 'Why our Janey?'

'I wish I could answer that,' said Neef softly. 'Although in Jane's case there will be some kind of an answer. It's just a question of time before the public health investigators find out why your daughter contracted the disease. I'm so sorry.'

Lees shook his head silently. His wife sobbed into her handker-chief. Neef pushed the tissue box nearer to her. A nurse came in and nodded at Neef's questioning look.

'Nurse Lawrie here has organized some tea for you and I think the chaplain's going to join you to talk about Jane. I think you'll find it helps. Don't hold back. Remember the good times you had together, the family holidays, the Christmases, the fun, the daft things she did. Speak about them. That way, you can go on keeping Jane alive inside you.'

As the couple stood up to follow the nurse out of the room, Mr Lees blew his nose loudly and turned to Neef. 'I'd just like to thank you for all you did for Janey, Doctor. I think I was a bit out of order the last time we spoke. None of this was your doing and I was too angry to thank you properly. I didn't really know what I was saying. We're both grateful, Martha and I.'

'I wish it could have been more,' said Neef.

Neef watched the door close behind the Leeses. He stared at it for a few moments, grateful for the silence in the room as he considered what he still had to do before going home. There came a knock. Eve Sayers put her head round the door. 'Can I come in?'

Neef nodded.

'I came to see Neil. I couldn't make it earlier this afternoon. I saw Mr and Mrs Lees out there,' said Eve. 'Is it what I'm thinking?'

'Jane Lees died a short time ago,' said Neef.

'The second victim,' said Eve.

Neef gave her a look that questioned her choice of phrase, but then considered it justified. 'Yes, the second victim.'

'Do you know what really worries me? There's something out there killing these kids and everyone in authority seems to be sitting around on their backsides waiting for number three to happen.'

'I'm sure that's not true,' said Neef.

'So what exactly *are* public health doing?' asked Eve.

Neef looked at her dispassionately and shrugged as if he had no heart for an argument. He was still thinking of Jane Lees.

Eve suddenly realized that she was kicking a man when he was down. She looked up at the ceiling as if seeking divine guidance.

'I'm sorry,' she said. 'I didn't think. I've been getting the run-around from the Public Health Department all day and I just didn't stop to think. You've had a bad day too, probably a lot worse than mine.'

Neef shrugged philosophically. 'I've had better,' he said.

'You've only had one of my three recipes. Want to try for number two?'

Neef relaxed a little and gave a weak smile. 'It's my turn. Why don't I take you out to dinner? It'll have to be out. I don't cook.'

'Neither of us really feels like going out to eat,' replied Eve. 'Come home with me?'

Neef was at first reluctant, but then nodded his assent. 'All right. Thank you,' he said.

When they got to the car park, Eve said, 'Leave your car. I'll drive you home later.'

Neef did not offer any argument. He felt strangely detached from what was happening, as if he had tripped out some emotional overload switch. He was a spectator to what was going on rather than a participant.

o   o   o

125

They did not speak as Eve negotiated the traffic and drove expertly across town, using the Golf GTi's acceleration to advantage when small gaps appeared in the traffic ahead. They still didn't speak as they stood on opposite sides of the elevator that took them up to Eve's apartment but they looked each other in the eye rather than at their feet or the floor-indicator above the doors. It didn't feel uncomfortable. Eve's gaze was positive; Neef felt that his own must look slightly puzzled.

Eve unlocked her door. She kicked aside the mail that was lying behind it and led Neef to the drinks tray where she poured him a large gin and tonic. 'Drink that,' she said.

Neef downed the gin without question.

'Come.'

Eve led Neef to the couch, where she pushed him gently backwards on to it and took off his shoes. 'Now relax,' she whispered. 'Nothing awful is going to befall you. I've been watching you, Michael Neef, and quite frankly you are a fake. You gave me a lecture on how to handle the mind-destroying amounts of grief your job entails, when the truth is you can't handle it yourself. You've been pretending. It really does get to you, doesn't it? I suddenly saw it in your eyes back there. You can't go on like this indefinitely, bottling it all up inside you. You'll make yourself ill. You need to talk it out. It's too much to carry all on your own.'

Neef stared up at the ceiling for a few moments. He said simply, 'It used to be Elaine. I could tell her when the going got tough.'

'Elaine?'

'Elaine was my wife. She died four years ago.'

'I'm sorry.'

'I still miss her,' said Neef. It sounded so pathetically inadequate, he thought, to distil all that loneliness and pain into four little words. 'She was always there when I needed her and then, suddenly, she wasn't. I've learned to cope with most things but occasionally, just occasionally, I find myself in a situation where . . .'

'You can't cope.'

'I can't cope,' agreed Neef slowly.'

Neef closed his eyes and rested his head on the back of the couch.

'Well, I'm not Elaine,' said Eve softly. 'But you're a nice man, Michael Neef, and if you need a shoulder to cry on, feel free.'

Neef opened his eyes and nodded with a slight smile. 'Thanks,' he said. 'I appreciate it.'

'Don't appreciate it,' said Eve softly. 'Use it. Talk to me. What got to you today? Jane Lees?'

'No . . .' Neef began hesitantly. 'I know what's going to happen to the kids and I can cope with that. I'm prepared. It's their parents who sometimes get to me. It's their parents' grief I can't handle.'

'Go on.'

'It's as if it's infectious. More often than not they're nice ordinary people who can't understand why it happened to their child. I can feel their hurt and, for some reason I can't fathom, it becomes mine. I know I should be able to stop it happening, put up some kind of barrier against it, but sometimes I just can't manage. I soak it up like a sponge and it drains me of everything . . . energy, optimism, hope.'

Neef looked directly at Eve. 'Well, counsellor? What's the answer?'

Eve stayed silent for a moment while she thought about the question. Eventually she took a deep breath and pronounced, 'I think you should run away and join the circus.'

Neef broke into a smile and Eve joined him. 'No easy answers,' she said.

'At least we're agreed on that.'

'How about recipe number two?' she prompted.

'Sounds good.'

Eve drove Neef home shortly after midnight. He had taken full advantage of not having to drive and although not completely drunk, he felt, 'pleasantly relaxed', as he put it.

'Have you got your key?' asked Eve.

Neef fumbled in both his coat pockets before holding it up triumphantly.

'What time do you have to be at the hospital in the morning?' asked Eve.

'Don't worry, I'll call a taxi in the morning.'

'I can come over on my way to the office,' said Eve. 'Pick you up around eight thirty?'

'I can get a taxi.'

'Nonsense. This is all my fault,' said Eve.

'Fault?' exclaimed Neef. 'I can't tell you the last time I felt this good. I'm indebted to you.'

'I'm glad you enjoyed yourself,' said Eve softly. She leaned over and kissed Neef lightly on the cheek.

Neef turned towards her hesitantly and said, 'You know, you're very beautiful.'

'Well, thank you.' Eve smiled. 'Tell me again when you're sober.'

'I'm not dru—'

Eve placed a finger lightly on his lips. 'Ssh,' she said, kindly. 'You've also got something to do about a ghost. Be off with you. I don't know what Dolly's going to say when she sees the state you're in.'

Neef manoeuvred himself out of the car with some difficulty, again protesting that he wasn't drunk.

'Sorry,' said Eve. 'Pleasantly relaxed.'

'Exactly,' said Neef, turning to look back inside the car.

'See you at eight thirty.'

'I can get—'

'Eight thirty.'

She wasn't going to take no for an answer.

Eve was as good as her word. She picked Neef up promptly at half past eight and took him to the hospital. On the way they talked about Neil.

'I'd like to take him out this Sunday if that's all right,' said Eve.

'Sounds fine,' said Neef. 'He's still quite stable and he's obviously very comfortable with you. I think your visits are doing him the world of good.'

'I'd like to think that was true,' she said. 'He's so easy to get attached to.'

Neef half turned his head as if to say something but Eve got in first. 'I know, I know,' she said. 'You really don't have to warn me.'

'Sorry,' said Neef. 'Have you thought what you two might do together?'

'The forecast for the weekend sounds reasonable. I thought we might try for a picnic by the river.'

'Sounds good.'

'Why don't you join us?'

'Me?' exclaimed Neef.

'Why not you?'

Neef didn't get more than a couple of words out when he stopped and reconsidered. He said, 'I was about to say something pompous about not getting personally involved with the patients, but I thought better of it.'

'Good. Then you'll come?'

'I'd love to,' said Neef. 'What would you like me to bring?'

'Just yourself. I'll fix the picnic. I'll also pick Neil up from the hospital. You can meet us somewhere. Better still, we'll pick you up from home.'

'I look forward to it,' said Neef.

'If I don't get a chance to speak to you before then, I'll see you at ten thirty on Sunday morning. You'll tell the nurses?'

'I'll tell Kate when I get in.'

'Sister Morse?'

'Yes.'

'I don't think she likes me.'

'She's suspicious of your motives. You're a journalist.'

'Guess that doesn't put her in a minority of one,' said Eve.

Neef shrugged.

Eve dropped him off outside the main gates and he waved to her as she drove off.

Neef hung up his jacket in his office and called into the duty room to warn Kate about Neil's picnic. She wasn't there. The night staff nurse said that she had called in. Her husband had taken a turn for the worse. She was up at University College Hospital.

Neef phoned the hospital and spoke to one of the housemen on the ward where Charlie Morse was a patient.

'Mr Morse has been moved to ICU. He was transferred last night with severe breathing difficulties.'

Neef felt a dark cloud come over him. He asked to speak to Clelland, the physician he had spoken to last time.

'I'll ask the switchboard to page him,' replied the houseman.

There was a thirty-second delay before the operator said, 'Still paging Dr Clelland for you.'

After another thirty seconds Clelland came on the line.

'Doctor, it's Michael Neef. I understand Charles Morse's condition has deteriorated.'

'He's very ill; he's not been responding to antibiotic therapy.'

'Did the lab confirm your Klebsiella diagnosis?'

'I'm afraid not,' replied Clelland. 'They found no evidence of bacterial involvement at all.'

Neef closed his eyes and rubbed his forehead lightly. He could sense a nightmare coming true. 'So where do you go from here?' he asked quietly.

'There's not much we can do,' confessed Clelland. 'If it's not bacterial it must be viral. It's just a case of keeping him as comfortable as possible and hoping he pulls through. We'll keep him on broad-spectrum antibiotics of course, to make sure secondary infection doesn't set in.'

'I don't think he has pneumonia at all,' said Neef.

'I'm sorry. I don't think I understand.'

'I don't think I do, either,' said Neef. 'But Charles Morse is displaying the exact same symptoms as two young girls who have recently died from cancer after being exposed to some unknown carcinogen. They both presented as severe pneumonias but no bug was isolated and they didn't respond to antibiotics.'

'The story in the local papers?'

'Yes.'

'Have I got this right? You're telling me that Mr Morse has cancer?'

'I hope to God I'm wrong but yes, I am. I think you'll find his pneumonia symptoms subside when you try him on steroids instead of antibiotics. Once the inflammation goes down you'll be able to find the tumours on X-ray.'

'Look, his wife's here at the moment,' said Clelland. 'I don't think I want to tell her this without knowing something more. It's a very awkward situation, if you see what I mean.'

'I understand,' said Neef. 'I don't think I want to say anything to Kate at the moment either. I could be wrong but it seems one hell of a coincidence.'

'But if you're right it would mean that Morse had been exposed to the same carcinogen as the two girls,' said Clelland.

'I suppose it would,' agreed Neef. 'Another connection for the public health service to ponder.'

'Maybe this will make it easier for them.'

'Maybe,' said Morse, reluctant to see any good coming out of Charlie Morse's misfortune. 'Will you give steroids a try?'

'Nothing to lose.'

'Good. I'll hold off saying anything to Kate until you've tried it. If it doesn't work we'll know I was wrong. If it does, I'll tell her.'

'Might be best coming from you.'

Where have I heard that before? thought Neef.

Nine

Frank MacSween called Neef just after eleven and said that he was carrying out the post-mortem on Jane Lees. 'Thought you might like to attend?'

'I didn't think you'd be doing it till Monday,' said Neef.

'The public health people are anxious to have the report. I said I'd do it today.'

'I'll come down,' said Neef.

Neef was just about to leave the unit when Kate Morse arrived. She was in uniform.

'You shouldn't be here,' said Neef.

'I wasn't doing much good up at Uni College,' said Kate. 'They said they'd call me if there was any change in Charlie's condition. I just don't understand it. He's not been responding to treatment at all. I know it's ridiculous but I keep thinking about Jane Lees. She was admitted as a pneumonia and didn't respond to antibiotics and the other girl . . . Mary . . . Marlene . . .'

'Melanie,' said Neef, feeling uncomfortable at keeping a secret from Kate. 'Melanie Simpson.'

'Yes, Melanie. They both had severe pneumonias that didn't respond to treatment. Mike, I'm scared.'

Neef couldn't fob Kate off with false reassurances but he didn't want to confide his own fears in her in case they turned out to be groundless. 'Maybe he'll turn the corner today,' he said with more sadness in his voice than conviction. 'I'll be down in Pathology for a while if anyone needs me.'

'Same as before,' announced MacSween as Neef entered the PM suite, doing up his gown. 'The cancer is more advanced of course, but there are multiple primary foci just like Melanie Simpson and no involvement of any organ other than the lungs. There's much less inflammation but that's because of the steroid therapy I see you wrote her up for.'

'Would you still go for a true viral pneumonia on this one?' asked Neef.

'A toughie,' said MacSween, and shrugged. 'I was pretty sure with Melanie but with Jane Lees I'm in a bit of a quandary. There's no doubt that she did respond to immuno-suppression with the steroids but on the other hand there are still definite signs of viral pneumonia.'

'So what side of the fence are you going to come down on?' asked Neef.

'Neither,' said MacSween.

'Neither?'

'I'm going to have to go for both. The girl's lung condition was caused by both viral pneumonia and cancer.'

'You're an obstinate old bugger, aren't you?' said Neef. 'You're determined to stay with viral pneumonia.'

'I'm just saying what I see,' retorted MacSween. 'That's what you have to do if you're a pathologist. Cold hard facts are what you get. If it's bullshit you're after, ask a psychiatrist.'

'But both these girls have been exposed to a powerful carcinogen. Everyone agrees about that, right?'

'Agreed,' said MacSween.

'It must have been something they inhaled because the condition's confined to the lungs and there are no signs of radiation burns on the skin.'

'Agreed.'

'Then surely it's reasonable to accept that the inflammation of the lungs is caused by an immune response to the cancer rather than viral pneumonia,' said Neef.

'Perfectly reasonable,' agreed MacSween.

'Then why persist with the viral-pneumonia angle?' asked a puzzled Neef.

'Because that's what I see. Logic or reason doesn't come into it. It's simply my observation.'

'You know what troubles me about that?' asked Neef.

'What?'

'It's not logical and it's not reasonable but it's the opinion of the best pathologist I know.'

'Well, thank you for that,' said MacSween.

'Until the virology lab report comes in and they don't find any viruses,' added Neef with a smile.

'The report for Melanie Simpson came in this morning,' said MacSween.

'And?'

'They found evidence of three or four viruses, just as we thought they would. The usual everyday sort of stuff. Rhinovirus, adenovirus and the like. Nothing unusual. No big killer bug.'

'So?'

'Nothing changes,' said MacSween. 'I see what I see.'

'What would you say if I told you I thought Charlie Morse is going to be case number three?' said Neef.

MacSween looked up from the table, the wrinkles prominent round his eyes as he screwed them up. 'You're not serious?'

'There are jsut too many similarities to be coincidence. I suggested to his doctor this morning that he might like to try Charlie on steroids.'

'My God,' said MacSween. 'Does Kate know what you think?'

'Not yet. I'm waiting to see if he responds. I'm hoping I'm wrong.'

'I hope you are too,' said MacSween. 'Have you mentioned this to Lennon?'

'Not yet, and for the same reason.'

'I think maybe you should. These guys need all the help they can get. They're still getting nowhere.'

'If Charlie *is* going to respond to steroids we should see an improvement by this afternoon. If that happens, they should be able to get some decent pictures of his lungs. If he really has bronchial carcinoma I'll call Lennon immediately. I'll check with Uni College around four and give you a call at home if you like.'

'I won't be there,' said MacSween. 'I'm spending the weekend with my daughter and son-in-law up in Yorkshire. We weren't due to go up until next month but young Nigel hasn't been too well this week and Betty thought she'd like to go.'

'I'll catch you on Monday then. Enjoy your weekend if you can.'

'I think your suspicions about Charlie have put paid to that,' said MacSween. 'Maybe if I gave you my daughter's phone number, you might call me if there's any news?'

'Of course,' said Neef.

Neef walked slowly back to the Oncology Unit. He was just about to go in through the door when David Farro-Jones pulled up in his car and got out.

'I was just coming to see you,' said Farro-Jones. 'I wanted to ask you how your trial patients are getting along?'

'Come on in. Let's get some coffee,' said Neef.

'You sound as if you need it,' said Farro-Jones. 'One of those days when nothing goes right?'

'They all seem to be "one of those days",' replied Neef. 'It's just one damned thing after another.'

'Sounds like I've picked a bad time to call,' said Farro-Jones. 'Maybe I should—'

'No,' insisted Neef. 'It's okay. The trial patients are all on Gancyclovir now so, according to Max, we should start to see an improvement any day now.'

'I tried calling Max yesterday,' said Farro-Jones. 'He wasn't around.

'He went back to working in the lab,' said Neef. 'As he said, there wasn't much for him to do around here until we start to see results. Apart from that things have been a bit difficult between us since I had to ask you to check out his virus preps.'

Farro-Jones made a face and said, 'I thought that might be the case but I'm sure you did the right thing. You just can't be too careful. Don't worry about Max, he'll come round. His sort always do. Maybe you'd let me take a look at the trial patients before I go.'

'Of course,' said Neef. His look must have betrayed puzzlement because Farro-Jones smiled and said, 'As a molecular biologist, I have a personal interest in seeing my field come into its own, even if I'm not personally involved!'

Neef accompanied Farro-Jones on an impromptu tour of the unit and introduced him to the gene-therapy children. This was a big success. The kids took immediately to the tall blond man who looked like the prince from a fairy tale. He also had a personal charm which coaxed smiles from children who were otherwise low in spirit. Neef was exchanging smiles with the nurse who had been attending Thomas Downy when he saw Thomas break into a fit of giggles at something Farro-Jones had whispered to him.

'We'll have to have you along more often,' said Neef when the time came for Farro-Jones to leave. 'You're good for morale.'

'I have a similar affinity for dogs and drunks,' smiled Farro-Jones. 'But I would like to come back and see how they're getting on if that's all right?'

'Of course. Any time.'

'Give Max my regards when you see him. Jane and I would love to have him to dinner if he can find the time.'

'I'll pass on the message,' said Neef. 'But he seems to work all the time.'

Neef was about to tell Kate Morse that Eve would be taking Neil Benson out for a picnic on Sunday when he saw she was in conversation with Lawrence Fielding. He couldn't hear what was being said but he sensed that something was wrong. Both of them looked in his direction and stopped talking. Kate walked towards him. 'Could I have a word?' she asked. 'In private.'

'Of course.'

Neef glanced at Fielding as he turned to follow Kate back to his office. He thought he looked apologetic about something.

'I just called Uni College. Charlie has been put on steroids,' said Kate. Her eyes were full of accusation. 'I mentioned this to Lawrence and he said that was probably your idea. Is that true?'

'I'm afraid it was, Kate,' said Neef softly.

'You think Charlie has the same thing as the two girls, don't you?'

'I don't know, Kate,' said Neef apologetically. 'That's why I didn't say anything to you earlier. I was waiting to see what effect the steroids would have. I didn't want to upset you unnecessarily.'

'I was right,' said Kate. 'There are similarities to Jane Lees and the other girl, aren't there?'

'There are. That's why I spoke to Clelland. I don't pretend to understand how all this came about but there are very definite similarities.'

Kate sank down into the chair in front of Neef's desk and rubbed her forehead nervously. 'My God, Charlie. He's going to die, isn't he?'

'I could still be wrong.'

Kate shook her head wistfully. 'But you're not,' she said. 'I can feel it. My Charlie is going to die.'

Neef felt totally helpless. Kate knew as much about Charlie's chances of surviving extensive lung cancer as he himself. They were virtually zero. 'I don't know what to say, Kate,' he confessed. 'I can't bullshit you. You know too much.'

'When will they know for sure?'

'I'll call Clelland around four.'

Kate nodded and got up to go. 'You'll tell me?'

Neef saw the look of naked vulnerability on Kate Morse's face and felt a lump come to his throat. 'Of course.'

Lawrence Fielding came in when Kate had left. He looked very uncomfortable. 'I'm afraid I rather put my foot in it, I'm afraid.'

'Not your fault,' said Neef. 'Trying to keep a secret from a friend, even with the best of intentions, is usually doomed to failure.'

'You really think that Charlie has the same thing as Jane Lees?'

Neef nodded. 'I'm afraid I do, although at this moment I think I'd give everything I own just to be wrong.'

'Amen to that. Mind you, statistics must be on the side of being wrong.'

'What do you mean?'

'If Charlie Morse has the same condition as Jane Lees and Melanie Simpson it means that he's been exposed to the same carcinogen.'

'Yes.'

'Then don't you think it's the strangest of coincidences that the third person to present with this condition happens to be one of the staff when in theory it could have been anyone in the city?'

Neef nodded and said, 'I think you've just put your finger on what's been making me feel distinctly uncomfortable about this whole business. There's something just not right about it if Charlie Morse really is the third case.'

'It would be different if cancer was an infectious condition, but it isn't,' said Fielding.

'No, it isn't,' agreed Neef. 'So it would be so much easier all round if I was just plain wrong.'

'Agreed,' said Fielding.

'We'll know later this afternoon. How are our patients?'

'I've just been assessing their scans,' said Fielding. 'I suppose it's a bit early to reach any firm conclusions but I would say that four of them are not showing any signs of improvement as yet while one is looking more hopeful.'

'Which one?'

'Thomas Downy. I think there may even be a slight reduction in the size of his tumour.'

'That must be the first piece of good news I've heard in a long time,' said Neef. 'Can I see the scan?'

'I'll get it,' said Fielding. He left the room and was back within a few moments carrying two CT scans. He also carried a clear plastic ruler. He spread them on Neef's desk where a space had been cleared for them.

'If you measure Thomas's tumour along this axis,' said Fielding, placing the ruler on the surface of the scan, 'It measures thirteen millimetres. That was taken before his op to introduce the Menogen virus. Now, if you measure the tumour across the same axis on this scan done this morning I think you'll find it slightly smaller.'

Neef placed the ruler across the image of the tumour and measured. 'Eleven and a half, maybe twelve?' he said.

'But not thirteen,' said Fielding.

'Definitely not thirteen,' agreed Neef, sounding pleased. 'A regression!'

'Looks like it, although it could be just a positioning artefact of the scan. We'll find out when we do the next one on Tuesday.'

'Personally, I'm going to believe this is a true regression. I need to have some good news in my life. Pity about the others, but, as you say, there's time enough yet.'

'Will you tell Max?'

'When I see him,' replied Neef. 'Maybe we shouldn't spread this around in case Tim Heaton gets wind of it and puts it in the Sunday papers.'

'Good point,' agreed Fielding. 'He'd overlook the fact that we have four other patients who aren't making progress at all.'

'Exactly. When all five are in regression we can call in the press.'

'That would be just so good,' said Fielding with such obvious feeling that it made Neef smile. 'It certainly would,' he agreed.

Neef found himself becoming more and more anxious as the time grew closer to four o'clock. He was just about to pick up the phone when a knock came to his door. It was Max Pereira.

'Can I come in?'

Neef looked at the receiver in his hand and then decided to put off the moment. 'Of course,' he said. 'I was beginning to wonder when we'd see you again.'

'I went back to the lab and did some work. I guess I was having withdrawal symptoms.'

'What are you working on?' asked Neef.

'The next generation of virus vectors.'

'You're not happy with the ones you've got?'

'Not by a long shot,' replied Pereira. 'If you have to open up the back of a kid's head to deliver the vector there's plenty of room for improvement.'

'I suppose when you put it that way . . .' agreed Neef.

'The real goal is to be able to deliver gene therapy by a simple one-off injection in the arm and have the bloodstream deliver the gene to exactly the right kind of stem cell so that the new gene is expressed in only the cells you want it expressed in and it will be maintained in these cells for the rest of the patient's life.'

'How far are you away from that?' asked Neef.

'With the competition as fierce as it is and the prize that big, I would guess at three to five years.'

'That soon?'

'I think so. A lot of guys are burning the midnight oil.'

'For all the wrong reasons,' said Neef.

'Like I said before, it doesn't matter. If you are the patient, why should you care what the motivation was? Stop fighting human nature, Mike. It's easier to go along with it. Don't expect too much of your fellow man and you won't be disappointed – well, not as often.'

'I'll try to bear that in mind,' said Neef.

'How are our guinea pigs doing?'

'One of our guinea pigs is showing signs of tumour regression already. Nothing from the others just yet.'

'Which tumour?'

'The cerebellar. Thomas Downy.'

'Wow,' said Pereira. 'I didn't think he'd be the first. I thought maybe the hepatoma. Any pictures?'

Neef pointed to the scans lying on the side of his desk. 'It's not much but I think it's definite.'

Pereira, who still had his beret on, pushed it back a little so he could slip his glasses on over his ears. He used the ruler and a magnifying lens. 'About a millimetre and a half, right?'

'That's what we made it,' agreed Neef.

'Ace,' said Pereira.

'Ace,' agreed Neef with a smile.

'Is the kid okay? I mean no ill effects from the surgery or the injection?' asked Pereira.

'He seems fine,' said Neef. 'David Farro-Jones came by to ask how things were going. Thomas was laughing and joking with him. David sends his regards, by the way. He and his wife extend a dinner invitation to you.'

'That's nice,' said Pereira.

Neef glanced up at the clock on the wall and saw that it was five past four. Pereira noticed him do it and got up from his chair. 'I'll get out of your way,' he said. 'I'm taking up your time.'

'I've just got some calls to make,' said Neef. 'Why don't you stick around? Maybe we could have a drink together. Celebrate Thomas's progress.'

'Okay, I might do that.'

Neef called Clelland at University College Hospital. 'It's Michael Neef, here. How did Charles Morse respond?'

'There's been quite a marked improvement in his lung condition,' replied Clelland. 'The inflammation's subsided; we've been able to get some decent X-rays.'

'And?'

'I'm looking at one right now,' said Clelland. 'I'm afraid you were right, Doctor.'

'He has lung cancer?'

'He's riddled.'

Neef let out his breath in a long sigh.

'Just what you didn't want to hear,' said Clelland, apologetically.

'Quite so,' said Neef, feeling as if he'd just had the stuffing knocked out of him.

'You'll tell his wife?'

'I'll tell her.'

Kate had her back to him when Neef found her talking to one of the nurses. He was waiting until they had finished but the other nurse looked at him over Kate's shoulder and Kate turned round. Neef saw immediately that she had read in his eyes what he had to say. She finished with the nurse and followed Neef back to his office.

'You were right? Charlie has cancer?'

'I'm afraid so,' said Neef softly. 'I'm so sorry.'

Kate put her hand to her mouth as if afraid to speak, then she said hesitantly, 'I suppose I've known all day yet I've been clinging to the hope that it was all some crazy mistake. Charlie would get better and we'd all be back to normal. I've watched so many other people do this in my time and yet, when it happened to me, I'm no different.'

Neef nodded. 'None of us are,' he said.

'I think I'd like to go see Charlie now if that's all right.' said Kate.

'Of course,' said Neef. 'If there's anything I can do, you only have to ask. You know that.'

Kate nodded and said, 'I know.'

Neef watched Kate leave his office and wished there was something more he could do, but there wasn't. He called Lennon at the Public Health Department and told him that Charles Morse was the third case.

'One of the staff you say?' exclaimed Lennon.

'He's chief technician in our pathology lab,' replied Neef. 'He's in his mid-thirties and his wife is my head nurse here in the unit.'

'Good God,' said Lennon. 'Of all the people in the city it could have been, the third case turns out to be someone on the staff of the hospital.'

'You're not the first person to point this out,' said Neef. 'My registrar, Lawrence Fielding, made the same comment. What do you think?'

'Just coincidence, I suppose,' said Lennon. 'But this could be the lead we need. There can't be too many things that a thirty-five-year-old man and two teenage girls have in common in the way of habits and haunts. We must be able to discover where their paths crossed, providing we can speak to this man?'

'Maybe not tonight,' said Neef. 'His wife's just left to be with him. Maybe tomorrow when they've both had time to come to terms with it.'

'I'll go up to University College in the morning then,' said Lennon. 'Please God, we'll discover the source this time. It's driving us to distraction.'

'I can imagine,' said Neef.

'Do the press know about this yet?' asked Lennon.

'Not from me and I don't think Uni College will be saying anything. The truth is we've only found out ourselves in the last hour.'

'Good,' said Lennon. 'We could use a bit of breathing space after last week's attention.'

'I imagine it wasn't too comfortable down there,' said Neef. 'We've had our moments with the press ourselves.'

'You wouldn't believe some of the calls we got after the story,' said Lennon. 'We've had reports of Martians landing on the common. It was the exhaust from their spaceship that was causing the cancer.'

'I hadn't considered that,' said Neef dryly.

'One woman thought the government were poisoning the water. Another thought it was the increase in dog shit that was the problem. She said it was the smell on sunny days that had given the kids cancer.'

'I hadn't reckoned on calls from nuts,' said Neef.

'You don't know the half of it.'

'Makes you worry what's out there,' said Neef.

'You can say that again,' said Lennon. 'God knows what we'll get when the press hit the panic button over number three.'

'Let's hope they don't get hold of it.'

'Chance would be a fine thing,' replied Lennon.

'Let me know how you get on. I'll be off tomorrow but I'll be back on Monday.'

'Lucky you,' said Lennon. 'I haven't had a day off since this thing started.'

Neef looked for the piece of paper with Frank MacSween's daughter's telephone number on it. He found it in the second pocket he searched in and punched up the numbers. There was no reply. He folded it up again and slipped it into the breast pocket of his shirt. He would try again later. It was time he went to find Max Pereira, assuming he was still around. He found him in the duty room reading one of the nurses' magazines.

'Sorry I was so long. Still fancy that drink?'

'Only reason I'm still here,' replied Pereira.

'What's with Sister Morse?' asked Pereira as they left the hospital and walked over to the pub on the corner. The Two Dragoons was the local for the staff of St George's. 'She seemed kind of upset when she left.'

'She's just found out her husband has cancer.'

'Shit. What kind?'

'Lung.'

'Shit. Heavy smoker?'

'Aged thirty-seven, never smoked in his life.'

'Lousy luck,' said Pereira.

'Luck had nothing to do with it. It's the same thing as Jane Lees. Remember? You saw her scans.'

'The kid in your unit? Sure, I remember. A real mess.'

'I'd appreciate it if you'd keep this to yourself in the meantime. The public health people are having a hard enough time as it is.'

'Mum's the word.' Pereira took a sip of his bourbon. Neef could almost sense what he was thinking. 'You know,' said Pereira, 'that sounds like some kind of weird coincidence.'

'That hasn't escaped our attention,' said Neef. 'But we can't read anything into it. Can you?'

Pereira played with the leather band of his beret as he considered. 'I guess not,' he said. 'What kind of things have your public health guys been looking for?'

'Something that gives off a gas,' said Neef. 'The cancer in all three cases is confined to the lungs and there are no signs of radiation burns.'

'How about asbestos?' suggested Pereira.

'There were no fibres in the lungs; that's what makes PH think it must have been a gas or fumes of some sort. They've been looking for a chemical that's been illegally dumped.'

'Must be like looking for a needle in a haystack,' said Pereira.

'They're hoping that Kate Morse's husband will help them narrow down the possibilities.'

'I wish them luck. Another drink?'

'Thanks, another gin,' said Neef.

Pereira returned from the bar with the drinks.

'So how are you going to spend your Sunday?' asked Neef.

'In the lab,' replied Pereira.

Neef smiled and asked, 'When do you find the time to go diving?' He nodded at the motif on Pereira's T-shirt, which advertised yet another diving school. This time it was an Israeli outfit on the Red Sea.'

'Two weeks in February, every year.'

'What about summer holidays?'

'I don't take any.'

'But you must go to scientific meetings and conferences. They're usually held in pretty nice places.'

'I don't go to them.' replied Pereira. 'If anyone has anything at all worth saying they publish it in the journals. Some guys just like to hear the sound of their own voices. They spend half their life trotting round the world in the same little club talking about work without actually doing any. I'm not one of them. You can get away with that sort of shit in universities but not in business. Mind you, every time I publish something on the vectors I get mail from half a dozen of these bozos suggesting, "collaboration".'

'Which you decline,' offered Neef, stating the obvious.

'Damned right. They can hitch a lift on some other guy's train.'

'It sounds a pretty monastic existence,' said Neef.

'I like it that way.'

'Another drink?'

'No, I've got some cultures to check on. I'd better be going.'

'See you on Monday?'

'Yeah. I'll come in. If the brain tumour's responding already, the others shouldn't be far behind.'

'I hope you're right,' said Neef.

'Trust me.' Pereira smiled as he got up to go, slinging his leather jacket over one shoulder.

The irony wasn't lost on Neef.

Neef drove home, filled Dolly's food bowl and then called Frank MacSween's daughter again. Once more there was no reply. He shrugged and went off to find himself something to eat. This meant hunting through the freezer among the packet meals. Neef bought these by the armful on his monthly trips to the supermarket. He picked something involving chicken and read the instructions after grabbing a cold beer out of the fridge.

To his surprise, Dolly decided to acknowledge his presence this evening and jumped up to join him on the couch. She lay along it with her head resting on his right thigh.

'Well, well, well,' murmured Neef. 'I'm honoured, Miss Day-dream.' He scratched Dolly behind the ears, and pretty soon she purred her appreciation.

'I hope you've had a better week than I've had, little friend,' sighed Neef.

Neef considered moving the cat so that he could put on some music or turn on the television but decided against it. Dolly did not bestow her affection lightly or often. The moment was to be honoured. Neef put his head back on the couch and closed his eyes. He tried letting his mind go blank but events of the past week kept intruding, not least Charlie Morse's cancer. He tried not to imagine what Kate and Charlie were going through at that moment but it was impossible. Eve Sayers had been right in her observation, he did carry too much on his shoulders and it was going to make him ill if he didn't find a way of dealing with it.

What were his options? he wondered. Booze was the easiest, but also one of the most dangerous. He had seen a number of doctors use drink to lighten the load in his time. The pathologist up at Uni College, Eddie Miller, was a case in point. Transcendental meditation? Eastern religion? A holiday, perhaps? Somewhere far away with blue skies and endless beaches where he could sit on a rock and fish all day, sip rum punch in front of scarlet sunsets.

It had been a long time since he had taken a proper holiday and he knew why. He couldn't face going alone. His last holiday had been with Elaine in Mexico. They had spent three glorious weeks just enjoying each other's company away from the cares of the world. It had been Garden of Eden stuff, a treasured memory and a carefully guarded one. Nothing and no one had been allowed to intrude on it. But maybe the time had come to let go a little. The pain and guilt associated with such a thought was this time tempered by insistent logic. Elaine had been dead a long time and she wasn't coming back. He had to let go sometime.

This train of thought brought Neef to thinking about Eve Sayers. He was certainly attracted to her but something always seemed to stop him thinking beyond this. Maybe it was just Elaine's ghost or maybe there was more to it than that if he was truthful with himself. Eve was a much more independent spirit than Elaine, a career woman with strong opinions of her own, an intelligent challenging woman, whereas Elaine had been content to be a home-maker and play second fiddle to his career. He wasn't at all sure how he would cope in a relationship with someone like Eve. Maybe it even scared him a little.

At ten thirty, just before turning in for an early night, Neef decided to call Frank MacSween's daughter one last time. On this occasion the call was answered, not by Frank's daughter but by his wife, Betty.

'Betty? It's Michael Neef. Frank asked me to call him. I've been trying since five o'clock.'

'I'm sorry, Michael, we've been out.'

Neef felt instant alarm as he detected a sob in Betty's voice. 'Is something wrong?' he asked.

'It's our grandson, Nigel,' replied Betty. 'He fell ill last week;

that's mainly why we came up to Yorkshire so soon after Clare's visit to us. But he got worse around teatime today and was taken into hospital.'

'I'm sorry to hear that,' said Neef.

'He died an hour ago,' said Betty.

'Oh Betty, I'm so sorry. That's absolutely awful. This has been the most hellish week for bad news. Do they know what it was?'

'Not yet,' said Betty. 'There'll be a PM of course but I still can't believe it myself. He was such a gorgeous baby. We all doted on him.'

'I won't intrude any more Betty,' said Neef.

'Do you want me to give Frank a message? I don't think he can speak to anyone right now.'

'It'll wait,' said Neef.

Ten

Next morning at ten thirty, Eve Sayers pulled up outside the door of Neef's cottage with Neil on board. The boy's face was pressed up against the window of the car when Neef emerged and he broke into a crooked smile. Eve had obviously told him who they had stopped to pick up.

'Hi, Tiger,' said Neef, ruffling the boy's hair as he got in beside him. 'I think it's probably a while since either of us were out on a picnic.'

'Make that the three of us,' added Eve. 'Don't I get a Hi.'

'Hi, Eve,' said Neef, leaning over to give her a peck on the cheek.'

Neil giggled and the tone was set for the day.

'I thought we might go down to Floxton Mill,' said Eve. 'Unless there's anywhere you would rather go?'

'Anywhere's fine by me,' replied Neef. 'I don't think I know that place.'

'You'll like it,' said Eve as she turned to concentrate on driving the car. She was wearing a white shirt and denim jeans and her hair fell loose about her shoulders. She had a relaxed air about her that put Neef at his ease. He needed a stress-free day, preferably with no mention of the hospital at all but particularly with no mention of the latest victim of the cancer.

Floxton Mill was just over an hour's drive from the city and, when he saw it, it took Neef's breath away. It was more picturesque than any place had a right to be. What was more, the sun was shining and there were no other people around.

'How did you know about this place?' asked Neef, his voice full of wonder.

'I've been coming here as long as I can remember,' replied Eve. 'Do you see that white cottage over there?' she asked, pointing through the willow trees to a small whitewashed cottage with a thatched roof.

'Yes.'

'My parents used to bring me there for holidays when I was very little and the mill was still working. We used to come every year for two weeks in July. The mill stopped working about ten years ago and was sold for conversion into a private home along with the surrounding land. I contacted the owners and explained how much the place meant to me. They agreed I could come here for picnics when I felt the need. It's four years since I was last here.'

'Let's hope the owners remember you,' said Neef.

'I called them yesterday,' said Eve.

Neef reflected that he should have known Eve would have done that.

'Who's hungry?' asked Eve.

Neil and Neef put up a discordant chorus of 'Me!' that made Eve laugh. It was the first time Neef had heard her laugh out loud. He liked the sound.

Eve had gone overboard with the food, with the emphasis heavily on what small boys would like. Sausage rolls and crunchy snacks were in abundance, and there was a chaos of coloured packets and bags to be opened by eager fingers. This didn't stop Neef participating with great enthusiasm. When he and Neil had eaten all they could, Neef lay back on the ground holding his stomach as if it were about to burst. Neil decided to do the same and both of them rolled around on the ground as if unable to get off their backs, making groaning noises. Eve pretended to be annoyed, which only incited them to greater heights and, eventually, gales of laughter.

'I think we should all have a snooze in the sunshine,' suggested Eve. 'Give our digestion time to recover.'

'Good idea,' agreed Neef. He lay flat with his head touching Neil's. Neil did the same, seeing it as a game. Eve joined in and all three lay flat on the ground like a three-pointed star. The sky above them was cloudless and the sun warm on their faces. The initial chat faded away until a long silence ensued. Neef was the one facing directly into the sun so he had to keep his eyes shut. This sharpened his other senses. He was aware of the sound of buzzing insects as they passed nearby and he could smell that the grass surrounding the mill had been cut recently.

'Neil,' whispered Eve.

There was no reply.

'Neil, are you awake?'

No reply.

'He's fast asleep,' said Eve. 'He is all right, isn't he?'

Neef rolled over on to his front and propped himself up on his elbows to look at Neil. 'He's fine,' he assured Eve. 'He just ate too much, like me. That was an excellent picnic.'

'I'm glad you enjoyed it. I'm ever so glad you decided to come along today. It's just perfect, isn't it?'

'Absolutely,' said Neef.

'So what's troubling you?' asked Eve.

Neef looked surprised. 'Nothing,' he said. 'What made you say that?'

'Your eyes,' replied Eve. 'They're a dead giveaway.'

Neef looked at Eve, preparing to rubbish the notion, but her steady gaze made him change his mind. 'Do you remember the day we went to lunch at Frank MacSween's? There was a baby there, Nigel, Frank's grandson.'

'Of course,' said Eve.

'He died last night.'

'My God, what happened?' asked Eve.

'They don't know yet. Frank and Betty had gone up to Yorkshire for the weekend to stay with Clare and Keith. I spoke to Betty last night. The boy was rushed to hospital yesterday afternoon; it sounded like he died within hours of admission.'

'What an awful thing to happen,' said Eve. 'His parents must be devastated.'

Neef nodded. 'Frank will be taking it really hard, too. He doted on his grandson. He'd already built him a gang hut in his garden.'

'Poor Frank,' said Eve. 'Poor Betty, too. She's lovely.'

Neef nodded.

'So what kind of illness kills a baby that quickly?' asked Eve.

'I wouldn't like to hazard a guess,' said Neef. 'But young children can sometimes succumb very quickly to infection. I suppose this must have been one of those times.'

'Will they carry out a post-mortem?'

'Yes, they'll have to establish the cause of death for the death certificate.'

Eve shuddered and said, 'I'd hate anyone to cut open my baby like that. The idea seems so awful.'

Neil woke up and Eve made a fuss of him, teasing him about eating so much. She pretended she could feel each individual item of food in his stomach. 'A sausage roll there,' she said. 'And another one . . . and another one! How many sausage rolls did you have?'

'Neil giggled as he tried to defend himself from Eve's probing fingers. 'Help me!' he appealed to Neef.

'I think you'll have to make a run for it, Neil. Quick!' Neef held out his hand and Neil grabbed it and pulled himself away from Eve. He started to run towards the river, still holding Neef's hand as Eve pretended she was about to give chase. 'I'm coming to get you,' she growled.

Neil and Neef ran right down to the water's edge and fell down on their stomachs to look down into the slow-flowing current where they lay for a minute without speaking.

'What can you see?' asked Neef.

Neil looked carefully, then pointed with his finger excitedly, saying, 'Fish!'

Neef saw that he was right. There were three or four sticklebacks darting in and out of the shadows. 'Well spotted,' he said. 'There's nothing wrong with your eyes.' He looked sideways at Neil, while the boy was intent on looking for more fish, and concentrated on examining the growth on his face. There was something about it that disturbed him. It was different somehow. He hoped to God it was imagination, but it seemed to have got a little bigger. Neil became aware that Neef was staring at him. He looked up at him questioningly.

'I think we should have a boat race. What do you say?' said Neef, anxious that nothing should ruin the day.

Neil's eyes lit up with approval.

'Right, then. First we have to select our boats.' Neef reached out and broke off a long reed from the water's edge. He trimmed it down until it was about six inches long. 'Right, I've got mine,' he said. 'How about you?'

Neil broke off a reed just as Neef had done and prepared it the same way. He nodded.

'Right, then, when I give the word, we both throw them in and follow them down to the bridge. First to the bridge is the champion. All right?'

Neil nodded enthusiastically. 'Ready, steady . . . go!'

Both reeds hit the surface of the water and started to drift slowly downstream, accompanied by yells of encouragement from both Neef and Neil. Eve came down to see what the noise was about. 'I'll judge the winner,' she said and hurried on ahead to the footbridge where she took up stance in the middle of the span, leaning over the parapet, chin on her hands as she concentrated on the imminent approach of the reeds.

'And the winner is . . . Neil!'

Neef feigned disappointment while Eve cheered and Neil danced up and down in delight.

As they walked back to the rug and the picnic basket, Neil scampered on ahead and Eve said to Neef, 'I can't remember the last time I enjoyed myself so much.'

'Me neither,' agreed Neef, putting his arm round her shoulders. It seemed entirely the natural thing to do.

And the moment would have been perfect had it not been for an awful doubt he now had about whether Neil's remission had come to an end.

By the following Tuesday, Neef had confirmation of his worst fears over the status of Neil's tumour: it had started growing again. Lawrence Fielding had carried out an extensive range of tests on the boy after Neef had told him of his suspicions and now there was no doubt: Neil's remission was over. There probably wouldn't be another.

Neef, of course, had known all along that this had been bound to happen sooner or later, but he still felt a great sadness come over him as he realized that now all he could do for Neil was to keep him as comfortable as possible as the inevitable approached.

He wasn't looking forward to telling Eve; she would take it badly. She had become very attached to Neil despite the warnings; but with a charismatic child like Neil it had been almost inevitable that she would. He wondered for a moment if it had been wise to allow Eve to start visiting Neil in the first place, but the doubt was quickly dispelled by the memory of the two of them playing together on the picnic. It *had* been the right thing to do. He was absolutely sure of it.

During the course of the morning, Neef heard that Frank MacSween was back on duty. He went down to Pathology just after lunchtime to offer his condolences. He found MacSween sitting in his office next to the PM suite. Being in the basement, the room had no windows and was lit by the same daylight-like fluorescent lights as the PM suite itself. MacSween appeared particularly pallid and a shadow of grey-white stubble covered his cheeks and jowls. He seemed distant and preoccupied.

'I came to say how sorry I was about your grandson,' said Neef. 'An absolute tragedy.'

MacSween nodded and Neef noted how haunted his eyes looked.

It alarmed him. MacSween shouldn't have come back on duty so soon. He obviously needed some kind of medical help to get him through the crisis.

'Are you okay, Frank?' Neef asked gently.

MacSween stared at him and Neef thought for a moment that he hadn't heard his question.

'That wee laddie meant so much to me,' said MacSween. 'I know he was only a baby but he symbolized the future for me somehow.'

Neef thought of the hollowed-out hedge hideaway in MacSween's garden and his plans for a tree house.

'When I held him it was as if I was holding the life force itself. It seemed to vibrate in him, tingling in his tiny arms and hands. Can you imagine what it's like to feel that when you spend most of your life touching dead flesh?'

Neef shook his head unsurely. He had known that MacSween was going to take the death of his grandson badly, but not this badly.

'And his breath. Have you ever smelled a baby's breath, Mike? It's beautiful . . . absolutely beautiful. And d'you know what?'

'What?' asked Neef quietly.

'I killed him.'

'You did what?' exclaimed Neef, totally taken aback by the comment.

'I killed him,' said MacSween. 'I don't know how and I don't know when exactly, but I know I did.'

'Frank, I really don't think you should be on duty. You've had an awful shock and you need time—'

MacSween held up his hand and looked Neef straight in the eye. 'I'm not out of my mind, Mike. I just know that I did. You see, I had a phone call just before you came in.'

'What sort of a phone call?' asked Neef as MacSween paused and his eyes seemed to glaze over.

'It was from the hospital up in Yorkshire, the one they took Nigel to. They had the results of the PM.'

'And?' prompted Neef.

'Bilateral pneumonia ... obscuring extensive bronchial carcinoma.'

'Jesus Christ,' exclaimed Neef. 'What the hell's going on?'

'I don't know,' said MacSween distantly. 'But there's no way a baby could have inadvertently been exposed to a carcinogen like Melanie Simpson or Jane Lees. The carcinogenic agent must have been still in the girls' bodies and somehow I must have taken it home and contaminated Nigel with it.'

'That doesn't make sense, Frank. Everything points to the inhalation of fumes being responsible.'

'Then that must be wrong,' said MacSween.

'But if it had been something particulate, your people would have found it when they examined the sections under the microscope. There was nothing out of the ordinary. No particles. No fibres.'

'This is not a coincidence,' insisted MacSween. 'Common sense simply will not wear it!'

'You're right,' agreed Neef quietly. 'But blaming yourself isn't the answer.' He was thinking of Charlie Morse. MacSween didn't yet know of the confirmation of Charlie's cancer. He almost balked at the thought of piling more misery on to MacSween but he felt he had to. 'I didn't get a chance to tell you about Charlie Morse,' he said.

MacSween looked at him strangely as if not understanding the words. 'My God, I'd forgotten about Charlie,' he said. 'He's got it too?'

Neef nodded and said, 'I'm afraid so. Charlie's riddled, to use their words.'

'What the fuck is going on?' exclaimed MacSween, his voice a hoarse mixture of anger and frustration.

'We'd better get the public health people over here right away,' said Neef. 'We've got to try and make some sense of this before we have a major outbreak on our hands.'

'A major outbreak of what?' asked MacSween, looking as puzzled as he sounded.

Neef understood MacSween's dilemma. He had used the phrase

without thinking. You had outbreaks of food poisoning, not cancer. You couldn't have an outbreak of cancer. 'To tell you the truth, I've no bloody idea.'

Neef returned to his own office and called Lennon at the Public Health Department. He wasn't in the building but, on hearing who was calling, his office gave Neef a mobile number. Lennon answered against a background of traffic noise.

'I think we should have a meeting as soon as possible,' said Neef. 'There's been another development.'

'Another case?'

'Yes, a baby in Yorkshire.'

'Would you repeat that?'

'You heard correctly. The baby was the grandson of our pathologist, Frank MacSween.'

'Bloody hell,' said Lennon. 'I can get there about five.'

'That's fine. We have to talk.'

Neef looked at his watch. It was three thirty. If Eve was in visiting Neil this afternoon, he would tell her about the remission being over. Neil hadn't been feeling too well that morning. She'd probably suspect that something was wrong anyway. Better to tell her outright. He called through to the duty room on the internal line and asked the staff nurse if Eve was in the unit.

'Miss Sayers arrived about three o'clock,' replied the nurse.

Neef walked along to Neil's room and paused when he saw Eve through the glass. She was reading Neil a story. He was not his usual self. He was lying quietly beneath the blankets on his bed, his eyes peeping out over the top. They never left Eve.

Neef entered the room quietly and approached the bed. 'Hello, you two,' he said softly, squatting down on his haunches beside Eve, who was sitting on a chair with the story book across her knees. 'I suppose I'm interrupting as usual.'

'You certainly are,' replied Eve. 'We were just getting to the bit where the wolf starts to huff and puff.'

Neef looked at Eve and saw in her eyes that she knew something was wrong. She was acting a part.'

'In that case, I'd better not interrupt any more,' said Neef. 'Perhaps we could have a word before you go,' he said to Eve.

Eve nodded with something approaching suspicion in her eyes. 'Of course,' she said.

'See you later, Neily,' said Neef to Neil, who blinked in reply.

Neef used the intervening time to tell Lawrence Fielding about Frank MacSween's grandson.

'There's something dreadfully wrong about all this,' said Fielding. 'Charlie Morse getting it was stretching coincidence to the limit but now Frank MacSween's grandson, a baby . . . Makes you think we're all at risk . . . from something we don't really understand.'

Neef nodded. 'If it's any comfort I feel the same.' He told Fielding about the meeting to be held at five. 'I'd like you to be there,' he said. 'But not a word to anyone else. A staff panic is the last thing we need.'

A gentle tap came to the door and Neef knew it was Eve. 'Come in,' he said softly.

She entered and crossed the floor to his desk looking as if she was walking on burning coals. 'Neil's remission's over, isn't it?' she said quietly.

'I'm afraid so,' replied Neef. 'I suspected it when I looked at the side of his face by the river on Sunday. Lawrence Fielding's confirmed it; the tumour's started to grow again.'

'What kind of a God would let that happen to a kid like Neil? It makes no sense,' said Eve. 'It makes you feel that life's just so pointless.'

Neef nodded and said, 'I know how you feel. I've been there a hundred times myself.'

Eve looked at him and shook her head. 'I've said it before but I'll say it again. I really don't understand how you do it day in day out.'

'Neil needs you now more than ever,' said Neef. 'Are you up to it?'

'I promised,' said Eve. 'It's going to break my heart but I'll be there for him every step of the way.'

'Good, and I'll be here for you.'

Eve stretched her hand across the desk and rested it on top of Neef's. 'I think I'm going to need you. I said I'm up to it but, to tell the truth, I'm not at all sure. Is there nothing at all you can do to help him?'

'Not in the way of treatment but we can deal with the pain.'

'I don't think I've ever felt this way in my life before,' said Eve. 'I'm absolutely full of anger and frustration but I don't know who to blame. I don't know who to vent it on. I want to hit something or somebody but there's nothing and nobody. What do I do?'

Neef shrugged and said, 'People have to find their own way of dealing with it. I'm sorry. That's not much help.'

'Maybe I'll work on my editor. Get him to mount some kind of campaign to raise funds in Neil's name. I don't want Neil to be forgotten. That wouldn't be right.'

Neef nodded. He could feel Eve's hurt.

'Have you seen Frank MacSween yet?' asked Eve

'I saw him earlier today,' said Neef.

'How is he taking it?'

'Badly.'

'Poor man. Did they discover what the child died of?'

'Not yet,' Neef lied. There was no way round it. It was the first outright lie he'd told Eve and he felt bad about it, but he didn't want her to know about the latest developments. He diverted his eyes. He could feel Eve looking at him, wondering, appraising him – or was that his own conscience accusing him?

'I'd better be going,' she said. 'Will you be leaving soon?'

'I've got a meeting. We seem to have more and more meetings these days,' said Neef weakly.

'Good night, then,' said Eve. 'I'll probably see you tomor-row.'

Lennon was ten minutes late for the meeting, which Frank MacSween

had convened in the Pathology Department lecture theatre, hoping
that it wouldn't attract too much attention if it was held down there.
It was in one of the oldest parts of the building, a semicircular room
with tiered seating reaching almost to the high ceiling, its wooden
benches polished by the backsides of generations of medical students.
At floor level there was a blackboard fronted by a long table and a
lectern. The room was badly lit by individual bulbs hanging from long
cords. The only concession made to modern times was an overhead
projector.

'Damned traffic,' said Lennon as he entered. 'Sorry I'm late.'

Neef introduced Lennon to Lawrence Fielding and said, 'There's
just going to be the four of us. There wasn't time to set up anything
bigger.'

'That'll come later,' said Lennon. 'In the meantime it's important
we have an exchange of views and information. Maybe I should start
by writing up what we know?'

'Good idea,' said Neef.

Lennon deposited his coat and briefcase on the desk in front of
the blackboard and ran his hand along the channel in front of the
board until he found some chalk.

'There have now been four cases: Melanie Simpson, Jane Lees,
Charles Morse and . . .?'

Neef looked to MacSween who said, 'Nigel Barnes.'

Lennon wrote the name up on the board. 'Four people who have
been exposed to a powerful carcinogen. We don't know what or
where it is but our assumption has been that it was a gas of some
sort. This has now been thrown into some doubt.'

'Correct,' said MacSween. 'There's no way my grandson could
have been exposed to chemical fumes. He must have become
contaminated through me. I must have taken something home on
my clothes.'

'It could have been Charlie Morse,' said Neef, realizing there was
something they had overlooked.

MacSween looked at him questioningly.

'Nigel came into contact with Charlie at a lunch you and your wife gave a couple of weekends ago. I remember Charlie trying to get Nigel to go to sleep. He was walking up and down with him on his shoulder. Remember?'

MacSween remained silent as he digested this.

'Gentlemen, I really have to point out that you are talking about this as if cancer were a transmissible disease. Cancer is not infectious or transmissible. It's not something you catch from somebody else. All four people must have come into contact with the prime source, the carcinogenic substance itself.'

'That's why we're saying it couldn't have been any kind of gas,' said MacSween. 'It had to be something we could have carried on our person or clothes.'

'I agree a gas now seems unlikely,' conceded Lennon. 'So what are you suggesting?'

'I carried out the PMs on both Melanie Simpson and Jane Lees,' said MacSween.

'So?'

'I must have contaminated myself with the carcinogen. It was probably in the girls' lungs.'

'But you didn't find anything in the dead girls' lungs,' Lennon reminded him. 'There was no foreign material found after extensive microscopy.'

MacSween shook his head in frustration. 'There must have been something,' he said.

'I think we should put Charlie Morse into isolation, just in case,' said Neef.

'On the grounds that he might be harbouring an invisible carcinogen which has given him cancer?' said Lennon.

'For want of a better explanation, yes,' said Neef.

'I agree,' said Fielding. 'We can't take any chances with something like this.'

'Whatever it is,' said Neef.

'That just about sums it up,' said MacSween. 'We've really no idea. Have we?'

There was silence in the room but it spoke volumes.

'I'm sure we'll get to the bottom of it soon,' said Lennon. 'Let's not be defeatist.'

Neef nodded his head but more through hope than conviction. MacSween just stared down at the floor.

'What do I tell the press?' asked Lennon.

'I think you'll have to play that by ear. Try to play it down as much as possible.'

'I suppose,' agreed Lennon. 'I wish we could get some kind of a break before they get hold of this.'

'So where is such a break going to come from?' asked Fielding.

Lennon said, 'If what Dr MacSween's saying is true, and either he or Charles Morse contaminated the baby with traces of the carcinogenic substance picked up from Melanie Simpson or Jane Lees, we should be able to find that substance with more detailed analysis and searching. Has Jane Lees's funeral taken place yet?'

'No,' replied MacSween. 'Her body's still in the mortuary.'

'Good,' said Lennon. 'And Charles Morse is still alive of course, so we have two chances of identifying the carcinogen. I'll arrange for a team of forensic pathology technicians to help you, Doctor. They'll be here tomorrow. I suggest we meet again on Friday.'

'We'll have to tell University College Hospital what's going on,' said Neef. 'They're treating Charlie Morse.'

'Of course,' said Lennon. 'We need their full cooperation. I'll contact them as soon as we're finished here.' And he added, it without trace of foreboding, 'And I think we should widen the scope of the next meeting to include all interested parties of both hospitals.'

Neef was surprised to find Kate Morse sitting in the duty room when he got back to the unit. She wasn't in uniform but she was sitting behind her desk.

Neef's first thought was to say all the usual things in the circumstances, but he stopped himself. He knew Kate too well for that. He knew she shouldn't be there; she knew she shouldn't be there so there was no need to say it. He said simply, 'Hello Kate. Want to talk?'

Kate nodded with a slight smile. 'You'd think with my background I'd be handling this better,' she said. 'I'm not. I'm falling apart.'

'It's different when it's your own,' said Neef.

'One minute everything's normal. Our life's going on as usual, then suddenly Charlie's in hospital and he's dying. I wasn't ready. I'm not prepared for it.' Kate put her hand to her head and paused as if trying to put her thoughts in order. 'The worst thing is not being able to understand it. All right, I know cancer can hit anyone at any time but something tells me that isn't what happened in Charlie's case. There's more to it. The fact that he has the same thing as Melanie Simpson and Jane Lees suggests that he ... got it from them?' Kate looked at Neef as if she had just managed to articulate something that had been eluding her. 'I know it's not possible but I'm scared all the same. Tell me it's not possible.'

'We've been considering that the carcinogenic substance was still present on Melanie or Jane, perhaps in their lungs, when they underwent autopsy and Charlie contaminated himself with it while working in the lab.'

'I see,' said Kate.

'They're going to put Charlie in isolation while they conduct another analysis of the path specimens from Jane Lees.'

'How long will that take?'

'They're bringing in extra help. We should know by Friday. We've arranged another meeting for then.'

Kate nodded and said wistfully, 'Not that any of it will help Charlie.'

'I'm afraid not,' said Neef. 'I don't know if you know this but Charlie wasn't the only one to be affected in such a secondary way.'

'What do you mean?'

'Frank MacSween's grandson.'

'Nigel? Oh no.'

'He died at the weekend.'

'Oh, Mike,' sighed Kate. 'How awful. What on earth is going on?'

'I wish I knew,' said Neef.

Neef filled the basket of the percolator with coffee taken from the jar on the shelf above the sink and topped up the jug with water. He switched it on.

'I see Neil's remission is over,' said Kate quietly, looking at the case notes in front of her.

'Afraid so,' said Neef.

'I'm sorry. He's a bit special to you.' Neef didn't deny it. 'And the trial patients aren't doing so well.'

'Apart from Thomas Downy. He's doing amazingly well. His tumour's still shrinking.'

'Does that mean the trial's a success or a failure?' asked Kate. 'One out of five doesn't sound that good but it's better than none out of five, and Thomas Downy's chances before the treatment were zero.'

'How does Dr Pereira feel about it?' asked Kate.

'I haven't seen him for a couple of days. He seems to spend all his time in the lab working on new virus vectors.'

'That's dedication for you,' said Kate.

'He's dedicated to making himself rich and famous.'

'At least he doesn't pretend anything else,' said Kate. 'That's something in his favour, and if what he does works for the patients does it really matter?'

'You sound exactly like Max,' smiled Neef.

'He makes a change from traditional British hypocrisy.'

'You sound as if you've brushed with authority,' said Neef.

'I saw our Minister of Health on television last night,' said Kate. 'I don't think I'd mind so much if politicians were honest about what they were doing. It's their constant need to dress up shitty objectives with high-sounding motives that really gets my goat. Don't you think?'

'I've stopped thinking about it,' Neef confessed. 'I've stopped wasting energy being angry. I fight my corner for the unit and that's it. My world begins and ends at that door. These are the people I care about.' Neef indicated to the children with his arm.

'That's bad, Mike,' said Kate. 'You should have outside interests. You *need* outside interests.'

'You're not the first person to point this out recently,' said Neef.

'Let me guess. Miss Sayers?' Neef smiled and nodded. 'You two get along then?'

'I think so,' said Neef.

'You only think so?'

'I'm just not sure,' said Neef. 'Neil plays a big part in our relationship. It's hard to define how big.'

Kate said, 'I've had to revise my opinion of Miss Sayers. I doubted her commitment to Neil but I was wrong. I'm told she never misses a visit and Neil absolutely adores her.'

'She's become very attached to him,' said Neef.

'Oh,' said Kate slowly. 'The warnings fell on deaf ears.'

'With a kid like Neil, they were bound to,' said Neef.

'And now you're starting to feel responsible?'

'No,' said Neef firmly. 'I thought about that but I have no regrets. It was good for both of them to have known each other.'

'Good,' said Kate. 'I'm sure you're right.'

'Is there anything I can do for you?' asked Neef.

'I don't think so, Mike, but thanks. I'd better get home. Mrs Redpath's looking after the children.'

Eleven

Max Pereira phoned the unit a couple of times during the week to ask about the children on the gene-therapy trial but did not actually come in until the following Friday morning, when he had arranged to meet Neef and Fielding. David Farro-Jones, who had kept up his interest in the trial patients, was also invited to attend.

'I just don't understand it,' said Pereira when they had finished assessing the scans and biochemical tests. 'The one I thought might do least well is doing really great while the others aren't improving at all.'

'Who did you think would do best?' asked Neef.

'Rebecca Daley,' replied Max without hesitation. 'I would have bet my ass on the hepatoma getting zapped.'

'The best-laid schemes of mice and men, eh, Max?' said Farro-Jones, getting a puzzled look from Pereira in reply.

'The question is, how long do we persist with the treatment for the four kids who aren't getting anything from it ... as yet?' said Neef.

'Personally, I don't think it's going to work for them,' said Fielding. 'I think we might be better off – or rather *they* might be better off – if we tried them on Antivulon. John Martin's still doing well and so are the others. It's proving much less toxic than conventional therapy, so the kids feel better.'

'What do you think, David?' asked Neef.

'I'm flattered to be asked,' replied Farro-Jones. 'I have to say, I think Lawrence here might be right. If gene therapy had been going to work we should have seen some improvement by now. Sorry, Max.'

'You gotta call it like you see it,' said Pereira. 'I think I even have to agree with you. I don't understand it but at least Thomas is getting something out of it.'

'It's a pity that the failure of the others is tending to detract from that,' said Neef. 'Thomas Downy's progress has been nothing short of remarkable.'

'It's unfortunate he's a single case,' said Farro-Jones. 'Statistically speaking that is.'

'I don't think I follow,' said Neef.

'I just meant that, from the point of view of validating the therapy, with only one success it's impossible to say for sure that gene therapy was responsible. The medical community at large might see it as just one of those things. I guess we're still looking for the breakthrough, Max.'

'I guess,' said Pereira.

'I don't think Thomas Downy's parents are going to be too concerned with statistics,' said Neef. 'It's my guess they're going to be over the moon with their son's progress, and rightly so. For what it's worth, Max, no one is going to convince me it was just one of those things. It was gene therapy that did the trick. Well done.'

'Thanks, Mike. I'd better get back to the lab. I've got lots to do.'

'Still after that million, Max?' said Farro-Jones, smiling.

'I'm prepared to work for it,' said Pereira. He turned to Neef and asked, 'Do you mind if I take a look at Thomas Downy on the way out?'

'Of course not,' replied Neef. 'It's thanks to you he's still there.'

Pereira left the room and Farro-Jones said, 'I take it you'll both be going along to the meeting this evening with the public health gurus?'

'We'll be there,' said Neef.

Pereira stopped at the foot of Thomas Downy's bed and waited till he had the boy's attention. Thomas was doing a jigsaw puzzle. The lid lying beside him on the bed said that it was of animals drinking at a water hole.

'Who are you?' asked Thomas unsurely when he finally looked up and saw Pereira standing there. Pereira was wearing his usual T-shirt and jeans. His leather jacket was over one arm and his beret squeezed up in his right fist.

'Nobody special, kid. I just wanted to see how you were.'

'Are you a doctor?'

'Not the kind you mean.'

'I'm feeling very well, thank you, sir,' said Thomas going back to his jigsaw.

'Good to hear it, kid,' said Pereira, turning to go with a shrug. He found a nurse standing in the doorway. 'I guess the Pied Piper can still sleep nights,' he said as he passed her. As he reached the exit he came upon Eve Sayers outside on the stairs. He half smiled in the way that people do when they know each other vaguely by sight and Eve smiled back. 'Dr Pereira?' she said.

'Yes.'

'I wonder if you could spare me a few moments.'

'I'm sorry, I don't seem to—'

'I'm Eve Sayers.'

'Of course,' exclaimed Pereira. 'You're the journalist friend of Michael Neef.'

'How about a cup of coffee?'

Pereira shrugged his shoulders. 'Why not.'

The two of them walked along to the hospital coffee shop and sat down. 'How's the trial going?' asked Eve.

'Are you asking as a journalist?'

Eve shook her head. 'Mike and I have an agreement. When I'm in his unit everything I hear is confidential.'

'It's nice you guys can trust each other. One of the kids is doing really well, the others not so good.'

'I can see you're disappointed.'

'I thought they'd all do well but maybe I was being over-optimistic. It's a failing of mine.

'Maybe there's time enough yet,' said Eve, playing with her teaspoon in its saucer.

Pereira looked at her appraisingly and said, 'Are you going to come to the point Miss Sayers?'

Eve conceded with a shrug. 'I know I shouldn't be saying this and Michael would be very angry if he found out, but when I saw you back there I just felt I had to ask you personally.'

'Ask me what?'

Eve looked Pereira straight in the eye and blurted out, 'Is there absolutely nothing you can do to help Neil Benson?'

'That's the kid with the melanoma, right?' Eve nodded. 'Not at the moment. We're working on vectors for that kind of tumour but they're not ready yet. I'm sorry.'

'I suppose I knew you'd say that,' said Eve. 'I just had to ask you face to face, just to make sure that I'd done absolutely everything I could.'

'Neil Benson is really special to you, huh?'

'Yes,' agreed Eve.

'That's tough but I guess you were warned what to expect at the outset.'

'Oh yes,' she agreed. 'I was warned.' She started rummaging in her handbag for a handkerchief. 'Michael warned me, and Sister Morse did, too, but here I am blubbing like a schoolgirl.' She pressed a tissue to her eyes.

'Sister Morse is doing her own share of weeping at the moment,' said Pereira.

'What do you mean?' asked Eve.

'Her husband's dying,' said Pereira. 'Cancer.'

'Michael didn't mention anything about that,' said Eve looking puzzled. 'How strange,' she murmured thoughtfully.

A look of unease appeared in Pereira's eyes. He had just remembered Michael Neef asking him to say nothing about Charles Morse's cancer.

Neef hadn't realized that the Friday-evening meeting was going to be so large. There were about twenty people in the lecture theatre when he arrived but there was no sign of Lennon. He nodded to Tim Heaton and Frank MacSween as he made his way through groups of people, and was joined by David Farro-Jones as he sat down to wait. Farro-Jones leaned over to say in his ear, 'The word is they've come up with nothing new. They're not one inch further forward.'

'Who are all these people?' asked Neef.

'Lots of them are public health scientists from out of town. I think the Department of Health is represented as well.'

'That serious,' exclaimed Neef.

'Looks like it. It seems we're all waiting for the good Doctor Lennon.' He looked at his watch. 'He's fifteen minutes late already. Let's hope this means he's come up with something. I'll speak to you later.'

Farro-Jones left Neef and went over to rejoin the group of University College physicians he had been with. Neef recognized one of them as Charlie Morse's doctor, Mark Clelland. He nodded to him. Neef was joined by Frank MacSween, who had been talking to Eddie Miller but broke off when someone said, 'Lennon's here.'

A few minutes later, Lennon entered the room, looking harassed. He flung off his coat and asked everyone to take their seats.

'Ladies and gentlemen,' he announced, 'I was delayed by the press. The cat's out the bag. They have the story. Eve Sayers was waiting for me this evening when I returned to my office.'

Neef felt a pang of embarrassment. He wanted to assure everyone in the room that he had had nothing to do with the leak. He could feel Frank MacSween take a suspicious sideways look at him.

'Miss Sayers seemed to know that Charles Morse was the third victim of the carcinogen. I saw no point in trying to deny it. I told her outright that there were actually four victims. She now knows about the baby. I also had to tell her that our efforts in tracing the carcinogen have come to nothing.'

A murmur of disappointment ran round the room.

'It's true, I'm afraid,' said Lennon. 'An entire team of path technicians has failed to find any clue at all as to the nature of the carcinogen. In effect, they confirmed the earlier findings of Dr MacSween's own lab.'

'Cold comfort,' murmured MacSween.

'The question is, where do we go from here?' said Lennon.

'I think we were hoping that you were going to tell us that,' said Tim Heaton. 'The bad publicity's going to damage all of us.'

'It was actually the cancer I was thinking about,' said Lennon.

'Of course,' said Heaton, looking chastened by the comment. 'But the public are liable to panic if this damned woman milks the story like these people do. I think our public relations people should be ready to issue reassurance.'

'How can we reassure people when we don't know what we're dealing with ourselves?' said Neef. He had been irked by Heaton's reference to 'this damned woman'.

'That's not the point,' said Heaton but he could sense that everyone else in the room thought that it was. He stopped talking.

Lennon said, 'I've prepared an updated summary of events. If someone could give me a hand with the projector . . .'

One of Frank MacSween's technicians moved forward to position the overhead projector and make the necessary electrical connections. Lennon put the first overhead in place with the palm of his hand and picked up a pointer.

'Melanie Simpson was our first case. Thirteen years old and a pupil at Longhill High School. She was admitted to University College Hospital with severe bilateral pneumonia. The rest you know.'

Lennon changed the acetate, at first putting in the new one upside down, then hastily swivelling it round.

'Our second case was Jane Lees, another thirteen-year-old and a pupil at Forest Green High School. She lived in the Polton Court flats which as you will see' – Lennon changed the acetate to one showing a hand-drawn map – 'is nowhere near Langholm Crescent, where Melanie lived. No common ground as far as we could determine, so we were unable to pinpoint an area where both girls might have come across the carcinogen.

'Our third case is, of course, Charles Morse, chief technician in Pathology here at St George's who, thankfully, is still alive. And our fourth is Nigel Barnes, baby grandson of Dr MacSween, pathologist here at St George's, who died last weekend. We've been working on the assumption that these last two cases were secondary and caused by traces of the carcinogen still being present in the girls' lungs when being examined pathologically. An extensive examination of the lungs, however, has failed to confirm this. This begs the question, how can you contaminate yourself with a substance that doesn't exist?'

'Was the search confined to path specimens taken from Jane Lees or have samples been taken from Charlie Morse as well?' asked Neef.

'We've had bronchoscopy samples taken from Mr Morse,' replied Lennon.

'Nothing found?'

'Nothing.' The room fell silent. 'I've prepared summary files with all the pathology details for anyone who wants one.' He held up a series of files bound in clear plastic. 'Help yourself later on the way out.'

'So what we're dealing with is an invisible, undetectable cancer-causing agent that no one's ever come across before. Is that right?' asked Alan Brooks, dean of the University Medical School.

'In a word, yes,' replied Lennon. 'Unless anyone has a better idea.'

'No, but I feel sure there must be one,' said Neef.

'I agree,' said Brooks. 'It's probably staring us in the face, and we just can't see the wood for the trees.'

'If anyone sees the wood, let me know,' said Lennon. It didn't get much of a laugh.

The meeting broke up with Neef determined to probe how Eve had found out about Charlie Morse. Had she been asking questions around the unit when she had been visiting Neil? Had she been going through his private papers when his back had been turned? Neef rested his elbows on the desk and allowed his head to sink into his hands. His imagination was threatening to run away with him.

The truth was that he was still smarting from some of the accusing glances he had seen at the meeting when Lennon announced the involvement of the press. Eve had made an agreement with him that she would not 'work' when she was in the unit. He had no reason to doubt her word.

Had he?

He still felt he had to ask her. He had to know for sure. He dialled Eve's home number. He was just about to hang up when it was answered.

'Eve Sayers.'

'Hello Eve, it's Michael. I was beginning to think you were out.'

'I was in the shower,' said Eve.

'I've just been to a meeting with the public health people. They said you'd found out about Charlie Morse and planned to run the story.'

'That's right,' said Eve.

Neef felt his throat tighten as he sensed they were about to fall out again. He heard the edge in Eve's voice.

'We had an agreement,' said Neef. 'You promised that anything you heard in the unit or from unit staff would be confidential.'

'We still have,' said Eve.

'How did you find out?' asked Neef.

'I don't think I feel inclined to tell you,' said Eve. 'It certainly wasn't from you, was it? You lied to me about Nigel's death. You knew perfectly well how he'd died when I asked you.'

'I was in a difficult position,' said Neef awkwardly. 'I didn't want to put you in one.'

'Well, thanks for nothing.'

'So you won't tell me?'

173

There was along pause before Eve sighed, and said, 'The truth is, I worked it out for myself. Max Pereira let slip that Charles Morse was dying of cancer and that made me wonder why you hadn't mentioned it earlier. I put two and two together and tried out my hypothesis on Dr Lennon. I told him I knew that Charles Morse was the third case and he confirmed it. He also admitted there was a fourth, Frank's grandson, Nigel.'

'Max Pereira told you Charlie had cancer?' exclaimed Neef, 'I didn't know you knew him.'

'We sort of knew each other by sight. I bought him a cup of coffee this afternoon.'

'To get information out of him.'

'No damn it!' exclaimed Eve. 'If you must know, I wanted to ask if he could do anything for Neil. I felt that desperate. I was prepared to get down on my bended knees and beg him, if you must know. It just slipped out somewhere along the way that Kate Morse's husband had cancer and I suddenly realised why you hadn't told me about it. You didn't trust me enough.'

'I didn't want to put you in a difficult position,' said Neef.

'Have you any idea how pompous you sound?' asked Eve.

'I think what you did was against the spirit of our agreement,' said Neef.

'If you people put as much effort into investigating this thing as you do in trying to hush everything up we might know just what the hell's going on by now,' said Eve. She put the phone down.

Neef put the receiver slowly back on its rest and leaned back in his chair. He closed his eyes and wished he'd never made the call. He tried telling himself that he had every right to be annoyed but there was no satisfaction to be had from that. He even had to consider for a moment that Eve had been right in her assertion about keeping things quiet. Avoiding scrutiny or publicity was a way of life in British society and there was no doubt in his mind that secrecy was often used by the incompetent to protect themselves. At least half the envelopes arriving on his desk had the words 'In Strict Confidence' marked on them when there was no need for it.

It was a case of the fewer who knew how the health service was run the better as far as the top echelons were concerned.

But surely allowing the public health people to carry out their investigations without the full glare of publicity on them was a different case altogether. Wasn't it? Neef couldn't come to a firm view on that any more. The fact was that they had got nowhere in their investigations and things didn't look like improving in the near future. He took the copy of the summary he had picked up at the meeting and put it in his briefcase along with other odds and ends from his desk. He would read it later. He was feeling low. He would go home, tell Dolly his troubles and have a few drinks before having an early night.

Neef's plan lasted as far as the car, then he changed his mind. One thing still niggled him about his conversation with Eve. It was her assertion that she had worked out for herself that Charlie Morse was the third victim. Was that really true or had she been protecting Max Pereira? There was a chance that Pereira would still be at the Menogen labs. He would drive over there and have it out with him before going home. He opened up his briefcase on the passenger seat and looked through his papers until he found something with a Menogen letterhead on it. Menogen Research was at 14, Langholm Road.

Neef parked the car in a side street off Langholm Road about two hundred yards from where the Menogen building was located. He took his briefcase from the passenger sent, located the car and approached the building. It was a modern low-rise structure protected by a chain-link fence with nothing much in the way of signing outside it apart from a green board that said MENOGEN RESEARCH. This was repeated on a brass plate on the wall next to an entry-phone system. Neef could see that there were lights on inside the building. He pressed the bell-push on the plate and waited. He had to do this a second time before the unmistakable sound of Pereira's voice said, 'Yeah?'

'Max, it's Michael Neef.'

'Yeah.'

'Can I come in?'

The door lock was released electronically and Neef stepped forward into an inner vestibule where he was confronted with another locked door. Pereira's voice, coming from a speaker in the ceiling, instructed him to step forward on to a tray charged with disinfectant to sanitize his shoes. He did this and the door in front of him opened to admit him into a small changing room.

'Change into gown and boots, Mike,' said Pereira. 'These are the rules. I'm in lab five.'

Neef left his shoes and topcoat in the changing room, picked up his briefcase and walked along the corridor to lab five in green gown and white wellingtons. He knocked once and entered. Pereira was seated on a stool in front of a laminar airflow cabinet. He was in the process of injecting a pink liquid into a cell culture bottle.

'Be with you in a moment,' he said from behind the surgical mask he wore.

Neef looked around him at the shelves laden with bottles and tubes. It looked just like any other lab as far as he was concerned, but very modern and tidy.

Pereira dropped the syringe he'd been using into a CINBIN container and stripped off his gloves. He opened a pedal bin with his right foot and let them fall in with an air of contrived drama.

'What can I do for you Mike?' he asked, pulling down his face mask.

'The press have got hold of the fact there's been a third cancer case caused by the mystery carcinogen and that Charlie Morse is the patient concerned. Eve Sayers is running the story.'

'Oh,' said Pereira, looking down at his feet.

Neef took this as an admission of guilt. 'I particularly asked you not to talk about that when I told you,' said Neef.

'I'm sorry, Mike,' said Pereira. 'I met Eve this afternoon and I let slip that Charlie Morse had cancer. I didn't think. That's as far as it went, honest. She must have worked out the rest from there. She said something about it being odd that you hadn't mentioned anything about it. She seemed to suggest you two had some kind of agreement about being straight with each other.'

Neef smiled wryly at Pereira's barbed comment. He sighed, 'Oh what a tangled web we weave when first we practise to deceive.'

'Shakespeare. Right?'

'Walter Scott.'

'I'm sorry if I'm responsible for this,' said Pereira. 'It was unintentional.'

'Not your fault,' sighed Neef. 'If I had told her in the first place she probably wouldn't have used it under the terms of our agreement. There have actually been four cases. The public health people came clean with her.'

'Four!' exclaimed Pereira. 'Are these guys no nearer finding out where this stuff is coming from?'

Neef shook his head and said, 'It's invisible and undetectable.'

'I don't think I believe that,' said Pereira.

'I don't think I do, either,' said Neef with a shrug.

'There must be some linking factor in four cases, for Christ's sake,' said Pereira.

Neef opened his briefcase and took out the summary that Lennon had prepared. 'See if you can spot it,' he said.

Pereira removed the half-frame spectacles that were hooked over the neck-band of his T-shirt and put them on. He rested his bare elbows on the bench as he read the summary.

'Jesus,' said Pereira when he'd finished. 'And you guys are looking for a chemical?'

'Why do you say it like that?' asked Neef.

'Because, you're looking for the wrong thing.'

'What do you mean?' asked Neef. He could see that Pereira was alarmed by what he'd read.

'It's as plain as day. It's a virus,' said Pereira. 'It's a fucking virus you should be looking for!'

Neef felt unsettled by the notion. He tried to remain rational and not be swept along by Pereira's assertion. 'Viruses don't give

177

you cancer. You can't catch cancer. It's not a transmissible disease,' said Neef.

'It is now,' said Pereira. 'You are looking for a virus that gave these folks their cancer. It's all there, man. It's been staring you in the face. MacSween's finding of bilateral pneumonia in both cases he autopsied . . .'

'I think that was an immune response to the cancer,' said Neef.

'I think you're wrong, Mike. It was a bit of both.'

Neef looked at Pereira. He was thinking about Frank MacSween's unwillingness to abandon his pneumonia finding, maintaining that his findings were consistent with both pneumonia *and* cancer. 'But there's no such virus,' he said.

'No *known* virus,' Pereira corrected. 'You've got a new one.'

'A virus that gives you lung cancer,' said Neef slowly as if the words pained him. 'You must be wrong,' he whispered. 'You *have* to be wrong.'

'Look on the bright side,' said Pereira. 'It's not highly infectious or you would have had more cases. It's my guess you need to inhale a fair few virus particles to develop the disease and maybe there's also a degree of natural immunity around.'

'But the virus lab did tests on Melanie Simpson and Jane Lees before and after death. They didn't find any new virus.'

'They weren't looking for a new virus,' retorted Pereira. 'They'd be looking for antibodies stimulated by known viruses. That's how diagnostic virology works.'

'But you'd think—'

'Not necessarily,' interrupted Pereira. 'People, even trained scientists, are reluctant to see new things, even when they're staring them in the face. Diseases can be around for anything up to a few years before labs start talking to each other and one of them admits they got some results they couldn't explain, then another says the same and it goes on from there.'

'But where could a new virus have come from?' said Neef.

'New viruses are evolving all the time, Mike. You know that.

'AIDS, Lassa fever, Marburg disease, Ebola. They keep cropping up all the time.'

'I thought the theory was that they weren't new, that they'd been there all the time and it's just with jungle areas of Africa being opened up and modern transport being so easy that they get carried into the community and trigger off an outbreak.'

'That's one of the theories,' said Pereira meaningfully. 'There are others. One thing's for sure.'

'What?'

'Old Africa isn't going to get the blame for this one.'

'I'll have to think about this, Max. I can't simply voice your theory at a routine meeting. If we were worried about panic before, this could make it a thousand times worse.'

'I guess it's still just a theory,' said Pereira, 'but it's where my money would go. It would be worth putting Charles Morse in isolation.'

'That's been done,' said Neef. 'Albeit not for this reason. Would you be willing to join the team, so to speak?' asked Neef. 'I think public health could use some help.'

Pereira shrugged his shoulders and said, 'I don't think I'd be too welcome, but I'm here for you if you want to ask anything.'

'Why do you say that?'

'Let's just say, previous experience with the British medical establishment has not been too ... positive. My face doesn't fit.'

'That must have made made life difficult,' said Neef.

'You could say,' agreed Pereira. 'Let's just say nobody does us any favours here at Menogen. Everything we do has to be done by the book, double checked, registered, licensed, recorded, you name it. There are plenty of people out there who would like to see us fall flat on our faces. We have one secretary working full-time on making sure all our paperwork is in order. We get more inspections in a year than one of your university labs would get in a decade, and God help us if we fall down on any of the safety procedures.' Neef nodded. 'Yet with the possible exception

179

of Birmingham, where the horse bolted some years ago, you and I both know that I could walk into just about any virus lab in the country and help myself.'

'So you feel you get a raw deal,' said Neef.

'On the contrary,' said Pereira. 'We get the right deal but it should be applied to the academic institutes as well. These jokers do what they damn well like and nobody says boo. Any mention of rules and regulations and they start throwing their hands in the air and screaming infringement of academic freedom. Infringement my ass! But it always works.'

'Am I allowed to ask what you're working on?' asked Neef.

'A new vector. I think it should work on melanomas. I'm also trying to figure out what went wrong with ones used on the four kids in the trial. I still don't understand it.'

Neef picked up on the word 'melanoma'. 'Do you reckon this new vector of yours could help Neil Benson?'

'That's what Eve wanted to know when she stopped me this afternoon,' said Pereira. 'I'm just developing it. It isn't licensed.'

'But would it work?'

'I reckon it's got a good chance,' replied Pereira.

'Neil's going to die within a month,' said Neef.

'I hope you're not asking what I think you are,' said Pereira. 'After what I just told you?'

'I suppose not,' said Neef. 'It just seems like such a shame ... How far along the way are you to getting it licensed?'

'It's brand-new,' said Pereira.

'So there's no chance of rushing it through the licensing procedure?'

'Rushing it through? You have got to be kidding. This is Menogen, remember? A nasty commercial affair. The establishment puts up hurdles specially for us, it doesn't take them down.'

'God, it's so galling to know that there's something that might help Neil and we can't do anything.' said Neef.

'It might not work, Mike,' said Pereira kindly. 'I would have put money on that other kid's hepatoma responding but it didn't.'

'Thanks, Max,' said Neef with a sigh. 'I'd better go and let you get on.'

'I'll see you to the door.'

Neef looked back at the Menogen building when he had crossed the street. He caught sight of Max Pereira through the lab window. He was gowning up to continue work.

Even after two gin and tonics, Neef was still on edge. He found it difficult to dismiss Pereira's virus idea. In fact, it seemed to gain increasing credence the more he thought about it. He considered telephoning Lennon if he could get his home number from somewhere. But what good would that do? Charles Morse was in isolation already and he was the only living patient. There were no other steps they could take except look for the virus itself. He would contact the hospital lab in the morning and ask about the reports on Melanie Simpson and Jane Lees. He'd ask if they had noticed anything out of the ordinary. He remembered that Frank MacSween had said at one point that he had seen a virology report on Melanie Simpson. He also remembered that there had not been anything remarkable in it but he would take a look at it in the morning if it was still available.

First thing in the morning, Neef went down to Pathology to seek out Frank MacSween. He found him preparing for the first post-mortem of the day.

'Hello, Michael, what can I do for you?'

Neef could not help but notice the change that had come over MacSween since the death of his grandson. It was as if he had no great interest in anything any more. He was going through the motions of life without having any heart for it.

'I was wondering if you still had a copy of the virology report on Melanie Simpson.' said Neef. 'I'd like to take another look at it.'

'Should do,' said MacSween. He walked through to his office and opened a filing cabinet. He pulled out a pink cardboard file and flipped it open. He extracted a single sheet and handed it over to Neef.

'Okay if I hang on to this for a little while?' asked Neef.

'Feel free,' replied MacSween. He didn't enquire why Neef wanted it. Neef didn't bother volunteering the reason. He wanted to say something to Frank as a friend but he had difficulty in knowing where to begin. 'Frank . . .'

'Uh huh.'

Neef saw that MacSween's eyes were dull and his look was distant. 'Oh nothing . . . I'll catch you later.'

Neef returned to his office and read through the virology report on Melanie Simpson. Three types of virus had been found in her lungs. Adenovirus, rhinovirus, and para-adenovirus. None had been reported present in any great number that would have signified infection. They were just reported as being present. There was no mention of any unidentified virus being found. There was no need for Neef to look up a virus text book. Adenoviruses and rhinoviruses were very common. They caused cold and flu-like disease but lots of people carried them without any ill effects. There was nothing in the report at all to support Max Pereira's notion of a new virus but it still worried Neef. He decided to call David Farro-Jones; he was an expert on the subject. He should have thought of that sooner.

'David? It's Michael Neef. I was wondering if I might come over and have a chat with you?'

'Of course. Can it wait till about eleven?'

'Fine, see you then.'

Twelve

It was raining heavily as Neef looked for a place near the medical school to park. A mixture of condensation and water on the car's windows made it difficult to reverse into the one space he had found being vacated on his third circuit of the block. It was very small; its previous occupant had been a Fiat Panda and he needed two attempts at getting the Discovery into it. This did not please the driver in the car behind, who displayed growing impatience with a blast of the horn. Neef glanced to the side as the other driver passed and saw it was a woman. She gave him a sour look and a shake of the head; he smiled pleasantly in reply.

Neef hunched his shoulders against the rain and ran across the road into the quadrangle. He slowed down on the cobbled surface, which looked treacherous but speeded up again when he came to the long flight of steps leading up to the tall, arched entrance, taking them two at a time. He paused just inside the doors to brush the rain from his hair and shoulders and then crossed the hall quickly past the reception desk. There were two men on the desk but neither paid him any attention. He walked straight past and into the elevator.

David Farro-Jones's lab was on the fourth and top floor of the building, which had been erected during the latter part of the nineteenth century and modified many times since. It retained its original high ceilings, which tended to dwarf people and contents, but the walls bore the bumps and scars of constant redesigning of

internal partitioning. Neef found Farro-Jones talking to a young man
with a straggly beard and glasses that made his eyes seem enormous.
He was wearing a sweatshirt bearing the logo of a brewery in Devon
and sandals over bare feet. Neef waited until they had finished before
approaching.

'Ah, Michael, be right with you,' said Farro-Jones. He picked up
a wire rack containing several rows of test tubes and said, 'I'll just
put these away in the fridge.'

Neef stood by the door looking at photographs pinned up on a
corkboard on the wall. They were electron micrographs of viruses,
blown up to enormous proportions. One of them looked like an
alien spacecraft. The caption said, 'T-Even Phage, Negative Stain,
Uranyl Acetate'.

'Sorry about that,' said Farro-Jones, joining him at last. 'Come
on into my office. Coffee?'

'Black, no sugar.'

Farro-Jones relayed the request to someone outside the door
whom Neef couldn't see. A few minutes later a middle-aged
woman with her grey hair tied back in a severe bun came in
with the coffee.

'Thank you, Marge,' said Farro-Jones.

'You're welcome, Doctor,' replied Marge, with a Welsh accent
and a smile of acknowledgement to Neef.

'Now then, what can I do for you?' asked Farro-Jones, swinging
his feet round and up on to the corner of his desk with a practised
ease. 'More problems with Max?'

'Not exactly,' said Neef. 'It's about this carcinogen business. I had
a talk with Max last night. I showed him the summary sheet we got
from public health. Max thinks . . .' Neef paused as if reluctant to
say the words.

'Max thinks what?' prompted Farro-Jones.

'He thinks we're dealing with a virus.'

The smile faded from Farro-Jones's face. 'A virus?' he exclaimed.
'You can't be serious?'

'Max was,' replied Neef.

'But that's crazy. Cancer isn't an infectious disease. How could it possibly be a virus?'

'I know, I know. We went through all that last night but Max has almost convinced me. He thinks it's a new virus and the fact is, he knows an awful lot more about viruses than I do. That's why I'm here. You're an expert too; you're also medically qualified. I'd value your opinion.'

Farro-Jones sat up straight and brought his hands to a peak over his nose and mouth. 'What can I say? I think the idea's ludicrous. I suppose with Charles Morse and Frank MacSween's grandson getting cancer in some secondary fashion it looks as if an infectious agent might be involved, but the fact is we'd have seen a lot more cases if that were true.'

'Pereira suggests that the virus might have a low infectivity rate,' said Neef. 'You need to inhale a lot of it. He also brought up the possibility of some people having natural immunity to it.'

'You'd certainly have to invoke something like that,' agreed Farro-Jones, his voice betraying his continuing scepticism. 'But there's been no mention of any new virus in the lab reports on the patients who've died.'

'I pointed that out too,' said Neef. 'Max said that hospital labs examine specimens for the presence of antibodies against known viruses, not actual viruses themselves. He seemed to suggest they might not pick up on anything new?'

'There's something in that,' conceded Farro-Jones. 'The main screening test is for antibodies against known viruses, an indirect indication of infection if you like.'

'So you couldn't test for antibodies against something you didn't know existed?'

'Quite so,' agreed Farro-Jones.

'How would you go about identifying a new virus then?' asked Neef.

'You'd have to examine samples directly, using the electron microscope. You'd actually have to look and see if anything resembling a virus was present.'

'Can that be done?'

'Of course.'

'I was thinking of samples from Charlie Morse. Do you think it's worth having a look?'

'If you like,' said Farro-Jones without much enthusiasm. 'Have you mentioned anything about this to public health?'

'Not yet. I thought I'd see what you thought first.'

Farro-Jones nodded and said, 'All right. If it would make you feel better, why don't I discreetly examine a few specimens from Charles Morse as you suggest and see what I come up with. If there's nothing there, as I suspect there won't be, we won't have to worry PH with Max's crazy idea. Can you imagine the panic if this notion got out? A virus that gives you cancer . . .'

'It doesn't bear thinking about,' said Neef.

Eve's story reporting the third and fourth cancer victims appeared on Saturday evening and Neef's telephone started ringing almost immediately. Tim Heaton was first; he was furious.

'Damn it! I've had the national papers on the line, radio and television, all wanting to know what St George's are going to do about the situation. This is a public health problem!' he exclaimed, 'but that woman has made it sound as if St George's is at fault. Can't you do something about her?'

'What do you suggest, Tim?' asked Neef coolly.

'I don't know. Think of something. She's a friend of yours, isn't she? This is doing the hospital no good at all. It's just the sort of thing we didn't need.'

'Eve believes she's just doing her job,' said Neef. 'There is a problem and we don't know where it's coming from. She's just reporting facts.' He felt uncomfortable at having to make out a defence for Eve that he didn't fully support, a bit like prosecuting an argument in a debating society because it had been picked for you. He reflected that barristers must often feel that way.

'But it's not our problem!' insisted Heaton. 'It's up to the public health service to work this thing out. All this stuff about doctors at St George's being puzzled is just sheer bad publicity for us.'

'With respect, Tim, with one of our staff members at death's door and the grandson of another already dead, it *is* our problem. It's everyone's problem.'

'We need to agree a policy.'

'If you say so.'

'I'm instructing our PR people to refer all press enquiries on the subject directly to public health, making it clear that it's their investigation, not ours. I'm instructing everyone else to say nothing at all.'

Neef understood that 'everyone else,' in the context of this conversation, included him. 'As you wish.'

'I don't suppose you have any good news about the gene-therapy trial that we could use to create a diversion, have you?'

Neef had to admire Heaton's one-track dedication to what he saw as his job. He said, 'At the moment, it looks like one success and four failures.'

Heaton sighed then said, 'I think I'm going to give Mr Louradis the go-ahead.'

'For what?' asked Neef in trepidation.

'He's been asked by one of the papers to write a layman's guide to gene therapy.'

'That vague?' asked Neef.

'Not exactly. The paper wants him to explain just exactly what you and Menogen are trying to do in the current trial.'

'Why doesn't Louradis go on the stage and be done with it,' snapped Neef.

'I feared you might see it that way,' said Heaton almost apologetically. 'But what harm can it do? None of the staff and patients will be identified by name and it might give the hospital a more positive image.'

'If you say so,' said Neef.

'Damn. You know the thing that really galls me?' continued Heaton. 'University College Hospital is getting off scot-free! Not a mention apart from the fact that they are the people treating our staff member! They've come up smelling of roses again. They're the star hospital. We're the baffled donkeys!'

'This will probably all be history in a few weeks' time,' said Neef. 'I think we should try riding it out with quiet dignity. If we start a slanging match it won't do anyone any good.'

'Oh absolutely,' said Heaton. 'I wouldn't dream of saying this to anyone else, you understand. They'd think I was paranoid or something.'

Neef grinned. He didn't say anything in case the amusement showed in his voice.

'There is one more thing, Michael.'

'Yes?'

'I was wondering if it might not be a good idea to deny Miss Sayers further access to the hospital. After all, she has no real business here, has she?'

Neef bit his tongue. Telling Heaton where to go might not be such a brilliant idea at this particular moment. 'I don't think that's wise, Tim,' he said. 'Eve has nothing at all against us. She thinks she's reporting the facts. I shudder to think what it might be like if she were suddenly to see us as the enemy.'

'Mmm, I hadn't thought of that,' conceded Heaton. After a few moments' thought he said, 'Perhaps you're right.'

'Apart from that, she's become very attached to one of the children in my unit. She visits him daily.'

'Oh well then. Just a thought.'

Neef closed his eyes and felt relief as the moment passed.

'I'm going to contact George Lancing at the Regional Health Authority now,' said Heaton. 'I want him to put pressure on the Department of Health to have this thing handled at top level. I don't think Lennon's up to the job.'

'It's a particularly difficult job for anyone at the moment,' said Neef. 'There's nothing to go on.'

'I don't think some extra help would go amiss. Action is what's needed, not understanding.'

'Up to you,' said Neef, and the conversation came to an end. Next to call was Eve Sayers.

'I've been trying to get through for ages,' she said.

'I had Tim Heaton on the line. He's our chief executive.'

'Not very pleased, huh?'

'You could say.'

'Are you very angry?'

'More numb than angry,' replied Neef.

'I just reported the facts, Mike.'

'Heaton thinks you made us look like donkeys.'

'That wasn't my intention.'

'I know.'

'He isn't going to ban me from the hospital, is he?'

'No, nothing like that,' replied Neef without further explanation. 'Just don't count on getting a Christmas card from him.'

'Will I get one from you?'

'You might.'

'I'm sorry for hanging up on you the last time we spoke.'

'We were both pretty angry as I recall.'

'Pax?'

'Pax,' agreed Neef.

'Want to come over?'

'If you're not too fussy about what we eat, why don't you come over here and I'll find us a delicious packet from the freezer.'

'What are we having?' asked Eve an hour later, as she came in and sniffed the air appreciatively.

'Something with an appetizing picture on the packet,' said Neef.

'They're all pretty good at that,' said Eve.

'I particularly liked the look of rapture on the faces of the people on the front of this packet,' said Neef.

Eve picked up the empty packet and looked at it. 'Irresistible,' she agreed. 'Looks like they just had sex instead of Salmon in Puff Pastry.'

The meal wasn't wonderful but it was palatable and washed down with a good wine that Eve had brought.

'Did you see Neil today?' asked Neef.

Eve nodded. 'He wasn't too well. I think Lawrence had upped his medication. I read him a fireman story and he dozed on and off and held my hand. It was nice, as if we didn't need to talk somehow.'

Neef nodded.

'The sparkle's going from his eyes. It's like watching a flame start to flicker and die. God! I'd give anything to be able to help him. I really would.'

Neef put his hand on top of Eve's. 'Hang in there,' he said gently. 'For his sake.'

'Of course. I'm sorry,' said Eve, pulling a paper tissue from her handbag and blowing her nose. 'Let's talk about something else.'

As if on cue, Dolly made her first appearance of the evening and walked across the floor to take up her customary position in front of the french windows.

'Do you think she's jealous of me?' asked Eve.

'I doubt it,' said Neef. 'Dolly's too self-possessed and confident to even imagine anyone else as a rival.'

'What a comfortable feeling that must be,' said Eve. 'How do I make contact with her?'

'The orange fish,' said Neef.

'Pardon?'

'It's her new toy. I stuffed it down the back of the couch.'

Eve went over to the couch and extracted the orange fish, complete with cane rod and line. She held the cane in her right hand and dangled the fish at Dolly's side. Dolly responded immediately and started to chase the fish, which Eve swung across the floor and round the room.

'Come on, Dolly!' urged Eve as she moved the fish even faster and Dolly gave a display of feline ability when it came to a chase. 'She certainly can move.'

'Cats are like that,' said Neef, joining her on the couch. 'Their agility can really take you by surprise.'

'Like this, you mean,' said Eve, sitting up straight and kissing Neef full on the lips. She drew back slightly as if waiting unsurely for a response. There was a hint of vulnerability in her eyes. Neef wrapped his arms round her and kissed her long and hard, his senses heightened by the sudden desire that came over him. It had been such a long time. 'If you like,' he said.

'I like,' replied Eve.

Eve rolled over on to her front and propped herself up on her elbows to look at Neef's face. His eyes were closed but there was a smile on his lips that said he wasn't actually asleep. She pushed the hair back from his forehead and said, 'This, of course, is another way of dealing with stress and tension.'

'I think I like it,' murmured Neef.

'Do you?' Eve teased. She ran her fingers lightly across his closed eyelids.

'God, yes.'

Eve looked at the trail of clothes and underwear that stretched out through the door of the bedroom. She rested her head on Neef's chest and said, 'I must say, I'm feeling quite relaxed myself.'

The telephone rang just before three in the morning. Eve, being disorientated, picked it off the bedside table and almost answered it before she remembered where she was and handed it to Neef.

'Neef.'

'It's Lennon. There's been another case.'

'Who?'

'An electrician on the staff at St George's.'

'Another staff member,' murmured Neef. 'Pereira must be right.'

'Right about what?' asked Lennon.

'I talked to Max Pereira on Friday night. He's the research scientist who's running our gene-therapy trial. He's an expert on viruses. He said our problem looked like a virus was responsible, not a chemical.'

'A virus?' exclaimed Lennon. 'But how?'

'I know, I know,' sighed Neef.

'Have you mentioned this to any of the university people?' asked Lennon.

'I asked David Farro-Jones for his opinion.'

'What did he say?'

'Like you, he didn't think much of the idea but he agreed to have a look at samples from Charlie Morse under the electron microscope to see if he could spot any sign of a new virus.'

'I see,' said Lennon.

Neef detected a coolness in the comment. He added, 'I was going to tell you if he found anything. It seemed such a weird idea that I didn't want to bother you with it unless we could back it up but now that there are five cases . . .'

'When will Dr Farro-Jones have the results of his search?'

'David thought Monday but I could call him in the morning and ask if things could be hurried up.'

'I'm sure the idea of an infectious source must have flitted across all of our minds during this business but we dismissed it because it simply isn't possible,' said Lennon. 'Cancer cannot be transmitted from person to person.'

'Certainly not in the past,' said Neef. He thought about what Pereira had said about people not wanting to consider anything new. 'We really should keep an open mind at this stage,' he said.

'Naturally,' replied Lennon.

'But let's hope Max is wrong.'

'I'm sure he must be.'

'What have you done in the light of the new case?' asked Neef.

'I've put out a general alert to all hospitals warning them to be on their guard about cases of viral pneumonia.'

'Good,' said Neef.

'I'm also going to try and set up another full meeting for this afternoon to discuss the implications of the new case.'

'What about the press?' asked Neef. He looked at the 'press' lying beside him in bed, wide-eyed as she listened to the conversation.

'I don't think it's worth even trying to keep quiet about the latest case,' said Lennon, 'but I think we should keep the virus notion very definitely under wraps.'

'Agreed,' said Neef, his eyes not leaving Eve.

After bidding Lennon goodnight, Neef passed the phone back to Eve, who replaced it on the table. 'You heard?' he asked.

Eve nodded. Neef waited for her to say something.

'I heard. I won't use any of this, if that's what you're worried about.'

'What I'm worried about is not a newspaper story,' said Neef. 'It's the very real possibility that we have a virus on the loose which is capable of spreading lung cancer like it was chicken pox.'

'Then you believe the virus hypothesis?'

'I'm a damned sight more worried about it than Lennon seems to be.'

'What can you do if it is a virus?'

'Very little,' conceded Neef. 'There's nothing we can do at all for people who already have it. Our only hope lies in trying to contain it and stop it spreading. We'll have to isolate the victims and public health will have to trace all their contacts; but most important, we'll have to determine the source of the outbreak and wipe it out. That's easier said than done. To the best of my knowledge no one's ever found out where a new virus came from.'

'Oh Mike,' said Eve, cuddling into Neef. 'I have such a bad feeling about all this.'

Neef didn't admit it but he was thinking exactly the same thing. 'Get some sleep,' he whispered.

Neef was at the hospital by eight, all thoughts of spending a relaxing Sunday with Eve having been dispelled by Lennon's middle-of-the-night phone call. It wasn't as if he had a definite plan of action to follow – he just felt he should be there. He was very much on edge. Lennon called again at nine thirty. 'I think I know how the electrician got it,' he said. 'His work sheet shows that he was called to Pathology to work on a faulty extractor fan. The request was made by Charles Morse.'

'Well done,' said Neef.

'There's more. I had a bit of luck.'

'Long overdue,' said Neef.

'I went down to Pathology this morning to look around and the duty technician came in while I was there. She told me that Morse and the electrician, Cooper, had some sort of a mishap while the repair was being done. Apparently the cowling came off the fan and showered them both with accumulated dirt from inside the ducting. It hit them full in the face and from what she said there's a fair chance they both inhaled a good deal of it.'

'I see.'

'They thought it a bit of a joke at the time but on further investigation I found out that this extractor was above table four in the PM room and that's where Frank MacSween conducted the autopsies on both Melanie Simpson and Jane Lees.'

'It's the one he prefers,' said Neef.

'It's my guess that the carcinogen was concentrated in the dirt behind the cowling because of the fault in the fan. Does MacSween wear a mask when he's cutting?'

'Always when an infectious disease has been present,' replied Neef.

'So he would wear one when doing Simpson and Lees?'

'I know he was,' replied Neef. 'I was present on both occasions for a short time.'

'You wore one too?'

'Yes. We were assuming that viral pneumonia had been involved.'

'Just as well,' said Lennon. 'I'm having the dirt from inside the ducting examined for the presence of carcinogenic substances.'

Or a virus, thought Neef as he put down the phone. He reflected on this latest piece of information. It meant that Frank probably hadn't given the disease to his grandson. It had been Charlie after all.'

'Almost certainly,' said Pereira when Neef called to tell him of the latest development.

'But what we still don't know is how Melanie Simpson gave it to Jane Lees when they didn't know each other – and, most important of all, how Melanie Simpson got it in the first place.'

'Is Lennon going to look for a virus in the dirt from the duct?' asked Max.

'He said he was having it examined for carcinogenic substances,' replied Neef. 'I assumed he was going to have the virology lab take a look at it, too.'

'If you say so,' said Pereira. He didn't sound convinced.

'Why don't you come along to the meeting this afternoon?' suggested Neef.

'I won't be finished here in the lab until well after two.'

'I'll pick you up at three. What do you say?'

'Okay.'

Neef tried phoning Farro-Jones at home but his wife, Jane, said that he had gone into the medical school. Neef called him at his lab and Farro-Jones replied.

'David? It's Michael Neef. I tried calling you at home. Jane said you were working.'

'I'm screening these samples from Charles Morse,' replied Farro-Jones. 'I thought the sooner the better.'

'Good, that's really why I was calling,' said Neef. He told Farro-Jones about the new case.

'This is beginning to look more and more like a nightmare.'

'Lennon was wondering if you might have a result by the time of the meeting this afternoon? I think he's planning on making some kind of statement to the press afterwards.'

'I can't promise,' said Farro-Jones. 'But I'll certainly do my best.'

* * *

Neef picked up Max at the Menogen labs at three o'clock. He found him excited. 'The new melanoma vector's looking real good,' he announced. 'Like I said, there's no way we could get the paperwork done in time to help your kid but I was thinking, maybe *you* could.'

'I don't understand,' said Neef.

'If a special request for licensing was to be made by the hospital maybe there's a chance they would listen?'

'That's certainly worth a try,' said Neef. 'You'll have to tell me what to do, who to approach, that sort of thing.'

'I'll call lovely Lillie at home when I get back and get her to call you. She'll tell you all you need to know.'

'Lovely Lillie?'

'Her name's Miss Langtry,' said Pereira. 'She's the lady who deals with all our licence applications.'

The venue of the meeting had been changed at the last minute from St George's to the Public Health Department offices in Sutton Place. This had been done at the insistence of Tim Heaton, who had withdrawn permission to use the hospital when he heard that a press briefing was to be given afterwards. He had done this on the grounds that continual association of St George's with the public health problem was doing the hospital's reputation no good at all.

It being Sunday, the traffic was mercifully light and Neef and Pereira were only five minutes late in getting to Sutton Place. As they made their way along to the Public Health Department offices Neef saw Eve standing on the pavement outside with a group of other journalists. He caught her eye and she smiled. He pointed to his watch to signify that they were late and mouthed the words, 'See you later.' Eve nodded in reply.

'I must apologize for the cramped conditions this afternoon,' announced Lennon, 'but we had a few last-minute problems to contend with.'

The room that had been pressed into service for the meeting was a bit small for the twenty or so people who attended. Neef found it unpleasantly hot and stuffy.

'Some of you know, of course, about the latest development but others may not. There's been another case: an electrician on the staff of St George's. We think we know how this man was affected and, because of this, it's become untenable to propose contamination at a common primary source. We must in fact, consider that the carcinogenic compound has been still present on or in the patients when admitted to hospital.

'A most interesting and unfortunately alarming alternative has been proposed by Dr Max Pereira of Menogen Research, who's currently collaborating with staff at St George's in a gene-therapy trial on cancer patients. Dr Pereira suggests that we should be looking for a brand-new virus as the agent responsible for our outbreak.'

There was a sudden hubbub in the room as people hearing the idea for the first time made all the objections that had been voiced before. Lennon held up his hands for calm.

'I know, ladies and gentlemen, this is heresy, but the suggestion has been made by someone I understand is an expert in such matters, so it's only right that we consider it.'

Another hubbub broke out.

'In the interim, I have issued an alert to hospitals, asking them to isolate all suspected viral pneumonias and to notify public health so that contacts can be traced and advised.'

'Don't you think this is all a little bit premature?' asked a man Neef knew to be a member of the Regional Health Authority. 'If you're proposing the existence of a virus completely unknown to medical science, don't you think you should wait until you have at least a shred of evidence to support it?'

There was murmured agreement for his comment. 'All you apparently have to go on is the word of this Pereira man.'

'I believe Dr Pereira is with us,' said Lennon, catching sight of the small swarthy man standing beside Neef.

'I'm here,' said Pereira.

'Perhaps you'd care to comment.' Lennon suggested.

'Do you know how long it took the medical establishment to acknowledge the existence of the AIDS virus?' Pereira asked.

'Surely you're not suggesting that this is anything like—'

'Who's to say?' interrupted Pereira. 'I think a few precautions are just common sense. Don't you?'

'There's a world of difference between taking precautions against a known risk and causing widespread public panic over something you've just made up!' retorted the Health Authority member. Neef noticed the man had gone red in the face. Pereira had an unsurpassed talent for rubbing people up the wrong way, he conceded. 'I'm against anything that causes unnecessary public alarm,' said the man.

There were murmurs of agreement all round.

'Yeah, yeah, the mushroom approach to the public,' said Pereira.

'What do mushrooms have to do—'

'Keep 'em in the dark and feed 'em bullshit.'

'Gentlemen, please,' interrupted Lennon. 'We all want to see this thing resolved as soon as possible. Bickering among ourselves is not going to help. Is Dr Farro-Jones here?' he asked. He wasn't. 'The reason I asked, ladies and gentlemen, is because Dr Farro-Jones has been conducting an electron-microscope search on lung-tissue samples taken from Charles Morse in an effort to detect the presence of any such new virus. He's been working all day on it. I hoped he might be here with some news but apparently not. In the meantime I'll furnish you with details of the new case and his relationship to the old ones. I apologize for the hastily rigged screen. Copies of the summary will be available as you leave.'

As the first overhead appeared on the screen, Pereira whispered to Neef, 'I'm off, I'll catch you tomorrow.'

Neef nodded. He saw that, as Pereira opened the door to leave, David Farro-Jones entered. The two had a brief whispered word, then Pereira left and Farro-Jones sidled quietly into the room. He joined Neef to watch the succession of overheads.

Neef now felt that he knew them off by heart. He looked away for a moment but then caught sight of the expression on Farro-Jones's face. He had obviously seen something up on the screen that had shocked him to the core.

Thirteen

Lennon finished his update on the persons affected and asked if there were any questions or comments.

'It does look uncannily like the work of an infectious agent,' said Alan Brooks, dean of the Medical School. The ensuing silence suggested this was not a popular comment.

'But there's no established link between the first and second cases,' said Lennon, catching the mood of the meeting. 'That's absolutely vital, and we looked hard enough, believe me. We're pretty sure that these two girls never met.'

No one else seemed keen to promote the infectious-agent argument.

Neef said, 'Dr Farro-Jones has arrived.'

Lennon turned up the lights again and turned away from the screen. 'Ah, Doctor, any news?'

Farro-Jones said distantly, 'I've spent the entire day examining uranyl acetate preps of lung secretions from Charles Morse. I found no evidence at all of any new virus being present.'

The room was filled with general murmurs of relief. Neef did not join them; he was wondering what Farro-Jones had seen earlier. He still looked preoccupied.

Lennon said, 'I think I can speak for everyone when I say that I'm mightily relieved to hear it, Doctor. I'm due to brief the press after this meeting and my biggest fear was the prospect of having to announce the birth of a nightmare in the form of yet another new virus for humanity to contend with.'

There was laughter in the room as the mood relaxed.

'My findings, of course, are not absolutely conclusive,' said Farro-Jones. 'There's always the possibility when looking for something entirely new that the staining conditions were not quite right or some step in the preparation wasn't quite what it should have been.'

Neef found Farro-Jones's rider a little puzzling. He hadn't liked the idea of a new virus in the first place. Why was he being so guarded about a negative finding?

'Quite so, Doctor,' said Lennon. 'But I'm sure your findings are correct. We're most grateful to you.'

'Did you find anything else in the samples?' asked Neef. He was irked at how keen the meeting had been to dismiss the virus theory.

'Like what?' asked Farro-Jones.

'Like fibrous or particulate matter.'

'A good point,' said Lennon, nodding his head.

'No, nothing,' replied Farro-Jones.

'Nothing that looked like it might have been the carcinogen?'

'No.'

'Then we're no further forward,' Neef persisted.

'I'm afraid not,' agreed Farro-Jones.

'Do you have a point to make, Dr Neef?' asked Lennon.

'I'm sure we're all relieved that there was no sign of a new virus, but on the other hand there was equally no sign of any particulate matter either. We're no nearer knowing what gave the girls cancer, so we can't afford to dismiss either notion completely. It's essential that we keep an open mind.'

'As long as keeping an open mind doesn't mean coming out with scare stories to the press!' said the RHA member who had had the run-in with Pereira. Neef now knew him to be Peter Baroda. He had asked one of the men standing beside him after Pereira left. It sounded as if Baroda had plenty of support in the room.

'We must avoid unnecessary alarm,' said a woman's voice.

Neef didn't recognize who it was but it made him wonder uncharitably if anyone had ever defined what *necessary* alarm was. He saw the woman's comment as part of the background noise of British public life, like calls for 'a full public inquiry' and demands that 'something be done'.

'Talking of unnecessary alarm, ladies and gentlemen,' said Lennon, 'I will be seeing the press after our meeting. I will have to inform them that there are now five recorded cases and give them details of who they are, but I see no point in mentioning anything about the virus theory as Dr Farro-Jones seems to have put that to rest for the moment at least. On the other hand, I'll have to bite the bullet and admit that we've not as yet been able to identify the source of the problem. I will, of course, stress that our enquiries are continuing with vigour.'

Neef left the meeting feeling confused and apprehensive. Despite his protests that the virus theory should not be dismissed out of hand, he felt that those attending the meeting had little heart for it. They simply didn't want to consider anything new. Even Lennon, who had earlier seemed open-minded enough to investigate it, had seized on Farro-Jones's negative findings of the day as a basis for dismissing the notion. He felt that a lot of heads were comfortably in the sand.

David Farro-Jones caught up with him as he walked back to his car. 'We have to talk,' he said. 'I've had a change of heart.'

'How so?'

'I think there's something in the virus theory after all.'

'What did you see in there that changed your mind?'

'Something on Lennon's slide.'

'What?'

Farro-Jones hesitated for a moment before saying, 'I don't want to talk here in the street.'

'Stop off at St George's on the way back. We can talk in my office.'

Farro-Jones nodded. 'See you there.'

'He followed Neef back to the hospital and parked parallel to him outside the unit. Neef led the way inside and ushered Farro-Jones into his office.

'I realized something today at the meeting that scared me greatly,' said Farro-Jones. 'It made me totally reconsider my opposition to the idea of a new virus being on the loose. In fact, I now think I even know where it might have come from.'

'What!' exclaimed Neef.

'When Lennon was running us through his overheads of the patients I noticed that Melanie Simpson lived in Langholm Crescent.'

'So what?' asked Neef, feeling let down.

'The Menogen Research labs are in Langholm Road, just round the corner.'

'Neef's mouth fell open. 'My God, you're suggesting that the Simpson girl was infected by something that escaped from Max Pereira's lab?'

'Making new viruses is Menogen's business,' said Farro-Jones.

'Yes but they're transport vectors . . . they're not—'

'As I said before, the more efficient the vector, the greater the risk – and the risk is that they'll cause cancer.'

'Yes but—'

'It could be coincidence,' conceded Farro-Jones. 'But I think I should continue hunting for a virus in the meantime. What do you think?'

'Of course,' replied Neef. 'But I think it would be most unfair to say anything about this until there's any proof. Damn it, it was Max Pereira who brought up the idea. He'd hardly do that if he thought there was any chance of something having escaped from his own lab. Apart from that, I've seen the Menogen operation. It's well run; they're constantly under inspection and scrutiny.'

'You can always hide something,' said Farro-Jones. 'And Menogen are under a lot of pressure to succeed.'

'Shit,' sighed Neef.

'But you're quite right,' said Farro-Jones. 'We shouldn't say anything until there's some proof. I don't think anyone else has noticed the geographical factor yet so that gives us some time. I'll get a team of technicians on to the scanning work.'

When Farro-Jones had left, Neef went out into Ann Miles's office and found a street directory on the shelf behind her chair. He took it back into his own office and looked up Langholm Crescent. He made a little sketch of its relativity to Langholm Road and, after checking the number of Melanie Simpson's house from the summary notes Lennon had handed out, he added a cross to his sketch. He was doing this when a knock came to the door.

'Come.'

Eve put her head round the door. 'Bad time?' she asked.

'Of course not. Come on in.'

'The press briefing finished ten minutes ago. I've come to see Neil.'

Neef nodded. 'How did the briefing go?'

'Lennon told us about the new case and more or less admitted they were no further forward. He appealed for our understanding and cooperation but he didn't mention anything about Max's virus idea. Does that mean it's a non-starter?'

'People didn't like it,' said Neef. 'I don't think they liked Max, either, if truth be told. David Farro-Jones examined a number of samples from Charlie Morse and found no evidence of a new virus.'

'I see,' said Eve. 'So we don't have to evacuate the city after all. What's that you're doing?' She was looking at the sketch on the desk.

'I . . .' Eve held his gaze. 'I . . .'

'You don't want to tell me, right?'

'It's not that I don't want to tell you. It's just that you're a journalist and that makes things difficult.'

'I can't be trusted?'

'Oh, I didn't mean that. It's just that—'

'You don't have to explain. This is always going to come between us, isn't it?'

Neef shook his head and said softly, 'I don't want it to. I really don't. David noticed something at the meeting today. There may be nothing to it but we have to consider the implications.'

Eve's eyes widened as Neef explained the reason for his sketch. 'That is absolute dynamite!' she exclaimed.

'It is also absolutely confidential.'

'Of course. My God! I hope he's wrong.'

'Believe me, so do I. Max Pereira's not the most charming man on earth but I do think he's honest and responsible when it comes to work. When he told me about the rules and regulations he had to comply with, he wasn't complaining. He just wanted them applied universally to all researchers.'

Neef's phone rang and Eve took this as her cue to leave. She gave a slight wave of her hand as she closed the door.

'Neef.'

'Dr Neef, my name is Jean Langtry. Dr Pereira asked me to call you. He said it was quite urgent. I understand you need information about licensing procedures.'

'Yes, Miss Langtry, good of you to call. What do we do?'

Neef made a series of notes on his desk pad as Jean Langtry spoke. He finished by thanking her for her help.

'Good luck, Doctor.'

Neef called Tim Heaton's office but there was no reply. He tried his home number, which he extracted from his desk file.

'Tim? It's Michael Neef. I need your help. I want the hospital to make an emergency application for permission to use a new Menogen vector on one of my patients. I've got all the details you need for the application.'

'It's Sunday evening, Michael.'

'Sundays are running out altogether for my patient, Tim,' said Neef. 'This just might help him.'

Heaton succumbed to the moral blackmail, as Neef felt sure he would. 'Oh, all right,' he said. 'I'll come in, but what's to say this vector will be any more successful than the other ones?'

'I don't know,' confessed Neef.

'All right,' conceded Heaton. 'Unfair question.'

Neef made out a clearer summary of what was required from his notes and used Ann Miles's word-processor to type it up for Tim Heaton's benefit. He added patient details from Neil Benson's file and put the two sheets of paper in a large manila envelope. He walked over to the admin block and left it outside Tim Heaton's office. He knew there was no chance of the application going off that night, but, if Heaton became familiar during the course of the evening with all the requirements, it should be ready to go off on Monday without fail. Neef returned to the unit and sought out Eve. She was still with Neil.

He watched for a moment through the glass door. Eve had her back to him. He could see that she had one of Neil's fire engines on the bed beside her and it looked as if she was telling him a story about it. Neil was listening but he didn't have the energy to do anything more than that. His days of playing with his beloved fire engines were coming to an end. His medication had dulled all his senses as well as the pain. Neef swallowed and took a breath before going into the room. 'Hallo, you two,' he said cheerfully. 'What are you up to?'

'Reading a story,' said Eve brightly, responding to Neef's Mr Cheerful act.

'About a fireman by any chance?'

'Who else?' Eve smiled. 'His name is Maxwell. Maxwell Gunn.'

'And what's Maxwell been doing today?'

'He's been rescuing a cat named Dolly from a tall tree overhanging a river.'

'My Dolly?' exclaimed Neef.

'Yes, but don't worry, she's all right. Maxwell brought her down safely on his turntable ladder.'

'Thank goodness for that,' said Neef. 'I didn't think Neil knew I had a cat named, Dolly,' said Neef.

Neil nodded his head slowly.

'He does,' said Eve. 'I told him. Dolly often figures in our stories.'

'In that case, it's about time Neil met the real Dolly. What d'you think.'

Neil nodded his head slowly again.

'As soon as you're feeling a bit better, Tiger. I'll . . . we'll take you to see Dolly. Get some rest now. I'll see you in the morning.'

Eve followed Neef out of the room and back to his office. 'He's fading away,' she said.

'It's partly the medication,' said Neef. 'It makes him sleepy.'

'How long do you think he's got?'

'A few weeks, not much longer.'

'Do you know what I did when you left for the hospital this morning?' asked Eve.

'Tell me.'

'I went to church.'

Neef felt uncomfortable. He didn't know what to say.

'It's the first time since I left school, I think, apart from weddings and funerals and the like. I prayed for Neil. Are you religious?'

'No,' replied Neef.

'Neither am I, really. It just seemed like a good idea at the time, as they say. I suppose when you want something badly enough you do all sorts of strange things, try anything.'

'I suppose,' said Neef. He changed the subject because he didn't want to say anything about Pereira's new vector just yet. He didn't want to raise false hopes. 'I'm hungry,' he said. 'How about you?'

'A bit.'

'There's a good Chinese restaurant in Ayton Road. What do you say?'

'I'm game,' said Eve.

The restaurant was quiet on a Sunday evening. There was only one other couple in the place. The tinkle of Chinese music was pleasantly muted. Neef had a gin and tonic and Eve a Campari as they looked at the menu. 'What do you recommend?' asked Eve.

'Anything involving the black-bean sauce.'

'I'll try it,' said Eve. She glanced at her watch and Neef noticed.

'I'm sorry,' he said. 'Have I got you here under false pre-tences?'

'No, nothing like that,' said Eve. 'But I do have my story to write and not just for the *Citizen*.'

Neef raised his eyes.

'One of the nationals liked my first piece on the cancer scare so they've invited me to do a second. I want it to be good. This could be a big opportunity.'

'Is that what you'd like,' asked Neef, 'to work on one of the nationals?'

'I'd like to *edit* one of the nationals,' said Eve, laughing.

'You're ambitious,' said Neef. 'Like Max.'

Eve's smile faded a little. 'There's nothing wrong with that, is there?' she asked.

'Of course not, as long as it doesn't drive you too hard.'

They lapsed into silence for a few moments.

'Do you think ambition's been driving Max too hard?' asked Eve quietly.

Neef screwed up his face and replied, 'He's quite open about what he wants from life and he works extremely hard to achieve it. What worries David Farro-Jones is that we don't know how many corners he cuts, how many short cuts he and Menogen are prepared to take.'

'Would you buy a used car from Max Pereira?' added Eve.

'That sort of thing,' replied Neef.

'But you said yourself there are lots of inspections and safeguards in the business Max is involved in,' said Eve.

'There are,' agreed Neef. 'I saw the place the other night. I was impressed. It struck me as being a well-run organization. Max has a bee in his bonnet about the universities not having to comply with all the regulations that commercial concerns do. He thinks they get off lightly.'

'Do they?'

'Frankly, yes.'

'What if the worst should happen and it turns out that the

cancer outbreak has been caused by a new virus from Max's lab? What then?'

'Max will be thrown to the wolves,' replied Neef.

'As simple as that? No mitigating circumstances?' said Eve. 'His work seems to have saved young Thomas Downy's life from what I hear.'

'None,' said Neef firmly. 'If Menogen is shown to be responsible for Melanie's death and the others, they can close it down and melt the key as far as I'm concerned.'

'Don't get me wrong, Michael,' said Eve, 'and I know you're going to think me insensitive, but if the worst should turn out to be true would you release me from our agreement and allow me to break the story before anyone else gets it?'

'I suppose,' said Neef. 'But that's not going to happen.'

'Of course not.'

The food arrived.

Neef's first call on Monday morning was from Frank MacSween. He was calling from home. 'Betty and I are just about to leave for the Lake District,' said MacSween. 'I've decided to take some leave. Get away for a bit. The Pathology work's being transferred to Uni for a while.'

'I'm glad you're taking a break,' said Neef. 'It'll do you both the world of good.'

'I'm really calling to ask you to do me a favour.'

'Shoot,' said Neef.

'The Pathology Department at University College are giving Eddie Miller a retiral dinner this evening. I won't be going but I'd be grateful if you would go along in my place. I don't think too many people are going from St George's, if any, and it'll be a shame if there's a poor turnout. I know he's leaving under a bit of a cloud but, if there's any profession that excuses a bit of an affair with the bottle, it's pathology. I've known Eddie a long time. He was good in his day.'

'If that's what you want,' said Neef.

'You do know him?'

'Not that well,' replied Neef. 'But we've met a few times over the years.'

'The dinner's being held in the Connaught Rooms at the university. Black tie, seven thirty for eight.'

'I'll be there. I'll pass on your good wishes to Eddie.'

'Do that,' said MacSween.

'Damnation,' said Neef as he put down the phone and Ann Miles came in with some papers.

'Problems?' she asked.

'The last time I looked at my dinner jacket it looked like a popular holiday destination for moths.'

'Hire one,' said Ann.

'It's finding the time,' said Neef.

'Tell me your size. I'll call the place my husband uses. They'll deliver it.'

'Great,' said Neef. He told Ann what he wanted.

Tim Heaton telephoned to ask if Neef had seen Mark Louradis's piece in the *Mail*. Neef replied that he hadn't.

'It's excellent,' said Heaton. 'They gave it a good half-page with diagrams to explain what the Menogen vectors were designed to achieve. This is exactly the kind of coverage St George's needs. It lets people know we're right at the cutting edge of medicine.'

'Good,' said Neef without emotion.

Neef arrived at the university at seven forty-five. The Connaught Rooms were on the third floor of the oldest building in the quadrangle and were used for all formal functions where an aura of academic dignity was seen as a desirable ingredient. The retirement dinner of an academic staff member was just such an occasion. The entrance hall itself was imposing, even intimidating, thought Neef, as he looked across to the uniformed man at the desk, the only living being beneath all the portraits of past chancellors and royal patrons. The man looked up from his paper, noted Neef's black tie and waved him on up with a 'Good evening, sir.'

'Evening,' replied Neef. He crossed the marble floor to the huge staircase leading up to the first floor. The steps were in white Italian marble and diverged in two directions after the first dozen so that they spiralled left and right up to the open first landing. High above the central well, a glass cupola allowed light to flood down during the day. At night, wrought-iron chandeliers did the job.

There were thirty to forty people in the Connaught Rooms when Neef finally got there. They were standing drinking sherry in a small area outside the main dining room. Waitresses, wearing black and looking as if they'd be more at home in a 1930s tearoom, circulated among the throng with sharp eyes and blank expressions, at all times on their guard against carelessly flung-out arms and sudden backward steps.

'Drink, sir?' asked one.

Neef accepted with a smile and looked round for a friendly face. MacSween had been right: there weren't many people here from St George's. As if sensing his solitude, David Farro-Jones came across with his wife Jane on his arm. Jane was as pretty as Farro-Jones was handsome. She was also charming.

'I didn't know you were coming, Michael,' said Farro-Jones.

'Hello Michael, haven't seen you for ages,' said Jane. 'I keep telling David we must have you to dinner.'

'That would be nice,' said Neef with a smile. 'Actually I'm here under false pretences. Frank MacSween asked if I'd come in his place. He's taking some leave. He took the death of his grandson hard.'

'Poor Frank,' said Jane.

'An absolute tragedy,' said Farro-Jones.

'Actually,' confided Jane, 'I think a lot of people are here under false pretences. I gather the Pathology Department will be glad to see the back of old Eddie. We're all here just to put a brave front on things.'

For Neef, the evening took on a surreal quality as they struggled through a dinner that was largely uneatable. The meat was tough, the vegetables mushy and the whole lot was cold because the kitchens were a very long way from the dining room. People pretended that nothing was amiss, not wishing to spoil things for Eddie on his last night. Complaints did not rise beyond exchanged glances and raised eyebrows. There was a lot of silent chewing.

The same series of glances and knowing looks carried on through the speeches as the dean praised Eddie's distinguished service to the university and the pathology department in particular. His selfless devotion to duty was held up as an example to all, especially the young, of whom there were none present, Neef noted. The eulogy culminated in the presentation of a clock to Eddie by the vice-principal and a bouquet of flowers to Eddie's wife, Trudy. Eddie, who had sat throughout the proceedings with downcast eyes and a beaming smile on his lips, got up to reply and almost toppled over backwards. He was drunk already. It was the waitresses' turn to exchange knowing looks. The diners waited with fixed smiles and buttocks clenched in embarrassment for Eddie to say something.

'Friends,' began Eddie, with a slur that confirmed the waitresses' suspicions. 'I dunno what to say.'

Tears of emotion ran down Eddie's cheeks as he launched into a thank-you speech that would have put an Oscar-winner to shame in terms of rambling length and boredom. Everyone was profoundly grateful when the vice-principal seized upon a pause in Eddie's delivery and started a chorus of 'For He's a Jolly Good Fellow'. People joined in with gusto, determined to make sure Eddie would not get another word in.

'Is it really over?' whispered Jane to Neef.

'Please God,' replied Neef.

People started to circulate and Farro-Jones took the opportunity of having a word with Neef about the virus hunt.

'Nothing yet,' he confided. 'But we've got all three electron microscopes working on it.'

'What have you told the staff?' asked Neef.

'I made the preps myself so no one knows that the samples came from Charlie. I just asked for a visual report on all viruses.'

'Good.'

'What are you two whispering about?' said a loud voice behind Neef, startling him. A heavy hand clamped down on his shoulder. It was Eddie.

'I'm not sure if you two know each other,' said Farro-Jones awkwardly.

'Don't tell me,' said Eddie, waving an unsteady finger at Neef. 'It's Oncology One, St George's . . . Neef.'

'That's right,' said Neef. 'We have met a couple of times before. Frank MacSween asked me to come along tonight and deliver his sincere apologies, Eddie. He and Betty have gone off to the Lake District for a bit of a break.'

'Poor Frank, losing his grandson like that,' slurred Eddie.

'Very sad,' agreed Neef.

'When are these buggers at public health going to trace the bloody source?' asked Eddie.

'They're not doing too well,' agreed Neef.

'Not doing well?' repeated Eddie with a theatrical raising of the eyebrows. 'A blind man on a foggy night could do better.'

'Can I tear you away for a minute, darling?' asked Jane Farro-Jones, seemingly appearing from nowhere, taking her husband's arm and pulling him gently to the side in a rescue mission. Neef, the only casualty of the manoeuvre, was left alone with Eddie.

'They've been totally unable to find out how the first patient contaminated herself,' said Neef.

'First patient?' slurred Eddie.

'Melanie Simpson,' said Neef, wondering why in God's name he was having this conversation.

Eddie tapped the side of his nose three times and shook his head. 'Not the first,' he said.

Neef felt goose pinples break out on the back of his neck but Eddie's speech was so slurred that there was a chance he might have misheard. 'I'm sorry?'

'It was me,' announced Eddie with a look of quiet triumph. 'I had the first patient.'

'What are you saying, Eddie?' asked Neef. 'You saw a case before Melanie Simpson?'

Eddie gave an exaggerated nod of the head. 'Certainly did.'

'Who?' asked Neef. Eddie started looking round for another drink. He was becoming bored. 'Who was this patient? When was this, Eddie?' insisted Neef.

'Few weeks ago.' Eddie was becoming more agitated at not being able to spot the source of his next drink.

Neef fought off the desire to pin him to the wall and choke the answers out of him. 'Why don't I fetch you a drink, Eddie?' he said pleasantly. His mind was racing. This was not going to be easy. Nobody wanted to talk to Eddie but the moment he left him alone someone was bound to feel duty-bound to join the guest of honour and the moment would have passed. He had to get the information out of Eddie now. He couldn't risk going to the bar; it would take too long. He glanced to the side and saw that the three people standing there had a small table beside them with drinks on it. The table stood in front of one of the marble support pillars. Neef took three steps round behind the pillar, dropped to his knees, reached round and lifted one of the drinks off the table. As he did so, he ran out of luck: the woman nearest him looked down and saw what he was doing. 'Well, really!' she exclaimed.

Neef shrugged awkwardly and rejoined Eddie as the woman related to her friends what had happened. Because it was university, Neef was relying on this being as far as things would go. Talk but no action was the norm. He pressed the drink into Eddie's hand.

'Thanks, Neefy old boy,' said Eddie.

'Eddie, did I understand you right? There was a case before Melanie Simpson and you reported it as bronchial carcinoma at the time?'

'Not officially. Officially it was lung congestion but I saw the tumours. I spotted them.'

'Who was this patient, Eddie?'

'Girl.'

'A girl? Young? Melanie's age?'

'About.'

'Why didn't you report the tumours, Eddie?'

Eddie took a drink and looked at Neef. 'Come on, Neefy,' he said. 'This is my party. I'm supposed to enjoy myself. Come and meet Trudy, my wife. Stood by me through thick and thin.' He made to move forward unsteadily.

Neef stopped him gently. 'Just tell me why you didn't report the tumours, Eddie?'

'Let me tell you something, Neefy,' confided Eddie. 'The secret of a quiet life is . . . tell them what they wanna hear. That's it, my son . . . tell them what they wanna hear. He didn't wanna hear anythin' 'bout tumours so I didn't report anythin' 'bout tumours. Nice and simple. Didn't make any difference.' Eddie gave a giant hiccup before continuing his slurred monologue. 'Little kid was dead anyway. Wasn't gonna bring her back.'

'Who didn't want to hear anything about tumours, Eddie?'

Eddie looked at Neef as if he was simple. 'He didn't,' he exclaimed.

'Who's he, Eddie?'

'Excuse me old boy,' said a waspish, male voice behind Neef. This was accompanied by a tap on the shoulder. 'My wife says you took her drink. The bar's over there you know.'

'Piss off,' hissed Neef through gritted teeth and the man recoiled backwards. 'I say,' he exclaimed.

'What's this about you taking someone's drink?' inquired Eddie. He pushed Neef aside with his forearm and called to the waspish man, 'What's this, Harold? Let me get you all a drink. This is my party. No one goes without a drink at my party.'

Neef saw the moment slip away as Eddie lumbered towards the three people who were looking daggers at him. He felt acutely embarrassed and turned away. He walked over to the bar and bought himself a large gin and tonic, which he downed in two gulps.

'That bad?' said a voice at his shoulder. It was David Farro-Jones.

Neef shook his head but couldn't say anything.

215

'What you need is a wife like Jane,' said Farro-Jones. 'She's trained to rescue me from all such occasions.'

'I noticed,' said Neef.

'Come and join us.'

'Eddie says that Melanie Simpson was not the first patient,' said Neef.

'What?' exclaimed Farro-Jones.

'He says there was an earlier one but he didn't report it.'

'Why not, for God's sake?'

'He says someone didn't want to hear it.'

'Why? Why?'

'I couldn't get any real sense out of him. He's as pissed as a newt.'

'He's been permanently pissed for the last eighteen months,' said Farro-Jones. 'Are you sure he's not just talking rubbish?'

'Maybe,' conceded Neef. 'But I think we have to follow it up.'

'Absolutely,' agreed Farro-Jones. 'He said earlier he was coming in tomorrow to clear out his desk and make his last farewells. We should get hold of them then while he's relatively sober and see if we can get any sense out of him.'

'I'll come over about ten,' said Neef.

'What are you two plotting?' asked Jane Farro-Jones as she joined them and linked her arms through theirs.

'How to bring an end to this fun evening,' replied Farro-Jones in a stage whisper.

'Make it soon,' pleaded Jane.

Eddie was now being physically supported by two of his colleagues from the Pathology Department, one on either side. They brought him to the centre of the floor and the vice-principal commanded – in the loud voice that goes with being a vice-principal and driving a Volvo estate car – that everyone form a circle.

Strange hands were linked nervously and the dean led off the singing of 'Auld Lang Syne'. Eddie hung between his supporters like a boned chicken while a tide of academics swept in and out on him. All it needs is for him to throw up now, thought Neef.

But mercifully it didn't happen and the evening ended in general back-slapping, coat-donning and the sounds of 'Splendid evening!' through the marble halls. The air outside smelled good to Neef as he walked off into the night. He'd get a taxi soon, but right now he needed to be alone.

There was a note behind the door from Eve. She had come round to the cottage earlier but had found him out. She had left a copy of the newspaper carrying her story on the cancer scare. Neef berated himself for not having told Eve that he was going to Eddie's retirement dinner, but if he was honest with himself he would have to admit that it had not been entirely an oversight. He had been a little peeved about Eve having rushed off the previous evening to work on her story. He knew it was childish but he had felt the need to express his independence. Now, after the awful evening he'd just had, he no longer felt the need. He wished she was here.

He picked up the paper and settled down to read her work.

Fourteen

Neef had a management meeting first thing on Monday morning. There was very little to discuss, although an appeal for more night nurses was made by Carol Martin, the director of nursing services. Carol had been lobbying individual consultants over this for some weeks. Too much responsibility was falling on too few nurses, she maintained. Neef had promised his support and gave it. Heaton and the gangly Phillip Danziger said they would see what could be done.

Mark Louradis was congratulated by Tim Heaton on his article on gene therapy.

'Now that's what I call positive journalism,' said Heaton. 'It associates St George's with state-of-the-art research in the public perception. GPs will see that we're a go-ahead hospital. They'll be happy to refer their patients here.'

Neef noted that Louradis avoided eye contact with him throughout the meeting. It gave him some satisfaction to know that he felt some guilt about his behaviour in seeking publicity for himself. For Neef the time for anger was past. He philosophically accepted that some people were just made that way.

Heaton was particularly pleased that cancer-scare attention had been diverted from St George's to the Public Health Department, where it rightly belonged in his opinion. He brought up the subject and was in turn applauded for his firm stand over moving the Sunday press briefing.

'What did you think of the press coverage of the cancer scare by the way?' asked Heaton.

'Alarmist, for the most part,' said Carol Martin. 'You'd think the carcinogen was a slimy, green, scaly monster who hid up dark alleys to trap the unwary, to read some of these reports.'

'Might be easier if it was,' said Neef. 'At least we'd know what we're dealing with.'

'What did you think of the coverage, Michael?' asked Heaton.

'I suppose they portrayed the authorities as being less than brilliant but that's almost a national pastime these days. I didn't think anything was too unfair.'

'I thought they were very unfair to the public health people,' said John Marshall. 'They haven't got the easiest of jobs at the moment.'

'But the unpleasant fact of the matter is that they're no nearer establishing the cause of the outbreak today than they were immediately after the first report,' said Neef.

'That's not necessarily their fault,' said Marshall.

'I'm not saying it is,' countered Neef. 'In fact, I agree with you but it doesn't alter the fact. They're not making progress.'

Neef looked at his watch. It was nine thirty-five. He was due at University College at ten.

'Busy day, Michael?' asked Heaton, who had seen the gesture.

'Aren't they all?' Neef replied.

'Well, if no one has anything else to report . . .'

There was a general shaking of heads.

'Let's start the week.'

Heaton came over to Neef and told him that he had put the emergency-permission request in motion.

'I'm grateful,' said Neef.

'You genuinely believe this one could work?'

'I'm optimistic. I have to be.'

Heaton grinned. 'I suppose in your position you can't afford to be anything else or you'd go mad. It can't be easy but I think you said you'd had one success on the trial when I spoke to you last.'

'Thomas Downy,' said Neef. 'A cerebellar tumour that's been regressing quite remarkably. He's having another scan done this morning. I'll let you know how he's progressing.'

'Please do,' said Heaton enthusiastically. 'This sort of story would be the perfect follow-up to Mark's article. The successful application of gene therapy to cancer would put us at the forefront of medical science. St George's would be regarded as a centre of medical excellence all over the world. We'd be up there with the best of them. Money would flow in. Patients would be clammering at our gates.'

'Perfect,' said Neef in neutral tones.

'Seriously, Michael, if this gene-therapy business brings off a complete cure in this child's case, I think we must consider show-boating it to the press. The hospital needs good publicity. What do you say?'

Neef was amused that Heaton was collecting on his Sunday-evening favour so soon. 'I agree, Tim,' he said. 'If it's a complete cure and not just a remission I think we and Menogen deserve some attention.'

Heaton seemed taken aback that Neef had agreed so easily and without argument. 'Excellent,' he enthused. 'I'll have John Marshall make out a preliminary draft and send it over.'

It was five past ten when Neef entered David Farro-Jones's lab.

'Just in time for coffee, Michael.'

'Miller's not in yet?' asked Neef.

'I've phoned down a couple of times. No answer. Mind you, considering the state of him last night, it'll be a wonder if he wakes up at all!'

Neef smiled and said, 'I think the long and happy retirement the dean spoke of must be wishful thinking. He must be on a bottle a day.'

'More,' said Farro-Jones. 'He'll be lucky if he sees the year out.'

'How does his wife cope?'

'Trudy? I think she's waiting for Eddie to die so she can get on with her life, or what's left of it. They've got a son in New Zealand. She'll probably go out there.'

Farro-Jones's secretary came in with the coffee. 'Black, no sugar isn't it, Doctor.'

'What a memory,' said Neef. 'Thank you.'

'Marge puts elephants to shame,' said Farro-Jones.

'I'm not at all sure how to take that, Doctor,' said Marge. 'And me on a diet.'

Both men laughed and Marge left.

'Maybe we should go down to pathology and wait for him,' suggested Farro-Jones when they'd finished their coffee and had said everything that could be said about the nightmarish dinner.

'Good idea,' said Neef.

The Pathology Department at University College Hospital was much larger than that at St George's by virtue of the fact that it was used for teaching purposes. First-year medical students came there to complete their anatomy and physiology courses, so it had to have extensive lab space. Farro-Jones took a short cut to Eddie's office through the main dissection lab a long, low-ceilinged room with frosted-glass windows. It could accommodate forty students working in pairs. Neef wrinkled up his nose at the smell of formaldehyde.

'Anyone home?' asked Farro-Jones after knocking on Eddie's door. He pushed open the door and entered. Neef followed him inside.

'Not here yet,' said Farro-Jones.

'His jacket's here,' said Neef, finding it hanging on the back of the door.

'Maybe it's one he leaves here,' said Farro-Jones.

'His briefcase, too,' said Neef, pointing towards a black document case lying in the corner of the room next to the filing cabinet.

'Strange. Maybe he's saying his goodbyes.'

'Let's ask around, shall we?'

Neef knocked on a door along from Eddie's.

'Come,' said a voice with an Indian accent.

'I'm looking for Eddie Miller. Have you seen him this morning?'

'I saw him half an hour ago. Who are you please?'

Farro-Jones popped his head round the door and said, 'It's all right, Vijay, he's with me. We came to say goodbye to Eddie.'

'Ah, David. Eddie's around somewhere.'

'Is he okay?' asked Farro-Jones.

'A bit of a sore head, I think.'

'Thanks, Vijay. We'll keep looking.'

Neef and Farro-Jones worked their way round the entire department. Several people had seen Eddie but not in the last half-hour. They returned to Eddie's office and saw that his jacket and briefcase were still there. They decided to wait until he came back. Ten minutes passed with still no sign of Eddie.

'Come on, Eddie,' said Farro-Jones, looking at his watch. 'I've got work to do.'

'Let's have another look for him,' suggested Neef. 'Maybe he's wandering around having a last nostalgic look at the old place. We could split up and I'll meet you back here.'

'Beats sitting around,' agreed Farro-Jones.

Neef followed a clockwise route that took him first through the pathology teaching museum, a silent room full of polished mahogany and glass cases displaying the organs of man, ravaged by disease and malformation. He paused in front of a particularly damaged foetus and read the legend, 'Radiation Damage'.

A small, bent man wearing the uniform of a university servant sat at a desk at the head of the room. Neef said, 'I'm looking for Doctor Miller. Have you seen him?'

'I saw him earlier,' replied the man in a high-pitched asthmatic wheeze. 'About an hour ago.'

Neef continued through the museum and out along the corridor leading to the PM suite used by the hospital pathologists and the area forensic service. This was off limits to students, being financed by the hospital trust rather than the educational budget. He looked in. One pathologist was at work. She looked up from the cadaver she was dissecting and asked, 'Who are you?

Neef looked apologetically at the large red-headed woman with the florid face and scalpel in her hand. The fact that she didn't smile made him feel uncomfortable. 'I'm sorry for intruding,' he said. 'I'm Michael Neef from St George's. I'm looking for Eddie Miller.'

'He's not here,' said the woman, resuming work.

'No, indeed,' said Neef, quietly backing out through the door. He let out his breath in a sigh. Once again he was reminded that he didn't like pathology or what it did to the people practising it. The stress the woman was under had been almost palpable. No wonder Eddie had finished up the way he had.

Neef passed through the body-vault room with its rows of heavy fridge doors on either side. He paused for a moment, feeling a strange compulsion to open one of the doors and examine the contents but then he fought the notion as being ridiculous and walked on. It was this place; it had put him on edge. He had had enough of wandering around it. He remembered the route back to Eddie's office through the dissection lab and took it.

Halfway across the room, he came to a halt when he heard a metallic clunk. After a few seconds it came again. 'Is anyone there?' he asked. There was no reply. The sound came again and Neef started to move towards where he thought it was coming from. He was a consultant physician but he felt nervous in this place, almost like a medical student about to encounter dead flesh for the first time. The feeling irked him; he saw it as a weakness. But on the other hand he felt convinced something was wrong. He could feel it in his bones, although it was his skin that gave an outward sign with goose-flesh coming up on the back of his neck.

There was a partition screen at the head of the room. The sound was coming from behind it. He rounded it slowly and came upon a row of what looked like bath tubs. They were formalin tanks for the preservation of corpses being used by the class students. As Neef looked along the row a sudden metallic clunk above the end tank caused his heart to miss a beat. He looked up and saw that the vent window above it was not properly fastened. The wind was catching it and rattling it against its retaining rod. This had been the source of the sound.

Feeling slightly embarrassed at his nervousness, Neef walked to the end of the row and looked around for something to stand on in order to close the vent. There was nothing suitable. Maybe the corner of the tank, he thought but as he looked down at it a sudden flurry of bubbles broke the surface of the formalin and made Neef catch his breath. When they settled he found himself looking down into the pale, dead face of Eddie Miller. Another burp of bubbles erupted from Eddie's mouth. Air that had been trapped in his lungs was escaping to the surface.

'Jesus Christ,' whispered Neef, unable to take his eyes off the awful sight. The dean's words, 'a long and happy retirement', sprang to mind like some hellish joke.

Neef went quickly in search of Farro-Jones and told him what he'd found. They returned to the scene together.

'Christ,' said Farro-Jones. 'What a way to go. But how?'

Neef looked up at the flapping vent, as the wind caught it again. He said, 'Eddie must have climbed up to fasten it and lost his footing. He probably fell backwards into the tank and hit his head on the end.'

Farro-Jones nodded. 'What awful luck,' he said.

'Where does this leave us?' asked Neef.

'Still wondering if what Eddie said was true,' said Farro-Jones.

'Right,' said Neef. 'It would have been nice to confront him when he was sober. I can't think why he would have made up something like that, even if he was stoned out of his skull.'

'No,' agreed Farro-Jones.

'Well,' said Neef, looking down at the floating corpse. 'We'll never know now.'

'Why don't I take a look through Eddie's PM records?' suggested Farro-Jones. 'I could see if there were any likely candidates for what he was claiming. He didn't give a name I suppose?'

'No, I kept asking him,' said Neef, 'but all I could get out of him was that it was a girl around Melanie Simpson's age.'

'That should be enough,' said Farro-Jones. 'It's worth a try.'

It was after lunchtime before Neef could return to his unit, having answered all the questions the police had put to him and completed the necessary paperwork in the form of a university hospital incident form. Farro-Jones asked him if he wanted to go to lunch but he declined, saying that too much of the day had been wasted already. Lawrence Fielding was waiting to see him when he finally got back.

'Take a look at these,' said Fielding excitedly. 'They're Thomas Downy's latest scans.'

Neef saw immediately why Fielding was excited. Thomas's tumour was down to the size of a pea. 'Absolutely bloody marvellous,' said Neef.

'To be quite honest,' said Fielding. 'I didn't really think this would happen. I hoped it would work of course, but I didn't really believe it. But now . . .'

Neef smiled and asked,' What about the others?'

'A disappointment, I'm afraid. Not one of them's shown any signs of improvement at all. I have to say again that I think we should return all of them to either conventional therapy or Antlvulon where appropriate.'

'All right,' said Neef. 'Let's not delay any more. Let's do just that.'

'You don't have to confer with Max Pereira or the management board?'

'No, the patients' welfare is my province and I say we count our blessings on this one. We've had one success and four failures . . . but what a success.'

Fielding smiled. 'At this rate,' he said. 'The tumour will be totally destroyed by next week. I understand Thomas's parents will be here this afternoon. Would you like to speak to them?'

'You do it,' said Neef. 'It's not that often we get the chance to impart some good news round here.'

'Thanks,' said Fielding. 'It's just so bloody good.'

Neef grinned. This was the first time he had ever heard Lawrence Fielding swear. 'Max Pereira has come up with a new vector. He thinks it might help Neil Benson. The hospital's applying for an emergency licence so we can use it.'

'I see,' said Fielding. His eyes betrayed his doubts.

'I know,' sighed Neef. 'It's a bit late in the day for Neil, but I'm still going to try.'

Fielding nodded. 'Right you are.'

'I haven't told Eve yet. I didn't want to raise false hopes. She's going through enough as it is over Neil.'

'I'll remember,' said Fielding.

'Any word from Kate Morse?'

'I spoke to her this morning. She was very down. I don't think Charlie's got long to go.'

'Maybe that's for the best,' said Neef.

'There's a rumour going around that a staff member died up at Uni College this morning,' said Fielding.

'Word gets around,' said Neef. 'It was Eddie Miller, the pathologist. He was closing a window in the dissection lab when he slipped and fell back into a vat of formaldehyde.'

'My God.'

'I was at his retirement dinner last night. He only came in to pick up a few personal belongings this morning,' said Neef.

'You never know what's round the corner, do you?' said Fielding.

Neef phoned Farro-Jones just after four to ask if he'd had any luck with the hunt for a virus.

'I'm afraid not,' said Farro-Jones.

'So Menogen are in the clear?'

'Not exactly. Just because we haven't found a new virus in the conventional sense doesn't mean to say that there isn't something there.

'I don't understand,' said Neef.

'It could be a different form of infectious particle.'

'Like what?'

'I was thinking of prions when I said it,' said Farro-Jones. 'As you know, those things are implicated in BSE – or mad-cow disease as our friends in the press like to call it – and of course in its so-called human equivalent, Creutzfeldt-Jakob disease . . .'

'I know *something* about prions, David, although, of course, they're more your speciality than mine but—'

'What I'm saying, Michael,' Farro-Jones, interjected, 'is that BSE is an infectious condition for which no bacterium or virus has ever been found. All right, we know that these prions – these proteinaceous infectious particles – can't be seen under a microscope, can't be cultured artificially. But they're there all right. And current thinking has it that a prion is responsible for BSE, CJD and the one they find in sheep—'

'Scrapie.'

'Precisely.'

'You're not saying that Max Pereira's created one of these things in the lab and it's got out, are you?'

'That's a bit science-fictionish,' said Farro-Jones. 'But when we play around with DNA in test tubes, even with all the precautions we take, we're really not a hundred per cent sure what's going on. That's the nature of research by definition, I suppose. You're constantly probing the unknown.'

'My God,' sighed Neef. There would be no way of tracing something like that back to the guilty lab either, I suppose?'

'No.'

'Do you really believe that could have happened?'

'The regulations are good, but, when you add commercial pressures and ambition to the equation, you've got a dangerous cocktail.'

'I suppose,' said Neef. 'Will you keep looking?'

'One more day,' said Farro-Jones. 'Apart from anything else, we can't take any more samples from Charles Morse. He's on the final furlong, I'm afraid.'

'So I hear,' said Neef. 'I don't suppose you've had a chance to look at Eddie Miller's post-mortem records?'

'Not yet. We wasted so much time with the police and form-filling this morning, I'm still trying to catch up on the day. I'll get on to it as soon as I can.'

Neef put down the phone, rested his elbows on the desk and rubbed his eyes. When he opened them again, Eve was standing there. 'I did knock,' she said. 'Am I welcome or are you still trying to avoid me?'

'I was not trying to avoid you,' insisted Neef, getting up and coming round to meet her. He kissed her lightly. 'I had to go out to a retirement dinner last night. It was a sort of last-minute thing. I went in place of Frank MacSween. It was a nightmare and to compound things the guest of honour took a header into a vat of formaldehyde this morning and killed himself.'

'You're serious?' exclaimed Eve.

''Fraid so. I spent most of the morning with the police.'

'Why you?'

'I found him,' said Neef. 'I went up there this morning to ask him about something he said last night.'

'How awful for you.'

Neef nodded and said, 'It wasn't very pleasant. Been to see Neil?'

Eve nodded. 'He's not very well today,' she said. 'The nurse told me he was sick a lot last night.'

'I heard.'

'But he still wanted a story. Maxwell Gunn was at the docks today, saving Captain Cod's fishing boat after it caught fire. Captain Cod was so grateful he gave Maxwell a big fish to take back to the fire station for his tea . . .' Eve looked away to the side and removed a tissue from her handbag. She held it briefly to her face before turning back to face Neef with an almost defiantly brave look.

Neef felt a lump come to his throat. 'Maybe we could go home,' he suggested softly.

'That would be nice,' said Eve.

'You didn't say what you thought of my story,' said Eve later as they lay together. Rain had just started to patter against the cottage windows and Dolly had paused at the bedroom door to look in on her way from the hall to the kitchen. She glanced disapprovingly at them before continuing.

'I thought it was good,' said Neef. 'Factual and not too fanciful.'

'Praise from Caesar,' said Eve. 'The paper liked it.'

'The national?'

'Yes. I think they might offer me a job on the staff.'

'What would that mean if they did?'

'Leaving the *Citizen*. Probably moving away.'

'I see. How soon?'

'They haven't offered me one yet,' protested Eve. 'I've only filed the one story.'

'But if they did?'

'Almost immediately, but don't worry. I wouldn't consider going anywhere while Neil still needs me.'

Neef grunted and said, 'I wasn't going to tell you this but now I'm going to on the grounds that I can't carry everything on my shoulders alone. Someone told me that not so long ago.'

Eve smiled and said, 'Obviously a lesson learned.'

'Max Pereira has come up with a new virus vector that he thinks might help Neil. Menogen has no chance of clearing it through the usual channels so the hospital's making an emergency application for a licence to use it. It was lodged today.'

'Michael, that's wonderful!' exclaimed Eve, sitting bolt upright.

Neef put a finger on her lips. 'Not so fast,' he said. 'It really is very late in the day for Neil. The odds are still stacked heavily against him . . . and us. Apart from that, the vector itself may not work. Four out of five didn't work in the official trial.'

'But it worked for Thomas Downy,' said Eve.

'Yes, it did.'

'Why weren't you going to tell me?'

'I didn't want to see you hurt by raising your hopes and then seeing them dashed again if the therapy failed.'

'I'm glad you told me,' said Eve, putting her head back down on the pillow. 'We should share everything where Neil's concerned. He means so much to both of us. Do you think you'll get permission?'

'I don't see why not,' replied Neef. 'It's just a question of how long it takes to come through.'

'I'm willing to bet that you feel better already for having told me that,' said Eve.

'You're right,' said Neef. 'I do.'

'Anything else you'd like to share with me while I'm here?' She pointed to her shoulder. 'It's not broad but it's very absorbent.'

'Lots,' smiled Neef. 'David didn't find any sign of a new virus in the samples they were examining.'

'Does that mean that Max is in the clear?'

'I thought so but David brought up the possibility of a new kind of infectious particle that doesn't show up under the microscope.'

'So the suspicion remains?'

'I'm afraid so but I'm reluctant to believe Max would deliberately do anything dangerous or irresponsible.'

'It's a difficult situation if Menogen can neither be cleared or convicted,' said Eve. 'People will think, no smoke without fire.'

'That's why we've kept this to ourselves,' said Neef. 'It wouldn't be fair to Menogen to point out the geographical connection. People would jump to just that conclusion.'

'Is David going to continue with the search?'

'For one more day. It looks like they're not going to come up with anything.'

'Anything else bothering you?'

'What is this?' said Neef with mock protest. 'The Spanish Inquisition?'

'This is for your benefit,' insisted Eve. 'I'm teaching you to share your troubles. It's good for you.'

'I didn't tell you why I went up to Uni College Hospital this morning.'

'No, you didn't. Why?'

Neef told Eve about Eddie Miller's retirement dinner and

Miller's assertion that he had seen an earlier case than Melanie Simpson.

'What?' exclaimed Eve. 'But that would put a totally different complexion on everything.'

'It would,' agreed Neef.

'But he died before you could quiz him about it?'

'Right, but there was probably nothing to his story. I couldn't get a name out of him and he seemed more interested in convincing me there was some kind of conspiracy against him. It was probably just the paranoid ramblings of an old drunk. David's checking Eddie's records just in case there should be anything there.'

'Anything else you'd like to confess to?' asked Eve.

'I think you've got absolutely everything out of me,' said Neef.

'And don't you feel better for it?'

'Actually, I think I do,' said Neef. 'Do you have to go home tonight?'

'Not if you don't want me to,' said Eve.

'I don't.'

Max Pereira came into the unit on the following afternoon and was delighted to see the improvement in Thomas Downy's CT scan.

'Lawrence took this yesterday,' said Neef.

'It's doing the business,' said Pereira wearing an ear-to-ear grin.

'It's damned nearly done the business,' said Neef. 'It's going to be all gone by next week.'

'They should all have been like this,' said Pereira, shaking his head. 'I've checked out the other four vectors till I'm blue in the face and they're okay. So why didn't they work? That's what I want to know.'

Neef shook his head and said, 'There are more things in heaven and earth, Horatio, than are dreamt of in your philosophy.'

'Can I take that as a don't know?' asked Pereira.

'You can,' said Neef.

'How's your public health problem?' asked Pereira. 'Have these bozos come up with the virus yet?'

'They didn't take too kindly to your suggestion,' said Neef.

'That guy Lennon couldn't find his dick in his pants,' said Pereira. 'If we'd had an electron microscope I would have looked for you. Didn't anyone bother?'

Neef felt uncomfortable. 'Yes,' he replied. 'David Farro-Jones had a good look at lung samples taken from Charlie Morse.'

'And?'

'Nothing, I'm afraid.'

'Shit. It's got to be a virus. I'm tellin' you, man.'

'For what it's worth, I think you're right,' said Neef carefully. He was watching Pereira for any sign of self-consciousness. 'But it's much harder to prove than to say.'

'Don't see why,' said Pereira.

Neef wondered about the man facing him. He obviously didn't know about Melanie Simpson's house being so close to the Menogen labs, and the fact that he kept pushing the virus idea suggested that he hadn't considered for a moment that his own lab might have been responsible for the creation of a new and deadly one. Or was Pereira just an incredibly good actor? Maybe his self-confidence came from knowing that no one could actually trace the problem back to Menogen. Neef didn't want to believe that but he couldn't entirely dismiss the notion either.

'I brought these,' said Pereira. He brought out two glass vials from his battered briefcase.

'The new vector?'

'Yeah. You might as well keep them here in the fridge for when you get permission, then you'll be able to get a quick start on your kid.'

'That was thoughtful,' said Neef.

'I suggest you keep one in the unit and one down in Pharmacy as a back-up, same as last time.'

Neef smiled wryly as he recalled the broken vial in theatre.

'Will do.'

Pereira left and Neef was torn by mixed emotions about the man. It was so easy to get uptight about his general rudeness and lack of sensitivity but, on the other hand, he was usually just saying what he felt was true without pausing to edit it it for social nicety. It made him realize how seldom other people actually did this.

The phone rang and interrupted his train of thought. It was Tim Heaton.

'I've got some bad news, I'm afraid.'

'Just what I don't need,' said Neef, wearily. 'Tell me.'

'Your application for an emergency gene-therapy licence has been blocked.'

'What?' exclaimed Neef, feeling as if his head was about to explode. 'Why?'

'It had to go before a sub-committee of the Regional Health Authority before I could submit it. I thought they would rubber-stamp it but I was wrong. They turned it down, refused to endorse it.'

'Our own bloody health board?' exclaimed Neef.

'They said an emergency application was not something to be made lightly. Menogen had already been granted considerable latitude in St George's. They wanted to see a full report on the first gene-therapy trial before they'd consider applying for any widening of remit. I'm sorry, Michael.'

'Jesus Christ,' said Neef. 'I've got the vector in the fridge. It could save Neil Benson's life and a bunch of old farts bleet about full reports and not asking lightly.'

'I really am sorry,' said Heaton.

'Was there more to it?' asked Neef.

'What d'you mean?'

'Are you telling me everything or was there more to it?'

There was a long pause that almost answered Neef's question before Heaton said, 'It was blocked by one member. The others would have passed it but for this one man who chose to make an issue of it.'

'Do you know his name?'

Another pause. 'If I tell you, you won't do anything silly will you?'

'I won't. I promise.'

'Peter Baroda.'

'Jesus Christ! It was personal!'

'What d'you mean?'

Baroda and Max Pereira had a bit of a run-in at the last public health meeting. They clearly didn't like each other. Baroda must have seen Pereira's name on the application. That's why the bastard blocked it.'

'That would be hard to prove,' said Heaton. 'But if that's the reason Baroda blocked the application, I agree with you. He's a bastard.'

'Oh Christ,' sighed Neef, as he saw Neil's last chance evaporate. 'What a world.'

'I'm sorry,' repeated Heaton. 'I don't have to remind you that there's no question of using the new vector without a licence.'

'No you don't.' replied Neef.

Neef was sitting with his head in his hands when Ann Miles came in with some letters to sign. 'Are you all right?' she asked.

'I'm fine,' said Neef.

'Coffee?'

'Please. And Ann?'

'Yes?'

'Would you see if Miss Sayers is in the unit and ask her to come along if she is?'

'Of course.'

Time seemed to stand still for Neef as he stared into space for the next thirty seconds or so. He heard Eve's voice as she returned with Ann.

'Duly summoned,' said Eve with a smile. 'He's a bit better today. What's the problem?'

The smile faded from Eve's face and her eyes filled with questions. 'Something's wrong, isn't it? Is it Neil?'

'The Health Authority refused to endorse the application for an emergency licence.'

Eve's mouth fell open. She shook her head in disbelief. 'But why?' she asked.

'Officially they didn't think it a good idea that we use any more Menogen vectors until they've assessed how the first trial turned out.'

'I see,' said Eve. 'And unofficially?'

'Max Pereira got up the nose of one of the board members at the last meeting with the public health people. This is him getting his own back.'

'He's letting a little boy die over something like that?' asked Eve, her eyes wide with disbelief.

'He probably doesn't see it that way,' said Neef. 'Max does have a habit of rubbing people up the wrong way.'

'Who is this board member?' asked Eve.

Neef looked at her suspiciously. 'You're not planning to do anything, are you?' he asked.

'Frankly, I'd cut his balls off if I thought it would help Neil, but it probably wouldn't, so no, I'm not planning anything. I'd just like to know.'

'His name's Baroda.'

'Peter Baroda?'

'You know him?'

'I know *of* him,' replied Eve. 'Big noise in local business circles, but he's not a doctor.'

'You don't have to be to sit on the board,' said Neef.

'Just a big wheel around town?'

'Something like that.'

'I can't believe this,' said Eve, shaking her head. 'We can't let something like this stop Neil getting a last chance. Do you have this new vector?'

'I do, but forget it. We can't use it without a licence.'

'Why not?' demanded Eve.

'Because it's not just a case of getting a piece of paper. The application has to be screened by experts who might spot some flaw in it that we can't see. That's what gene-therapy vetting is all about.'

'But Neil's going to die without treatment!' Eve protested.

'You don't have to point that out,' retorted Neef. 'Don't make things worse.'

Eve got up and looked at Neef as if she she had suddenly lost all respect for him. Without saying anything more, she turned on her heel and left.

Neef went home alone and sat looking out at the garden with a drink in his hand. He couldn't be bothered making himself anything to eat. He had little heart for anything. Despite knowing that he was right in what he'd said, he was tortured by the look of disgust on Eve's face before she left. In her eyes he was letting Neil die while he was in a position to save him. Maybe he should have played the hero so beloved by films, the man who said to hell with rules and regulations and did his own thing.

Crap! If everyone did that, there would be anarchy. Medicine would be full of charlatans injecting their latest elixirs and cure-alls without fear of comeback. It might have been different if he had the assurance of someone other than Max Pereira that the vector was safe, but, with suspicion hanging over Pereira, that was a non-starter.

After two drinks he fell asleep in the chair. When he woke up he found Dolly lying in his lap. He scratched her behind the ears and said, 'At least you haven't left me, little pal . . . or are you thinking of going too?'

Dolly was clearly in the mood for some attention. She rolled over in an invitation to Neef to scratch her tummy. The attention was cut short when the phone went.

'Neef.'

'It's Eve. I'm sorry, I shouldn't have stormed out like that. It was just . . . I was so . . .'

'I know,' said Neef. 'Let's forget it.'

'I've got some news.'

'What?'

'The application's going ahead after all.'

'What?' exclaimed Neef.

'I asked around my colleagues about Baroda and one of them came up with something useful. I've just used it.'

'What do you mean, you've used it?' asked Neef uneasily.

'I phoned Baroda and said I was doing a piece about saunas in the area being used as a front for brothels. I asked him if he'd like to tell me why his green Jaguar is regularly parked outside the Executive Sauna in Melton Place.'

'Good Lord.'

'In the end, we came to an arrangement. He withdraws his objection to the licence application and I develop amnesia over his car.'

'That's blackmail.'

'Yes.'

'Well done.'

'He said the application would be forwarded tomorrow. I said it would be nicer if it went off in the post tonight.'

'Frightening,' said Neef.

'What is?'

'You are, when you're in pursuit of something you want.'

'It's that kind of a world,' said Eve.

'You sound more like Max Pereira every day.'

'Anyway, I *am* sorry about my behaviour earlier. Will I see you tomorrow?'

'See you tomorrow,' agreed Neef.

Neef felt hungry all of a sudden.

Fifteen

Charles Morse died at eleven the next morning. Kate was with him. Neef was warned by Mark Clelland at University College that it was about to happen and took the opportunity of going over to be there for Kate if she needed him. When Kate came out of Charlie's room and saw Neef standing there she came forward, put her hands on his chest and allowed him to wrap his arms round her. Her tears flowed freely.

'I am so sorry, Kate,' Neef whispered.

Kate nodded mutely against his shoulder. Clelland acknowledged his presence with a nod of thanks.

A nurse ushered them into a small sitting room and brought tea. Neef poured it and Eve gradually composed herself. 'I still can't believe it,' she said. 'It's all happened so quickly.' She got up slowly and walked over to the window, holding the cup in her hand.

'Look at them,' she said. 'Buses, cars, taxis, people going about their business as if nothing has happened. But it has. My Charlie is dead. Why don't they realize?'

Neef got up to go towards her but Kate turned and stopped him. 'It's all right, Mike, really. I've been preparing myself for this. It doesn't look like it but I have. Just give me a few moments.'

Kate took slow steady breaths in an attempt to compose herself but she failed; the tears started to flow freely down her cheeks. 'Oh, Mike,' she sobbed. 'What am I going to do without him. He was everything to me, my whole reason for . . . being. What's the point in going on without Charlie?'

'I know, I know,' soothed Neef, wrapping his arm round her shoulders. 'You need time Kate. Hang in there.'

Kate eventually calmed down and took a sip of her tea. 'Are they any nearer to finding out how Charlie got his cancer?' she asked in a voice she was struggling to keep the tremble out of. She flicked at imaginary dirt on her knee with her fingernails.

Neef shook his head. 'No, it's still being investigated.'

Kate was silent for a while, then she said, 'For God's sake, tell me something happy.' She was half laughing, half sobbing.

Neef decided to take her at her word. 'Thomas Downy's cerebellar tumour has almost completely disappeared.'

'You're serious?'

'Yup. No doubt about it.'

'I take back everything I thought about Dr Pereira,' said Kate.

Neef nodded. 'Maybe we were a bit hard on him. Thomas Downy certainly owes his life to him.'

'Thank God there's still some good news in the world,' said Kate, trying to smile through her tears.

'Come on, I'll run you home,' said Neef.

When Neef got back to the unit, Ann Miles told him that Tim Heaton had been trying to get in touch. 'I thought he might be,' he replied. He returned Heaton's call, hoping that he could sound surprised when he had to.

'Michael, I've got some good news for you. Peter Baroda has apparently changed his mind. Your application has gone in after all.'

'It has?' exclaimed Neef, suddenly realizing that an acting career wasn't for him. 'That's marvellous.'

'I don't know why he changed his mind but he did, and that's the main thing.'

'Absolutely,' agreed Neef. 'Wonderful news.'

'Thought you'd be pleased. By the way, I forgot to ask yesterday about your brain-tumour patient. Still progressing satisfactorily?'

Neef screwed up his face. It wasn't Heaton who had forgotten to ask – as Heaton well knew: it was he who had forgotten to call Heaton and tell him.

'Tim, it completely slipped my mind in the excitement,' he said. 'Progress has been more than satisfactory. The tumour's shrunk to the size of a pea. With a bit of luck it'll be completely gone by next week.'

'Splendid!' said Heaton. 'John Marshall's been working on a press release I asked him to draft, just in case.'

'Fine,' said Neef.

'This is just what the hospital needs,' said Heaton. 'A cure for cancer.'

'Hang on . . .'

'It's a start,' said Heaton. 'You can't deny that.'

'I suppose not,' agreed Neef.

'I'll let you know the minute we hear anything about the application.'

Neef's last call of the day came from David Farro-Jones.

'I've been through Eddie Miller's autopsy records for the past three months, Michael. There's absolutely nothing there to back up his story.'

'That's a relief,' said Neef.

'I'll say,' agreed Farro-Jones.

'And still no new virus?'

'No new virus. We're going to have to stop looking. It's taking up too much time.'

Charles Morse's death sparked off a new round of newspaper attention the following day. CANCER DEATH TOLL RISES AS AUTHORITIES CONTINUE TO GROPE IN THE DARK, was the headline in the *Citizen* and this tack was followed by virtually all the others. One of the papers had managed to corner the local Member of Parliament and put him on the spot. He assured his constituents that he had written to the Health Secretary demanding immediate action and that he had assured him that appropriate steps were being taken.

During the course of the day, Neef was to discover what this meant. Lennon called to say that he was no longer in charge of the investigation. A team of specialists had arrived from the Department of Health to take charge. They counted among their number a scientist from Porton Down, the government's chemical and biological defence establishment.

'They've also removed Charles Morse's body,' said Lennon. 'They want to carry out their own pathological investigation.'

'Can they do that?' asked Neef.

'Under their terms of reference, they can do pretty much what they damned well please,' said Lennon. 'They've virtually taken over everything down here at Sutton Place and put an immediate ban on all press briefings. I dare say you'll be meeting them soon enough. A man named Klein is in charge.'

Two hours later Ann Miles announced that Drs Klein and Waters were outside.

'Send them in.'

'Klein, a tall thin man with a prominent Adam's apple that bobbed disconcertingly above a stiff Bombay-stripe shirt collar, appeared first and held out his hand. 'John Klein.' He came across as being neither friendly nor rude, just businesslike. His companion, a head shorter, with sloping shoulders and a downturn to the left side of his mouth that suggested a slight stroke in the recent past, introduced himself as Malcolm Waters. Neither man smiled.

'Thank you for seeing us at short notice, Doctor,' said Klein. 'As you probably know already, we're heading a team sent in by the Department of Health to deal with your problem.'

'I'd rather you didn't call it mine,' said Neef, hoping to lighten the atmosphere.

'Quite,' said Klein without a trace of humour. 'I meant you in the general sense of the area. We're just acquainting ourselves with all the local medical and scientific personnel who've been involved in the investigation so far. I understand from Dr Lennon that it was you who raised the possibility of a virus being responsible for the cancer outbreak.'

'One of my colleagues suggested it,' corrected Neef. 'I just passed it on.'

'This would be . . .' Klein paused while he thumbed through a sheaf of papers. 'Dr Pereira.'

'That's right.'

'What made Dr Pereira suspect a virus?'

Neef shrugged and said, 'Case pattern, I think; failure to establish any other cause.'

'If all else fails, blame a virus,' said Waters with a smirk.

Neef and Frank MacSween had often made the same kind of comment but somehow, coming from Waters, it seemed to Neef offensive. He took a dislike to the man.

'There were other things,' said Neef. 'But you'll have to ask Dr Pereira; he's the expert on viruses, not me.'

'But you actually got as far as looking for this supposed virus, I understand.' said Klein.

'Not personally,' said Neef. 'Another of my colleagues did some electron microscopy on lung samples taken from Charles Morse. He didn't find anything.'

'That would be . . .' Klein referred to his notes again. 'Dr Farro-Jones at the university medical school?'

'That's right.'

'Is Dr Pereira here at the moment?' asked Waters.

Neef said not. 'Dr Pereira's not actually on the staff. He's an employee of Menogen, a commercial biotechnology company. We're conducting a trial of their gene-therapy vectors at the moment.'

'We know,' said Waters. 'I just thought he might be here.'

'He only comes in a couple of times a week,' said Neef.

'Why was Dr Pereira's opinion sought in the first place?' asked Klein.

'The subject came up in conversation, I suppose,' said Neef

'In conversation?' said Klein. 'Do you often discuss confidential medical matters with outsiders, Doctor?'

'I regard Dr Pereira as a colleague. He's also an expert virologist who had an opinion to offer at a time when no one else did. I'm sure Dr Lennon valued his contribution too.'

'Dr Lennon is no longer in charge of this investigation,' said Klein coldly.

Neef chose not to comment.

'We must point out that there's a question of confidentiality at stake,' said Klein. 'Dr Pereira is an outsider.'

'I don't understand,' said Neef. 'How is this a problem?'

'The department has instructed us to enforce a total information ban while we conduct our inquiry. No member of the hospital or university staff will be permitted to say anything at all to the press, and you, of course, will no longer be at liberty to discuss any aspect of the problem with Dr Pereira.'

Neef had to consider for a moment before the full implication of what Klein was saying dawned on him. 'Or what?' he challenged.

'I sincerely hope it won't come to that, Doctor,' said Klein. 'It's all for the best. I'm sure the last thing either of us wants is to create unnecessary fear and alarm among the general public.'

Here we go again, thought Neef. 'So you think it's a virus too,' he said, giving Klein a jaundiced look.

'I think we can do without rash statements like that, Doctor.'

'Are you here to investigate the problem or cover it up?' asked Neef, his hackles rising.

'The department has only the public interest at heart,' said Klein.

'A comfort,' said Neef.

'I had hoped we might have a better working relationship than we appear to be developing,' said Klein.

'All you've done since you came in is tell me to keep my mouth shut,' said Neef. 'Why did you bother to come all the way over here to do that?'

Klein and Waters exchanged looks. 'We understand you have an association with a journalist,' said Klein. Klein made the word sound obscene.

'Miss Eve Sayers,' added Waters, referring again to his notes.

'So what?'

'We just wanted to make sure you understood how important the department considers confidentiality in this matter and how seriously it would view unwelcome publicity should it arise.'

'Just so there's no misunderstanding,' added Waters.

Neef had difficulty keeping rein on his temper but he managed. Instead of arguing, he looked at his watch and said, 'You'll have to excuse me. I'm rather busy.'

'We may want to speak to you again, Doctor,' said Waters.

'My secretary, Mrs Miles, will arrange an appointment,' said Neef curtly.

Waters gave a lopsided smile and Klein said, 'Thank you for your time, Doctor.' They left.

Neef picked up the phone and called David Farro-Jones. 'I've just been interviewed by the bloody gestapo,' he said.

'Klein and Waters? They're not exactly Morecambe and Wise, are they?'

'Pompous pricks,' said Neef. 'What exactly are they?'

'Klein's an epidemiologist from DOH. He's been given charge of the investigation. Waters is a virologist from Porton Down.'

'Looking for his next "defensive" weapon,' sneered Neef.

'Careful, the phone might be tapped,' said Farro-Jones in a joking whisper.

'Wouldn't surprise me,' said Neef. 'You didn't say anything about the Langholm connection, did you?' asked Neef.

'It wouldn't have been fair to Max,' said Farro-Jones. 'We didn't come up with any evidence so I saw no point in telling them. They may, of course, spot it themselves.'

'Well, if they alienate everyone as much as they have me they're going to have to spot just about everything for themselves,' said Neef.

'Let's wait and see how it goes,' said Farro-Jones.

Neef discovered that Eve had been in to visit Neil earlier. He had missed her but she had left a message inviting him over for dinner. If he couldn't make it, he was to leave a message on her answering machine. He could, so there was no need. It was something to look forward to for the next few hours while he waded through paperwork, most of which he regarded as unnecessary.

It was a pity, he thought, that someone in government couldn't have foreseen what the laudable-sounding phrase, 'accurately monitoring performance', actually meant in practice – assessments, appraisals, audits, endless form-filling. The practice of medicine was now very much secondary to the administration of it.

Neef arrived at Eve's apartment to find her hopping mad.

'What on earth's going on?' she asked.

'Hello to you too,' Neef replied.

'I'm sorry,' said Eve with a guilty look. 'It's just been such a frustrating day. I went down to Sutton Place to get an update on the story and there's been some kind of *coup d' état*. Lennon's not in charge any more and the men from the ministry are saying nothing. Has there been some dramatic new development?'

'Not that I know of,' said Neef. 'The men from the ministry, as you call them, were sent in in response to some MP calling for action. They came to see me this afternoon and warned me to keep my mouth shut, especially where you were concerned.'

'And people call this a free country,' said Eve. 'The more I see of government departments the more convinced I become that no one working in them actually knows what they're doing. As soon as the spotlight falls on them, their knee-jerk response is to find ways of turning it off, rather than be pleased to show the public how well they're dealing with things.'

'So what will you do?' asked Neef.

'I'll write a protest story about unnecessary government secrecy; the other papers will do the same and the powers that be will end up in a worse mess than if they'd spoken to us in the first place,' said Eve.

'I seem to remember hearing once that the government had powers to stop the press writing anything at all about certain things if the notion took them,' said Neef.

'They'd really have to have a good reason to slap a D-notice on us. They'd have to know a lot more about this thing that they've been letting on. Do they?'

'I don't think so,' said Neef. 'But I got the feeling *they* think it's a virus, too. One of the fun people I met today was from Porton Down.'

'The germ warfare place?'

'Defence establishment,' corrected Neef.

'Looking for new toys?' said Eve.

'My thought, too,' said Neef.

'You shouldn't be telling me this,' said Eve.

'We have an agreement as individuals,' said Neef. 'I'll tell you what I want.'

'They really did get up your nose, didn't they?'

'Yes.'

As they sat eating, Eve said, 'I won't be in to see Neil tomorrow. I told him today. He understands. I'll be there the day after.'

'You've been in every day since you started,' said Neef.

'And I'll be in every day until he gets better,' said Eve. 'It's just that tomorrow I have to do something rather special.'

'Oh?'

'The *Express* wants to talk to me face to face. I think they might offer me a job.'

'Wonderful,' said Neef. 'Just what you wanted.' His voice betrayed disappointment.

'Don't worry,' said Eve, softly. 'We'll work something out. Be happy for me?'

'Of course,' said Neef. 'Best of luck.'

Neef had hoped that the next day would bring permission to start Neil Benson off on Pereira's new vector, but it didn't. He asked Tim Heaton if he could hurry up proceedings with a few phone calls. Heaton said that he would see what he could do but there was still nothing by the end of the day. There was no word from public health about how the new regime was handling the investigation and Eve did not call to say how she had got on at her interview.

A thoroughly unexciting and unsatisfying day, thought Neef as he left the unit.

Dolly was the only one to benefit from Neef's quiet day. With nothing else on his mind, he remembered to go to the pet shop on the way home and pick up a supply of cat food and litter. He also bought her a new toy; her fascination with the orange fish had begun to wane.

If Neef had known what lay in store for him on the following morning he might have been well pleased to accept another uneventful day in lieu. He stopped off on the way to the hospital to pick up his morning paper and a picture on the front page of the *Express* caught his attention. He thought he recognized the building in the photograph. When he looked closer he saw that he was right. It was the Menogen Research building. Neef lifted the paper off the rack and opened it out. KILLER CANCER BUG ESCAPES FROM RESEARCH LAB, screamed the headline.

Unsure of which emotion to heed first – shock, a sense of betrayal, fear, alarm – Neef bought the paper and returned to his car to read the rest. The story was credited to, 'Our Special Reporter', and said that unnamed official investigators were considering the possibility that the recent outbreak of cancer cases had been caused by a virus escaping from the Menogen Research Laboratories in Langholm Road. It noted that the first victim had been Melanie Simpson, who had lived in Langholm Crescent. Official sources were refusing to confirm or deny the reports and had placed a news blackout on the story. It had come to the paper's attention, however, that one of the investigators brought in by the government was a virus expert from the Porton Down defence establishment. Steven Thomas, managing director of Menogen, had dismissed the claims as 'ludicrous'.

Neef felt sick in his stomach. Had Eve's career been so important to her that she'd done this? He felt stupid and hurt at the same time. He desperately tried to think of an alternative explanation. Was it conceivable that Klein and Waters had seen the Langholm Road – Langholm Crescent tie-up right away and had leaked the story to the papers? But why? They were actively trying to keep things *out* of the papers. Unless of course . . . they saw the opportunity to blame everything on Menogen and get public health and the Department of Health off the hook in one fell swoop.

Neef, surprised at the deviousness of his own thoughts, tried calling Lennon as soon as he got in. Not surprisingly the line was engaged. He asked Ann Miles to keep trying but it took about thirty minutes before he heard Lennon's West Country burr at the end of the line.

'I know the investigation's officially out of your hands,' said Neef. 'But there's something I'd really like to know.'

'Shoot,' said Lennon.

'When did Klein and Waters first see the connection between Menogen's address and Melanie Simpson's?'

'When they read it in the paper this morning,' said Lennon acidly.

It was what Neef had feared hearing. 'You're sure they didn't know?'

'Certain. Perhaps I can ask you something?'

'Go ahead.'

'Did you?'

Neef closed his eyes. It was a reasonable question in the circumstances and he felt embarrassed at having kept Lennon in the dark. 'I knew,' he confessed. 'But there wasn't a shred of evidence to suggest it was anything more than a coincidence. There still isn't.'

'Someone obviously disagrees with you,' said Lennon. The word, 'someone' was pronounced in a manner to suggest to Neef that Lennon thought he knew exactly who.

'What's happening?'

'I'm not sure I should tell you in the circumstances,' said Lennon.

'I see,' said Neef weakly. 'If it's any comfort, I'm as shocked as you are. I knew nothing about the story.'

'Klein and Waters are following up on it. I don't suppose they'll be too displeased if the public thinks it was them who worked this one out. It's almost too good for them to pass up, really.'

'I don't understand,' said Neef.

'If they play their cards right, they're going to come out of this looking like hotshots. They've cleared up the mystery within two days of arriving. They spotted something the bumbling local bloke – me – failed to see and Menogen will probably now be sacrificed to the flames of public anger.'

'But Klein and Waters didn't spot anything!' protested Neef. 'And the chances are that nothing' escaped from the Menogen labs at all!'

'You really don't understand much about human nature, do you Neef?' said Lennon just before he put the phone down.

Neef reflected on what Lennon had said. The man was right. He really didn't.

Neef's first post of the day arrived and with it permission to try Menogen's new vector out on Neil. He read the technical report that came with the official go-ahead and saw that both scientific reviewers had been enthusiastic about Pereira's vector. One had called the work 'brilliant', the other, 'highly ingenious.' He wondered how Max Pereira was feeling right now. He called the Menogen number but there was no reply, not even an answerphone message.

Neef wanted to start Neil off right away with an injection of the vector. He went in to the duty room to tell Staff Nurse Williams, Kate Morse's temporary replacement, and found Kate there herself. She was wearing uniform and smiled at him when he came in.

Neef raised his eyes.

Kate said, 'I'm all right, Mike. I'd rather be her than sitting at home wondering when they'll allow me to bury my husband.'

'I heard,' said Neef.

'Charlie's gone and I've accepted it. I've got two kids, a mortgage and a career to pursue so I'm here to get on with it.'

'Good,' said Neef. 'We've missed you.' He told Kate about the new vector for Neil Benson.

'Sounds good,' said Kate.

Neef suddenly realized that she hadn't seen the story in the paper. The smile faded from his face. This wasn't going to be easy. 'Kate, there's something I think you should read. It's a newspaper story.'

Neef returned to his office and reappeared with the paper. He handed it to Kate and stood by while she read it.

'Is this true?' asked Kate in a barely audible whisper when she'd finished.

'As far as I'm concerned, it's not,' said Neef. 'The only fact in that story is the coincidence of the addresses. It's a totally irresponsible and highly damaging load of rubbish.'

Kate looked at Neef as if trying to make up her mind. 'If I thought that little bastard was responsible for my Charlie's death . . .'

'I know Pereira isn't the most personable character in the world, Kate, but I've come to trust him in spite of everything.'

'Very well,' said Kate. 'Who wrote the story?'

Neef couldn't reply. He looked away and made a gesture of hopelessness with his hands.

'Not Eve Sayers?' said Kate. Neef shrugged. 'Oh Mike, I'm so sorry.'

Neef nodded. He smiled wryly and said, 'About Neil Benson. Can you get him ready?'

Neef was making some final calculations on how much viral suspension to inject, based on the current volume of Neil's tumour, when Ann announced that Max Pereira was outside.

'Send him in.'

Pereira had a copy of the the morning paper in his hand and was clearly upset. 'Have you seen this shit?' he stormed. 'The bastards have shut us down! Would you fucking believe it?'

'Calm down, Max,' said Neef. 'Tell me what's happened.'

'The fucking authorities have revoked all our licences. They've closed us down, pending a full inquiry. They've padlocked the gates. What killer virus for Christ's sake?'

'I hate to remind you in the circumstances, but you were the one who suggested a virus in the first place,' said Neef.

Pereira put his hands to his head as if he was close to breaking point. 'Okay, okay,' he said. 'I do think a virus is responsible but there's nothing in the Menogen labs even close to being a candidate, and even if there were we have so many safety regulations to comply with that there is no way, *no way, man*, that anything could get out of there.'

'I believe you,' said Neef.

'Thank Christ somebody does.' Max pointed to the paper. 'Who writes this shit?'

Once again, Neef couldn't reply and looked away.'

'You're kidding,' said Pereira. 'Not Eve. Shit, I thought she was a friend of mine.'

'Join the club.'

Kate Morse came in to confirm that things were ready for Neil's injection. She froze when she saw Pereira sitting there but quickly recovered, although her face was like a mask. Neef noted that there was no suggestion of guilt or embarrassment about Pereira.

'I was sorry to hear about your husband,' said Pereira.

'Thank you,' said Kate coldly. She turned towards Neef and looked him in the eye, saying, 'If you're quite sure about this, Neil will be ready when you are.'

Neef nodded.

'Neil?' exclaimed Pereira. 'Neil Benson? The melanoma kid?'

'Permission came through this morning,' said Neef.

'Then I won't kill myself just yet,' said Pereira. 'That's good news.' He caught sight of the way Kate Morse was looking at him and the smile faded. He said, 'You read the story in the papers this morning, didn't you? And now you're wondering if I killed your husband. I didn't, nor did anyone else at Menogen. If you never believe anything else in your life, lady, believe that.'

'I'll try, Doctor,' said Kate. She turned on her heel and left the room.

Pereira appeared totally preoccupied for a few moments before he turned to Neef and said, 'I'd like to be present when you inject the kid, if that's okay.'

'Of course,' replied Neef. 'It's really your work we're dealing with here.'

The virus had been brought out from the unit fridge and Neef and Pereira were putting on gowns when Ann came towards them with a memo in her hand. 'I think you should read this,' she said to Neef.

Neef read the note and swore. 'It's from Tim Heaton,' he said. 'The health authorities have pulled the plug on all Menogen products,' he said. 'A total ban.'

Pereira took the note from his hand and read it too. 'Looks like we've been tried, convicted and sentenced before we even had a chance to say anything,' he said. He started taking off his gown. Neef followed suit but stopped halfway through and put it back on again. 'We're going ahead,' he said.

'Are you out of your mind?' exclaimed Pereira. 'You can't do this. You'll destroy your career, man.'

'I read the expert scientific reports that came with the licence this morning,' said Neef. 'They were excellent. These are the opinions that really matter, not the half-arsed, reflex action of some government-sponsored clown in response to a bloody newspaper story.'

'Don't do it, Mike. Half-assed or not, the pen-pushing clerks of this world will destroy you.'

'If Neil lives, it'll be worth it.'

'Wow,' said Pereira under his breath. 'And I thought you guys didn't really give a shit about your patients.'

'Am I doing this alone or are you with me?'

'Count me in,' said Pereira.

Kate Morse and one other nurse were in the side room with Neil when Neef and Pereira entered. Neil was lying on an examination couch, already sedated and seemingly peaceful. The grossly disfiguring tumour on the side of his face stood out like some horrible parasitic growth from a different world against the surgical sheeting enfolding him.

Neef took the virus suspension from the junior nurse and charged the syringe. He said to Pereira, 'I calculated the volume on the same basis as last time, using the same formula. It worked out at Six-point-five millilitres.'

'Sounds about right.' said Pereira. 'Are you really sure you want to go through with this?'

'I'm sure.'

'Then you may want the nurses to leave.'

Neef looked at him, then realization dawned on his face. 'Of course,' he said, 'I wasn't thinking.'

Kate Morse, who had been looking thoroughly confused, turned to her junior nurse and said, 'Thank you, Nurse. I don't think we'll be needing you any more.' The young girl left the room. Kate said, 'Would someone mind telling me what's going on?'

Neef looked as if he was struggling for words. Pereira beat him to it. 'Against my advice, your boss here is about to inject one of my virus vectors into this child, knowing that permission to use it has been revoked. If you stay in the room, Sister, you may be held responsible, too, should there be any comeback. That's why I suggested the nurses leave.'

'Is this true?' Kate asked Neef.

'It is.'

'Then you must have good reason to do this. I'll stay if you don't mind.'

Pereira raised his eyes to the ceiling. 'Don't you guys know what you're doing to a cynicism that's taken me a lifetime to build?' he asked.

'Let's get on with it,' said Neef.

After the injection, Neil was taken back to his own bed and Neef and Pereira returned to Neef's office. Neef asked Kate Morse to join them.

'I feel as if we've just robbed a bank,' said Kate.

'It's probably worse,' said Pereira.

'It was my decision, my responsibility,' said Neef. 'I'm going to have Ann draw up a document stating that this was the case and that you assisted out of loyalty to me, Kate, and that I did what I did against all your advice, Max. I'll sign it.'

Any response from Pereira or Kate was cut short by a knock at the door. Ann said, 'Miss Sayers is here, Doctor.'

The three of them exchanged looks of total disbelief.

Pereira shook his head and said, 'She's got neck, I'll give her that.'

'I don't believe it,' said Kate.

'I don't think I do, either,' said Neef.

Kate and Pereira got up to go. Kate led Pereira out through the door that led into the unit rather than have them meet Eve in Ann's office. 'We'll be in the duty room,' she said.

A few moments later, Eve stood in the doorway. 'Can I come in?' she asked.

'I'm not sure we have anything to say to each other,' said Neef. His features would have made the sphinx seem animated.

'So little faith, Neef?' asked Eve.

Neef saw that her gaze was level and unyielding. 'What do you mean?'

'I didn't write the story.'

Neef's face was a picture of disbelief. 'Sure,' he said.

'I did not write the story,' repeated Eve slowly in an unvarying monotone.

Neef said, 'Only three people knew about the Langholm address connection.'

'Someone else must have,' said Eve.

'Did you get the job?' asked Neef.

'I didn't take it.'

'Why not?'

'They showed me the story they were going to do about Menogen and asked if I would do the follow-ups. I refused.'

'You refused?'

'I told them I thought the Menogen story was irresponsible journalism. They were going to destroy a company's reputation without having any evidence against them at all. They showed me the door.'

'Why didn't you call last night?'

Eve said, 'It was late when I got back and my damned phone was out of order. I was feeling so low, I didn't have the heart to go out to a call box. I took a sleeping pill and went to bed.'

'Christ! What a day,' said Neef slumping back in his chair and putting his hands behind his head.

'Can I go and see Neil now?' asked Eve.

'No, I'd rather you didn't,' said Neef.

Eve looked suddenly vulnerable, as if he'd struck her. 'You're not going to stop me seeing him?'

'Nothing like that,' said Neef. 'He's just been injected with Menogen virus.'

'You got permission?' asked Eve, her whole expression changing.

'Yes . . . and, no,' replied Neef. He told Eve what he'd done.

'You injected him without a licence?' exclaimed Eve. 'But you said you'd never do that.'

'I said I couldn't do it without the proposal being screened by experts. It was screened by them and approved. That was good enough for me. The ban was invoked by politicians in response to your . . . the story in the papers. That wasn't good enough for me, or Neil.'

'Thank God,' said Eve.

'Max Pereira's out in the duty room with Kate Morse. They both think you wrote the story. This morning Kate thought Pereira had killed her husband. I think Max believes he'll never work again.'

Eve closed her eyes. 'What can I say?,' she said.

'Nothing,' said Neef. 'If you didn't write the story.'

Sixteen

Neef made Eve wait while he summoned Pereira back into the room. Kate Morse had gone off to deal with some problem in the unit.

Pereira looked at Eve as if she was a curious, alien life-form.

'She didn't write the story,' said Neef.

'And I'm playing quarterback for the Giants next season,' said Pereira softly.

'I'm serious,' said Neef.

'I didn't write it,' said Eve. 'I knew it was going in; they asked me to do the follow-up but I did not write the story that appeared in the paper this morning.'

'Then who did? How many closet journalists do you have on the staff in this goddam hospital?' asked Pereira.

'They didn't get the story from a journalist,' said Eve. 'Or they wouldn't have asked me to carry on with it. An insider gave them the information and an *Express* staffer wrote it up.'

'So, who on the staff would want to put out a story like that?' said Neef, thinking out loud.

'And why?' added Pereira.

'Tim Heaton's always looking for press attention,' said Neef. 'But this wouldn't make sense. The story isn't going to do St George's any good at all. The Louradis article on gene therapy has already associated St George's with Menogen in the public mind. This is going to be as damaging to us as it is to Menogen.'

'But maybe not so costly,' said Pereira. 'You don't think it could have been Louradis himself do you?'

'But why?' asked Neef.

'He called me up to ask a few things when he was writing his "plain man's guide to gene therapy" article. The man obviously craves press attention. He struck me as the kind who'd say anything to stay in the limelight.'

'I don't think he knew about Melanie living next to Menogen,' said Neef. 'Apart from that, it's hard to see how this story would help Louradis in his quest for stardom.'

'So we're still looking for a motive,' said Eve. 'Maybe someone wanted to seriously damage Menogen. Did you upset anyone that much, Max?'

Pereira shrugged.

'Or maybe it was some kind of deliberate diversion,' said Neef. He was thinking of Heaton's tactics in the past of using a good-news story to counteract the damage caused by bad publicity.

'But a diversion from what?' said Eve.

'That's what we have to work out,' said Neef. 'Let's take it one step at a time. If someone wants Menogen blamed for the cancer outbreak it might just be that that same someone knows the real reason behind it and wants it covered up.'

'But no one's even thought of an alternative possibility, have they?' asked Eve.

'No,' admitted Neef.

'I don't suppose there's any chance you could find out from the newspaper who gave them the story?' Pereira asked Eve.

Eve shook her head and said, 'None at all. They'll protect their source. Apart from that, we didn't exactly finish up on good terms.'

'Why don't we have a think about this and meet again tomorrow?' suggested Neef, looking at his watch. 'We'll be doing Thomas Downy's last scan in the morning. You'll probably want to be here for that anyway, Max?'

'Yeah,' replied Pereira. 'I'm looking forward to that.' He got up to go.

'What are your plans Eve?' asked Neef as the door closed.

'Right now I'm going down to Sutton Place. It's my guess that this morning's story will have forced the hand of Messrs Klein and Waters. They're going to have to make some kind of press statement. I plan to make it an uncomfortable experience for them.'

'Good for you,' said Neef. 'Will I see you later?'

'If you like.'

They arranged that Eve would come over to Neef's cottage when she had finished writing up her piece for the *Citizen*.

Tim Heaton called shortly after four. He was not in a good mood.

'I've spent all bloody day trying to get sense out of these ministry people and I've failed. They admit that they weren't investigating Menogen Research before the newspaper story broke but they refuse to kill the story. It's as if they *want* the public to believe it!'

'It takes the heat off them,' said Neef.

'But St George's is associated with Menogen!' exclaimed Heaton. 'Just as we were about to capitalize on Mark Louradis's groundwork and go public with our St George's cancer-cure success, this has to happen! It's all gone sour. University College Hospital Trust will think we're a laughing stock. What GP fund-holders in their right minds will refer patients to us now when we're associated with a discredited company like Menogen?'

'The story's not exactly done the company much good either,' said Neef. 'They're absolutely adamant that nothing from their lab could have caused the outbreak. The trouble is, no one's going to listen to them.'

'Bloody newspapers.'

'Before you ask, it wasn't Eve Sayers who wrote the story.'

'That's something, I suppose. You got my memo about the ban on Menogen products?'

'I did.'

'I know you were keen on trying out that last one but that's how it goes.'

'I suppose,' said Neef. Now was not the time to tell Heaton what he'd done. Unauthorized treatment of a patient at St George's with an experimental product from Menogen Research was not exactly the light relief he was looking for. The fact that the patient was a young boy without mother or father to look after his interests would make him an exploited helpless guinea pig as far as the tabloids were concerned. Truth wouldn't get a look in.

Eve arrived at the cottage around eight.

'Are you hungry?' asked Neef.

'I had some pasta before I wrote up my report,' replied Eve.

'Did you pick up anything useful at Sutton Place?'

'Klein spoke to us. He said their inquiries were continuing. Everyone wanted to know about the killer virus and how it had escaped from Menogen's labs. Klein and Waters went into a bullshit routine; they didn't have the decency to admit that they had no evidence of this at all, so I gave them a hard time.'

'How so?'

'I asked them publicly if they knew about the Langholm address link before it appeared in the papers. Klein talked round the question for a bit but in the end I pinned him down and he admitted he hadn't. The staffer from the *Express* then saw his chance and tried to get Klein to say that his paper had been instrumental in providing a valuable lead in the investigation. I said there was no evidence at all to back up their claims, and the *Express* story had been malicious rather than helpful.'

'Good for you,' said Neef.

'The *Express* man wasn't too pleased,' said Eve. 'Asked me whose side I was on. I then asked Klein if he had shut down a perfectly responsible company solely on the say-so of an unsubstantiated newspaper report. He said not so I asked what his reasons were. He said he couldn't divulge them at present. It wouldn't be in the public interest.'

'You mean he hasn't thought of any yet.'

'That would be my guess, too,' said Eve. 'Just for good measure, I asked him if it was true that Menogen Research were taking legal action over the closure.'

'Are they?' asked Neef.

'I've no idea but I would if I were them. Friend Klein turned a whiter shade of pale and said that he couldn't comment.

Neef poured two gin and tonics and handed one to Eve. 'Sounds like you've been at war with everyone,' he said.

'Feels like it, too,' said Eve, taking a sip of her drink. 'You know, something's been bugging me all day.'

'What?'

'You said that only three people knew about the Langholm address link?'

'Yes.'

'You, me . . . and David Farro-Jones?'

'Yes.'

'Supposing it was David Farro-Jones who leaked the story to the papers.'

Neef looked at her in silence for a moment. 'You can't be serious,' he said.

Eve shrugged. 'I know he's a friend of yours but, if it wasn't you and it wasn't me, that only leaves him.'

'But why would he do that?' protested Neef.

'That's what I've been wondering about,' said Eve. 'David Farro-Jones is a molecular biologist like Max, making gene-therapy vectors like Max . . . but maybe not so good.'

Neef's eyes widened. 'You're suggesting that David wanted to damage Menogen because of jealousy; they were more successful than he was?'

'I'm not sure of his reasons,' said Eve. 'But it's a thought. You said yourself there's a lot of money to be made out of successful vectors for gene therapy. Anything that damaged Menogen would benefit the competition, including David Farro-Jones.'

Neef shook his head as if he was unwilling to contemplate Eve's suggestion, but he found he could not dismiss it altogether. 'I suppose it's a possibility.'

It was a possibility that was to prevent Neef from getting a good night's sleep. He lay awake in the small hours wondering if David Farro-Jones was capable of doing such a thing. It seemed so totally out of character. He always seemed to have the best interests of the patients at heart. Yet David had been the one to warn him about Max Pereira's driving ambition, suggesting that Max couldn't be trusted. What if it was really he and not Max who was being driven by greed and ambition?

One thought led to another. If Farro-Jones had been intent on damaging Menogen, maybe he been prepared to go further than just leak information to the papers. The question now was, had he actually been prepared to impede the investigation of the outbreak so that suspicion would remain with Menogen? After all, David had been in charge of the hunt for the virus. He was also, as Neef suddenly thought, the investigator of Eddie Miller's claim that there had been an earlier cancer case than Melanie Simpson.

He gave up trying to sleep and got up to make some coffee.

Neef got in at eight the next morning to discover that Neil had had a bad night. He went immediately to see him and find out for himself. Neil's eyes were dull; the spark had gone from them. It was something he had seen so often before in terminally ill patients. Neil's life had started to ebb away. 'Hi, Tiger, how're you doing?' he asked softly as he sat down on the edge of the bed and ran his forefinger along Neil's forehead. Ostensibly it was an affectionate gesture but it told Neef something about the feel of Neil's skin. He found nothing reassuring there.

'That injection we gave you yesterday is going to make you all better,' said Neef. 'Then we'll go see Dolly at my place. Would you like that?'

Neil did not respond. He continued to look into space with lacklustre eyes.

'Maybe we'll even go on another picnic with Eve,' he continued. 'We'll eat too many sausage rolls again and race our boats in the river. You're not going to win this time!'

Neef still couldn't elicit a response.

Suddenly Neil said quietly, 'Want Eve.'

'She'll be here soon,' said Neef. 'I promise.'

'Want Eve,' whispered Neil.

Neef got up and looked down at the boy with a sinking feeling in his stomach. Maybe Eve was going to be too late.

Neef hurried back to his office and tried phoning her. There was no answer, so he left a message on her answerphone for her to call him urgently. He tried calling the offices of the *Citizen* but was told Eve wasn't there.

Max Pereira came in at eleven and Neef told him about Neil.

'Shit,' said Pereira. 'There was always a chance he was too far gone to be helped.'

Neef nodded.

'It may be a reaction to the virus we injected yesterday,' said Pereira.

'How so?' asked Neef.

'Although the virus wouldn't do him any harm it would still challenge his immune system and make him feel under the weather. If he wasn't feeling that great to begin with . . .'

'He wasn't,' confirmed Neef.

'Then he would feel pretty bad.'

'I hope to God it's just that,' said Neef, 'but I fear not. I think he's letting go, and I don't think we can do anything about it. I tried this morning without success.' He looked at his watch. 'He asked for Eve but I haven't been able to contact her. I'll never forgive myself if she doesn't get a chance to see him one more time before . . .'

Lawrence Fielding came in with Thomas Downy's CT scan in his hand. The expression on his face said it all. 'He's cured,' he announced. 'No sign of the tumour at all.'

Neef took it and examined it before saying, 'Bloody marvellous.'

He handed the scan to Pereira, checked his watch again and swore under his breath.

'Something wrong?' asked Fielding.

Neef told him about Neil and his own failure to contact Eve.

'Have you tried public health?' suggested Fielding. 'Journalists seem to hang out there these days.'

Neef was about to pick up the phone when it rang. It was Eve.

'I just called home to check my machine and found your message. What's the problem?'

'It's Neil. Can you come right now?'

'On my way,' said Eve without further question but Neef heard the alarm in her voice. She was there within fifteen minutes.

'What's happened?' she asked anxiously.

'I think he's having to give in to his cancer,' said Neef. 'He's just had too much to cope with for too long. It was such an unequal struggle and now he's tired himself out. He was asking for you.'

'But what about this new vector thing?' asked Eve, her eyes pleading the case.

'I think it's come too late,' said Neef.

Eve swallowed and took a moment to compose herself before asking, 'Can I see him now?'

Neef nodded. 'Go on through. I'll join you soon.'

Neef waited until Pereira had finished checking Thomas Downy's scan before saying, 'I'd like to have a talk, if you could spare me a few minutes?'

'I've got all day,' replied Pereira. 'They closed down my lab, remember?'

'That's partly what I wanted to talk to you about,' said Neef. 'There were three people who knew about Melanie Simpson living next to the Menogen labs. Me, Eve Sayers and the man who spotted the link in the first place, David Farro-Jones.'

Pereira's eyes widened with what Neef construed as dismay, but he didn't say anything.

'I've noticed from time to time that you appear to dislike David. Would you mind telling me why?'

'He's full of shit,' said Pereira. 'All front and no substance.'

'I've always found him a pleasant and extremely helpful colleague,' said Neef.

'You've never been in direct competition with him,' said Pereira. 'Lots of people are pleasant and charming when you're not standing in their way or going after something they want.'

'I take it you *have* stood in his way at some time?' said Neef.

'When we were post-docs together in the States we were both in the running for a medal that the science faculty awarded annually to the most promising young researcher. David wanted it badly. To cut a long story short, it went to me.'

'And David wasn't very pleased?'

'Outwardly he couldn't have been more charming, but later, at a reception, he had a bit too much to drink and I met the real David Farro-Jones, the one who called me a little Jewish bastard and accused the awards board of being infested with kikes. That, he explained, was how I really got the prize.'

'Farro-Jones said that?' said Neef.

'It's not the sort of thing you forget,' said Pereira. 'Next morning he was back to being his charming old self again, behaving as if nothing had happened.'

'I see,' said Neef. 'So you would have no problem with the notion that it was David Farro-Jones who leaked the story to the papers?'

'None at all,' said Pereira.

'Then the question is, how far has he been prepared to go to ensure that suspicion stays on Menogen?' said Neef.

'What d'you mean?'

'David was in charge of the hunt for the virus. When I suggested that his failure to find one put Menogen in the clear he brought up the possibility of a new kind of infectious agent one you couldn't see under the microscope. He mentioned a prion.'

'No chance,' said Pereira dismissively. 'That was a red herring. Prion disease is nothing like we're seeing here. If the agent is

invisible, it's invisible for another reason. Either it's not there or
... maybe it's because we can't see the wood for the trees ...'

'What are you thinking of Max?'

'David wasn't the only one looking for the virus was he?' asked
Pereira, ignoring Neef's question.

'No, he had a team working on it.'

'And none of them noticed anything out of the ordinary ...
Interesting. Was the original virology analysis on the early patients
done by Farro-Jones's lab?' asked Pereira.

'No, the hospital lab did it,' said Neef.

'Could you get me a copy of the reports on any of the patients?
Preferably all of them.'

'I think so. Why?'

'I'll tell you when I've seen them,' said Pereira. 'I don't suppose
you can get me some lung samples?'

'From the cancer patients?'

'Yeah.'

'I can try.'

Neef went along to join Eve in Neil's room. When he entered he
was amazed to see that there was a tiny spark of life in Neil's eyes.
Eve had captured his interest. She was telling him a story about
Maxwell Gunn.

'Now if you're going to grow up and be a big strong fireman like
Maxwell you're going to have to concentrate on getting better,' said
Eve. 'Isn't that right?'

Neil nodded and Neef smiled. She was getting through to
him.

'Get some rest now,' said Eve. 'I'll see you later and we'll have
another story.'

Neil nodded and closed his eyes. Eve stood up; Neef could see
that there were tears starting to form in her eyes. She followed
Neef outside.

'I could feel him slipping away from me,' she said. 'I could reach
him but I couldn't hold on to him. It was as if he was being pulled

away from me by some . . . power. It wasn't malevolent, just insistent, and I didn't know how to fight it.'

'You did really well,' said Neef. 'You made contact. I couldn't get near him at all.'

'I'll be back later,' said Eve. She kissed Neef on the cheek.

When Neef returned to his office, he sat for a few moments in thoughtful silence before turning his attention to Pereira's request. With Frank MacSween away on leave he had no idea how he could lay hands on any pathological material taken from victims of the outbreak. Apart from Frank, the only other person he had known in Pathology was Charlie Morse, and he was now a victim himself. After a few minutes he realized that the pathology department was not the only source of infected material. The electrician up in University College Hospital was a possibility. With any luck Mark Clelland, the physician who had looked after Charlie, would be involved in the case.

Neef called University College and asked to speak to Clelland.

'Mark? It's Michael Neef at St George's.'

'Hello there,' replied Clelland. 'I've been meaning to call you. I wanted to thank you for coming over the other day when we lost Charles Morse. I appreciate it. I'm sure his wife did, too. What can I do for you?'

Neef hadn't realized that Clelland had considered his going across a favour. This made things easier. 'Mark, I was wondering if you could get me a lung biopsy from the electrician who was infected at the same time as Charlie.'

'Douglas Cooper? Hmmm, that could be a bit difficult. Normally it would be no problem but these ministry chaps have put a ban on any pathological material being sent to any lab other than their own.'

'I see,' replied Neef. He hadn't considered this difficulty. 'Oh well,' he said, sounding disappointed. 'I was hoping to have some new slides made for teaching purposes and the carcinoma in these cases is just so widespread that I thought they would be ideal. Still . . . if it can't be done, it can't be done.'

There was a pause before Clelland took his cue from Neef's disappointment. 'Leave it with me, I'll see what I can do.'

'Thanks, Mark. I'll owe you one.'

Neef's thoughts strayed back to Neil Benson. He was losing his battle for life and the prospect of his death filled him with dismay. In spite of his constant professional denials, Neil was as special to him as he was to Eve. He was only a little boy but he was a symbol of courage in the human spirit. He deserved to win his battle, not lose it.

But he was going to die and it seemed so unfair, the sort of injustice that came dangerously close to making him lose heart for the struggle. Neef saw the danger in this line of thought and broadened his horizon. Neil wasn't the only one on the danger list who needed consideration: the four kids on the Menogen trial who hadn't responded to gene therapy were also fading.

This last thought made him wonder why. It seemed strange that Thomas Downy had done so well on the new treatment when the others had done so badly. It was almost as if four of the five had received no therapy at all . . .

Neef felt a thin film of cold sweat break out on his brow as an awful thought crossed his mind. There *had* been a difference in their treatments! Thomas Downy had been treated with a back-up supply of vector because of the accident in theatre with the original vial. All the other children had received the original preparations . . . the ones taken away and tested by David Farro-Jones!

Neef tried putting his suspicions down to paranoia brought on by stress, but they persisted. If Farro-Jones had really wanted to discredit Menogen he could easily have done so by making sure their vectors wouldn't work. He could have inactivated them while ostensibly screening them for safety . . . At my request! thought Neef, putting his head in his hands. If the nurse hadn't dropped Thomas Downy's vial in theatre there would have been no need to use the back-up vial from Pharmacy and there would have been five failures out of five!

Neef hesitated about what to do. Should he think about this a bit longer, maybe discuss it with someone? Or should he jump right in and act on instinct? His earlier conversation with Max Pereira swung things in favour of the latter. He called in Lawrence Fielding.

'I'm putting our four failures back on the gene-therapy trial,' he said.

'You're what?' exclaimed Fielding.

'I want you to fix up theatre bookings as soon as possible. We're going to start all over again using the back-up vials from Pharmacy.'

'But why?' asked a bemused Fielding. 'What's going to be different this time?'

'I think there was something wrong with the vials the first time,' said Neef.

'What exactly?' asked Fielding.

'I'm not sure but we had to use a back-up vial on Thomas and it worked.'

Fielding looked doubtful. 'I hope you know what you're doing,' he said. 'Any results obtained will be invalid because of the digression from agreed protocol. You won't be able to publish the results.'

'I don't give a damn about publication,' said Neef. 'I want the kids to have a chance.'

'What a perfectly bloody awful day,' sighed Neef as he rested his head on Eve's shoulder. They were sitting together on the couch in her flat. 'I talked to Max about your Farro-Jones idea.'

'And?'

'He wasn't in the least surprised. He seemed to think it would be typical of the man.'

'So?'

'How could I have been so wrong about him?' said Neef.

'It can happen to the best of us,' said Eve.

'I keep thinking about the damage he could have done.'

'To Menogen?'

'Not just that. I keep wondering just how far he was prepared to go to discredit Menogen.' Neef told Eve about his suspicions over the vials for the trial.

'Do you really think he would do that?' exclaimed Eve, her voice betraying disbelief.

'I don't know what to believe,' confessed Neef. 'Having been so wrong about him once it's difficult for me to judge.'

'We don't know that you were wrong,' Eve reminded him. 'It was just an idea.'

'It's one that I feel obliged to follow up after talking to Max,' said Neef. 'And I don't like where it's taking me.'

'What do you mean?'

'I keep wondering whether or not he would be prepared to interfere with the public health investigation to stop them finding out the real truth about the cancer outbreak.'

'How so?'

'He was the one I told about Eddie Miller's assertion that there'd been an earlier case than Melanie.'

'So?'

'The next morning Eddie had an accident and was dead before I could ask him any questions.'

'Surely you are not suggesting that—'

Neef held up his hands. 'I don't know,' he said. 'I just know that it happened that way and then it was David who checked Eddie's records and said there was nothing to worry about.'

'I can see him leaking a simple story to the papers to show Menogen in a bad light, but to go to these lengths just doesn't seem real, somehow,' said Eve.

'Agreed,' said Neef. 'If it's true, it suggests that he wasn't just out to damage Menogen. There was a completely different reason for his behaviour, something we haven't even considered.'

The two of them sat in silence for a while until Eve broke it. 'Are you absolutely sure Eddie Miller didn't mention this first patient's name at any time?' she asked.

'Not absolutely sure,' conceded Neef. 'He was very drunk and his speech was slurred. His whole assertion took me so much by surprise that it threw me at the time. I know I asked him a number of times for a name but he always seemed to wander off at a tangent.'

'What else did you ask him?'

'Lots of things,' said Neef. 'I asked him when he'd seen the "real" first patient. He claimed it was a few weeks before Melanie. I kept pressing him for details but all I got out of him was that she was a girl about the same age as Melanie.'

'Nothing else?' asked Eve.

Neef shook his head as he tried hard to remember. 'I asked him why he didn't report it at the time.'

'And?'

'He gave me a lecture about telling people what they wanted to hear. He said this was the way to a quiet life. He said that someone didn't want the tumours reported so he didn't report them.'

'As simple as that?'

'He made it sound that way. He said the little kid was dead anyway. What did it matter? Making out a report wasn't going to bring her back.'

'The little kid,' repeated Eve. 'Were these his exact words?'

'As far as I remember. Why?'

'We are talking about a girl of thirteen or fourteen. Right?'

'Yes, I suppose so. What are you getting at?'

'Not so "little", wouldn't you say?'

Neef thought about this in silence, then sat up with a start.

'You're right!' he exclaimed. 'Eddie didn't say the little kid, he said the *Little* kid. Little was her surname! It *must* have been!'

'Well, I suppose it could be,' said Eve, doubtfully.

'It's worth a try, don't you think?' said Neef.

'Yes, let's be positive,' urged Eve. 'Where do we go from here?'

'We'll have to think about that,' said Neef. 'Knowing the girl's name would enable us to make enquiries but it's odds on that her file's been removed. It would just alert people to what we were up to. We need another way.'

'But not tonight,' said Eve. 'It's late.'

Neef looked up at her and pulled her mouth down gently on his.

'No, not tonight,' he agreed.
'First, call the hospital. Find out how Neil is.'
Neef made the call.
'He's holding his own.'

Ann Miles came in with coffee and put it on his desk. Neef smiled his thanks. It had been another busy day but all four children who had failed to respond in the initial gene-therapy trial had been reinoculated with vector viruses, this time from the stocks held in the hospital pharmacy. Neef's sense of satisfaction was tempered by the thought that he seemed to be getting potentially deeper and deeper into trouble. Neil's current treatment was definitely illegal; there was a distinct possibility that reinstating the four trial patients on Menogen products was, too. Neef let out a long sigh. His only defence was that he was doing everything with the best of intentions. This wouldn't be enough to satisfy a medical investigation board should it come to that, but it did keep his conscience clear.

He turned his thoughts to the Little child, assuming there was one, and how he was going to get information about her. It wasn't just a case of getting information. He needed to do it without anyone knowing, especially David Farro-Jones. That immediately eliminated any kind of official approach to University College Hospital. He supposed he could make a request for a list of all teenage girls who had died in Uni College in the past few months, but that might be a bit obvious. What he really needed was some other way, a way that would arouse no suspicion at all. After a few minutes' thought, he had it. The local newspapers! The chances were that the girl's death would have been listed in the columns of the local newspaper. He could check back issues without anyone being any the wiser. Feeling pleased with himself, Neef set off for the offices of the local paper. Once he was there, it didn't take long to find what he was looking for.

Susan Mary Little, beloved daughter of Ann Little and the late Charles Little, aged 13 years, after a long illness bravely borne. Grateful thanks to the doctors and nurses of University College Hospital for their devoted care. Family flowers only. Donations to the Cystic Fibrosis Trust.

There followed details of the cremation arrangements

Neef stared at the words 'cystic fibrosis'. This was Farro-Jones's special research interest. Was this a link? Had Susan Little been one of the patients on the University College Hospital gene-therapy trial? he wondered. Eddie Miller had said he had recorded the cause of death as lung congestion, but she had really died of bronchial carcinoma. Someone hadn't wanted it known. What did it all mean? Just how deep did Farro-Jones's involvement go? There was no family address attached to the death notice. Neef resolved to look the Littles up in the phone book.

There were seven Littles within the catchment area for University College Hospital. Neef knew that this wasn't foolproof in itself because cystic-fibrosis patients would be referred here from all over the county. But, on the other hand, he had noted that the cremation was held locally. The first name 'Charles' narrowed the possibilities down to two. There were no numbers registered to an Ann Little.

Seventeen

Neef found a small package sitting on his desk. It had been delivered by the hospital van service and was addressed to him personally in black marker pen. He opened it and found a plastic specimen vial labelled, 'D Cooper, bronchoscopy tissue.' The slip wrapped round it read, 'From a well-wisher to an amnesiac. Neef mentally thanked Mark Clelland and wrapped up the vial again for storage in the fridge until Pereira came for it. He phoned Pereira to tell him and he was there within twenty minutes. He seemed both surprised and pleased that Neef had got him the sample.

'It wasn't easy,' said Neef. 'Public health have put a ban on the movement of any pathological material from the victims.'

Pereira smiled wryly. 'But you still got it,' he said quietly.

Neef looked puzzled. 'Yes,' he replied.

'You're saying it wasn't easy, but it was. It always is for you guys. When the rules don't suit you, a phone call here, a phone call there, and you get round them. Anyone so much as removing a paperclip from Menogen without permission would be in deep shit, but it's us they end up closing down.'

Neef reflected ruefully on what Pereira had said and understood his bitterness. 'Does that mean you don't want the sample?' he asked with an embarrassed smile.

'I want it,' replied Pereira. 'I'll be gone for a few days. I've called in a favour. One of those other awful commercial establishments has given me some lab space.'

Neef watched the door close and reflected that Pereira had every right to feel aggrieved . . . but people with chips on their shoulders could be a real pain.

Eve came in to sit with Neil and Neef joined them after a short while. Eve was telling Neil of the latest exploits of Maxwell Gunn. His station had been given a brand-new fire engine and Maxwell had been given the honour of driving it for the very first time to a fire. It had no fewer than three different sirens and Maxwell operated them from three buttons above the windscreen. On the way back from the fire and very late at night Maxwell had hit all three buttons by accident and woken up everybody in the city. Next day everyone was yawning because of this.

Neef saw a slight suggestion of a smile at the corner of Neil's mouth, but it was very weak. Eve yawned to punctuate her story and Neef followed suit. Neil looked as if he might do so as well, but in the end he just closed his eyes.

Eve looked at Neef and Neef saw the pain in her eyes. 'He's still fighting,' he said. 'You're working wonders.'

'It's not enough, is it?'

'No one could do any more. Every day he survices gives Pereira's virus a little more time to do its job, but he's getting very tired. He has the heart of a tiger but he's really just a little boy who's been through more than any little boy should have to.'

Eve rested her head on Neef's chest and couldn't hold back her sobs any more. She apologized and sobbed alternately.

'Sssh,' soothed Neef. 'There's nothing to be sorry about.'

Neef arranged to see Eve later at her apartment. As soon as she was gone he took out the paper on which he had written the two addresses and called the first Charles Little. A woman answered.

'Mrs Little, it's about your daughter, Susan.'

'You must have a wrong number.'

'I'm sorry.'

Neef dialled the other number. Again a woman's voice answered.
'Mrs Little?'
'Yes.'
'I'm sorry to trouble you; it's about your daughter, Susan.'
'I don't have a daughter named Susan or anything else for that matter.'
'I do apologize. Wrong number.'
Neef cursed. Where did he go from here? Either he was wrong about the family being local or they didn't have a telephone. That was a possibility he hadn't considered.
Before leaving the unit, Neef gave instructions that he was to be informed if there was any deterioration in Neil's condition. He left Eve's number for them to try if he wasn't at home.

'I tried persuading my editor to take Menogen's side in this affair,' said Eve.
'That was brave of you,' said Neef.
'Tell me about it,' said Eve. 'He thinks we've been far too constrained as it is. Everyone else has been going for Menogen's throat. He gave me a lecture about telling the public what they want to hear.'
'Where have I heard that before?' said Neef. 'And right now they want to hear about a big bad research company that's been manufacturing killer viruses.'
'More or less.'
'Thomas Downy no longer has a tumour in his brain,' said Neef.
'That's wonderful,' said Eve.
'I agree,' said Neef. 'It is, but I don't think the papers will be too interested to hear that it was a Menogen virus that cured him. That would be a bit embarrassing, would it not?'
'I'll have another go at the editor if you like,' said Eve.
Neef smiled and suggested she leave it for a bit. 'There is something you could help me with though,' said Neef. 'How do I go about finding Susan Little's family?'

'Susan? Then you managed to find out something today?'

Neef told her how he'd come by the information.

'Why didn't *I* think of that?' exclaimed Eve. Neef smiled. 'You say she was a cystic-fibrosis patient?'

Neef nodded and said, 'I'm sure that must be some kind of link to David Farro-Jones. That's his special interest.'

'Any ideas?' asked Eve.

Neef shook his head but said, 'I think Max may be on to something. He asked for pathology specimens from the cancer patients. I managed to get him a lung biopsy from Douglas Cooper, the electrician who got infected at the same time as Charlie Morse. He's taken it away somewhere to work on. In the meantime it might be helpful if I could speak to Susan Little's family.'

'Cystic fibrosis is a high-profile disease,' said Eve. 'It's popular in terms of fundraising.'

'What are you getting at?' asked Neef.

'It's possible that the *Citizen* or one of the local freebies covered Susan's death at the time. I'll check in the morning if you like?'

'Good idea.'

At two in the morning Eve and Neef were woken by the phone ringing. It was John Duncan, one of the housemen at the unit.

'Dr Neef? I understand you asked to be informed if Neil Benson's condition worsened.'

'Yes.'

'It has, sir. I don't think he'll see morning.'

Eve was already out of bed getting dressed. Neef followed and they were at the hospital within fifteen minutes of Duncan's call.

Neef let Eve be alone with Neil while he spoke to Duncan. There was nothing medical to be done and Eve had the best chance of reaching him.

'I'm very sorry, sir,' said Duncan. 'I understand the boy's a particular favourite of yours.'

'I don't have favourites,' replied Neef without looking at Duncan. He was watching Eve whisper to Neil.

'No, sir, of course not,' replied Duncan.

Neef stood in the doorway of Neil's room and listened. 'Maxwell's depending on you, Neil,' he heard Eve say. 'He keeps asking me when you'll be well enough to help him out. There's just so much work for him to do at the fire station. He needs all the help he can get. He told me he'll try to come round tomorrow to show you the new fire engine. Won't that be good? Promise me you'll try to be well enough to see him?'

Neef watched as Neil's head made a tiny nodding gesture on the pillow. Eve was trying desperately to keep the sob out of her voice.

'I think you've reached him again,' said Neef.

'I'm going to stay here,' said Eve. 'If that's all right.'

'Of course,' said Neef. 'I'll stay, too.'

Eve put a hand on his chest and said, 'Go home. You can't stay for them all.'

Neef knew that she was right. 'I'll see you in the morning,' he said. He kissed Eve lightly on the cheek and held her close for a long moment before walking away.

Neef didn't sleep; he was back in the unit shortly before seven. He found Eve still beside Neil. She was kneeling on the floor beside his bed and her head was resting on the pillow, although her eyes were open and she was whispering to Neil. Neef smiled at her before checking with John Duncan about the other patients. He told Duncan he could go off early.

'He's still hanging on,' said Duncan. 'It's amazing. Miss Sayers talked him through the night.'

'It is,' agreed Neef.

Neef made some coffee using the equipment in Ann Miles's office, and then said to Eve, 'Breakfast. Neil's sleeping.'

Eve got up stiffly and watched as Neef knelt to examine the boy. 'How is he?' she asked.

'Holding his own,' replied Neef. 'Well done.'

Eve took coffee with Neef in his office and then said she was going to go back to her flat to shower and change. 'I'll have to go into the office,' she said. 'But I'll keep checking with you.'

'Of course,' said Neef. 'If anything should change, I'll get word to you.'

He gave instructions that Neil was not to left alone. It was worth trying to capitalize on the time Eve had gained for them by continuing to stimulate his interest in what was going on around him, as she had done. The nurses took turns reading to him, telling his stories, showing him pictures and talking about his fire engines. Every hour that passed was more time for the Menogen virus to work on his tumour. Just before noon, Neef looked in on Neil. Despite the best efforts of the nurses, he still felt they were fighting a losing battle. Eve phoned to ask how things were going.

'Touch and go,' admitted Neef.

'I'll be in soon,' she said. 'But first I'm going along to the local fire station. I've half persuaded them to do some kind of visit for Neil this afternoon. At least, the station officer's agreed to talk to me.'

'That's a good thought,' said Neef. 'That might be just what we need.'

'I also checked up on Susan Little for you. One of the freebies did cover her death. She lived with her parents in the Combe Tower flats, not the most salubrious part of town. Got a pen?'

'Ready.'

She gave him the address. 'When she died, the neighbours started up a fund to commemorate Susan. They raised two hundred and fifty pounds, which they donated to research into cystic fibrosis at University College Hospital.'

'I see,' said Neef. 'I'll check it out.'

Hunger pangs reminded Neef that he hadn't had anything to eat since early the previous evening. Breakfast that morning had been a cup of black coffee. He went along to the staff restaurant and, after a quick look at the board, opted for smoked haddock. There was nothing wrong with it but his appetite seemed to' disappear after a couple of mouthfuls. He was joined at the table by Tim Heaton.

'Heard anything from public health?' Heaton asked.

'Not officially. I think we're included in their publicity ban.'

'Rumour has it they're on to something.'

'What makes you say that?'

'Up until now, the public health people have been seeking voluntary cooperation from contacts of patients affected by the cancer. Now it's mandatory. All contacts have been confined to their homes until further notice. Fumigation squads have been sent in, certain personal effects confiscated. Medical and nursing staff treating the surviving patients have had the same restrictions slapped on them. What do you think?'

'They think it's a virus,' replied Neef.

'Only think?'

'Maybe they know,' conceded Neef. 'Do any of the new sanctions affect us?'

'Any member of staff reporting sick with a cold or flu-like illness has to be notified to public health. They'll take appropriate action to isolate and investigate.' Neef nodded thoughtfully. 'I'm surprised they aren't doing more,' said Heaton. 'If they think it's a virus why isn't the entire staff being vetted?'

'I think it's a question of time,' said Neef. 'If any of us were going to get it, it would have shown up by now.

'Lucky,' said Heaton.

'And strange,' said Neef.

'Why strange?'

'You'd think if it was a new virus no one would have immunity to it, but it seems that some of us, if not most of us, have.'

'Thank God for that,' said Heaton. 'That's all I can say.'

'Amen to that.'

'How's your little patient, the one you were going to treat with the new vector?'

'He's hanging on by his fingertips,' said Neef.

'I'm sorry.'

Neef saw that he was drifting into a conversation he'd rather not be in. He looked at his watch and said that he'd have to go.

'Me too,' said Heaton. 'Monthly budget meeting time and that damned Martin woman is still on my back for more nurses.'

'She probably needs them,' said Neef.

'You medics and nurses are all in cahoots, I know you are,' Heaton joked.

'Get rid of us and the place would run smooth as clockwork,' said Neef.

Heaton gave him a furrow-browed look and left.

Neef returned to the unit – and to a bad moment he had not anticipated. Ann wasn't in her office to warn him. He opened the door to his office and found David Farro-Jones sitting there. Neef swallowed and hoped his face wasn't showing the discomfiture he felt.

'There you are.' Farro-Jones smiled. 'Your secretary said you'd be back soon, so I thought I'd wait. Hope you don't mind.'

'Of course not,' said Neef, trying appear normal as his pulse rate climbed.

'I was passing. I thought I'd look in and see how your brain-tumour patient was doing. Still a success story?'

'Absolutely,' said Neef. 'He's just been given the all-clear. Let me show you his latest scan.'

'Absolutely marvellous,' said Farro-Jones. 'I'm so pleased for you chaps. Max must be over the moon.'

'He's pleased,' agreed Neef. 'But this other business has taken the shine off it for him and Menogen.'

'I suppose so,' said Farro-Jones, his voice apparently filled with concern. 'These bloody newspapers have a lot to answer for. I hope the company's going to sue.'

'I don't know,' confessed Neef. 'I haven't seen Max to ask him. They closed down the Menogen labs.'

'I heard,' said Farro-Jones solicitously. 'Talk about jumping the gun. You know, in a way I feel responsible.'

'How so?' asked Neef, almost choking.

'I was the one who spotted the coincidence in the addresses of Menogen and young Melanie.'

'But you didn't tell anyone,' said Neef.

'No, of course not,' said Farro-Jones with a smile that made Neef feel uncomfortable. 'It's just that I keep worrying I may have left something lying around on my desk. Maybe someone saw it and decided to make themselves some pocket money by leaking it to the press.'

'It's water under the bridge now,' said Neef. 'The damage has been done, however it happened.'

'I suppose so,' sighed Farro-Jones. 'Are you going to show me that scan?'

'Of course.' Neef brought out Thomas Downy's last CT scan and let Farro-Jones examine it.

'Absolutely amazing,' said Farro-Jones. 'It's really hard to believe that this patient was actually dying of a brain tumour only a few weeks ago.'

'It certainly is.'

'You have to admit it, Michael, this is the therapy of the future. It's going to change the whole face of medical science.'

'I'd find it hard to argue,' agreed Neef.

Farro-Jones returned the scan. 'I'd best be getting back, now that I've see what the competition can do!'

Neef tried to laugh along but it was difficult. He felt a flood of relief when the door closed behind Farro-Jones. It was short-lived. His eyes fell on the address of the Little family he'd left lying on his desk. It was half tucked under his desk diary but the name Little was clearly visible. Could Farro-Jones have seen it? Neef couldn't decide. There was no way of knowing where Farro-Jones's eyes might have strayed during the time he'd been alone in the room.

Neef decided to act quickly. There was a chance that David had not seen the memo but there was equally a chance that he had. If he wanted to know the truth about the man's involvement in the cancer deaths, the sooner he spoke to Mrs Little the better.

The Combe Tower estate was one of the worst areas in the city. It suffered all the social ills of the day, from high unemployment to heroin addiction and gang warfare. The authorities were content to contain the area rather than police it, however much they denied this publicly. Neef took a look behind him at the Discovery, wondering how much of it would be left when he returned. The burnt-out wreck of a Ford Cortina at the far end of the car park did not fill him with confidence.

Both lifts were out of action and a group of women, weighed down with plastic shopping bags, were complaining about it in the hallway as he sought the door leading to the stairs.

'Two bloody days!' were the last words he picked up as he started to climb. At each landing, he had to pick his way through accumulated rubbish. Beer cans and crisp packets predominated, although in the gloom of the third landing corner he saw a syringe lying among the debris, the dried blood of its user colouring the plastic barrel brown.

As he approached the fourth floor he heard voices at the top of the stairs. It wasn't reassuring; it was the sound of a group of young men. As Neef reached the landing the sound suddenly stopped and the eyes of four youths who were playing cards stared up at him.

'You got a problem?' asked one.

'No problem,' said Neef passing by, hoping that would be an end to it. He was relieved to hear the conversation start again behind him as he sought out flat number three and knocked on its chipped and battered door.

A middle-aged woman with sunken cheeks and straight grey hair answered. She wore a woollen V-necked jumper with a gold crucifix hanging round her bare neck, a shapeless skirt that seemed to have pleats where no pleats were intended and slippers with a large furry ball on each.

'Mrs Little? I'm Dr Neef from St George's hospital.'

The woman's face took on a puzzled look. 'What d'you want?'

'I'd like to talk to you about your daughter.'

'Susan? What's there to talk about?'

'I'm sorry, believe me, but I'd like to ask you about her treatment. There are some things I have to know.'

'Susan wasn't treated at your hospital. It was University College.'

'Could I come in for a few minutes, Mrs Little?' Neef asked. He was aware of neighbours beginning to take an interest in what was going on.

'Suppose so,' agreed the woman reluctantly. 'I was doing my ironing.'

Neef was led into the living room, where an ironing board stood with a blouse straddled across it. A wooden clothes horse stood beside it with various items, already ironed, hanging on it. There were no children's clothes.

'Was Susan an only child, Mrs Little?' asked Neef.

Ann Little nodded. 'She was all I had left. Her dad died three years ago.'

'I'm sorry,' said Neef. 'And she had cystic fibrosis?'

'From the time she was born.'

'Was she looked after by University College Hospital from the beginning?'

'A wonderful place,' said Mrs Little. 'They were all so good to her, especially the – what d'you call 'em? – the physios who cleared her lungs.'

'Was there ever any mention of a cure for Susan?' asked Neef.

'Last year,' replied Mrs Little, sitting down on the edge of a chair facing Neef. She shook a cigarette free from a packet that had been sitting on the mantelpiece and lit it. 'They tried out a new treatment for people like Susan but it didn't come to anything.'

'Was that the gene-therapy trial?' asked Neef, excited at the prospect of making the connection with Farro-Jones.

'That was it,' agreed the woman, blowing out a cloud of smoke. 'They were going to put some new gene into Susan's lungs so she wouldn't need the physio any more but something went wrong. It didn't work out.'

'A pity,' said Neef.

'Everyone was so disappointed,' said Mrs Little, looking wistful. 'Especially Dr Farro-Jones. I think he designed the new treatment.'

'Yes, he did,' said Neef, his pulse rate rising. 'Did you see Dr Farro-Jones after that?' he asked.

'He came to visit. Ever such a nice man, a real gentleman. He really cared about the patients. He came to see how Susan was getting on.'

'He came here?' asked Neef.

'Yes.'

'When?'

'The first time was just after the new treatment failed, about a year ago, I suppose. He said it wouldn't be long before they'd sorted out the problems and they'd have another go at curing her.'

'Did you see him again?'

'Two or three months ago.'

Neef felt his mouth go dry. 'He came here again?'

'Yes, he'd been working on a new treatment and said he was offering Susan first chance of it before they'd even started using it in the hospital. Susan was really pleased. She liked Dr Farro-Jones. He's very good-looking, you see, and her being of an age . . .'

Neef smiled. 'What happened?'

Dr Farro-Jones came here to treat her. It was our secret, he said.

'What sort of treatment?' asked Neef.

'It was very simple,' said Mrs Little. 'He just put a couple of small tubes up her nose and made her breathe deeply for a few minutes. There was no pain or anything.'

Neef swallowed. Here was the gas that public health had started out looking for, but it wasn't a gas: it was obviously a virus suspension being administered by nebulizer, one prepared by an over-ambitious son of a bitch who had bypassed all the rules.

'Then what happened?' he asked.

'Susan didn't get any better. In fact her illness took a turn for the worse and she had to be admitted to the hospital. Her lungs had filled up, you see. Dr Farro-Jones said the new treatment had come too late to save her. He was very upset. He even attended the funeral. Such a nice man, dedicated if you know what I mean.'

Neef nodded. He knew what she meant. He also understood what Pereira meant when he had called Farro-Jones a few other things.

'Did Susan know a girl named Melanie Simpson?' asked Neef.

'There was a girl called Melanie; they were in the Girl Guides together. I don't know if her last name was Simpson. Why?'

'Did Melanie ever come here?'

'She came to visit Susan just before she went into hospital for the last time. She'd been sent by the Guides to wish her well. You should have seen the flowers they sent.'

'How about Jane Lees?'

'Jane came too,' said Mrs Little.

'How did Susan know Jane?'

'Jane lives next door to my mother. Susan used to play with her when we went over there on a Wednesday and Sunday. They were good friends, the two of them.'

'Did you know that Jane had died?' Neef asked.

Mrs Little nodded. 'Cancer,' she said.

'Melanie, too,' said Neef.

Mrs Little looked shocked. 'I didn't know about Melanie,' she said. 'What an awful . . .' Her face suddenly showed confusion and uncertainty. 'Why are you here?' she asked. 'Why are you asking all these questions? What's going on?'

At that moment the doorbell rang. Neef stiffened. He listened as the door was opened.

'Dr Farro-Jones! What a surprise. We were just talking about you.'

'Really?' said Farro-Jones's voice. 'Can I come in?'

'Of course, Doctor. Maybe someone round here will tell me what this is all about.'

Farro-Jones entered the room ahead of Mrs Little. He smiled uneasily at Neef. 'Hello, Michael, I didn't expect to find you here.'

'Really?' replied Neef with cold accusation in his eyes.

'What has Mrs Little been telling you?'

'Everything,' replied Neef flatly.

Mrs Little looked confused. 'Will someone please tell me what's going on?' she pleaded.

Neef and Farro-Jones ignored her.

'So what now?' asked Farro-Jones, still managing a smile, but Neef thought his eyes told a different story. He saw trepidation there. The smile was just bravado. 'How deep shit am I in?'

'Terminally deep,' said Neef. 'I know what you did.'

'I see.' Farro-Jones began to ring his hands nervously and run his fingers through his hair. 'I don't suppose it'll do any good to point out that I did it for the best?'

Neef shook his head. 'You did it for yourself, nobody else. And you've ended up killing several people.'

'I didn't mean for any of this to happen. It was just fate, just bloody bad luck. I didn't know the vector virus was going to turn out to be carcinogenic for Christ's sake, and there was certainly no way I could have foreseen it becoming infectious through DNA repair. How could I? I thought when Susan got cancer, it was just a bit of bad luck and that was an end to it.'

'Cancer?' exclaimed Mrs Little. 'My Susan had cancer?'

'Dr Farro-Jones's new treatment gave her cancer, Mrs Little,' said Neef without taking his eyes off Farro-Jones. 'She didn't die of cystic fibrosis. Dr Farro-Jones just pretended she had.'

'I explained there was a risk,' said Farro-Jones.

'Was Eddie Miller just bad luck too?'

'Drunken sot,' said Farro-Jones under his breath.

'I think it's time we spoke to the police,' said Neef.

'Face the music, eh?' said Farro-Jones attempting to produce a smile again. 'I think not.'

Neef felt the hair on the back of his neck rise as he saw the look in Farro-Jones's eyes. 'You can't seriously believe that you can get away with it?' he asked, sounding braver than he felt.

'Everything that could convict me is sitting in this room right now,' said Farro-Jones.

Mrs Little was totally bemused. 'What's going on?' she almost screamed. 'Will someone please tell me what is going on?'

Both Neef and Farro-Jones ignored her.

'You're wrong,' said Neef. 'I wrote a letter to Frank MacSween before I came over here. Frank won't rest until you're brought to justice. You're resposible for killing his grandson.'

'MacSween's still away on leave,' said Farro-Jones. 'Let's stop playing silly buggers shall we?'

Farro-Jones suddenly picked up the iron that was sitting on the ironing board beside him and hurled it at Neef.

It was only a distance of ten feet; Neef had no time to avoid it. It hit him high up on the left temple and a sudden sharp pain was replaced by blackness.

Neef came round to a world of pain, suffocating heat and the sounds of a woman screaming. He tried to move from where he lay on the floor but pain ignited inside his head and made him retch. He tried again and found he couldn't breathe when he tried to sit up. The flat was on fire and the air was full of smoke. Suddenly very much awake, he sank back down to floor level again where he could find some air and started to crawl towards where he thought the screams were coming from. He found Mrs Little in the hallway; she had been trying to reach the door but her slippers had caught fire and she was hopping around in agony as she tried to pull them off.

Neef could see that the blaze had been started in the hall. There had been deliberate intent to block access to the outside door. There was no way out. He pulled Mrs Little, who was hysterical, down to floor level and tore her slippers off. Next he pulled her along the floor back into the living room as far away from the main blaze as possible. She kept trying to resist, seeing the door as her avenue of escape.

'Stay down,' he yelled against the noise of the fire, pushing Mrs Little's face down to to floor level. 'There's air down here!'

Neef grabbed one of the articles from the clothes horse and wet it with water from the jug Mrs Little had been using to fill her steam iron from. He pressed the wet cloth to his face and crawled across to the living room door. It was ablaze but he pushed what was left of it shut in an attempt to keep the flames at bay a little longer. He could see that Mrs Little was now deeply in shock. Her eyes were wide open but she wasn't seeing anything. She lay on the floor, shaking from head to foot, biting a corner of her sweater, which she had pulled up to put in her mouth.

'It's going to be all right,' said Neef. 'The fire brigade will be on their way. We just have to hang on a little while longer.'

He looked up at the window, unsure whether to break it. He had visions of suddenly creating a flue for the fire to race out through, engulfing them in flames. He'd wait another few moments, if they had that long.

The heat was becoming unbearable and the air they found at floor level was scorching their lungs. Somewhere above the noise of the conflagration he thought he could hear the sound of sirens. 'Please God!' he prayed.

Despite the fact that the flat was full of fumes, Neef could smell burning hair and skin. He looked at Mrs Little and saw that her hair was smoking. He would have to break the window. They had only seconds before they would become part of the holocaust. As he prepared to stand up and break the glass he noticed the flower vases sitting at either end of the fireplace. Their contents had succumbed to the heat but it was what they were sitting in that interested him. Neef crawled across the floor on his stomach and put his hand into the first vase. His fingers touched water. He dragged both vases over to the window and emptied most of the contents of the first one over Mrs Little's head. He then doused himself and took a swig of the water. In the circumstances, it was cool and delicious.

The sirens were now very loud and he could hear something scrape against the wall of the building outside. Help was coming. Neef knew that the next few seconds were going to be crucial if they were to survive. The firemen, coming up the ladder outside, would break the window. He and Mrs Little would be at risk from both flying glass and the possible creation of a fire storm rushing through the room to meet the up-draught. He considered trying to stand up and show himself to the firefighters but he might not be immediately visible and consequently get the full force of the breaking glass in his face followed by possible immolation as the flames engulfed him.

He opted instead to remain close to the floor with Mrs Little. As a last resort, he crawled over to the clothes horse and pulled it over on its side. He gathered as much clothing as he could and used it to cover all the exposed areas of Mrs Little's and his own body as they huddled on the floor. A brief impression of a dark shadow through the smoke and fumes told Neef that someone was outside the window. He closed his eyes and shielded as much of Mrs Little as he could.

The window shattered and a sudden draught of searing heat almost dragged the last breath from his body as it swept out through the window. He struggled to his feet as water came cascading into the room. He had to press himself against the wall at the side of the window frame to avoid being hit by the force of the jet. If it struck him the chances were he would be thrown clear across the room and probably through the blazing door out into the hall. As the jet from the hose moved slowly towards the other side of the room, Neef moved across the window frame and caught the attention of the fireman outside on the ladder. There was a gap of about two metres between the ladder platform and the wall of the building. This had been forced by the metal window frame of the flat buckling outwards when the glass had been smashed. Neef could see that this was going to be a problem.

There was no way the ladder could move in closer.

Eighteen

'How many?' yelled the fireman.

'Two of us.'

'Are you together?'

'Yes.'

'I'm going to have to get cutting equipment to get nearer,' shouted the man through cupped hands. He pointed to the tangled window frame.

'No time!' shouted Neef in reply.

The fireman and Neef both looked at the gap between the building and the ladder. It was not an encouraging sight.

'I'll get the woman,' cried Neef. 'She's not heavy.'

Neef disappeared briefly back inside the blazing room and pulled Mrs Little to the window. He prepared to pass her over to the fireman. At first there didn't seem to be a problem. Neef could support Mrs Little, who was still in shock, quite easily. He was holding her with one arm and leaning out to bridge the gap when she suddenly came to her senses and all at once realized where she was. She screamed when she looked down and saw that there was nothing beneath her feet. She began kicking and struggling, suddenly and dramatically increasing the burden on Neef's arm.

'It's okay, I've got her,' yelled the fireman as he leaned out as far as he could and caught hold of the writhing woman. 'Let go of her!'

Neef let go and Mrs Little appeared to pass safely into the fireman's care. At the last moment, however, she kicked out hysterically with both legs and broke free of his grip. She slipped from his grasp and for a moment hung suspended from her skirt, which the fireman, to his credit, had managed to grab a handful of. There was an agonizing moment when it seemed the situation might be saved before the material suddenly gave way and Mrs Little spiralled down to her death.

'Jesus Christ!' yelled the fireman, putting a hand to his visor as he looked down at the spreadeagled body below. He looked across at Neef, his face contorted with anguish and remorse in the firelight. 'Was that your—?'

'No,' cried Neef above the noise of the fire. 'And it wasn't your fault. There was nothing you could do!' He watched as the fireman took a few moments to compose himself, then quickly the man was back on top of his job.

'Think you can make it?' he shouted to Neef.

'Yes,' replied Neef, knowing that he had no option. He hoisted himself up into the gap left by the window frame and felt his senses reel as he looked down. His eyes sought desperately for reference points.

'Take your time,' yelled the fireman. 'Prepare yourself!'

Just as Neef had worked up the courage to jump, an old sofa in the room behind him exploded and a great cloud of black smoke engulfed him, burning his eyes and throat with toxic fumes. He steeled himself to remain motionless, trying not to breathe until the air had cleared. When he found he could breathe again he slowly opened his eyes and blinked several times to clear them of tears.

'Are you okay?' shouted the fireman.

'Yes,' replied Neef. 'I'm coming across.'

This time, as he prepared to jump, the ladder suddenly swung away from him, increasing the gap by yet another half a metre.

'Just the wind!' yelled the fireman. 'It'll come back.'

Neef's nerves would not take any more. He watched the ladder swing gently back and then launched himself across the gap. He landed with both feet firmly on the ladder platform and the fireman's arms around him. He stood there for a long moment in a bear-hug with the fireman.

'Does this mean we're engaged?' asked the fireman.

'I just can't begin to thank you enough,' gasped Neef.

'No need,' said the fireman. 'Think you can make it down on your own?'

Yes,' replied Neef. He started out on a descent that seemed to take for ever.

When he reached the ground and turned to look at the jumble of hoses, vehicles and flashing blue lights circled there, he felt totally disorientated until ambulance personnel reached him. 'Any injuries sir?'

'No, I'm fine,' replied Neef, shrugging off the blanket that was being draped round his shoulders. He looked around for Mrs Little's body and spotted a stretcher between two of the fire appliances; it was covered by a tarpaulin but there was an unmistakable human shape underneath. He walked towards it.

'I really don't think you should, sir,' said a policeman, putting a restraining hand on his arm.

Neef freed himself, saying, 'Just give me a moment, will you?'

Assuming that Neef must be in some way related to the dead woman, the police and firefighters remained in a huddle in the background while Neef knelt down and drew back the cover from Ann Little's broken body. Surrounded by the emergency vehicles, she seemed so small and insignificant, just like a rag doll. Neef was consumed with anger. Farro-Jones had come into this woman's life, conned her into trusting him and used her only daughter as a guinea pig to further his research career. He had murdered her daughter just as surely as he had murdered her, the bastard. But such a gentle-man . . . he really cared about the patients . . . he had even turned up at Susan's funeral . . . such a nice man. Neef stood up and took a deep breath. He felt he knew where Farro-Jones must have gone.

An ambulance technician appeared at his elbow. 'Are you ready now, sir? It's best if you come along and have a check-up even if you feel okay right now.'

'I'll be with you in a moment,' said Neef without taking his eyes off Mrs Little.

The ambulance man moved back to be replaced by a policeman. 'I'm afraid we need to ask you a few questions, sir, if you feel up to it?'

'Can it wait?' said Neef. 'I'm going up to the hospital for a check-up.'

'Of course, sir. Maybe just your name and address for the time being?' Neef complied. 'You're a doctor?'

'At St George's.'

As the policeman put his notebook back in his pocket and turned to walk back to his colleagues, Neef saw that, for the moment, no one was actually looking at him. He seized the opportunity and moved swiftly round the back of one of the fire appliances. Shielded from view by it, he started running to the car park where he'd left his car. He was relieved to find the Discovery still with all its wheels. It started first time and he was on his way, tyres squealing in protest.

He felt sure that Farro-Jones would have gone straight to Pathology at St George's to look for the letter he had lied about sending to Frank MacSween. The fact that it didn't exist meant that he'd probably still be hunting for it down in MacSween's office. In all probability he would be under the impression that he and Ann Little had died in the fire.

The sight of Farro-Jones's car outside Pathology at St George's brought a knot of fear to Neef's stomach. It was only a car but it had come to symbolize much more than that. For the first time in his life he felt that he was coming up against real evil. He should have realized something earlier but he hadn't. There was only one explanation for Farro-Jones's attempt to kill him and Ann Little at the flat the way he had. He was mad. This was not a comforting thought to nurture as he made his way downstairs to the pathology lab.

He stopped at the foot of the stairs and listened for a moment. He couldn't hear a thing. Then he remembered that Frank MacSween's compassionate leave and Charlie Morse's death had meant that hospital pathology work was temporarily being carried out over in University College Hospital. The St George's technicians had been sent over there, too. Neef looked along the basement corridor and saw a light coming from under Frank MacSween's door. He stared at it, a thin horizontal strip of light in the darkness that said he had been right. Farro-Jones was here.

Neef noted the broken lock and pushed open the door, his bulk almost filling the doorway.

Farro-Jones looked up, shocked. He was sitting in Frank MacSween's chair and had been rummaging through the pile of papers that had been accumulating in MacSween's absence.

'You won't find it. I sent it to his home address.'

Farro-Jones got up slowly from the desk and moved backwards, his eyes looking left and right as if to assess his options. He had only one and that was to open the connecting door behind him that led directly to the PM room. This he did.

'It's over,' said Neef, moving towards him. 'The police are on their way and you, you bastard, are going to prison for the rest of your life.'

Farro-Jones spread his hands in front of him as if to appease Neef's anger. 'Like I said, Neef, I didn't mean for any of this to happen. It was all just bad luck, that's all. It all went wrong; I panicked and everything just seemed to get worse.'

'You treated the Littles as if they were lab animals. They trusted you and you killed them! And you call it bad luck!'

'So Ann Little is dead,' said Farro-Jones. His eyes had taken on a different look as if he had just realized something. 'And you expect me to believe that if the police were coming they would have let you come on ahead on your own? Come on, Neef. You're playing the Lone Ranger. You're the only one who knows.'

'That's enough,' said Neef, still stalking Farro-Jones. They had passed the PM tables and were backing towards the body vaults.

'You know what, Neefy, old son? I don't think there's any letter, either. Fancy your chances? Come on then.'

Farro-Jones had now adopted an agressive stance. He had stopped backing off and was prepared to fight it out with Neef. Neef had the advantage of height, weight and probably strength but Farro-Jones had the build of a natural athlete. He was light on his feet. Farro-Jones made a feint to the left and Neef blocked the move. He was gradually backing Farro-Jones into the far corner of the room, where there would be no escape. Farro-Jones could see it. He dummied a move to the right then corrected and came straight at Neef. Neef was a ready – he sidestepped and caught Farro-Jones on the side of the face with a vicious right hook. Farro-Jones went down. He remained on his knees, rubbing his cheek.

If Neef had known anything about street fighting he would have gone for Farro-Jones with his feet and finished the fight there and then, but it wasn't in his nature. He waited for Farro-Jones to concede. Farro-Jones remained on the floor until he had got his breath back and then began to get up. 'All right, Neef. You win,' he said as he continued to rise. Neef relaxed ever so slightly and Farro-Jones lunged at him, head first. He caught Neef in the midriff and knocked the wind out of him as his back was slammed against the doors of the body vault. Neef recovered quickly and slammed both his fists into Farro-Jones's ears at the same time. He tried to finish the move off by raising his knee into Farro-Jones's face but missed as he backed off.

There was still no way that he could get round Neef and his headlong assaults were not paying dividends. He looked around him with darting glances as Neef waited for him to try again. His eyes fell on a jar of lubricant that the mortuary porter used for the hinges on the body-vault doors. It was sitting on a window-sill to his right. He quickly averted his eyes from and started circling in that direction. Two or three feinted moves later he was within range. Without taking his eyes off Neef, he shot out his arm behind him, grabbed the jar and let fly with it. Neef simply moved his head a little to the left and it sailed harmlessly past to shatter on the body-vault door and fall to the ground.

For the first time, Neef saw defeat in Farro-Jones's eyes and it lifted his spirits. It even made him a little careless. He had avoided the flying missile with such ease that he had overlooked the fact that its contents had spilled out on to the floor behind him. Farro-Jones saw what had happened and the look in his eyes changed again. Neef did not have time to work out why before Farro-Jones faked a lunge towards him and made him step backwards into the spreading puddle of lubricant. His feet slid away from him and he toppled over backwards against the body-vault door. His head hit the heavy metal clasp securing the door and he almost lost conciousness for a few moments.

It was enough for Farro-Jones to seize the initiative. He was on Neef in a flash, raining blows on his head until Neef was lying supine on the floor in a black world of his own.

When he came round he was bound hand and foot with surgical tape. Farro-Jones was in the far corner of the room looking at the paper work clip hanging above three coffins that sat in readiness for residents of the body vault. He must have seen Neef move, out of the corner of his eye, and came over.

'Well, Neef, this is a sad day for you. You're being cremated at four thirty this afternoon.'

Neef felt his insides turn to water. The look on Farro-Jones's face said that he wasn't joking.

'For Christ's sake, man, you can't hope to keep getting away with killing people. Common sense should tell you that. Where is killing me going to get you?'

Neef's appeal to reason only brought a smile to Farro-Jones's face. 'With you and Ann Little out of the way, no one can prove anything. No one who knows me saw me at the flats today and no one will ever see you again after you take the place of – Farro-Jones looked at the wad of papers he was holding – 'James Henry Todd . . . at his cremation this afternoon. Come on!'

Farro-Jones put his hands under Neef's armpits and dragged his body across the floor towards the wooden trestles where the three coffins sat. 'It's going to be a tight fit; Mr Todd was a good bit shorter than you, but I'm sure we'll manage.'

Neef was still groggy from the blows to his head, but panic was bringing life to his limbs. He strained at the tape that secured him but could make no impression on it.

'I thought you'd be unreasonable about this,' sneered Farro-Jones, 'so while you were out cold I nipped out and got a little something to calm you down.' He started to fill a syringe. 'Nothing too drastic. I wouldn't like you to miss your own funeral.'

There was nothing Neef could do to stop the injection going ahead. Amost immediately he felt his muscles go weak and his resolve slip away. He was not truly unconscious, just too weak to move. Farro-Jones forced some tissue into Neef's mouth and then gagged him with surgical tape. He removed the lid of the coffin intended for James Todd and propped it up against the vault door.

'In you go,' he grunted as he struggled to lift Neef's apparently lifeless body, and finally loaded him untidily into the coffin.

'As I thought,' said Farro-Jones. 'A bit tight.' He bent Neef's legs this way and that until he had them both inside the coffin. Finally he packed the area around Neef's head with surgical gowns so that he was held totally immobile, even if he had been *capable* of moving – which he was not.

Farro-Jones seemed to see from his eyes that Neef was still conscious. 'Good,' he said. 'You're going to experience the whole bit, Neef. The drive to the crematorium, the service, the organ music, the hymns – what's the betting it's the twenty-third psalm, eh? You may even hear a few tears being shed before that electric motor starts and you feel yourself sink down to where the ovens are. The clank of the fire door opening and then . . . in you go.'

Farro-Jones lifted the lid of the coffin and Neef was aware of its shadow coming over him before all the light disappeared and he could hear Farro-Jones insert the screws one by one in their pre-drilled holes. He could already feel the temperature start to rise.

He felt his own breath rebound off the lid against his face. The air supply must be limiting, he thought. With any luck it would run out before a live cremation became a possibility. It all depended on whether Farro-Jones was going to screw the lid down. Please, God, let him screw it *right* down. Asphyxia must be by far the better option.

'I'll just leave you a little gap, Neef,' he heard Farro-Jones say. 'Wouldn't like you to smother before the big event.'

Neef could see a thin chink of light where Farro-Jones had left the lid loose and wedged it open with the screwdriver he'd been using.

Neef's nightmare situation was now beginning to threaten his sanity, so great was his sense of absolute terror. Why in God's name had he not let the police handle it? He hadn't even told anyone where he was going! No one knew where he was and no one would ever know what had happened to him. True, there would be a bit of a scandal when the mortuary attendants discovered that they still had the body of someone named Todd, who should have been cremated. But by then it would be too late to wonder who or what had really been in the coffin that had been consigned to the flames. He could hear Farro-Jones moving about; he heard the sound of the body-transporter trolley being raised and lowered as Todd's body was returned to the vault.

'Soon be time, Neef. The hearse will be here in a few minutes,' said Farro-Jones. 'Then all my troubles will be over and it's back to the rigours of the research lab. You know, I thought it was a hellish quirk of fate when Frank MacSween's grandson became infected but, if he hadn't been, I wouldn't have been able to tidy up things here so nicely. When all's said and done the number of people who've died might be said to be unimportant when you think about the benefits my research could bring when the teething troubles have been sorted out. Don't you think?'

The gag in Neef's mouth prevented any kind of reply to the rambings of the madman outside. The muscle relaxant Farro-Jones had used on him was beginning to wear off a little and his limbs were now racked with pain at being crammed and twisted into such a confined space. Cramp was already threatening in his calf muscles.

'Time to batten you down, old son,' said Farro-Jones. 'They'll be here any moment now.'

Neef saw the crack of light disappear as Farro-Jones removed the screwdriver from the crack and started screwing the lid down. His voice was further away now. Suddenly there were other voices.

Neef's terror soared to almost unbearable heights as he imagined that the undertakers had arrived. If they were here this soon, he was going to be conscious throughout. His brain was screaming instructions to his limbs but they refused to respond. He had no way at all of alerting the people outside.

Neef felt the coffin rock slightly on its trestle. Someone had touched it. He waited for it to be lifted, his eyes wide with fear in the darkness. There was an agonizing silent pause when nothing at all happened, then Neef realized that the lid screws were being undone. As the lid was slid away, he blinked against the light and looked up into the face of a policeman.

Neef was helped up into a sitting position. He saw Farro-Jones being held between two uniformed policemen while another in plain clothes cautioned him.

'How on earth?' he gasped as his gag was removed.

'I guessed,' said Eve appearing at his side and hugging him with relief.

'But how did you know I was here?'

'When I looked out of the window earlier to wave goodbye to the firemen who'd been to visit Neil I saw your car parked outside Pathology. David's car was parked beside it. That worried me. Ann Miles told me that you'd gone out, so I thought it odd that your car was back but you weren't. I was about to phone the police when they arrived; they were looking for you in connection with . . . a fire?'

'It's a long story,' said Neef, rubbing his forehead weakly at the thought of it. He suddenly felt awfully tired and couldn't fight the feeling. The effects of the injection Farro-Jones had given him and thoughts of what had so nearly happened to him conspired to make him lose consciousness.

Within minutes of waking up in a small side ward in the hospital, Neef was having an argument. He had declared himself fit and wanted to leave but this apparently was not an option open to him. The nurse present when he woke up had no wish to enter into any real argument with a consultant physician, so she called the young doctor who had dealt with Neef's admission.

'A few nasty bumps on the head and probably a hangover from what was injected into you – but apart from that, no damage.'

'Good,' said Neef. 'Now I'd like to go. I've got lots to do.'

'I'm afraid that's not possible yet, sir. The police and some ministry people are insisting that you stay where you are until you're . . . debriefed, I think the word was.'

'How long is that going to take?'

'They've been informed that you've come round, sir. It shouldn't be long.'

'Look I have to at least phone someone,' said Neef, making for the door and opening it. There were two policemen standing outside. Neef closed the door again.

'Sorry,' said the doctor, shrugging. 'They'll probably be here soon.'

He was right. Four men wearing civilian clothes but showing warrant cards arrived within ten minutes and spent the next four hours questioning Neef. He was both exhausted and exasperated by the time they were through.

'Can I please go now?' he asked.

'I'm afraid not, sir, not just yet,' replied one of the policemen.

'Why the hell not?'

'We'd like you to wait here until we've found Dr Pereira.'

'Pereira? Where the hell does he come into this?'

'We've been looking for him for some time, sir. It shouldn't be long before we find him and then we can sort this whole thing out.'

Neef saw that further argument was useless. He watched as the four men left and resigned himself to more waiting.

It was almost midnight before a commotion outside the door said that something was happening at last. When the door finally did open, Neef got up to welcome Max Pereira.

'What the hell's going on, Mike?'

'I'm not sure myself,' replied Neef. He told him about the fire and Farro-Jones's subsequent arrest.

'Jesus!' exclaimed Pereira. 'You've had quite a day.'

'Farro-Jones had been experimenting with an unlicensed virus,' said Neef. 'He was using one of the cystic-fibrosis kids as a guinea pig.'

'I know about the virus,' replied Pereira, but he didn't elaborate.

One of the policemen who had interviewed Neef earlier came in to say that a meeting had been convened down in the pathology lecture theatre. The two of them were 'requested' to attend.

Neef and Pereira accompanied the policeman in silence, their footsteps echoing through the deserted corridors at that time of night. When they got to the lecture theatre they found that chairs had been brought in and positioned round the long table that normally sat in front of the blackboard for student demonstrations. Klein sat at the head with Waters to his right. The other ten or so places were taken by DOH and police officials. Neef and Pereira were placed together at the foot of the table facing Klein.

Klein welcomed them and said, 'Gentlemen, I'm sure we all regret the happenings of the last twenty-four hours. I think I speak for all of us when I say that we must do all in our power to minimize the resulting damage.'

Neef and Pereira exchanged glances.

'But however awful the experiences have been – particularly for Dr Neef, I understand – we must keep a sense of proportion and priority, so first I have some good news. We appear to've contained the cancer outbreak. There've been no new cases reported among the contacts we've been keeping in isolation. One more week and I think we can confidently raise the restrictions and consider this outbreak over.'

'Good,' said one of the public health people.

'I'm sure everyone will be glad to get back to normal, so it's just a question of how we can put all this behind us as quickly and as painlessly as possible and with a minimum of lasting damage to all parties.'

Neef and Pereira exchanged another glance.

'I'm talking about a damage-limitation exercise, gentlemen,' said Klein. 'I'm sure you'll all agree with me that it serves no real purpose to prolong this unfortunate business with lengthy enquiries, the preparation of reports and the encouragement of prurient press interest, which will only serve to promote fear and alarm in the general public.'

Perish the thought, mused Neef. It's keep-your-mouth-shut time again. He saw Pereira had reached the same conclusion.

'Frankly, I'm asking for your cooperation in putting an end to this business,' said Klein, looking at Neef and Pereira.

'What exactly are you proposing, Dr Klein?' asked Neef.

'In return for your cooperation and silence, we in turn will take no further action in bringing a prosecution against Menogen.'

'What?' exploded Pereira. 'You know damn' well that Menogen had nothing whatever to do with it!'

'Absolutely!' agreed Neef, equally angry. 'It was all down to Farro-Jones and his damned ambition.'

'Unfortunately Dr Farro-Jones can't be here to defend himself,' said Klein.

'Only because he's in police custody!' stormed Neef.

'I understand that Dr Farro-Jones has undergone some kind of mental breakdown. He's been transferred to a secure hospital. It may be some time before we can question him, but of course we accept your assertion that he has been engaged in illegal experimentation on Susan Little,' said Klein. 'Most reprehensible and most regrettable, but there is no actual evidence that links these experiments to the cancer deaths.'

'Jesus!' said Pereira.

'Susan Little was the link between Melanie Simpson and Jane Lees,' said Neef, exasperation in his voice. 'They both visited her.'

'But there is no actual evidence to show that Susan Little died of lung cancer at all,' said Klein.

'Farro-Jones had the pathologist, Miller, cover it up,' said Neef.

'The pathologist in question being unfortunately dead,' said Klein acidly. 'And I must remind you that no virus has yet been found to be responsible for the deaths. We still feel that the most likely event was the escape of some unidentified infectious agent from the premises of Menogen Research. We're prepared to accept that this was in no way due to negligence on the part of the staff at Menogen, and that it was a one-off occurrence that no one could have foreseen. That's why we're prepared not to prosecute in return for your cooperation.'

Neef could hardly believe that Klein was being so obtuse.

'No deal,' said Pereira quietly.

It had much more effect than if he had said it angrily. Neef had the distinct impression that Pereira had been holding something back. A number of men moved uncomfortably in their seats. Klein seemed more discomfited than most. 'I'm sorry you feel that way,' he said. 'But you leave me no alternative—'

'You know, don't you?' interrupted Pereira. He was looking at Waters, who had remained silent throughout.

The downturn to Waters's lips quivered slightly. 'I don't know what you mean,' he said.

'Yes you do,' said Pereira. 'You're a virologist like I am – a good one, too, otherwise you wouldn't be at the Porton fun factory.'

'I really must ask you to come to the point, Doctor Pereira,' said Klein.

Neef could see that he was rattled. He felt himself relax as he realized Pereira must be holding some kind of ace up his sleeve.

Pereira said to Waters, 'You saw the virology reports just as I did. You took Charlie Morse's body away for investigation. What you didn't know is that I had a sample from Douglas Cooper's lungs to work on.'

Waters and Klein looked at each other. This was clearly unwelcome news to them. Klein swallowed. 'What are you suggesting?' he asked, as if he feared the answer.

Pereira said, 'The routine virology reports on the dead patients showed the presence of rhinovirus, adenovirus and para-adenovirus, all viruses that you might expect to appear in any virology report on a patient with pneumonia. But the *para*-adeno virus caught my attention. I analysed it as best I could in the time available. It wasn't an ordinary example of para-adeno virus at all. It was obviously one that had been modified for use as a gene-therapy vector. The technicians who were looking for a new virus wouldn't have realized this at the time. I think Farro-Jones created a virus vector, based on para-adeno virus, that would carry the CF gene into the host cells of cystic-fibrosis patients and integrate it into their chromosomes. But it's my guess that wasn't good enough for him. He wanted to go one step better and give the vector a specific target site on the DNA. Unfortunately, it seems the target he came up with happened to be a proto-oncogene. When the virus integrated it caused the cell to become cancerous. Somewhere along the line he had the double misfortune of the disabled virus becoming active again. In short, he created a virus that turned lung cancer into an infectious disease.'

'So that's why some people were immune to it,' said Neef. 'If it was based on an ordinary virus like adenovirus, lots of us would have antibodies to it.'

'Depending on when you last had a cold or flu,' said Pereira.

'But some of us wouldn't,' said Neef.

'Presumably why our friend from Porton Down is interested in it,' said Pereira. 'And why these guys are now doing their best to pretend it doesn't exist.'

Klein interrupted. 'If what you say is true, Dr Pereira, we

really must insist that you hand over your isolate of this virus immediately.'

'Menogen Research does not use para-adenovirus as a vector. It never has,' said Pereira flatly. He said it as a challenge.

Klein cleared his throat and said, 'I think we can accept in the light of this . . . revelation that Menogen Research were in no way to blame for this unfortunate outbreak.' Pereira kept staring at Klein. 'And that we were perhaps precipitate in revoking their licence . . .'

Pereira stared on. 'It's cost us a bundle.'

'And that perhaps financial compensation for their losses might be in order.'

'Good,' said Pereira quietly. 'We've started talking to each other. Now, would you really like me to hand over this virus that you've already got down at Porton or will I just chuck it in the sterilizer?'

'We would like the virus,' replied Klein, refusing to admit anything to Pereira. 'Some of these gentlemen will accompany you when you leave here.'

'Just as you like,' said Pereira, enjoying his moment. 'And our licence?'

'Will be restored in the morning.'

'Along with a press release clearing us of all blame?'

'Yes,' said Klein as if he'd said the word without opening his mouth. 'There will be no other kind of press release,' added Klein coldly.

The tone of Klein's voice told Neef that he would rather not know about the threat behind it. Pereira had pushed his luck as far as it would go. He looked at Pereira, who was about to rise to the bait, and interrupted first. 'I'm sure that Dr Pereira and I would be the last people on earth to wish to cause unnecessary fear and alarm to the general public. You can be assured of our complete silence.'

'Good,' said Klein. 'Public peace of mind is so important.'

❖   ❖   ❖

Outside the room, Pereira lit a cigarette and inhaled deeply.

'You did well in there,' said Neef. They were talking together while two police officers waited to accompany Pereira to the lab where he had propagated the virus.

'I had to,' replied Pereira. 'Didn't I?'

'Yes, you did,' admitted Neef thoughtfully. 'When I first met you I thought you were filled with a totally unnecessary cynicism. It appears I was wrong. I'm sorry.'

Pereira smiled. 'When I first met you, I thought there was no such thing as a genuinely dedicated doctor who always put his patients first. I was wrong. I'm sorry, too.'

The two men shook hands and Neef watched as Pereira left with the policemen.

Neef yawned and made his way back to his unit, where he found Lawrence Fielding catching up on some paperwork at his desk. The unit was on night lights. Fielding was working in a pool of light from his desk lamp.

'Hello,' said Neef wearily. 'How are things?'

'You look like you've been in the wars,' said Fielding, seeing the mark on Neef's head where the ashtray had hit him earlier.

'You could say,' agreed Neef. 'More than that I cannot say.'

Fielding nodded his understanding. 'I gathered something's been going on. Can I assume that the cancer scare's now been resolved?'

'You can,' said Neef.

'Well, that's the main thing I suppose.'

Neef nodded and asked, 'How's Neil?'

'Good,' replied Fielding. 'We'll have to include the fire brigade in our list of recognized therapies. Their visit did him the world of good. He's found a new grip on life.'

'Good. How are the four we restored to the trial. Any ill effects?'

'They seem okay for the moment. They should certainly make it through to the Gancyclovir treatment.'

Neef nodded his satisfaction. 'Any other news?'

'John Martin's doing really well on Antivulon. I think we could up his dose.'

'Excellent. I think we might have lost him by now on conventional treatment.'

'All in all things are looking pretty good at the moment,' said Fielding.

'Can't ask for more than that,' said Neef. 'But tomorrow is another day as they say. Seen Eve?'

'She went home about ten. She said you should call her if you turned up. She's been worried sick about you.'

'I'll phone her.'

Neef called Eve from his office.

'Thank God!' she exclaimed when she heard his voice. 'No one would tell me anything about you except that you were "helping the police with their enquiries".'

'I'm free now,' said Neef. 'I'm at the unit.'

'Can you come over?'

'On my way.'

Neef held Eve in his arms for a long time. It was just so good to touch her and smell her perfume, feel the softness of her hair against his cheek.

'Your poor face,' said Eve reaching up to touch his bruised forehead.

'It's nothing. I owe you my life,' said Neef.

'You can't tell me about it, can you?' said Eve, sensing a slight awkwardness about Neef.

'Max and I had to agree to keep silent, but you know most of it anyway. Please God I never have another day like this one in my entire life,' said Neef with obvious feeling.

'Did you see Neil?'

'I saw him before I left the unit. Lawrence tells me he's come through the crisis, thanks to you and the fire brigade.'

Eve nodded with a smile. 'They were a big success. What do you think his chances are now?' she asked.

'It's all going to be up to the Menogen vector now,' replied Neef. 'But it's going to be given a fair chance to do its stuff.

We'll start him on Gancyclovir the day after tomorrow. I'm optimistic.'

'You have to be,' said Eve.

'Apart from that . . .'

'I'd give anything for the three of us to have another picnic like the one we had down at the mill.'

Neef agreed, holding Eve closer. 'I've been thinking,' he said. 'If Neil should come through this he's still going to need love and support, ideally in a real family background. I was thinking maybe you and I . . .'

'Yes?'

'Well, you know, maybe we could . . .'

'What?'

'You know.'

'Not good enough, Neef.'

'All right,' said Neef. He took both Eve's hands in his. 'It's true that when I first met you I was still in love with my wife Elaine.'

'Your wife?' prompted Eve.

'My *late* wife,' conceded Neef. 'Elaine is dead and gone. I'll never forget her or what we had together, but that's all in the past. This is the present and I'm alive. I'm also very much in love with you. I just can't bear to contemplate a future without you. I would be the happiest man alive if you'd be my wife.' Neef brought Eve's hands up to his mouth and kissed each in turn. 'What do you say?'

Eve smiled.

'Yes,' she said.